The Secret of the Old Clock

"The Crowley clock at last!" Nancy exclaimed

NANCY DREW MYSTERY STORIES

The Secret of the Old Clock

BY CAROLYN KEENE

PUBLISHERS *Grosset & Dunlap* NEW YORK

A NATIONAL GENERAL COMPANY

*This new story for today's readers is based
on the original of the same title.*

Contents

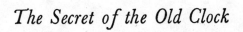

The Secret of the Old Clock

CHAPTER I

The Rescue

NANCY DREW, an attractive girl of eighteen, was driving home along a country road in her new, dark-blue convertible. She had just delivered some legal papers for her father.

"It was sweet of Dad to give me this car for my birthday," she thought. "And it's fun to help him in his work."

Her father, Carson Drew, a well-known lawyer in their home town of River Heights, frequently discussed puzzling aspects of cases with his blond, blue-eyed daughter.

Smiling, Nancy said to herself, "Dad depends on my intuition."

An instant later she gasped in horror. From the lawn of a house just ahead of her a little girl about five years of age had darted into the roadway. A van, turning out of the driveway of the house, was barely fifty feet away from her. As the driver vigorously sounded the horn in warning, the child became confused and ran directly in front of the van. Miraculously, the little girl managed to cross the road safely and pull herself up onto a low wall, which formed one side of a bridge. But the next second, as the van sped away, the child lost her balance and toppled off the wall out of sight!

"Oh my goodness!" Nancy cried out, slamming on her brakes. She had visions of the child plunging into the water below, perhaps striking her head fatally on a rock!

Nancy leaped out of her car and dashed across the road. At the foot of the embankment, she could see the curly-haired little girl lying motionless, the right side of her body in the water.

"I hope—" Nancy dared not complete the harrowing thought as she climbed down the steep slope.

When she reached the child, she saw to her great relief that the little girl was breathing normally and no water had entered her nose or mouth. A quick examination showed that she had suffered no broken bones.

Gently Nancy lifted the little girl, and holding her firmly in both arms, struggled to the top of the embankment. Then she hurried across the road and up the driveway to the child's house.

At this moment the front door flew open and an elderly woman rushed out, crying, "Judy! Judy!"

The next second, the child lost her balance

"I'm sure she'll be all right," said Nancy quickly.

The woman, seeing Nancy's car, asked excitedly, "Did you run into her?"

"No, no. Judy fell off the bridge." Nancy quickly explained what had taken place.

By this time another woman, slightly younger, had hurried from the house. "Our baby! What has happened to her?"

As the woman reached out to take Judy, Nancy said soothingly, "Judy's going to be all right. I'll carry her into the house and lay her on a couch."

One of the women opened the screen door and the other directed, "This way."

Nancy carried her little burden through a hallway and into a small, old-fashioned living room. As soon as she laid the child on the couch, Judy began to murmur and turn her head from side to side.

"I believe she'll come to in a few minutes," said Nancy.

The two women watched Judy intently as they introduced themselves as Edna and Mary Turner, great-aunts of the little girl.

"Judy lives with us," explained Edna, the older sister. "We're bringing her up."

Nancy was somewhat surprised to hear that these elderly women were rearing such a small child. She gave her name and address, just as Judy opened her eyes and looked around. Seeing Nancy, she asked, "Who are you?"

"My name is Nancy. I'm glad to know you, Judy."

"Did you see me fall?"

Nancy nodded, as the child's Aunt Mary said, "She rescued you from the river after you fell in."

Judy began to cry. "I'll never, never run into the road again, really I won't!" she told her aunts.

Nancy said she was sure that Judy never would. She patted the child, who smiled up at her. Although Nancy felt that Judy would be all right, she decided to stay a few minutes longer to see if she could be of help. The child's wet clothes were removed and a robe put on her.

Mary Turner started for the kitchen door. "I'd better get some medication and wet compresses for Judy. She's getting a good-sized lump on her head. Nancy, will you come with me?"

She led the way to the kitchen and headed for a first-aid cabinet which hung on the wall.

"I want to apologize to you, Nancy, for thinking you hit Judy," the woman said. "I guess Edna and I lost our heads. You see, Judy is very precious to us. We brought up her mother, who had been an only child and was orphaned when she was a little girl. The same thing happened to Judy. Her parents were killed in a boat explosion three years ago. The poor little girl has no close relatives except Edna and me."

"Judy looks very healthy and happy," Nancy said quickly, "so I'm sure she must love it here."

Mary smiled. "We do the best we can on our small income. Sometimes it just doesn't suffice, though. We sold some old furniture to the two men in that van you saw. I don't know who they were, but I guess the price was all right."

Mary Turner's thoughts went back to little Judy. "She's so little now that Edna and I are able to manage with our small income. But we worry about the future. We're dressmakers but our fingers aren't so nimble with the needle as they used to be.

"To tell you the truth, Nancy, at the time Judy's parents were killed, Edna and I wondered whether we would be able to take care of Judy properly. But we decided to try it and now we wouldn't part with her for anything in the world. She's won our hearts completely."

Nancy was touched by the story. She knew what was in the minds of the Turner sisters—living costs would become higher, and with their advancing years, their own income would become lower.

"Unfortunately," Mary went on, "Judy's parents left very little money. But they were extremely bright people and Judy is going to be like them. She ought to study music and dancing, and have a college education. But I'm afraid we'll never be able to give her those things."

Nancy said reassuringly, "Judy may be able to win a scholarship, or get other financial aid."

Mary, finding Nancy a sympathetic listener, con-

tinued, "A cousin of our father's named Josiah
Crowley used to help us. But he passed away a
couple of months ago. For years he used to pay
us long visits and was very generous with his
money." Miss Turner sighed. "He always promised to remember us in his will—he loved little
Judy—and I am afraid Edna and I came to depend
on that in our plans for her. But he did not carry
out his promise."

Nancy smiled understandingly and made no
comment. But she did wonder why Mr. Crowley
had changed his mind.

"Josiah went to live with some other cousins.
After that, things changed. He rarely came to see
us. But he was here just last February and said
the same thing—that Edna and I were to inherit
money from him. He had always helped us and it
seemed strange that he should stop so suddenly."

Mary Turner looked at Nancy. "Maybe you
know our well-to-do cousins that he went to stay
with. They live in River Heights. They're the
Richard Tophams."

"Do they have two daughters named Ada and
Isabel?" Nancy asked. "If so, I know them."

"That's the family all right," replied Mary.

Nancy detected a hint of coolness in the woman's voice. "Do you like those two girls?" Miss
Turner asked.

Nancy did not answer at once. She had been
taught never to gossip. But finally she said tact-

fully, "Ada and Isabel were in high school with me. They were never my close friends. We—uh —didn't see eye to eye on various things."

By this time Mary Turner had selected a few items from the first-aid chest. Now she went to the refrigerator for some ice cubes. As she arranged the various articles on a tray, she said, "Well, when Cousin Josiah passed away, to our amazement Richard Topham produced a will which made him executor of the Crowley estate and left all the money to him, his wife, and the two girls."

"Yes. I did read that in the newspaper," Nancy recalled. "Is the estate a large one?"

"I understand there's considerable money in it," Mary Turner replied. "Some of Josiah's other cousins say he told them the same thing he told us, and they are planning to go to court about the matter." The woman shrugged. "But I guess a fight to break the will would be hopeless. Nevertheless, Edna and I cannot help feeling there *must* be a later will, although as yet no one has presented it."

Nancy followed Miss Turner into the living room. The cold compresses helped to reduce the swelling where Judy had hit her head on a rock. Convinced now that the little girl was all right, Nancy said she must leave.

"Come to see me again soon," Judy spoke up. "I like you, Nancy. "You're my saving girl."

"You bet I'll come," Nancy answered. "I like you too. You're a good sport!"

The child's great-aunts profusely thanked Nancy again for rescuing Judy. The visitor had barely reached the door when Edna suddenly said, "Mary, where's our silver teapot?"

"Why, right there on the tea table— Oh, it's gone!"

Edna ran into the dining room. "The silver candlesticks! They're gone too!"

Nancy had paused in the doorway, startled. "Do you mean the pieces have been stolen?" she asked.

"They must have been," replied Mary Turner, who was white with apprehension. "By those men who bought some furniture from us!"

Instantly Nancy thought of the men in the van. "Who were the men?" she asked.

"Oh, Mary, how could we have been so careless?" Edna Turner wailed. "We don't know who the men were. They just knocked on the door and asked if we had any old furniture that we wanted to sell. We'll never get the silver back!"

"Maybe you will!" said Nancy. "I'll call the police."

"Oh dear!" Mary said woefully. "Our phone is out of order."

"Then I'll try to catch up to the van!" Nancy declared. "What did the men look like?"

"They were short and heavy-set. One had dark hair, the other light. They had kind of large noses. That's about all I noticed."

"Me too," said Edna.

With a hasty good-by Nancy dashed from the house and ran to her car.

CHAPTER II

A Missing Will

THE BLUE convertible sped along the country road. Nancy smiled grimly.

"I'm afraid I'm exceeding the speed limit," she thought. "But I almost wish a trooper would stop me. Then I could tell him what happened to the poor Turner sisters."

Nancy watched the tire marks which the van driven by the thieves had evidently made in the dirt road. But a few miles farther on a feeling of dismay came over her. She had reached a V-shaped intersection of two highways. Both roads were paved, and since no tire impressions could be seen, Nancy did not know which highway the thieves had taken.

"Oh dear!" she sighed. "Now what shall I do?"

Nancy concluded that her wisest move would be to take the road which led to River Heights. There was a State Police barracks just a few miles ahead.

11

"I'll stop there and report the theft."

She kept looking for the van, which she recalled as charcoal gray. "I wish I'd seen the license number or the name of the firm that owns the van," Nancy said to herself ruefully.

When she reached State Police headquarters Nancy introduced herself to Captain Runcie and told about the robbery, giving what meager information she could about the suspects. The officer promised to send out an alarm immediately for the thieves and their charcoal-gray moving van.

Nancy continued her journey home, thinking of the Turners and their problems.

"I wonder why Mr. Josiah Crowley left all his money to the Tophams and none to his other relatives. Why did he change his mind? Those Tophams are well to do and don't need money as much as the Turners."

Nancy did not know Richard Topham, but she was acquainted with his wife, as well as his daughters. They were arrogant and unreasonable, and disliked by many of the shopkeepers in town. Ada and Isabel had been unpopular in high school. They had talked incessantly of money and social position, making themselves very obnoxious to the other students.

"I wonder," Nancy thought, "if a way can't be found so the Turners could get a share of the Crowley money. I'll ask Dad."

Five minutes later Nancy pulled into the double

garage and hurried across the lawn to the kitchen door of the Drews' large red-brick house. The building stood well back from the street, and was surrounded by tall, beautiful trees.

"Hello, Nancy," greeted the pleasant, slightly plump woman who opened the door. She was Hannah Gruen, housekeeper for the Drews, who had helped rear Nancy since the death of the girl's own mother many years before.

Nancy gave her a hug, then asked, "Dad home? I see his car is in the garage."

"Your father's in the living room and dinner will be ready in a few minutes."

Nancy went to say hello to her tall, handsome father, then hurried to wash her hands and comb her hair before the three who formed the Drew household sat down to dinner. During the meal Nancy related her adventure of the afternoon.

"What tricky thieves!" Hannah Gruen burst out. "Oh, I hope the police capture them!"

"They certainly took advantage of those Turner sisters," Mr. Drew commented.

"Mary and Edna are in financial difficulties," Nancy commented. "Isn't it a shame that Josiah Crowley didn't bequeath some of his estate to the Turners and other relatives who need the money?"

Carson Drew smiled affectionately at his only child, then said, "Yes, it is, Nancy. But unless a will written later turns up, that's the way it has to be."

"The Turners think there is another will," Nancy told him. "Wouldn't it be wonderful if it can be found?"

"I agree," spoke up Hannah. "It's well known in town that Mrs. Topham and her daughters were unkind to Josiah Crowley for some time before he died. Their excuse was that Josiah's eccentricities were extremely trying."

"The Tophams have never been noted for any charitable inclinations," Mr. Drew observed with a smile. "However, they did give Josiah a home."

"Only because they knew he was going to leave all his money to them," said Hannah. "If I'd been Josiah I wouldn't have stayed there." The housekeeper sighed. "But when people get old, they don't like change. And probably he put up with things rather than move."

She said the treatment the Tophams had accorded old Josiah Crowley had aroused a great deal of unfavorable comment throughout River Heights. Nancy had not known him personally, but she had often seen the elderly man on the street. Secretly she had regarded him as a rather nice, kindly person.

His wife had died during an influenza epidemic and after that he had made his home with various relatives. According to rumors, all these people had admitted that he had paid his board and done many favors for them. They in turn had been very kind to him, and though poor themselves, had tried to make Josiah Crowley comfortable and happy.

"Tell me everything you know about Mr. Crowley," Nancy urged her father.

The lawyer said that the old man had publicly declared he intended to provide in his will for several deserving relatives and friends. Then, three years before his death, the Topham family, who had never shown an interest in him, had experienced a sudden change of heart. They had begged Josiah Crowley to make his home with them, and at last he had consented. Shortly after he moved into the Topham house, Mr. Drew was told that the old man had decided to leave all his money to them.

Mr. Crowley, though failing in health, maintained a firm grip on life. But as time went on, he became more and more unhappy. He continued to live with the Tophams, but it was whispered about that he frequently slipped away to visit his other relatives and friends, and that he intended to change his will again.

"Then there must be a later will!" Nancy said hopefully.

Mr. Drew nodded, and went on, "One day Josiah Crowley became critically ill. Just before his death he attempted to communicate something to the doctor who attended him, but his words, other than 'will,' were unintelligible. After the funeral only one will came to light, giving the entire fortune to the Tophams."

"Dad, do you suppose Mr. Crowley was trying to tell the doctor something about another will which he had put some place where the Tophams couldn't find it?" Nancy asked.

"Very likely," the lawyer replied. "Probably he intended to leave his money to relatives who had been kind to him. But fate cheated him of the opportunity."

"Do you think anybody has looked for another will?" Nancy questioned.

"I don't know. But I'm sure of this. If another will shows up, Richard Topham will fight it. The estate is a considerable one, I understand, and they aren't the kind of people to share good fortune."

"Can't the present will be contested?" Nancy asked.

"I hear that other relatives have filed a claim, declaring they were told another will had been made in their favor. But unless it is located, I doubt that the matter will ever go further."

"But the Tophams don't deserve the fortune," Hannah Gruen remarked. "And besides, they don't need the money. It doesn't seem fair."

"It may not seem fair, but it is legal," Mr. Drew told her, "and I'm afraid nothing can be done about the situation."

"Poor Judy and her aunts!" said Nancy.

"There are others affected in the same way," her father remarked. "For instance, two young women who live on the River Road. I don't know their names. I understand they were not related to Mr. Crowley, but were great favorites of his. They are having a struggle and could use some extra money."

Nancy lapsed into silence. She felt strongly that a mystery lurked behind the Crowley case.

"Dad, don't *you* believe Josiah Crowley made a second will?" Nancy questioned suddenly.

"You sound like a trial lawyer, the way you cross-examine me," Mr. Drew protested, but with evident enjoyment. "To tell the truth, Nancy, I don't know what to think, but something did happen which might indicate that Mr. Crowley at least intended to make another will."

"Please go on!" Nancy begged impatiently.

"Well, one day nearly a year ago I was in the First National Bank when Crowley came in with Henry Rolsted."

"The attorney who specializes in wills and other estate matters?" Nancy inquired.

"Yes. I had no intention of listening to their conversation, but I couldn't help overhearing a few words that made me think they were discussing a will. Crowley made an appointment to call at Rolsted's office the following day."

"Oh!" cried Nancy excitedly. "That looks as though Mr. Crowley had made a new will, doesn't it? But why didn't Mr. Rolsted say something about it at the time of Mr. Crowley's death?"

"For one of many reasons," Mr. Drew replied. "In the first place, he may never have drawn a new will for Mr. Crowley. And even if he had, the old man might have changed his mind again and torn it up."

Before Nancy spoke again, she finished the delicious apple pudding which Hannah had made. Then she looked thoughtfully at her father. "Dad, Mr. Rolsted is an old friend of yours, isn't he?"

"Yes. An old friend and college classmate."

"Then won't you please ask him if he ever drew up a will for Mr. Crowley, or knows anything that might solve this mystery?"

"That's a rather delicate question, young lady. He may tell me it's none of my business!"

"You know he won't. You're such good friends he'll understand why you're taking a special interest in this case. Will you do it? Please!"

"I know you like to help people who are in trouble," her father said. "I suppose I could invite Mr. Rolsted to have lunch with me tomorrow—"

"Wonderful!" Nancy interrupted eagerly. "That would be a splendid opportunity to find out what he knows about a later will."

"All right. I'll try to arrange a date. How about joining us?"

Nancy's face lighted up as she said, "Oh, thank you, Dad. I'd love to. I hope it can be tomorrow, so we won't have to waste any time trying to find another will."

Mr. Drew smiled. "We?" he said. "You mean you might try to find a hidden will if Mr. Crowley wrote one?"

"I might." Nancy's eyes sparkled in anticipation.

CHAPTER III

An Unpleasant Meeting

"WHAT are your plans for this morning, Nancy?" her father asked at the breakfast table.

"I thought I'd do a little shopping," she replied. Her eyes twinkled. "There's a dance coming up at the country club and I'd like to get a new dress."

"Then will you phone me about lunch? Or better still, how about eating with me, whether Mr. Rolsted comes or not?"

"I'll be there!" Nancy declared gaily.

"All right. Drop in at my office about twelve-thirty. If Mr. Rolsted does accept my invitation, we'll try to find out something about Josiah Crowley's wills." Mr. Drew pushed back his chair. "I must hurry now or I'll be late getting downtown."

After her father had left, Nancy finished her breakfast, then went to the kitchen to help Hannah Gruen, who had already left the table.

"Any errands for me?" Nancy asked.

"Yes, dear. Here's a list," the housekeeper replied. "And good luck with your detective work."

Hannah Gruen gazed at the girl affectionately and several thoughts raced through her mind. In school Nancy had been very popular and had made many friends. But through no fault of her own, she had made two enemies, Ada and Isabel Topham. This worried Hannah. The sisters, intensely jealous of Nancy, had tried to discredit her in positions she had held in school. But loyal friends had always sprung to Nancy's defense. As a result, Ada and Isabel had become more unpleasant than ever to Nancy.

"Thanks for your encouragement," she said to Hannah a little later, giving her a hug.

"Whatever you do, Nancy, beware of those Topham sisters. They'd be only too happy to make things difficult for you."

"I promise to be on my guard."

Before leaving the house, Nancy phoned the Turners. She was glad to hear that Judy had suffered no ill effects from her fall. But she was disappointed that the police had found no clue to the thieves who had stolen the silverware.

"Please let me know if you learn anything," Nancy said, and Edna promised to do so.

Becomingly dressed in a tan cotton suit, Nancy set off in her convertible for the shopping district. She drove down the boulevard, and upon reaching the more congested streets, made her way skillfully through heavy traffic, then pulled into a parking lot.

"I think I'll try Taylor's Department Store first for a dress," she decided.

Taylor's was one of River Heights' finest stores. Nancy purchased several items for Hannah on the main floor, then went directly to the misses' wearing apparel section on the second floor.

Usually Nancy had no trouble finding a sales-clerk. But this particular morning seemed to be an especially busy one in the department, and an extra rush of customers had temporarily over-whelmed the sales force.

Nancy sat down in a convenient chair to await her turn. Her thoughts wandered to the Turner sisters and little Judy. Would she be able to help them? She was suddenly brought out of her rev-erie by loud-voiced complaints.

"We've been standing here nearly ten minutes!" a shrill voice declared. "Send a saleswoman to us immediately!"

Nancy turned to see Ada and Isabel Topham speaking to the floor manager.

"I'm afraid I can't," the man replied regretfully. "There are a number of others ahead of you. All our salespeople are—"

"Perhaps you don't know who we are!" Ada in-terrupted rudely.

"Indeed I do," the floor manager told her wearily. "I will have a saleswoman here in a few moments. If you will only wait—"

"We're not accustomed to waiting," Isabel Topham told him icily.

"Such service!" Ada chimed in. "Do you realize that my father owns considerable stock in Taylor's? If we report your conduct to him, he could have you discharged."

"I'm sorry," the harassed man apologized. "But it is a rule of the store. You must await your turn."

Ada tossed her head and her eyes flashed angrily. This did nothing to improve her looks. In spite of the expensive clothes she wore, Ada was not attractive. She was very thin and sallow, with an expression of petulance. Now that her face was distorted with anger, she was almost ugly.

Isabel, the pride of the Topham family, was rather pretty, but her face lacked character. She had acquired an artificially elegant manner of speaking which, although irritating, was sometimes amusing. It was her mother's ambition that Isabel marry into a socially prominent family.

"I pity any future husband of hers!" Nancy thought with a chuckle.

Suddenly Ada and Isabel saw Nancy, who nodded a greeting. Isabel coldly returned the nod, but Ada gave no indication that she had even noticed Nancy.

At that moment a saleswoman hurried toward

the Topham sisters. At once they began to shower abuse upon the young woman for her failure to wait on them sooner.

"What is it you wish to look at, Miss Topham?" the clerk said, flushing.

"Evening dresses."

The saleswoman brought out several dresses. Nancy watched curiously as the Tophams, in an unpleasant frame of mind, tossed aside beautiful models with scarcely a second glance. They found fault with every garment.

"This is a very chic gown," the saleswoman told them hopefully, as she displayed a particularly attractive dress of lace and chiffon. "It arrived only this morning."

Ada picked it up, gave the dress one careless glance, then tossed it into a chair, as the distracted clerk went off to bring other frocks.

The fluffy gown slipped to the floor in a crumpled mass. To Nancy's horror Ada stepped on it as she turned to examine another dress. In disgust, Nancy went to pick it up.

"Leave that alone!" Ada cried out, her eyes blazing. "Nobody asked for your help."

"Are you buying this?" Nancy asked evenly.

"It's none of your business!"

As Nancy continued to hold the dress, Ada in a rage snatched it from her hands, causing a long tear in the chiffon skirt.

"Oh!" Isabel cried out. "Now you'v
We'd better get out of here, Ada!"

"And why?" her haughty sister shr
was Nancy Drew's fault! She's always making
trouble."

"It was *not* my fault," Nancy said.

"Come on, Ada," Isabel urged, "before that
clerk gets back."

Reluctantly Ada followed Isabel out of the department. As they rushed toward a waiting elevator, Nancy gazed after them. At this moment
the saleswoman reappeared with an armful of
lovely frocks. She stared in bewilderment at the
torn dress.

"Where did my customers go?" she asked Nancy
worriedly.

Nancy pointed toward the elevator, but made
no comment. Instead she said, "I'm looking for
an evening dress myself. This torn one is very
pretty. Do you think it could be mended?"

"Oh, I don't know," the woebegone clerk
wailed. "I'll probably be held responsible and I
can't afford to pay for the dress."

"I'm sure Taylor's wouldn't ask you to do that,"
Nancy said kindly. "If there's any trouble, I'll
speak to the manager myself. What usually happens is that such a dress is greatly reduced."

"Thank you," the clerk replied. "I'll call Miss
Reed, the fitter, and see what can be done."

"First, let me try on the dress," Nancy said, smiling.

They found a vacant fitting room and Nancy took off her suit and blouse. Then she slipped the lovely pale-blue dance creation over her head and the saleswoman zipped it up.

"It's darling on you," she said enthusiastically.

Nancy grinned. "I kind of like myself in it," she said. "Please call the fitter now."

Presently Miss Reed, a gray-haired woman, appeared. Within seconds she had made a change in an overlap of the chiffon skirt. The tear was no longer visible and the style of the dress was actually improved.

"I told our manager what happened," said the saleswoman. "If you want the dress, he will reduce the price fifty percent."

"How wonderful!" Nancy exclaimed. Laughing, she said, "That price will fit into my budget nicely. I'll take the dress. Please send it." She gave her name and address. To herself she added, "Ada Topham did me a favor. But if she ever finds out what happened, she'll certainly be burned up!" Nancy suppressed a giggle.

"It's been a real pleasure waiting on you, Miss Drew," the saleswoman said after Miss Reed left and Nancy was putting on her suit. "But how I dread to see those Topham sisters come in here! They're so unreasonable. And they'll be even worse when they get Josiah Crowley's money."

The woman lowered her voice. "The estate hasn't been settled, but the girls are counting on the fortune already. Last week I heard Ada say to her sister, 'Oh, I guess there's no question about our getting old Crowley's fortune. But I wish Father would stop worrying that somebody is going to show up with a later will which may do us out of it.' "

Nancy was too discreet to engage in gossip with the saleswoman. But she was interested and excited about the information. The fact that Mr. Topham was disturbed indicated to her that he too suspected Josiah Crowley had made a second will!

The conversation reminded Nancy of her date. She glanced at her wrist watch and saw that it was after twelve o'clock.

"I must hurry or I'll be late for an appointment with my dad," she told the saleswoman.

Nancy drove directly to her father's office. Although she was a few minutes ahead of the appointed time, she found that he was ready to leave.

"What luck, Dad?" Nancy asked eagerly. "Did Mr. Rolsted accept your luncheon invitation?"

"Yes. We are to meet him at the Royal Hotel in ten minutes. Do you still think I should quiz him about the Crowley will?"

"Oh, I'm more interested than ever in the case." She told her father about the saleswoman's gossipy remarks.

"Hm," said Mr. Drew. "It's not what you'd call evidence, but the old saying usually holds good, 'Where there's smoke, there's fire.' Come, let's go!"

The Royal Hotel was located less than a block away, and Nancy and her father quickly walked the distance. Mr. Rolsted was waiting in the lobby. Carson Drew introduced his daughter, then the three made their way to the dining room where a table had been reserved for them.

At first the conversation centered about a variety of subjects. As the luncheon progressed the two lawyers talked enthusiastically of their college days together and finally of their profession. Nancy began to fear that the subject of the Crowley estate might never be brought up.

Then, after the dessert course, Mr. Drew skillfully turned the conversation into a new channel and mentioned some strange cases which he had handled.

"By the way," he said, "I haven't heard the details of the Crowley case. How are the Tophams making out? I understand other relatives are trying to break the will."

For a moment Mr. Rolsted remained silent. Was he reluctant to enter into a discussion of the matter? Nancy wondered.

Finally the lawyer said quietly, "The settlement of the estate wasn't given to me, Carson. But I confess I've followed it rather closely because of something that happened a year ago. As the present will stands, I do not believe it can be broken."

"Then the Tophams fall heir to the entire estate," Mr. Drew commented.

"Yes, unless a more recent will is uncovered."

"Another will?" Carson Drew inquired innocently. "Then you believe Crowley made a second one?"

Mr. Rolsted hesitated as though uncertain whether or not he should divulge any further information. Then, with a quick glance about, he lowered his voice and said, "Of course this is strictly confidential—"

CHAPTER IV

Racing the Storm

"CONFIDENTIAL?" Mr. Drew repeated, looking at Mr. Rolsted. "You may rest assured that whatever you tell us will not be repeated to anyone."

"Well, I'll say this much," Mr. Rolsted went on, "about a year ago Josiah Crowley came to me and said he wanted to draw up a new will. He indicated that he intended to spread out his bequests among several people. He expressed a desire to write the will himself, and asked me a number of questions. I took him to my office and told him exactly how to proceed. When he left, he promised to have me look over the document after he had drawn it up."

"Then you actually saw the will?" Mr. Drew asked in surprise.

"No. Strange to say, Crowley never came back. I don't know whether he ever wrote the will or not."

"And if he did, there would be a chance that it would not be legal?" Nancy spoke up.

"Yes. He might have typed it and signed the paper without a witness. In this state at least two witnesses are required and three are advisable."

"What would happen," Nancy asked, "if a person were ill or dying and had no witness, and wanted to make a will?"

Mr. Rolsted smiled. "That sometimes happens. If the person writes the will himself by hand and signs it, so there's no doubt the same person did both, the surrogate's office will accept it for probate."

"Then if Mr. Crowley wrote out and signed a new will, it would be legal," Nancy commented.

"That's right. But there's another thing to remember. It's pretty risky for someone who is not a lawyer to draw up a will that cannot be broken."

Mr. Drew nodded. "If Josiah Crowley left any loophole in a will he wrote personally, the Tophams would drag the matter into court."

"Yes. It's a foregone conclusion that the Tophams will fight to keep the fortune whether they have a right to it or not. I believe some other relatives have filed a claim, but up to the moment they have no proof that a later will exists."

Although Nancy gave no indication of her feelings, the possibility that Mr. Crowley had made a new will thrilled her. As soon as Mr. Drew paid the luncheon check, the three arose and left the dining room. Mr. Rolsted took leave of Nancy and her father in the lobby.

"Well, Nancy, did you find out what you wanted to know?" Mr. Drew asked after the lawyer had left.

"Oh, Dad, it's just as I suspected. I'm sure Mr. Crowley did make a later will! He hid it some place! If only I could find out where!"

"It would be like looking for a needle in a haystack," Mr. Drew commented.

"I must figure out a way!" Nancy said with determination. "I want to help little Judy."

She awoke the next morning thinking about the mystery. But where should she start hunting for possible clues to a second will? She continued pondering about it while she showered and dressed.

As she entered the dining room, she was greeted with a cheery "Good morning" from her father and Hannah Gruen. During breakfast Mr. Drew said, "Nancy, would you do a little errand for me this morning?"

"Why, of course, Dad."

"I have a number of legal documents which must be delivered to Judge Hart at Masonville some time before noon. I'd take them myself, but I have several important appointments. I'd appreciate it if you would drive over there with them."

"I'll be glad to go," Nancy promised willingly.

"Besides, it's such a wonderful day. I'll enjoy the trip. Where are the papers?"

"At the office. You can drive me down and I'll get them for you."

Nancy, wearing a yellow sunback dress and jacket, hurried away to get her gloves and handbag. Before Mr. Drew had collected his own belongings, she had brought her car from the garage and was waiting for him at the front door.

"I put the top down so I can enjoy the sun," she explained as her father climbed in.

"Good idea. I haven't heard you mention the Crowley case yet today," Mr. Drew teased as they rode along. "Have you forgotten about it?"

Nancy's face clouded. "No, I haven't forgotten, but I must admit I *am* stumped as to where to search for clues."

"Maybe I can help you. I've learned that the two girls on River Road who expected to be remembered in the will are named Hoover. You might look them up on your return trip."

"That's great. I'll watch the mailboxes for their name."

When they reached the building where Mr. Drew had his office, Nancy parked the car and waited while her father went upstairs to get the legal documents to be delivered to Judge Hart. Returning a few minutes later, he placed a fat Manila envelope in his daughter's hand.

"Give this to the judge. You know where to find him?"

"Yes, Dad. In the old Merchants Trust Company Building."

"That's right."

Selecting a recently constructed highway, Nancy rode along, glancing occasionally at the neatly planted fields on either side. Beyond were rolling hills.

"Pretty," she commented to herself. "Oh, why can't all people be nice like this scenery and not make trouble?"

It was nearly eleven o'clock when she finally drove into Masonville. Nancy went at once to Judge Hart's office but was informed he had gone to the courthouse. Recalling that her father had mentioned the necessity of the papers being delivered before noon, she set off in search of the judge.

Nancy had considerable trouble trying to see him, and it was twelve o'clock when at last she delivered the Manila envelope into his hands.

"Thank you very much," he said. "I'll need these directly after lunch."

Nancy smiled. "Then I'm glad I found you."

When Judge Hart learned that Nancy was the daughter of Carson Drew, he at once insisted that she have luncheon with him and his wife at their home before returning to River Heights.

She accepted the invitation and spent a very

pleasant hour with the Harts. During the meal the judge laughingly asked if Nancy was still playing aide to her father.

"Oh, yes," she said, and at once told him about the Drews' interest in the Crowley case.

"Did you know Josiah Crowley or ever hear of him?" she asked.

Both the Harts nodded. "A maid who used to be with them, came to work for us after Mrs. Crowley's death," the judge explained. "Jane herself passed away a short time ago."

"We never met Josiah," Mrs. Hart added, "but Jane pointed him out to my husband and me one time down on Main Street."

"Did he have relatives or friends in town?" Nancy inquired.

"I think not," the judge replied.

Nancy wondered what old Josiah had been doing in Masonville if he had no relatives or friends there. The town was not known as a spot for sight-seeing. Her interest was further quickened when Mrs. Hart remarked that she had seen Mr. Crowley in town at another time also.

"How long ago was that?" the girl asked.

Mrs. Hart thought a minute, then replied, "Oh, less than a year, I'd say."

When luncheon was over, the judge said he must leave. Nancy told the Harts she too should go. She thanked them for their hospitality, then said good-by. Soon she was driving homeward.

"Why had Mr. Crowley gone to Masonville?" she asked herself. "Could it have had anything to do with a later will?"

Nancy had chosen a route which would take her to River Road. Half an hour later she turned into the beautiful country road which wound in and out along the Muskoka River, and began to look at the names on the mailboxes. "Hoover," she reminded herself.

About halfway to River Heights, while enjoying the pastoral scenes of cows standing knee-high in shallow sections of the stream, and sheep grazing on flower-dotted hillsides, Nancy suddenly realized the sun had been blotted out.

"A thunderstorm's on the way," she told herself, glancing at black clouds scudding across the sky. "Guess I'd better put the top of the car up."

She pressed the button on the dashboard to raise the top, but nothing happened. Puzzled, Nancy tried again. Still there was no response. By this time large drops of rain had started to fall.

"I'll get soaked," Nancy thought, as she looked around.

There was no shelter in sight. But ahead, past a steep rise, was a sharp bend in the road. Hopeful that there would be a house or barn beyond, Nancy started the car again.

Vivid forked lightning streaked across the sky. It was followed by an earth-shaking clap of thunder. The rain came down harder.

"Oh, why didn't I bring a raincoat?" Nancy wailed.

When Nancy swung around the bend, she was delighted to see a barn with lightning rods about a quarter mile ahead. Farther on stood a small white house.

"I wonder if that's the Hoover place," Nancy mused.

By now the storm was letting loose in all its fury. The sky was as dark as night and Nancy had to switch on her headlights to see the road. She was already thoroughly drenched and her thought of shelter at this point was one of safety rather than of keeping dry.

Nancy turned on the windshield wipers, but the rain was so blinding in its intensity, it was impossible to see more than a few feet ahead. Almost in an instant the road had dissolved into a sea of mud.

Nancy had been caught in a number of storms, but never one as violent as this. She feared a bad skid might land her in a ditch before she could reach the shelter of the barn.

"How much farther is it?" she worried. "It didn't seem this far away."

The next instant, to Nancy's right, a ball of fire rocketed down from the sky.

"Oh! That was close!" she thought fearfully. Her skin tingled from the electrical vibrations in the air.

A moment later a surge of relief swept over Nancy. "At last!" she breathed.

At the side of the road the barn loomed up. Its large double doors were wide open. Without hesitation, Nancy headed straight for the building and drove in.

The next moment she heard a piercing scream!

CHAPTER V

A Surprising Story

NANCY froze behind the wheel. Had she inadvertently hit someone? Her heart pounding in fright, she opened the car door to step out.

At the same instant a shadowy figure arose from a pile of hay near her. "I guess I must have scared you silly when I screamed," said a girl of Nancy's age, stepping forward.

"You— You're all right?" Nancy gasped.

"Yes. And I'm sorry I yelled. I came out here to check on our supply of feed for the chickens. I didn't think it was going to be a bad storm, so I didn't bother to go back to the house."

"It's pretty bad," said Nancy.

"Well, the storm terrified me," the girl continued. "I didn't hear your car coming, and when it rushed in here, I panicked."

Nancy began to breathe normally again, then

told the stranger her name and the fact that the mechanism for raising the top of the convertible was not working.

"That's a shame," said the girl. "And you must get your clothes dried. The storm is letting up. Let's dash over to the house. Grace will help you too. She's my sister. My name's Allison Hoover."

Hoover! Nancy was tempted to tell Allison that she had been planning to call, but she decided not to mention it at the moment. It might be better to do her sleuthing more subtly.

Nancy smiled at Allison. "Thanks a million. But first I'd like to wipe out the car. Are there any rags around the barn?"

Allison produced several and together the two girls mopped the water from the cushions and floor. By this time the rain had stopped. As Nancy and Allison sloshed through a series of puddles to the farmhouse, Nancy had a better chance to study her companion. She was tall, with reddish-blond hair and very fair skin. Her voice was musical and she had an attractive, lilting laugh.

The girls reached the run-down farmhouse and stamped the mud from their shoes on the back porch. Then Allison flung open the door, and they entered a cheerful kitchen.

As the door shut behind them, another girl who was just closing the oven of an old-fashioned range turned toward them in surprise.

"Grace, I've brought a visitor," Allison said

quickly. "Nancy, I want you to meet my sister. She's the mainstay of our family of two."

Grace Hoover cordially acknowledged the introduction and greeted Nancy with a warm smile. Nancy judged her to be at least four years older than Allison. Her face was rather serious, and it was evident from her manner that responsibility had fallen on her shoulders at an early age.

Nancy was attracted to both girls and responded to their friendly welcome. She put on a robe which Allison brought her and Grace hung her wet clothes near the range. Presently Grace pulled an ironing board from a closet with the intention of pressing Nancy's garments. But Nancy would not hear of this and began to iron them herself.

"This is fun," she said to the sisters. "I don't know what I would have done without you girls."

"It's great for us," Allison spoke up. "We don't have much company. To tell you the truth, we can't afford it."

Grace stepped to the stove, removed a golden-brown cake from the oven, and set it on the table to cool.

"But today we're not talking about money. It's Allison's birthday and this is a birthday cake. Nancy, if you're not in too much of a hurry, I wish you'd join us in a little celebration."

"Why, I'd love to," Nancy said.

"Grace's cakes are yummy," Allison declared.

"I'm not much of a cook myself. My department is taking care of the barn and the chickens."

Soon Nancy finished pressing her clothes and put them back on. Meanwhile, the cake had cooled and Grace started to spread the chocolate frosting.

"Suppose you two go into the living room and wait," she suggested. "I'll bring in the cake and tea."

Nancy followed Allison to the adjoining room. Although it was comfortable, the room did not contain much furniture. The floor had been painted and was scantily covered with handmade rag rugs. With the exception of an old-fashioned sofa, an inexpensive table, a few straight-backed chairs and an old oil stove which furnished heat in cold weather, there was little else in the room. However, dainty white curtains covered the windows, and Nancy realized that although the Hoovers were poor, they had tried hard to make their home attractive.

"Do you two girls live here alone all the time?" Nancy inquired.

Allison nodded. "Grace and I have been living here since Father died. That was two years ago. Mother passed away just before that," the girl added with a slight catch in her voice. "Their illnesses took every penny we had."

"I'm terribly sorry," Nancy remarked sympathetically. "It must be dreadfully hard for two girls to run the farm by themselves."

"Our farm isn't as large as it once was," Allison said quietly. "We have only a few acres left. I know you are too polite to ask how we manage, Nancy. Grace helps a dressmaker at Masonville whenever she can get work. She makes all her own clothes and mine too. And I raise chickens."

From just beyond the doorway suddenly came the strains of "Happy Birthday to you! Happy Birth—"

By this time Nancy had joined in. She and Grace finished "—day to you. Happy Birthday, dear Allison. Happy Birthday to you!"

Grace set the cake with eighteen lighted candles on the table. She and Nancy sang the second verse with the words "May you have many more!"

Tears stood in Allison's eyes. When the song ended, she grasped her sister in a tremendous hug. Then she gave Nancy one.

"This—this is the nicest birthday I've had in years," she quavered.

"And it's one of the most enjoyable I've ever attended," Nancy said sincerely.

Suddenly Allison began to sing a tuneful old English ballad about the birthday of a village lass. Nancy listened entranced to Allison's clear, bell-like tones. When she finished, Nancy applauded, then said:

"That was perfectly lovely.   You have a beautiful voice, Allison!"

The singer laughed gaily.   "Thank you, Nancy. I've always wanted to take lessons, but as you know, voice training is pretty expensive."

At that moment Grace brought in a tray of fragrant tea.   As she poured three cups, Allison blew out the candles and served the cake.

"I've never tasted anything more delicious in all my life," Nancy said enthusiastically.

The three girls chatted like old friends.   Finally the sun broke through the clouds.   As Nancy rose to leave, she noticed an unusual picture on the wall opposite her and commented on its beauty.

"Uncle Josiah Crowley gave it to us," Allison told her.   "If he were only alive now, things would be different."

At the mention of the name, Nancy sat down again.   Was she going to pick up a clue to the possibility that Mr. Crowley had made a later will?

"He wasn't really our uncle," Grace explained. "But we loved him as much as though he were a relative."   Her voice broke and for a moment she could not go on.   Then, gaining control of herself, she continued, "He lived on the farm next to us— that was when Mother and Father were alive.   All of Allison's and my misfortunes seemed to come at once."

"He was the dearest man you ever saw," Allison

added. "Some people thought him queer, but you never minded his peculiar ways after you knew him. Uncle Josiah was very good to us. He always told me that he'd back me in a singing career."

"Yes," Grace added. "Uncle Josiah used to say Allison sang as sweetly as a bird and he wanted to pay for lessons with a famous teacher. But after he went to live with the Tophams, he never said any more about it."

"He never liked it with the Tophams, though," Allison declared. "They weren't kind to him, and he used to slip away to visit us."

"Uncle Josiah often said that we seemed like his own children," Grace spoke up. "He brought us many nice gifts, but we loved him for himself and not his money. I remember, though, the very last day we saw him alive, he told us 'I have planned a big surprise to make you girls happy. But I can't tell you now what it is. You'll see it in my will.' Those were his very words."

"And then the Tophams got everything," Allison said. "He must have changed his mind for some reason."

"It's hard to believe he would forget his promise to us," Grace said sadly.

"Oh, wouldn't it be wonderful if a later will could be found!" Allison exclaimed.

"Yes," Nancy replied slowly. "I've heard that

Mr. Crowley told other people he was leaving money to them. The Turner sisters, for instance. Do you know them?"

"Slightly," Grace answered.

"My dad," Nancy went on, "is a lawyer and he and I are very much interested in this case. He even mentioned you girls, and to tell the truth I was on my way here to talk to you."

Allison impulsively grasped Nancy's arm. "You say your father is a lawyer? Grace and I are positive Uncle Josiah made a later will. Oh, if we could only engage your father to help us prove this!" Then a sad look came over her face. "But I'm forgetting—we wouldn't have any money to pay him if we should lose the case."

"Don't let that worry you," said Nancy kindly. "This is your birthday and you must be happy, Allison. My special wish for you is that before you're one year older, you'll inherit some of the Crowley money, so that you can take those singing lessons!"

CHAPTER VI

An Exciting Appointment

THE HOOVER girls walked out to the barn with Nancy. "Do come to see us again," Grace called, as the young detective climbed into her car.

"Yes, please do," Allison added.

Nancy promised that she would. "As soon as I have some news," she said.

Although the weather had cleared, the River Road remained muddy and slippery. Nancy found it necessary to drive with extreme care for the next two miles until she reached the main highway.

"No wonder this River Road isn't used much," she thought. "And how do Grace and Allison get to town?" Nancy wondered. She had not seen a car at the Hoover home and knew that no bus passed their door.

"I certainly wish," she thought, "that I or somebody else could locate a later will of Josiah Crowley's by which the Hoovers and the Turners would receive some much-needed money. I must tell Dad about this latest development."

She decided to see if her father was in his office and drove directly there. Nancy parked the car in a nearby lot. She surveyed the convertible ruefully as she climbed out.

"Poor thing! It certainly needs a bath!"

Nancy found Mr. Drew in. As she entered his private office, he arose from the desk chair to kiss her. "I'm glad you're here—and safe," the lawyer said. "I was worried about you when that violent storm came up. When Hannah phoned me that you weren't back, I began to regret I'd sent you on the errand."

His daughter grinned. "I'm back, all in one piece. I delivered the papers to Judge Hart and learned that he and his wife saw Mr. Crowley in Masonville a couple of times. Also, I talked to the Hoover girls."

She described her meeting with Allison and Grace Hoover and ended by asking her father if he could help them.

"From what you say, it does look as though Josiah Crowley might have made another will which included them as beneficiaries," Mr. Drew commented thoughtfully. "I'll be glad to do anything I can to help the Hoover girls."

He asked whether the sisters had given Nancy any specific information about Mr. Crowley's habits or other helpful clues. When Nancy shook her head, Mr. Drew suggested that she invite the girls to his office for a little conference. "Perhaps if I ask them some questions, it will recall helpful incidents." The lawyer studied his desk calendar for a moment, then looked up at his daughter. "How about tomorrow afternoon at two-forty-five? I can give them about half an hour."

For answer, Nancy gave her father a hug and then asked if she might use his telephone to call the Hoovers at once.

Grace and Allison eagerly accepted the Drews' invitation, and Nancy said she would drive out to bring them to the conference and take them home afterward.

"You're a doll!" cried Allison, who had answered the telephone. "Nancy, I just know you're going to solve this mystery!"

Suddenly an idea came to Nancy. She asked Allison how long the girls would be able to stay in River Heights.

"Oh, as long as you need us," Allison replied.

"Good. Then I'd like you both to stay and have supper with us," Nancy said.

"Sorry I can't join you," Mr. Drew told his daughter as she hung up. "I have a dinner engagement and conference in the evening."

Just then, the mayor of River Heights was shown into the lawyer's office, and Nancy arose to leave. She spoke to the mayor for a moment, then said, "See you later, Dad."

Before Nancy returned home, she stopped at an old-fashioned house on a side street. It was the home of Signor Mascagni, a famous voice teacher who had retired to the small city the year before, but took a few outstanding pupils. Nancy introduced herself to the white bushy-haired, florid-faced man, then said:

"Signor Mascagni, would you be willing to listen to the voice of a friend of mine and give your honest opinion as to whether or not she might become a great singer? If she might, and she can obtain the money for lessons, would you be able to take her as a pupil?"

Signor Mascagni studied Nancy for several minutes before replying. Finally he said, "You do not look like the kind of girl who would come here on a foolish errand. Ordinarily I do not accept beginners. But in this case I would be willing to hear your friend sing." He laughed. "Mind you, I will give you nothing but the truth, and if your friend does not measure up, I hope her feelings will not be hurt too deeply."

Nancy laughed too. "I like honesty," she said. "As a matter of fact, this girl knows nothing about what I am asking you. Coming here will be a complete surprise to her. I'm probably no judge of voices, but I think she's a natural. However, we will both appreciate having your opinion, and will certainly abide by it."

She arranged for a meeting the following afternoon at four o'clock and left Signor Mascagni's house in an excited mood. "Maybe I'm going way out on a limb," Nancy mused, "but this is another one of those hunches of mine that Dad talks about, and I must carry through."

When she picked up the Hoovers the following day, Nancy did not mention the appointment with the voice teacher. The three girls went directly to Mr. Drew's office and at once he began to quiz Grace and Allison about Mr. Crowley.

"I understand that he was a rather eccentric man," the lawyer began. "Suppose you tell me everything you can remember about what Josiah Crowley did and what he said which would help us figure out where he might have secreted a later will."

"Uncle Josiah was rather absent-minded," Grace spoke up. "I often saw him hunting for his spectacles, which he had pushed up on his head."

"Did he ever hide things?" Mr. Drew asked.

"Oh, yes." Allison laughed. "Uncle Josiah was always putting articles away in what he called a safe place. But the places were so safe he never could find the things again!"

"Then," Nancy spoke up excitedly, "Mr. Crowley could have hidden a will and then forgotten where?"

"I suppose so," Grace replied. "While living with the Tophams, I'm sure that's just what he would have done. One day when he was calling at our house he talked about the Tophams and the way they were trying to get all his money. 'I guess they think—just because I stay on—that they're going to get everything. But they'll be fooled when they find I've made another will,' he said with that odd little chuckle of his. 'This time I'm not going to trust it to any lawyer. I'll put it away in a place that I know will be safe.' "

Allison asked Mr. Drew, "Do you think Uncle Josiah hid another will somewhere in the Tophams' house?"

The lawyer looked down at his desk for several seconds before replying. "If he did, we would have a great fight on our hands, I'm afraid, trying to persuade the Tophams to let us make a search."

Another thought had come to Nancy and she shuddered at the idea. Perhaps the Tophams had been alerted by all the talk of a later will, had searched for it, discovered one, and by now destroyed it!

She flashed her father a questioning look and got the impression that he had the same thought. But there was no point in discouraging the Hoover girls by telling them this.

Mr. Drew continued to question the sisters until three-thirty, then said he had another appointment. He would do all he could to help the girls and would not charge them for his services.

"Unless they bring results," he added with a smile.

"You're very kind, just like your daughter," said Grace as she arose and shook hands with the lawyer. "You have no idea how much Allison and I appreciate what you're doing for us."

When the three girls reached Nancy's car, she told the sisters she wanted them to meet someone special in town, and drove directly to Signor Mascagni's home. As they went up to the front porch they could hear the sounds of a soprano voice singing an aria from *Tosca*.

"How beautiful!" Allison exclaimed softly.

The girls were admitted by a maid and asked to wait in a small room while Signor Mascagni's pupil finished her lesson. Puzzled, Allison waited for Nancy to explain.

"I have a surprise for you," Nancy said with a grin. "Signor Mascagni has promised to listen to your voice. If you pass the test, he'll consider taking you as a pupil—that is, after we find the money for voice lessons."

Allison was too dumfounded to speak, but Grace cried out, "Oh, Nancy, what are you going to do next? We've known you only twenty-four hours and you've already boosted our morale sky-high."

At this moment the door to the studio opened. The young soprano came out, followed by Signor Mascagni. He said good-by to his pupil, then invited the three callers into the studio. Nancy quickly introduced the Hoover sisters.

"And you are the singer," the man said almost

at once, addressing Allison. "I can tell from your speaking voice."

Apparently the teacher sensed that Allison had been taken by surprise and was a little nervous. Accordingly he began to talk on other subjects than music. He showed the girls several paintings in the room and pieces of statuary which had come from Italy.

"I prize them highly," he said.

"They are exquisite," Allison remarked.

Signor Mascagni walked to a rear window and pointed out a lovely garden in back of the house. Then, evidently satisfied that Allison was at ease, he led the way to the grand piano and sat down.

"Now what would you like to sing?" he asked Allison with a smile. "Please stand right here facing me."

"Something very simple," she replied. " 'America the Beautiful'?"

The teacher nodded, asked her what key she would like it played in, then began to accompany her. Allison sang as though inspired. Her voice sounded even more beautiful than it had at the farmhouse, Nancy thought. When Allison finished the song, Signor Mascagni made no comment. Instead he asked her to try a scale, then to sing single tones, jumping from octave to octave.

"You have a very fine range, Miss Hoover," was his only comment.

For half an hour he had Allison try short songs

in various keys and at one point joined with her in a duet. At last he turned around on the piano bench and faced Nancy and Grace.

"I believe," he said slowly, "I believe that some day we shall know Allison Hoover as an operatic star!"

Before the girls could say anything, he jumped up and turned to shake Allison's hand fervently. By this time the full import of his words had dawned on the young singer. Tears began to roll down her cheeks.

"*Bravissimo! Bravissimo!*" he exclaimed. "You sing, you cry, you smile! *Magnifico!* You will also be a dramatic actress *splendida.*"

Nancy and Grace were nearly on the verge of tears also, they were so overwhelmed by the happy news. Then suddenly the three girls became serious, remembering that there was still the problem of money for lessons from this great man. They knew his fee per hour must be very high.

Allison suddenly began to talk and poured out her whole story to the white-haired teacher. "But I know," she declared with a brave smile, "that somehow I'm going to get the money for the lessons and I wouldn't want to take them from anybody but you, Signor Mascagni. I'll come back to you just as soon as I can. Thank you very, very much. Please, girls, I'd like to leave now."

As Allison rushed toward the front door, Signor Mascagni detained Nancy and Grace. "This Allison, she is wonderful!" he exclaimed. "I want to give her lessons to see that her training is correct." He threw up his hands and shook his head. "But I cannot afford to give the lessons free. Perhaps I could cut my price—"

"We'll find the money somehow, signor!" Nancy promised. Then she and Grace thanked the teacher and followed Allison outside.

At the Drew home that evening there were mixed emotions on everyone's part. Hannah Gruen had taken a great fancy to the Hoover sisters and the news of Allison's talent had thrilled her, as well as the girls. Conversation at supper was gay and animated. Nancy and Mrs. Gruen drove the sisters to their farm and on parting Nancy again promised to do all she could to help find a will from which the girls might possibly benefit.

But figuring out how to do this became a problem that seemed insurmountable to Nancy. At breakfast the following day, Mr. Drew suggested, "Nancy, perhaps if you'd give your mind a little rest from the Crowley matter, an inspiration about the case might come to you."

His daughter smiled. "Good idea, Dad. I think I'll take a walk in the fresh air and clear the cobwebs from my brain."

As soon as she finished eating, Nancy set out at a brisk pace. She headed for River Heights' attractive park to view the display of roses which was

Signor Mascagni shook Allison's hand fervently

always very beautiful. She had gone only a short distance along one of the paths when she caught sight of Isabel and Ada Topham seated on a bench not far ahead.

"They're the last people in the world I want to see right now," Nancy thought. "They'll probably say something mean to me and I'll lose my temper. When I think how Grace and Allison and the Turners could use just one-tenth of the Crowley money which the Tophams are going to inherit, I could just burst!"

Nancy had paused, wondering whether she should turn back. "No," she told herself, "I'll go on to see the roses. I'll take that path back of the Tophams and they won't notice me."

Nancy made her way along quietly, with no intention of eavesdropping on the two girls. But suddenly two words of their conversation came to her ears, bringing Nancy to an involuntary halt.

She had distinctly heard Isabel say—"the will."

In a flash Nancy's detective instincts were aroused and her heart pounded excitedly. " It must be Josiah Crowley's will they're talking about," she reasoned.

CHAPTER VII

The Angry Dog

WITH the instinct of a detective who dared not miss a clue, Nancy deliberately moved closer to the bench on which the Topham girls were seated.

"If there *should* be another will, I'm afraid we'd be out of luck." The words, in Ada's nasal voice, came clearly to Nancy.

Isabel's reply was in so low a tone that the young sleuth could just manage to catch the words, "Well, I, for one, don't believe Josiah Crowley ever made a later will." She gave a low laugh. "Mother watched him like a hawk."

"Or thought she did," Isabel retorted. "The old man got out of her clutches several times, don't forget."

"Yes, and what's worse, I'm sure Nancy Drew thinks he made a later will. That's why she's taking such an interest in those Hoover girls. I actually saw them go into Mr. Drew's office yesterday and it wasn't to deliver eggs! If Nancy gets her father interested, he might dig up another will. Oh, how I hate that interfering girl!"

At this Nancy could barely refrain from laughing. So the Tophams *were* concerned about the existence of a second will. With bated breath she listened further.

"You're such a worry wart, Ada. You can trust Dad and Mother to take care of things, no matter what happens," Isabel commented dryly. "They won't let that pile of money get away from us. It's ours by right, anyhow."

"You've got something there," Ada conceded. "We should have old Josiah's money after supporting and putting up with him for three years. That was pretty clever of Mother, never accepting any board money from Josiah Crowley!"

The conversation ended as Isabel and Ada arose from the bench and walked away. Nancy waited until they were out of sight, then emerged from her hiding place. Seating herself on the bench vacated by the Topham sisters, Nancy mulled over the remarks she had just overheard.

"There's no doubt in my mind now that if there is a later will, the Tophams haven't destroyed it. How thrilling! But where can it be?"

Nancy realized that to find it was a real challenge. "And I'd better hurry up before the Tophams stumble on it!"

For another ten minutes Nancy sat lost in

thought, sifting all the facts she had gleaned so far.

"There must be some clue I've overlooked," she told herself. Suddenly, with a cry of delight, she sprang to her feet. "Why didn't I think of that before! The Hoover girls and the Turners aren't the only ones who should have figured in this will. There are other relatives of Mr. Crowley who have filed a claim. I wonder who they are. If I could only talk with them, I might pick up a clue!"

Immediately Nancy set off for her father's office. He was engaged in an important conference when she arrived, and she had to wait ten minutes before being admitted to the inner office.

"Now what?" Mr. Drew asked, smiling, as she burst in upon him. "Have you solved the mystery or is your purse in need of a little change?"

Nancy's cheeks were flushed and her eyes danced with excitement. "Don't tease me," she protested. "I need some information!"

"At your service, Nancy."

The young sleuth poured out the story of the Topham sisters' conversation in the park, and told him of her own conclusions. Mr. Drew listened with interest until she had finished.

"Excellent deducting," he praised his daughter. "I'm afraid, though, I can't help you obtain the relatives' names. I don't know any of them."

Nancy looked disappointed. "Oh dear!" she sighed. "And I'm so anxious to find out right away. If I delay even a single day the Tophams may locate that other will—and destroy it."

The next instant her face brightened. "I know! I'll drive out and see the Turner sisters. They might be able to tell me who the other relatives are." Nancy arose and headed for the door.

"Just a minute," said the lawyer. "I wonder if you realize just what you are getting into, Nancy?"

"What do you mean?"

"Only this. Detective work isn't always the safest occupation in which to engage. I happen to know that Richard Topham is an unpleasant man when crossed. If you do find out anything which may frustrate him, the entire Topham family could make things extremely difficult for you."

"I'm not afraid of them, Dad."

"Good!" Mr. Drew exclaimed. "I was hoping you would say that. I'm glad you have the courage of your convictions, but I didn't want you to march off into battle without a knowledge of what you might be up against."

"Battle?"

"Yes. The Tophams won't give up the fortune without a bitter struggle. However, if they attempt to make serious trouble, I promise to deal with them myself."

"And if I do find the will?"

"I'll take the matter into court."

"Oh, thank you! There's no one like you in all the world."

After leaving her father's office, Nancy went directly home to get her car. When she told Hannah Gruen her plans, the housekeeper warned, "Don't become too deeply involved in this matter, dear. In your zeal to help other people, you may forget to be on your guard."

"I promise to be as careful as a pussycat walking up a slippery roof," Nancy assured the housekeeper with a grin, and left the house.

Quickly backing her car from the garage, she set off in the direction of the Turner home. The miles seemed to melt away as Nancy's thoughts raced from one idea to another. Before the young sleuth knew it she had reached the house.

"Hi, Judy!" she called to the little girl, who was playing in the yard with a midget badminton set.

The child looked very cunning in a pink play suit. The hand-embroidered Teddy bears on it were surely the work of her loving aunts.

"Hi, Nancy! I'm glad you came. Now I'll have somebody to play with," Judy said, running up to the visitor.

Obligingly Nancy took a racket and batted the feathered shuttlecock toward the child. "Hit the birdie," she called.

Judy missed but picked up the shuttlecock and whammed it nicely across the net. Nancy hit it back and this time the little girl caught the birdie on her racket and sent it over.

The game went on for several minutes, with

Judy crying out in delight. "You're the bestest batter I ever played with, Nancy," she declared.

After ten minutes of play, Nancy said, "Let's go into the house now, Judy. I want to talk to your aunties."

Judy skipped ahead and announced her new playmate's arrival.

"Hello, Nancy," the women said as she entered the living room.

"We were watching the game from the window," said Mary Turner. "This is a real thrill for Judy. Edna and I are very poor at hitting the birdie."

"It was lots of fun," Nancy replied. "I'm glad to see you all again."

She now asked whether the police had located the thieves who had taken the silver heirlooms from the house.

"Not yet," Mary answered. "And what's worse, we found that several other pieces had been taken too."

"What a shame!" Nancy exclaimed. "But I'm sure the stolen articles will be found." Then she added, "I came here on a particular mission."

"Yes?"

"Your story about Mr. Josiah Crowley intrigued me. Then, the other day, I met two girls, Grace and Allison Hoover, who told me of a similar promise from him regarding his will."

"How amazing!" Edna Turner exclaimed. "I

heard Josiah mention the Hoovers and Allison's beautiful voice."

"Dad and I have become very much interested in the case and are inclined to agree with you and the Hoovers that Mr. Crowley may have written another will shortly before his death and hidden it some place."

"Oh, wouldn't it be wonderful if such a will could be found!" Mary exclaimed. "It might mean all the difference in the world to Judy's future."

"What I want to do," Nancy went on, "is talk to as many of Mr. Crowley's relatives as I can find. Some place I may pick up a clue to where a more recent will is hidden. Tell me, do any of his other relatives live around here?"

"Yes. Three that I can think of," Edna answered.

She went on to say that two cousins, who had never married, lived on a farm just outside Titusville. "Their names are Fred and William Mathews."

Suddenly the Turner sisters blushed a deep pink. They glanced at each other, then back at Nancy. Finally Edna said:

"Many years ago Fred proposed to Mary, and William to me, and we came near accepting. But just at that time we had the great tragedy in the family and took Judy's mother to rear, so we decided not to marry."

An embarrassing pause was broken by Judy. "Some day my aunties are going to give me one of my mother's dollies, Nancy. Isn't that nice?"

"It certainly is," Nancy agreed. "And you must be sure to show it to me." Then she asked the sisters, "What relation are the Mathews to Mr. Crowley?"

"First cousins on his mother's side."

"Do you think they would mind my asking them some questions, even though I'm a stranger?"

"Not at all," Mary replied. "They're very fine gentlemen."

"And tell them Mary and I sent you," Edna added.

"How far is Titusville from here?" Nancy inquired.

"Oh, not more than five miles on Route 10A. You could drive there in a few minutes. It's on the way to Masonville. Nancy, won't you stay and have lunch with us?"

Eager to continue her work, the young sleuth was about to refuse, but Judy put in an invitation also. "Please, oh please, Nancy. And while my aunties are fixing it, you and I can play badminton."

"All right," Nancy agreed. "And thank you very much."

It was nearly two o'clock when she finally was ready to depart.

"Oh, Mary," said Edna suddenly, "we forgot to

tell Nancy about Josiah's wife's cousin, Mrs. Abby Rowen. She'd be apt to know more about the will than anyone else."

"That's right! You really should call on her, Nancy. She took care of Josiah one time when he was sick, and he thought the world of her. He often declared he intended to leave her something. She's a widow and has very little."

"Even a few thousand dollars would mean a lot to her," Edna added. "Abby must be over eighty years of age, and growing forgetful. She has no children and there's no one to look after her."

"Where shall I find Mrs. Rowen?" Nancy asked, hoping it was not far away.

"Abby lives on the West Lake Road," Edna responded. "It's a good many miles from here."

"Then I shan't have time to go there today," the young sleuth said. "But I'll surely see her as soon as I can. And now I must be going."

Nancy thanked the Turner sisters and said good-by. But before she could leave, Judy insisted upon showing how she could jump rope and do all kinds of dancing steps with a hoop on the lawn.

"Judy entertains us all the time," Mary remarked. "We believe she's very talented."

Nancy thought so too. As she drove off, she again hoped that money would become available for a very special education for Judy.

After Nancy had gone five miles along the designated route, she began to watch the mailboxes.

Soon she noticed one which bore the name *Mathews*. The farmhouse stood back a distance from the road and had a wide sweep of lawn in front of it. Near the house a man was riding a small tractor, mowing the grass.

Nancy drove down the narrow lane which led into the grounds, and stopped opposite the spot where the man was working. The man's back was toward her, and he apparently had not heard the car above the noise of the tractor, so she waited.

Looking toward the house, Nancy suddenly saw a sight that appalled her. Wedged between two stones of a broken wall was a police dog puppy whining pitifully. Nancy dashed forward and released the little animal. As it continued to whimper, she cuddled the pup in her arms and began to examine its paws.

"Why, you poor thing!" Nancy said, seeing a tear in the flesh of one hind leg. "This must be taken care of right away."

She decided to carry the puppy over to the man on the mower. As Nancy walked across the lane, she suddenly heard an angry growl near her. Looking back, she saw a huge police dog, evidently the pup's mother, bounding toward her.

"It's all right," Nancy called soothingly to the dog. "I'm not going to take your baby away."

She took two more strides, but got no farther. With a fierce snarl the dog leaped on Nancy, knocking her flat!

CHAPTER VIII

A Forgotten Secret

NANCY screamed for help, hoping to attract the farmer's attention. She expected momentarily to be bitten by the angry dog, but to her great relief the animal did not harm her.

The young sleuth's sudden fall had caused the puppy to fly from her arms. With a leap its mother was at the pup's side. She grabbed her baby by the back of its neck and trotted off toward the barn.

"O-o, that was a narrow escape." Nancy took a deep breath as she got to her feet, brushed herself off, and ruefully surveyed a tear in her sweater.

By this time the man on the tractor, having changed direction, saw the fracas and came running. He apologized for the dog's actions, but Nancy said quickly:

"It was my fault. I should have set the pup

down.   Its mother probably thought I was trying to dognap her baby!"

"Possibly."

Nancy explained why she had picked up the little animal and the farmer said he would look at the cut later.

"I'm glad you weren't hurt," he added. "Thanks for being such a good scout about it. Did you come to see me or my brother?" he asked. "I'm Fred Mathews."

Nancy gave her name, and added that she was acquainted with the Turner sisters and others who had been told they would benefit under Josiah Crowley's will.

"My dad—the lawyer Carson Drew—and I are working on the case.   We believe there might have been a later will than the one presented by Mr. Topham, and we'd like to find it."

"And you came to see if William and I could give you a clue?" Fred's bright blue eyes sparkled boyishly.

"That's right, Mr. Mathews.   Also, did Mr. Crowley ever tell you he was going to leave you some money?"

"Indeed he did."

At this moment another man came from the house and Fred introduced him as his brother William.   Both were tall, spare, and strong-muscled.   Though their hair was gray, the men's faces were youthful and unwrinkled.

"Let's sit down under the tree here and discuss this," Fred suggested, leading the way to a group of rustic chairs. He told William of Nancy's request, then asked him, "Did Cousin Josiah ever give you any idea he'd made a will in which we were not beneficiaries?"

"No. I thought one would come to light when he died. To tell the truth, Miss Drew, Fred and I were thunderstruck at the will which left everything to the Tophams. That wasn't what Cousin Josiah led us to believe."

"It certainly wasn't," Fred spoke up. "But I guess William and I counted our chickens before they were hatched. We just about make ends meet here with our small fruit farm. Help and equipment cost such a lot. One thing we've always wanted to do, but couldn't afford, was to travel. We thought we'd use the money from Cousin Josiah to do that."

"But our dream bubble burst," said William. "No trips for us."

Nancy smiled. "Don't give up hope yet. Dad and I haven't."

She was disappointed that the brothers could offer her no clues about a place to look for another will. A little while later she left the farm and returned home.

"No new evidence," she told her father. "Let's hope Mrs. Abby Rowen has some!"

Early the next morning she set off for the elderly

woman's home, and reached her destination by asking directions of people living along West Lake Road.

"This must be Abby Rowen's house," Nancy told herself. "It fits the description."

She climbed out of her car and stood before the one-story frame building which was badly in need of paint and repair. The yard around it was overgrown with weeds, and the picket fence enclosing the cottage sagged dejectedly.

"The place looks deserted," Nancy mused. "But I'll see if Mrs. Rowen is at home."

Nancy made her way up the scraggly path to the house and rapped on the front door. There was no response. After a moment, she knocked again.

This time a muffled voice called, "Who's there? If you're a peddler, I don't want anything."

"I'm not selling anything," Nancy called out reassuringly. "Won't you let me in, please?"

There was a long silence, then the quavering voice replied, "I can't open the door. I've hurt myself and can't walk."

Nancy hesitated an instant before pushing open the door. As she stepped into the dreary living room, she saw a frail figure on the couch. Abby Rowen lay huddled under an old shawl, her withered face drawn with pain.

"I am Nancy Drew and I've come to help you, Mrs. Rowen."

The old lady turned her head and regarded Nancy with a stare of wonder.

"You've come to help me?" she repeated unbelievingly. "I didn't think anyone would ever bother about old Abby again."

"Here, let me arrange the pillows for you." Gently Nancy moved the old woman into a more comfortable position.

"Yesterday I fell down the cellar stairs," Mrs. Rowen explained. "I hurt my hip and sprained my ankle."

"Haven't you had a doctor?" Nancy asked in astonishment.

"No." Abby Rowen sighed. "Not a soul has been here and I couldn't get in touch with anybody. I have no telephone."

"Can you walk at all?" Nancy asked.

"A little."

"Then your hip isn't broken," Nancy said in relief. "Let me see your ankle. Oh my, it is swollen! I'll bandage it for you."

"There's a clean cloth in the closet in the kitchen," Abby told her. "I haven't any regular bandage."

"You really should have a doctor," Nancy remarked. "Let me drive you to one."

"I can't afford it," the old woman murmured. "My pension check hasn't come, and it's too small, anyway."

"Let me pay the doctor," Nancy offered.

Abby Rowen shook her head stubbornly. "I'll not take charity. I'd rather die first."

"Well, if you insist upon not having a doctor, I'm going to the nearest drugstore and get some bandaging and a few other things," Nancy told her. "But before I go, I'll make you a cup of tea."

"There's no tea in the house."

"Then I'll get a box. What else do you need?"

"I need 'most everything, but I can't afford anything right now. You might get me some tea and a loaf of bread. That's enough. You'll find the money in a jar in the cupboard. It's not very much, but it's all I have."

"I'll be back in a few minutes," Nancy promised.

She stopped in the kitchen long enough to examine the cupboards. With the exception of a little flour and sugar and a can of soup, there appeared to be nothing in the house to eat. Nancy found that the money jar contained less than five dollars.

"I'll not take any of it," she decided.

Quietly the young sleuth slipped out the back door. She drove quickly to the nearest store and ordered a stock of groceries. Then she stopped at a drugstore and purchased bandages and liniment.

Reaching the cottage, she carried the supplies inside and adeptly set about making Abby Rowen more comfortable. She bathed the swollen ankle and bound it neatly with the antiseptic bandage.

"It feels better already," Mrs. Rowen told her gratefully. "I don't know what would have happened to me if you hadn't come."

"Oh, someone would have dropped in," said Nancy cheerfully. She went to the kitchen and in a short while prepared tea and a light lunch for the elderly woman.

As Abby Rowen ate the nourishing meal, Nancy was gratified to observe that almost immediately her patient became more cheerful and seemed to gain strength. She sat up on the couch and appeared eager to talk with Nancy.

"There aren't many folks willing to come in and help an old lady. If Josiah Crowley had lived, things would have been different," she declared. "I could have paid someone to look after me."

"It's strange that he didn't provide for you in his will," Nancy replied quietly.

She did not wish to excite the woman by telling her real mission. Yet Nancy hoped that she might lead her tactfully into a discussion of Josiah Crowley's affairs without raising hopes which might never be realized.

"It's my opinion that Josiah did provide for me," Mrs. Rowen returned emphatically. "Many a time he said to me, 'Abby, you'll never need to worry. When I'm gone you'll be well taken care of by my will.' "

"And then everything was left to the Tophams," Nancy encouraged her to proceed.

"That was according to the first will," Abby Rowen stated.

"You mean there was another will?" Nancy inquired eagerly.

"Of course. Why, I saw that will with my own eyes!"

"You saw it!" Nancy gasped.

The old woman nodded gravely. "Mind, I didn't see what was in the will. One day Josiah came to call and give me some money. Right off I noticed he had a bunch of papers in his hand. 'Abby,' he said, 'I've made a new will. I didn't bother with a lawyer. I wrote it myself.' "

"How long ago was that?" Nancy asked quickly.

"Let me see." Abby Rowen frowned thoughtfully. "I can't remember the exact date. It was this past spring. Anyway, Josiah hinted that he'd done well by me. 'But, Josiah,' I said, 'are you sure it's legal to write it yourself?' 'Of course it is,' he said. 'A lawyer told me it was all right, just so long as I wrote it myself and signed it. But I did have it witnessed.' "

"Do you know who witnessed the will?" Nancy broke in.

"No. He didn't say."

"Haven't you any idea what became of the will?" Nancy asked hopefully.

"Well, I remember Josiah did say something about putting it where nobody could get it unless they had legal authority. But I really don't know what became of it."

"Are you certain that was all Mr. Crowley said?" Nancy inquired gently. She recalled the Turners saying that Abby had become forgetful.

The elderly woman shook her head and sighed. "Many a night I've lain awake trying to think what else he did say about where he would put the will. I just can't recollect."

"Try to think!" Nancy begged.

"I can't remember," Abby Rowen murmured hopelessly. "I've tried and tried." She leaned against the cushions and closed her eyes, as though the effort had exhausted her.

At that very moment the clock on the mantel chimed twelve. Abby's eyes fluttered open and an odd expression passed over her face.

For an instant she stared straight before her, then slowly turned her head and fastened her eyes on the clock.

CHAPTER IX

Helpful Disclosures

NANCY watched Abby Rowen intently as the mantel clock finished striking. The elderly woman's lips had begun to move.

"The clock!" she whispered. "That was it! The clock!"

Nancy gripped the arms of her chair in excitement. "Josiah Crowley hid the will in a clock?" she prompted.

"No—no, it wasn't that," Abby murmured, sighing again. "I know Josiah said something about a clock, but whatever it was has slipped my mind."

Silence descended over the room. Nancy was wondering what connection the timepiece could have with the missing will. Mrs. Rowen was staring at the clock, evidently still trying to probe her memory.

Suddenly she gave a low cry. "There! It came to me just like that!"

"What, Mrs. Rowen?" Nancy urged quietly, lest she startle the old woman into forgetfulness.

"A notebook!" Abby exclaimed triumphantly.

Nancy's heart gave a leap, but she forced herself to say calmly, "Please tell me more about this notebook."

"Well, one day not long before he passed away, Josiah said to me, 'Abby, after I'm dead, if my last will isn't found, you can learn about it in this little book of mine.'"

"Do you know what became of the notebook, Mrs. Rowen?"

"Oh dearie me! There goes my memory again. No, I don't."

Although baffled, Nancy felt a growing conviction that the whereabouts of the Crowley will was definitely tied up with a clock of some kind. But, she pondered, why did the striking of the mantel clock remind Abby Rowen of the notebook?

Impulsively Nancy got up and went over to the mantel. She looked inside the glass front and in the back. There were no papers inside.

Returning to her chair, Nancy asked the elderly woman, "What became of the furnishings of the Crowley home when he gave it up?"

"The Tophams got 'most everything."

"There must have been a family clock," Nancy mused, half to herself.

"A family clock?" Abby repeated. "Oh, yes, there was a clock."

"Can you describe it?"

"It was just an ordinary mantel type, something like mine—tall, with a square face," the woman told Nancy. "Only Josiah's was fancier. Had some kind of a moon on top."

"What became of the clock?" Nancy questioned.

"I suppose the Tophams got it, too."

At last Nancy, sure she had done all she could for Abby, and that she had learned as much as possible for the present, rose to depart. After saying good-by, she stopped at a neighboring house and asked the occupants to look in occasionally on the ailing woman.

"I think maybe one of the county's visiting nurses should see Mrs. Rowen," she suggested.

"I'll phone the agency," the neighbor offered. "Meanwhile, I'll go over myself. I'm so sorry I didn't know about Mrs. Rowen."

As Nancy drove toward River Heights, she jubilantly reviewed the new facts in the case. "Now, if I can only locate Mr. Crowley's notebook—or clock—or both!"

Nancy's brow knit in concentration. How would she go about tracking down the old timepiece?

"I guess," she concluded, "if the Tophams *do* have the clock, I'll have to pay them a visit!"

While she did not relish the idea of calling on

the unpleasant family, Nancy was determined to pursue every possible clue. "I can just see Ada's and Isabel's expressions when I appear at their front door," Nancy thought wryly. "Well, I'll think of some excuse to see them."

She was still mulling over the problem when she pulled into the driveway of her home and heard a familiar voice calling her name.

"Why, Helen Corning!" exclaimed Nancy, as a slim, attractive school friend of hers ran up. "I haven't seen you for days."

"I've been busy lately," Helen explained, "trying to sell six tickets for a charity ball. But I haven't had much luck. Would you like a couple?"

A sudden idea flashed into Nancy's mind at her friend's words. "Helen," she said excitedly, "I'll buy two of your tickets and sell the rest for you."

The other girl stared in astonishment. "Why, that's a wonderful offer, Nance. But—"

Nancy's eyes danced. "I know you think I've lost my mind. I really mean it, though. Please let me take the tickets! I can't tell you my reasons yet—except my cause is a worthy one."

Helen, looking relieved but bewildered, handed over the tickets. "This is really a break for me," she said. "Now I can leave for my aunt's Camp Avondale this evening as I'd hoped. It's at Moon Lake. I thought I'd never get off, with those tickets unsold!"

Nancy smiled. "Have a grand time, Helen," she said.

"How about coming along? It's not expensive and there's room for lots more girls. We'd have loads of fun."

"I'd love to," Nancy replied, "but right now I can't get away."

"Maybe you can make it later," Helen suggested. "If so, just zip on up. I'll be there for two weeks before the regular summer camp opens."

The two friends chatted a little longer, then said good-by. Nancy put the car away, then walked slowly toward her house, looking meditatively at the charity tickets in her hand.

"These are to be my passport to the Tophams' stronghold!"

It was the following afternoon when Nancy approached the large pretentious house belonging to the Tophams.

Bracing herself for what she realized would be a trying interview, Nancy mounted the steps and rang the doorbell. "Here goes," she thought. "I must be subtle in this maneuver to keep from arousing the Tophams' suspicions!"

At that moment a maid opened the door, and with a condescending look, waited for Nancy to state her mission.

"Will you please tell Mrs. Topham that Nancy Drew is calling?" she requested. "I'm selling tickets for a charity dance. It's one of the most important functions of the year in River Heights," Nancy added impressively.

It seemed ages to the young sleuth before the maid returned and said that "Madame" would see her. Nancy was ushered into the living room, which was so bizarre in its decor she was startled.

"Such an expensive hodge-podge!" Nancy observed to herself, sitting down. She glanced at the pink carpet—which to her clashed with the red window draperies—and at an indiscriminate assortment of period furniture mixed with modern.

A haughty voice interrupted her thoughts. "Well, what do you want, Nancy?" Mrs. Topham had sailed grandly into the room and seated herself opposite Nancy.

"I'm selling—" Nancy began pleasantly.

"Oh, if you're selling things I'm not interested," the woman broke in rudely. "I can't be handing out money to every solicitor who comes along."

With difficulty Nancy suppressed an angry retort to the cutting remark. "Mrs. Topham," she said evenly, "perhaps your maid didn't make it clear. I am selling tickets to a charity ball which will be one of the loveliest affairs in River Heights this year."

"Oh!" A slight change came over Mrs. Topham's face. Nancy sensed that her words had struck a responsive chord. The woman was well known for her aspirations to be accepted by the best families in River Heights. "Well—"

To Nancy's dismay Mrs. Topham's response was cut off by the arrival of Ada and Isabel. The sisters entered the room, but did not at first notice Nancy's presence. They were intently carrying on a disgruntled conversation.

"Really!" Ada was complaining. "I'm positive that woman snubbed us deliberately."

Then she and Isabel caught sight of Nancy and stopped short. They stared coldly at the visitor.

"What are *you* doing here?" Isabel asked with a patronizing air.

Mrs. Topham answered her daughter's question. "Nancy is selling tickets to a charity dance, dear. It's to be a very important affair and I think it will be—er—beneficial—for us to be present."

Isabel tossed her head disdainfully. "Don't waste your money, Mother."

"Isabel's right," Ada chimed in. "We don't want to go to a ball just anybody can go to. We only attend the most exclusive affairs."

"Absolutely," Isabel declared in her haughtiest tone. "After all, Ada and I are very particular about the people we choose to meet."

Mrs. Topham hesitated, evidently influenced by her daughters' argument. Nancy's heart sank, and she feared her cause was lost. She fully realized that Ada and Isabel would stay away from the dance just to spite her.

As she debated what her next move should be, Richard Topham walked into the living room.

He was a thin man, with sparse graying hair. His manner was rather nervous. Mrs. Topham perfunctorily introduced Nancy to her husband.

"I gather you have some tickets to dispose of, Miss Drew," he said without ceremony. "How many?"

"Why, four," Nancy replied in some surprise.

"I'll take them all." Mr. Topham opened his wallet with a flourish and drew out a hundred-dollar bill. Here you are. Keep the change for your charity."

His daughters gasped and his wife exclaimed, "Richard! Have you lost your senses? All that money!"

"Listen," Mr. Topham retorted bluntly. "This donation will entitle us to have our names on the programs as patrons."

With this remark he slumped into a chair and buried himself in the financial section of the newspaper. His family stared at one another, but they knew that the matter was closed. They never dared disturb him when he was absorbed in the stock-market reports.

Nancy arose reluctantly. She still had not accomplished the real purpose of her visit, but she had no excuse for prolonging her stay. How could she find out about the Crowley clock? Was it the one on the mantelpiece?

"I must be going," she said. Then, looking at her wrist watch, she pretended that it had stopped and began to wind it. "What time is it, please?"

"There's a clock right in front of you—on the mantel," Ada said sharply.

Nancy looked at the timepiece. "So there is," she remarked casually. "Is it an heirloom, perhaps the old Crowley clock I've heard so much about?"

Mrs. Topham looked down her nose. "I should say not! This is a far more expensive one!"

Isabel also rose to Nancy's bait. "Cousin Josiah's old clock was a monstrosity. We wouldn't even have it cluttering up the attic!"

Nancy's hopes waned, but she asked quickly, "Oh, then you sold it?"

"No," Ada spoke up contemptuously. "Who'd give any money for that piece of junk? We sent it up to our bungalow at Moon Lake."

Moon Lake! The words hit Nancy like a thunderbolt. Not only had the Topham girl given Nancy the very information she sought, but Helen Corning's invitation to Camp Avondale provided a valid reason to visit the resort! Now if she could only figure out how to see the old clock!

As if Ada had read the visitor's thoughts, she said airily, "We have some really fine pieces up at the cottage, Nancy. If you ever get up that way, drop in to see them. The caretaker will show you around."

"Thank you. Thank you so much for everything," Nancy said, trying hard to conceal her excitement.   As the door closed behind her, Nancy grinned in anticipation.

"What luck!" she told herself.   "Moon Lake, here I come!"

CHAPTER X

Following a Clue

WITH soaring spirits, Nancy walked homeward. "I wonder," she thought, "how the Tophams will feel about Josiah Crowley's old clock if it costs them the inheritance they're counting on."

At dinner that night Nancy chatted with unusual animation, deciding not to tell of her exciting plans until after Hannah had served dessert.

Mr. Drew, however, sensed that big news was coming. "My dear," he said, laying a hand on his daughter's arm, "you look like the cat that swallowed the canary. What's the big scoop?"

Nancy giggled. "Oh, Dad. I can't keep any secrets from you." Then, as the table was cleared, the young sleuth told of her great stroke of luck. "And just think, Helen invited me to her aunt's camp!"

"Good," her father commented, smiling. "You

can combine business with pleasure, Nancy. Swimming and boating and fun with the girls will provide a much-needed vacation."

"May I start first thing in the morning?" his daughter asked.

"An excellent idea, Nancy. The change will do wonders for you. Go, by all means."

Hurriedly she packed a suitcase and the next morning was off to an early start.

Moon Lake was about a fifty-mile drive. One way to go was past the Hoover girls' farm and Nancy decided to stop there. As she approached the house, the young sleuth heard singing. It was coming from the barn.

"How beautiful!" Nancy thought, as the clear soprano voice went through a series of trills and flutelike scales.

In a moment the singer appeared and Nancy teasingly applauded. Allison's eyes danced. "Thanks. I was just trying to imitate some of the greats."

"You'll be great yourself one of these days," Nancy prophesied.

"Not unless I get some money to finance lessons," Allison said. "Any news, Nancy?"

"Sort of. I've had a little luck." At this moment Grace appeared and instantly invited Nancy to stay, but the young detective said she too had work to do. "I hope to have a good report for you soon," she added, and waved good-by.

Grace's face brightened and Allison declared cheerfully, "Then there's still hope? We are so lucky to have you as a friend, Nancy. Come see us again soon. Please."

Resuming her journey, Nancy soon branched off from the River Road and headed toward Moon Lake. As she drove along, her thoughts revolved constantly around the Crowley relatives and the Hoovers.

She sighed. "How different things would be for them now if Josiah Crowley hadn't been so secretive!"

Her reverie was ended by the sudden strange actions of her car. It kept veering to the left of the road in spite of her efforts to keep it in the middle. With foreboding, Nancy stopped and got out to make an inspection. As she had suspected, a rear tire was flat.

"Oh dear!" she murmured in disgust. "Such luck!"

Though Nancy was able to change a tire, she never relished the task. Quickly she took out the spare tire from the rear compartment, found the jack and lug wrench, and went to work. By the

time her job was completed, she was hot and a little breathless.

"Whew!" she exclaimed, as she started on her way again. "I'll be ready for a nice, cool swim in Moon Lake!"

It was after twelve o'clock when she came in sight of Camp Avondale, run by Helen's aunt. Through the tall trees Nancy caught a glimpse of cabins and tents. Beyond, the blue lake sparkled and glimmered in the sunlight.

As Nancy drove into the camp, a group of girls gathered about her car. Helen came running out of a cabin to greet her chum.

"Girls, it's Nancy Drew!" she exclaimed joyfully and made introductions. Nancy did not know any of the campers, but in no time they made her feel warmly welcome.

"Nancy," said Helen, "park your car back of the dining hall, then come have lunch."

"That sounds wonderful." Nancy laughed. "I'm nearly starved!"

First, she was escorted to the main building where she met Aunt Martha, the camp director, and registered.

"May she stay with me?" Helen asked.

"Certainly, dear. And I hope you have a splendid time, Nancy."

"I'm sure I shall, Aunt Martha."

As the two girls walked off Nancy told Helen

about selling the charity-dance tickets and gave her the money paid by Mr. Topham.

"He surely was generous!" Helen commented in surprise. Then she smiled wryly. "I have a feeling he did it more for social prestige than sympathy for the cause."

Nancy scarcely had time to deposit her suitcase under her cot and freshen up after the long ride when lunch was announced by the ringing of a bell. Campers hurried from all directions to the dining hall. The food was plain but appetizing and Nancy ate with zest.

The meal over, she was rushed from one activity to another. The girls insisted that she join them in a hike. Then came a cooling dip in the lake. Nancy enjoyed herself immensely, but the Crowley mystery was never far from her mind.

"I must find out where the Tophams' cottage is located," she reminded herself. "And next, manage to go there alone."

Nancy's opportunity to accomplish the first part of her quest came when Helen suggested about five o'clock, "How about going for a ride around the lake in the camp launch? There's just time before supper."

"Wonderful!" Nancy accepted readily. "By the way, can you see many of the summer cottages from the water?"

"Oh, yes. Lots of them."

Helen led her friend down to a small dock and with four other girls climbed into the launch, a medium-sized craft.

As one of the campers started the motor, Helen remarked, "It's always a relief to us when this engine starts. Once in a while it balks, but you never know when or where."

"Yes," spoke up a girl named Barby. "And when you're stuck this time of year, you're stuck. There are hardly any cottagers up here yet, so their boats are still in winter storage."

As the little launch turned out into the lake, Nancy was entranced with the beautiful sight before her. The delicate azure blue of the sky and the mellow gold of the late afternoon sun were reflected in the shimmering surface of the water.

"What a lovely scene for an oil painting!" she thought.

As they sped along, however, Nancy kept glancing at the cottages, intermingled with tall evergreen trees that bordered the shore line.

"The Tophams have a bungalow up here, haven't they?" she questioned casually.

"Yes, it's across the lake," Helen replied. "We'll come to it soon."

"Is anyone staying there now?"

"Oh, no, the cottage is closed. It's being looked after by Jeff Tucker, the caretaker. He's the tallest, skinniest man I've ever seen outside a circus."

"Is it hard to get to the place?"

"Not if you go by launch. But it's a long way if you take the road around the lake." Helen looked at her friend. "I didn't know you were particularly interested in the Tophams, Nancy."

"Oh, they're not friends of mine, as you know," Nancy returned hastily. "I was merely curious."

After a time, as the launch slowed down and chugged along close to shore, Helen pointed out a wide path through the woods. At the end of it stood a large, rambling white cottage.

"That's the Topham place," she said.

Trying not to appear too eager, Nancy looked intently at the bungalow. She made a quick mental note of its location.

"Tomorrow I'll visit that place and try to solve the mystery!" she told herself.

CHAPTER XI

An Unexpected Adventure

NANCY awoke the next morning to the fragrant odor of pines. Eager to start out for the Topham bungalow, she dressed quickly.

But in her plans she had reckoned without Helen Corning and her friends. From the moment breakfast was over, Nancy was swept into another whirlwind of activity by the campers of Avondale. The entire day passed without a chance for her to break away.

"Oh, Helen!" Nancy groaned as she tumbled into bed that night. "Tennis matches, canoe races, swimming, water skiing—it's been fun. But tomorrow I think I'll stay out of the activities."

Helen laughed gaily. "You'll change your mind after a sound sleep, Nancy. Wait and see."

For answer, Nancy murmured a sleepy good night. But even as she slipped into slumber, she vowed that in the morning she would not be deterred again from visiting the Tophams' summer place!

After breakfast the next day, Nancy stood firm in her resolve. When Helen urged her to accompany the girls on an all-day hike, Nancy shook her head.

"Thanks a lot, but please excuse me today, Helen."

Normally Nancy would have loved going on such a hike. But she had to achieve her plan of sleuthing. Helen, though disappointed, heeded her friend's plea and trudged off with the other campers into the woods.

As soon as they were out of sight, Nancy leaped into action. After obtaining Aunt Martha's permission to use the launch, she hurried down to the dock. Nancy had frequently handled motorboats and was confident she could manage this one.

"Now. Full speed ahead for the Tophams'!"

To her delight the motor started immediately, and Nancy steered out into the lake. As the launch cut through the water, a cool spray blew into her face. The young sleuth felt a thrill of excitement as she guided the craft toward her destination which might hold a solution to the mystery.

"If only the Tophams' caretaker will let me in when I get there!" she thought.

Nancy's heart beat somewhat faster as she neared her goal. But all of a sudden there was a sputter from the engine. The next instant, to Nancy's utter dismay, the motor gave one long wheeze and died.

"Oh!" she cried aloud.

Nancy knew that the tank held plenty of fuel, for she had checked this before departing. A moment later she recalled Helen's remark about the engine becoming balky at times.

With a sigh of impatience at the unexpected delay, Nancy examined the motor. For over an hour she worked on it, trying every adjustment she could think of. But her efforts were useless. There was not a sound of response from the motor.

"What miserable luck!" she said aloud. "Of all days for the motor to conk out! This means I won't get to the Topham cottage after all!"

For a moment Nancy was tempted to swim ashore. To be so close to the bungalow and not be able to reach it was tantalizing. But she resisted the impulse; she could not leave the boat stranded—it would drift off and she would be responsible.

"I'll just have to wait for a passing boat to rescue me," Nancy decided.

But fate was against her. The hours dragged by and not another craft appeared in sight. Nancy became increasingly uncomfortable as the hot sun beat down on her. Also, she was growing weak from hunger.

"And worst of all," Nancy thought gloomily,

"another whole day is being wasted. I want to get to the bottom of this mystery!"

To occupy her mind, Nancy concentrated once more on the motor. Determinedly she bent over the engine. It was not until the sun sank low in the sky that she sat up and drew a long breath.

"There!" she declared. "I've done everything. If it doesn't start now, it never will."

To her relief and astonishment, it responded with a steady roar as if nothing had ever gone wrong!

Nancy lost no time in heading back toward camp. She dared not attempt to visit the bungalow, since it would be dark very soon.

When finally she eased up to the dock, Nancy saw Helen and her friends awaiting her. They greeted her with delight.

"We were just going to send out a search party for you!" Helen exclaimed. She stopped abruptly and stared at her friend. "You're sunburned and covered with grease! What happened?"

Nancy laughed. "I had an extended sun bath." Then she gave a lighthearted account of her mishap as the campers trooped back to their cabins. When Helen learned that Nancy had had nothing to eat since breakfast, she went to the kitchen and brought back some food.

The following morning the young sleuth decided on her next move. Directly after breakfast she began packing.

When Helen entered the cabin she exclaimed in amazement, "Why, Nancy Drew! You're not leaving camp already!"

"I'm afraid I'll have to, Helen. Right after lunch. I may be back but I'm not sure, so I'd better take my bag with me."

"Don't you like it here?"

"Of course!" Nancy assured her. "I've had a wonderful time. It's just that there's something very important I must attend to at once."

Helen looked at her friend searchingly, then grinned. "Nancy Drew, you're working on some mystery with your father!"

"Well, sort of," Nancy admitted. "But I'll try to get back. Okay?"

"Oh, please do," Helen begged.

Nancy went to the office to pay Aunt Martha and explain her hasty departure. After lunch she set off in her car to a chorus of farewells from the campers, who sadly watched her depart.

She headed the car toward the end of the lake, then took the dirt road leading to the Topham cottage. Soon she came to a fork in the woods.

"Now, which way shall I turn for the bungalow?" she wondered. After a moment's hesitation, Nancy calculated that she should turn left toward the water and did so.

The going was rather rough due to ruts in the road. Two of them, deeper than the others, apparently had been made by a heavy truck.

"The tracks appear fresh," Nancy mused.

As she drove along, the young sleuth noticed a number of summer cottages. Most of them were still boarded up, since it was early in the season. As she gazed at one of them, the steering wheel was nearly wrenched from her hand by a crooked rut. As Nancy turned the steering wheel, to bring the car back to the center of the narrow road, one hand accidentally touched the horn. It blared loudly in the still woods.

"That must have scared all the birds and animals." Nancy chuckled.

Around a bend in the road, she caught sight of a white bungalow ahead on the right side of the road.

There was no sign at the entrance to the driveway to indicate who the owner was, but a wooded path leading down to the lake looked like the one she had seen from the water.

"I think I'll walk down to the shore and look at the cottage from there," Nancy determined. "Then I'll know for sure if this is the place Helen pointed out."

Nancy parked at the edge of the road and got out. To her surprise, she observed that the truck's tire marks turned into the driveway. A second set of tracks indicated that the vehicle had backed out and gone on down the road.

"Delivering supplies for the summer, no doubt," Nancy told herself.

She went down the path to the water, then turned around to look at the cottage.

"It's the Tophams' all right," Nancy decided.

Instead of coming back by way of the path, she decided to take a short cut through the woods. With mounting anticipation of solving the Crowley mystery, she reached the road and hurried up the driveway.

"I hope the caretaker is here," she thought.

Nancy suddenly stopped short with a gasp of astonishment. "Why, the Tophams must be moving out!"

The front and side doors of the cottage stood wide open. Some of the furniture on the porch was overturned and various small household items were strewn along the driveway.

Nancy bent to examine some marks in the soft earth. She noted that several were boot prints, while others were long lines probably caused by dragging cartons and furniture across the lawn.

"That must have been a moving van's tracks I saw," Nancy told herself. "But the Tophams didn't say anything about moving." She frowned in puzzlement.

Her feeling persisted and grew strong as she walked up the steps of the cottage porch. Nancy knocked loudly on the opened door. No response. Nancy rapped again. Silence.

Where was Jeff Tucker, the caretaker? Why wasn't he on hand to keep an eye on the moving activities? An air of complete desertion hung over the place.

"There's something very strange about this," she thought.

Curious and puzzled, Nancy entered the living room. Again her eyes met a scene of disorder. Except for a few small pieces, the room was bare of furniture. Even the draperies had been pulled from their rods and all floor coverings were gone.

"Hm! Most of the furnishings have been taken out," Nancy thought. "I suppose the movers will be back for the other odds and ends."

She made a careful tour of the first floor. All but one room had been virtually emptied. This was a small study. As Nancy entered it, she noticed that the rug lay rolled up and tied, and some of the furniture had evidently been shifted in readiness for moving.

"Funny I didn't hear anything about the Tophams deciding to give up their cottage," she murmured. "And I must say those moving men were awfully careless—"

A vague suspicion that had been forming in the back of Nancy's mind now came into startling focus. "Those men may not be movers!" she burst out. "They may be thieves!"

At once Nancy thought of the dark-gray van which had stopped at the Turners. "Those men may be the same ones who robbed them!"

That would explain, Nancy thought fearfully,

the evidences of the truck's hasty departure. "Probably the thieves were scared away when I sounded my horn!"

Nancy glanced about uneasily. What if the men were still nearby, watching for a chance to return and pick up the remaining valuables? The realization that she was alone, some distance from the nearest house, swept over her. A tingling sensation crept up Nancy's spine.

But resolutely she shook off her nervousness. "At least I must see if the Crowley clock is still here," Nancy reminded herself, and then went through the bungalow again.

She found no trace of the timepiece, however. "I guess the thieves took that too," Nancy concluded. "I'd better report this robbery to the police right now." She looked about for a phone but there was none. "I'll have to drive to the nearest State Police headquarters."

Nancy started toward the front door. Passing a window, she glanced out, then paused in sheer fright. A man, wearing a cap pulled low over his eyes, was stalking up the driveway toward the cottage. He was not tall and slender like the caretaker. This stranger was rather short and heavyset.

"This man fits the Turners' description! He must be one of the thieves who stole the silver heirlooms!" Nancy thought wildly.

CHAPTER XII

A Desperate Situation

FOR A moment Nancy stood frozen to the spot, positive that the man who was coming to the Topham cottage was one of the thieves.

But she hesitated only an instant. Then she turned and ran back into the study. Too late she realized that she had trapped herself, for this room had no other door.

Nancy started back toward the living room. But before she had taken half a dozen steps she knew that escape had been cut off from that direction. The man had reached the porch steps.

"It won't do a bit of good to talk to him," she reasoned. "I'll hide, and when he leaves, I'll follow him in my car and report him to the police!"

Frantically the young sleuth glanced about for a hiding place. A closet offered the only possible refuge. She scurried inside and closed the door.

Nancy was not a second too soon. She had scarcely shut the door when she heard the tread of the man's heavy shoes on the floor just outside. Peeping cautiously through a tiny crack in the door, she saw the heavy-set man come into the study. His face wore a cruel expression.

As he turned toward the closet where she huddled, Nancy hardly dared to breathe, lest her presence be detected. Apparently the man noticed nothing amiss, because his eyes rested only casually on the door.

Nancy's hiding place was anything but comfortable. It was dark and musty, and old clothing hung from nails on the walls. As dust assailed her nostrils, she held a handkerchief to her face.

"If I sneeze he'll surely find me," she told herself.

She felt around and once came close to ripping her hand on a sharp nail. Then she came upon something soft on a shelf and imagined it was a sleeping cat. She drew back, then touched it more cautiously.

"Only an old fur cap," she told herself in disgust. "O-oo, now I feel like sneezing more than ever!"

She held one hand over her mouth hard and waited in agony. But presently the desire to sneeze passed and Nancy breathed more freely.

When she dared to peep out through the crack a second time, she saw that two other rough-looking men had come into the room. One was short and stout, the other taller. Nancy was sure that neither of these two men was the caretaker, because Helen Corning had mentioned that the man was skinny.

The heavy-set man who had come in first seemed to be the leader, for he proceeded to issue orders. "Get a move on!" he growled. "We haven't got all day unless we want to be caught. That girl you saw, Jake, may be back any time from the shore. And she just might get snoopy."

The man addressed as Jake scowled. "What's the matter with you, Sid? Going chicken? If that girl comes around, we'll just give her a smooth story and send her on her way."

"Cut out the yaking," said Sid. "Parky, you and Jake take that desk out of here."

There was no doubt now in Nancy's mind. She was trapped by a clever gang of thieves! She could only continue to watch and listen helplessly from her hiding place.

The two men lifted the heavy piece of furniture and started with it to the door. But they did not move swiftly enough to satisfy the leader, and he berated them savagely.

Jake turned on him. "If you're in such a hurry, why don't you bring the van back to the driveway, instead of leaving it hidden on that road in the woods?"

"And have someone driving past here see us!" sneered the leader. "Now get going!"

Little by little the men stripped the room of

everything valuable. Nancy was given no opportunity to escape. Sid remained in the room while the others made several trips to the van.

"Well, I guess we have all the stuff that's worth anything now," Sid muttered at last.

He turned to follow his companions, who already had left the room, but in the doorway he paused for a final careful survey of the room.

At that same moment Nancy felt an uncontrollable urge to sneeze. She tried to muffle the sound, but to no avail.

The thief wheeled about. "Hey! What—"

Walking directly to the closet, he flung open the door. Instantly he spotted Nancy and angrily jerked her out.

"Spying on us, eh?" he snarled.

Nancy faced the man defiantly. "I wasn't spying on anyone."

"Then what were you doing in that closet?" the thief demanded, his eyes narrowing to slits.

"I came to see the caretaker."

"Looking for him in a funny place, ain't you?" the man sneered.

Nancy realized that she was in a desperate situation. But she steeled herself not to show any of her inward fears.

"I must keep calm," she told herself firmly. Aloud, she explained coolly, "I heard someone coming and I just felt a bit nervous."

"Well, you're going to be a lot more nervous,"

the man said threateningly. "This will be the last time you'll ever stick your nose in business that doesn't concern you!"

A fresh wave of fright swept over Nancy, but resolutely she held on to her courage. "You have no right to be here, helping yourself to the Tophams' furniture!" she retorted. "You should be turned over to the police!"

"Well, you'll never get the chance to do it." The ringleader laughed loudly. "You'll wish you'd never come snoopin' around here. I'll give you the same treatment the caretaker got."

"The caretaker!" Nancy gasped in horror. "What have you done to him?"

"You'll find out in good time."

Nancy gave a sudden agile twist, darted past the man, and raced for the door. The thief gave a cry of rage, and in one long leap overtook her. He caught Nancy roughly by the arm.

"Think you're smart, eh?" he snarled. "Well, I'm smarter!"

Nancy struggled to get away. She twisted and squirmed, kicked and clawed. But she was helpless in the viselike grip of the powerful man.

"Let me go!" Nancy cried, struggling harder. "Let me go!"

Sid, ignoring her pleas, half dragged her across the room. Opening the closet door, he flung her inside.

Nancy heard a key turn.

"Now you can spy all you want!" Sid sneered. "But to make sure nobody'll let you out, I'll just take this key along."

When Nancy could no longer hear the tramp of his heavy boots she was sure Sid had left the house. For a moment a feeling of great relief engulfed her.

But the next instant Nancy's heart gave a leap. As she heard the muffled roar of the van starting up in the distance, a horrifying realization gripped her.

"They've left me here to—to starve!" she thought frantically.

CHAPTER XIII

The Frustrating Wait

AT FIRST Nancy was too frightened to think logically. She beat upon the door with her fists, but the heavy oak panels would not give way.

"Help! Help!" she screamed.

At last, exhausted by her efforts to force the door open, she sank down on the floor. The house was as silent as a tomb. Bad as her predicament was, Nancy felt thankful that enough air seeped into the closet to permit normal breathing.

Although she had little hope that there was anyone within miles of the cottage, Nancy got to her feet, raised her voice, and again shouted for help. Her cries echoed through the empty house and seemed to mock her.

"Oh, why didn't I have enough sense to tell Helen where I was going?" she berated herself miserably. "The girls at camp will never dream that I came here."

Then Nancy remembered mournfully that her father thought she intended to remain at Camp Avondale for a week! He would not become alarmed over her absence until it was too late.

"Someone may find my car at the side of the road," Nancy reasoned, "but it isn't very likely. Few persons pass this way so early in the season."

She wondered, with a shudder, what had become of Jeff Tucker. The thief called Sid had hinted that the caretaker had received the same treatment as Nancy. If he was locked up somewhere, she could expect no aid from him.

"Those thieves will get so far away that even if I could get out of here, I'd be too late."

As the full significance of the situation dawned upon Nancy, panic again took possession of her. In a desperate attempt to break down the door, she threw her weight against it again and again. She pounded on the panels until her fingers were bruised and bleeding. At last she sank down again on the floor to rest and tried to force herself to reason calmly.

"I'm only wasting my strength this way. I *must* try to think logically."

Nancy recalled that it was sometimes possible to pick a lock with a wire. She removed a bobby pin from her hair, opened it, and began to work at the lock. But in the darkness she could not see and made no progress. After fifteen minutes she gave up the task in disgust.

"It's no use," she decided dejectedly. "I—I guess I'm in here for good."

She began to think of her father, of Hannah Gruen, of Helen Corning, and other dear friends. Would she ever see them again? As despondency claimed Nancy, she was dangerously near tears.

"This will never do," she reprimanded herself sternly. "I must keep my head and try to think of some way to escape."

The trapped girl began to rummage in the closet, hoping that by some lucky chance she might find a tool which would help her force the lock of the door. Nancy searched carefully through the pockets of every garment which hung from the hooks. She groped over every inch of the floor.

She found nothing useful, however, and the cloud of dust which she had stirred up made breathing more difficult than before. The closet had become uncomfortably warm by this time. Longingly she thought of the fresh air and cool lake water from which she was closed off.

Then, unexpectedly, Nancy's hand struck something hard. Quickly investigating with her fingers, she discovered a wooden rod suspended high overhead. It was fastened to either side wall and ran the length of the closet. Evidently it had once been used for dress and coat hangers.

"I might be able to use that rod to break out a panel of the door," Nancy thought hopefully. "It feels strong and it's about the right size."

She tugged at the rod with all her might. When it did not budge, she swung herself back and forth on it. At last, amid the cracking of plaster, one side gave way. Another hard jerk brought the rod down.

To Nancy's bitter disappointment, she found that unfortunately the rod was too long to use as a ram in the cramped space. But after further examination, she discovered that it had pointed ends.

"I might use this rod as a wedge in the crack," she thought hopefully.

The young sleuth inserted one end in the space between the hinges and the door, and threw all her weight against the rod. At first the door did not move in the slightest.

"That old Greek scientist, Archimedes, didn't know what he was talking about when he said the world could be moved with a lever," Nancy murmured. "I'd like to see him move this door!"

As she applied steady pressure to the rod a second time, she saw that the hinges were beginning to give. Encouraged, Nancy again pushed full force on the "lever."

"It's coming!" she cried.

Once more she threw her weight against the rod. A hinge tore from the casing and the door sagged. It was now easy to insert the wedge, and Nancy joyously realized that success would soon be hers. With renewed strength she continued her efforts.

Then, just as another hinge gave way, she was startled to hear footsteps. Someone came running into the study, and a heavy body hurled itself against the door of the closet.

For a moment Nancy was stunned. Could this be one of the thieves who had heard the noise she had made and had returned to make sure that she did not escape? She discarded the theory quickly. Surely the three men would want to get far away as quickly as possible. But who was this new-comer? One of the Tophams?

"So, one o' you ornery robbers got yourself locked up, did you?" came an indignant male voice. "That'll teach you to try puttin' one over on old Jeff Tucker. You won't be doin' any more pil-ferin'. I got you surrounded."

The caretaker! Nancy heaved a sigh of fervent relief. "Let me out!" she pleaded. "I'm not one of the thieves! If you'll only let me out of here, I'll explain everything!"

There was silence for a moment. Then the voice on the other side of the door said dubiously, "Say, you aimin' to throw me off, imitatin' a lady's voice? Well, it won't do you any good! No, sir. Old Jeff Tucker's not gettin' fooled again!"

Nancy decided to convince the man beyond doubt. She gave a long, loud feminine scream.

"All right, *all right,* ma'am. I believe you! No man could make that racket. This way out, lady!"

Expectantly Nancy waited. But the door did not open. Then she heard to her dismay:

"If that ain't the limit. The key's gone and I've left my ring o' extra keys somewhere. It's not in my pockets."

Nancy groaned. "Oh, Mr. Tucker, you must find it. Have you looked in every one of your pockets? Please hurry and get me out."

"Hold on, ma'am," the caretaker said soothingly. "I'll just check again."

Nancy was beginning to think she would still have to break down the door, when she heard Jeff Tucker exclaim, "Found it! You were right, ma'am. Key was in my back pocket all the time. It—"

"*Please* open the door!" Nancy broke in desperately.

A key turned in the lock and the bolt clicked. Joyfully Nancy pushed the door open and stepped out. For a moment the bright sunlight in the room almost blinded her. When her vision adjusted, she saw a very tall, thin, elderly man in blue shirt and overalls. He stared at her with concern and amazement.

"Mr. Tucker," she explained quickly, "I'm Nancy Drew. I was here looking for you when those awful thieves came and locked me in the closet." She paused and gazed at the caretaker. "I'm glad to see that you're all right. Their

leader told me they'd locked you up too." She
then asked the elderly man to tell his story.

Jeff Tucker seemed embarrassed as he began to
speak. "I was plain hornswoggled by those crit-
ters, Miss Drew. They pulled up here in a movin'
van, and told me I'd better get after some tres-
passers they'd seen nearby. So," the elderly man
went on with a sigh, "I believed 'em. One of the
men went with me down to the lake and locked
me in a shed. I just got out." He shook his head
sadly. "And all this time they was robbin' the
place. Guess I'll be fired."

Secretly Nancy was inclined to agree, knowing
the Tophams. But aloud she said reassuringly:

"Don't worry, Mr. Tucker. We'll report this
robbery to the State Police immediately. Perhaps
the troopers can catch the thieves before they get
rid of the stolen furniture."

The caretaker looked somewhat relieved. "And
I can sure give a good description o' those crooks.
I'd never forget their ugly faces!"

"Fine," said Nancy. A sudden thought struck
her. "Oh, before we go, Mr. Tucker, tell me, was
there an old clock in this house? A tall, square-
faced mantel clock?"

Jeff Tucker's bright blue eyes squinted. "Mantel clock? Hm. Why, sure enough!" He pointed
to the mantel over the living-room fireplace. "Sat
right up there. Got so used to seein' it, I couldn't

remember for a minute. Don't know how come they took that too. Never thought it was worth much. The Tophams never bothered windin' the thing."

Nancy's pulse quickened. Knowing that the clock had been stolen, she was more eager than ever to have the thieves apprehended. She urged Jeff Tucker to hurry out to her car.

"Where's the nearest State Police headquarters?" she asked him as they climbed into the convertible.

"There's none till you get to Melborne, Miss Drew."

"We'll hurry."

Nancy headed as fast as possible for the highway. Would she succeed in heading off the thieves and recovering the old Crowley clock, so she could learn its secret?

CHAPTER XIV

A Tense Chase

"WHICH way is Melborne?" Nancy asked the caretaker when they reached the highway.

"Down there." He pointed.

"That's the direction the thieves took," Nancy told him, noting the dust and tire marks which revealed the van's exit onto the highway. "But," she added, glancing at the dashboard clock, "they're probably too far away by this time for us to catch them."

"Yes, ding it," Jeff muttered.

Nancy drove as rapidly as the law permitted toward Melborne. All the while, Jeff Tucker peered from one side of the road to the other.

"Those rascal thieves might just have nerve enough to stop an' count their loot," he said to Nancy. "So I'm keepin' a sharp eye peeled."

Nancy smiled in spite of the gravity of the situation. "Maybe," she replied. "Though I doubt that those men would be so reckless."

"Oh, I don't mean out in plain sight. They might have pulled off the road, back o' some o' these closed-up summer places."

"We'll watch for their tire marks on any dirt side road," the young sleuth said.

Jeff became so absorbed in looking for the van's tire marks that he never asked Nancy why she had come to see him at the Topham house.

"Those fake movers," he said, as they neared the outskirts of Melborne. "I wonder how far they went."

Nancy did not reply until they came to a crossroad, then she pointed. "They turned north here on this dirt road. How much farther is it to Melborne?"

"Only a mile."

As they came into the little town, Nancy asked her companion, "Which way to State Police headquarters?"

"Go right down Central Avenue to Maple Street. Turn left, and there it is."

Reaching headquarters, Nancy parked the car and hopped out. Jeff Tucker followed as she walked briskly into the office.

"I want to report a robbery," she told the desk sergeant after identifying herself.

For a moment the officer, taken aback, looked in astonishment at Nancy. "You've been robbed?" he asked. "In *our* town?"

"No, no!" Nancy cried out. She then gave a

Nancy reported what had taken place at the Tophams' cottage

quick but complete resume of what had taken place at the Tophams' cottage. Jeff Tucker added his account.

The police officer needed no further urging. Immediately he summoned four men and issued orders. "Now," he said, turning to Nancy, "have you any idea which road the thieves took?"

"Yes, Officer. When we passed the road crossing a mile outside of town, I saw their truck tracks on the dirt road leading north. I'll be glad to show you."

"Good. Lead the way. But first I'll send out a general alarm."

"Hurry!" Nancy begged as she started out. "Those thieves have at least an hour's head start!"

Jeff Tucker had been advised to return to his home. Accordingly he telephoned his son to come and pick him up in his car.

"Good luck!" he called, as the others pulled away. "I sure don't know how I'm goin' to break this to the Tophams."

Nancy was sorry for him, but she felt a thrill of excitement as she proceeded up the street, the police car following close behind.

Beyond the town, Nancy chose the road which she felt certain the thieves had used. The two cars sped along until Nancy unexpectedly came to a fork. Both branches were paved and no tire marks were visible. Nancy stopped. The police car pulled up alongside.

"What's the matter?" asked the officer in charge, whose name was Elton.

"I'm not sure which way to go now."

The policemen sprang from their automobile and began to examine the road. Officer Elton said that if a moving van had passed that way, its tire marks had been obliterated by other vehicles. It was impossible to tell which route the thieves had traveled.

"It'll be strictly guesswork from here," Officer Elton said to Nancy.

"In that case," replied Nancy, "it's my guess that the van went to the left." She pointed to a sign which read: *Garwin, 50 miles.* "Isn't Garwin a fairly large city?" she queried.

"Yes."

"Perhaps the thieves headed that way to dispose of the stolen furniture."

The officer nodded approvingly. "Sounds reasonable," he said. "Well, in any case, we can't go much farther, because we're near the state line."

Nancy had another thought. "I'll take the road to Garwin and swing around toward River Heights." She smiled. "If I see those thieves, I'll let you know."

"Well, you watch out, young lady. Those men may lock you up again!"

"I will. Anyhow, there'll be plenty of traffic as soon as I reach the main highway."

Without giving the policemen an opportunity

for further objection, Nancy started up and swung her car to the left. She noted in her rear-view mirror that the squad car had turned onto the right-hand road.

"The officers must have picked up a clue," Nancy said to herself. "But I certainly wish I could spot that van and maybe find a chance to look in the old clock!"

Nancy soon reached the main road. As mile after mile of highway spun behind her, Nancy's hopes grew dim. There were a number of side roads, any one of which the moving van might have taken to elude pursuers.

The young sleuth decided to adhere to her original theory—that Sid and his pals had headed for Garwin—and kept on the main highway.

"Those thieves think Jeff and I are still locked up and won't suspect they're being followed," she assured herself. Smiling, she thought hopefully, "In that case they won't be on their guard!"

About ten minutes later Nancy stopped at a service station to have her car refueled, and on impulse asked the attendant, "Did you by any chance see a moving van pass here recently?"

"Sure did, miss," was the prompt answer. "About half an hour ago. I noticed it because the driver was going at a terrific speed for a van."

Heartened, Nancy thanked him and resumed her pursuit, going past the turn for River Heights. "If only I can overtake the truck and somehow examine the Crowley clock before I have to report to the police!" she thought.

Again time elapsed and Nancy still saw no sign of a moving van on the highway. It was growing dusk and she decided that she would have to admit defeat.

"I never caught up to them." She sighed in disappointment, and turning into the opposite lane, headed back for the River Heights road.

Just then Nancy recalled that a little beyond the service station where she had stopped, she had noticed a rather run-down old inn. It was a slim hope, she knew, but the thieves might have put their van behind it while having a meal there.

"I'll go in and ask, anyhow," she decided.

Nancy increased her speed as much as she dared and within a few minutes came in sight of the inn. It stood back from the road a short distance and was half-hidden by tall trees. In front of the building a battered sign bearing the name *Black Horse Inn* creaked back and forth from a post. There was no sign of the van. Beyond the inn Nancy glimpsed a garage and a large barn. The doors to both were closed.

"I wonder," mused Nancy, "if the moving van is parked inside either one."

At the far side of the inn was a small woods with a narrow road leading into it. For safety's sake, Nancy thought it best to park her car on this little-used road.

She turned off the car lights, pocketed the key, and walked back to the curving driveway leading to the inn. As Nancy made her way forward, her heart pounded. There were tire marks which could belong to Sid's van! They led to the barn!

"Maybe those thieves are eating," she thought. "I'll look."

As Nancy stepped onto the porch, the sound of raucous laughter reached her ears. She tiptoed to a window and peered inside. What the young sleuth saw made her gasp, but she felt a glow of satisfaction.

In a dingy, dimly lighted room three men were seated about a table, eating voraciously. They were the thieves who had robbed the Topham bungalow!

CHAPTER XV

Nancy's Risky Undertaking

"I MUST notify the police at once!" Nancy told herself as she recognized the three thieves.

Turning away from the window, she crept noiselessly from the porch. She was about to make a dash for her car when a sudden thought occurred to her.

"If the gang have parked their van in the barn, now's my chance to look for the Crowley clock. I'm sure those men will be eating for a while, or they may even be staying overnight."

Acting on the impulse, Nancy sprinted to her car. Hastily she snatched a flashlight from the compartment, since it was now dark outside.

She made her way cautiously to the rear of the inn. Reaching the barn, she tried the closed doors, her heart pounding. They had not been locked!

As she slid back one of the doors, it squeaked in an alarming fashion. Anxiously Nancy glanced toward the inn, but so far as she could tell, her actions were unobserved. There was no one in sight.

Focusing her flashlight, she peered hopefully into the dark interior. A cry of satisfaction escaped her lips.

In front of her stood the moving van!

"What luck!" she exclaimed, snapping off her light.

With a last cautious glance in the direction of the inn, she hastily stepped inside and closed the barn door. With it shut, the interior of the barn was pitch dark.

Nancy switched on her flashlight again and played it over the moving van. She saw that its rear doors were closed.

Securing a firm grip on the handle, she gave it a quick turn. To her dismay the door did not open. The thieves had locked the van!

"Oh dear! Now what shall I do?" she wondered frantically. "I'll never be able to break the lock."

Desperately Nancy glanced about. She dared not remain many minutes in the barn, lest the thieves return and find her there. But she had to find out whether the Crowley clock was in the van.

"Perhaps the keys were left in the ignition," Nancy thought hopefully.

She rushed to the front of the van and clambered into the driver's seat. But there were no keys hanging from the ignition lock.

Nancy's mind worked frantically. She must find the keys! Perhaps the men had not taken them into the inn but had concealed them in the truck. Suddenly she remembered that people sometimes hide automobile keys under the floor mat. It was barely possible that the thieves had done this.

Hastily she pulled up a corner of the mat. Her flashlight revealed a small ring of keys!

"Luck was with me this time," she murmured, and quickly snatching up the ring, she ran back to the rear of the van.

After trying several of the keys, she at last found one which fitted the lock. Turning it, she jerked open the door. Nancy flashed her light about inside the truck. To her joy she recognized the van's contents as the furniture stolen from the Topham cottage!

"What will I do if the clock is on the bottom of the load?" Nancy wondered as she surveyed the pile of furniture. "I'll never find it."

Dexterously she swung herself up into the truck and flashed the light slowly about on chairs, tables, rugs, and boxes. There was no sign of the Crowley clock.

Then the beam rested for a moment on an object in a far corner. With a low cry of delight, Nancy saw that her search had been rewarded. Protected by a blanket, an old-fashioned mantel clock rested on top of a table in the very front of the van!

The young sleuth scrambled over the pieces of furniture as she tried to reach the clock. Her dress caught on something sharp and tore. Finally she arrived within arm's reach of the blanket. She grasped it and carefully pulled the clock toward her.

One glance at the timepiece assured her that it fitted the description Abby Rowen had given her. It had a square face and the top was ornamented with a crescent.

"The Crowley clock at last!" Nancy whispered almost unbelievingly.

But as she stood staring at it, her keen ears detected the sound of voices. The thieves!

"I'll be caught!" flashed through her mind. "And I won't be able to escape a second time!"

Clutching the blanket and the clock tightly in her arms, Nancy scrambled over the piled-up furniture as she struggled to get out of the truck before it was too late.

Reaching the door, she leaped lightly to the floor. She could now hear heavy footsteps coming closer and closer.

Nancy shut the truck doors as quickly as possible, and searched wildly for the keys.

"Oh, what did I do with them?" she thought frantically.

She saw that they had fallen to the floor and snatched them up. Hurriedly inserting the correct key in the lock, she secured the doors.

But as Nancy wheeled about she heard men's angry voices directly outside. Already someone was starting to slide back the barn door!

"Oh, what shall I do?" Nancy thought in despair. "I'm cornered!"

She realized instantly that she could not hope to run to the front of the car and place the keys under the mat where she had found them. "I'll just put them on the floor," she decided quickly. "Maybe the men will think they dropped them."

Then, glancing frantically about for a hiding place, Nancy saw an empty grain bin. Running to it, still holding the clock, she climbed inside and dropped the blanket over her head just as one of the barn doors slid open.

One of the men was speaking loudly. Nancy recognized the voice instantly. It belonged to Sid, the ringleader of the thieves.

"You had enough to eat," he growled. "We're goin' to get out of here before we have the cops down on our heads."

He climbed into the cab and turned on the headlights. Nancy held her breath. Would her hiding place be discovered? But the men apparently did not even look toward the bin.

In a moment Sid cried out, "What did you do with those keys? Thought you put 'em under the floor mat."

"I did."

"Well, they ain't here."

"Honest, boss, I—"

"Then come and find 'em, and don't be all night about it either!"

"All right. Get out of the way and give me a chance!"

As Jake went to the truck and began a careful search for the keys, Nancy listened fearfully from her hiding place.

"Say, if you've lost 'em—" the leader did not finish the threat, for at that moment the third man announced:

"Here they are on the floor! You must have thought you'd put 'em in your pocket, Jake, and dropped 'em instead."

"I didn't!" the other retorted.

The thieves were obviously in a quarrelsome mood. Just then the leader interposed:

"Cut out the yaking! We ain't got no time for a fight unless we want to land behind bars!"

"And if we do, it'll be your fault, Sid Sax. You left that girl to starve—"

"Shut up!" the leader snarled.

After a few more angry words, the three thieves climbed into the front seat and in a moment the engine started.

In relief Nancy heard the men go. The moment they were a safe distance from the barn, she climbed out of the bin.

Nancy watched long enough to make certain that the van had taken the road to Garwin. Then, snatching up her flashlight and clutching the precious clock in her arms, she turned and ran. "I'd better cut through the woods," she decided.

As Nancy darted among the trees, she cast an anxious glance over her shoulder, but to her intense relief she saw that she was not being followed. There seemed to be no one in the vicinity of the Black Horse Inn.

"I had a narrow escape that time," the young sleuth told herself as she ran. "I hate to think what might have happened if I had been discovered!" She clutched the mantel clock more tightly in her arms. "But it was worth the risk I took! I found the clock and maybe the secret of Josiah Crowley's will!"

Reaching the car, Nancy sprang inside. She took the key from her pocket and inserted it in the ignition lock.

"I'll notify the police as fast as I can," she decided. "Perhaps the state troopers can catch those men before they dispose of the furniture."

Then, just as Nancy was about to start the motor, her glance fell upon the Crowley clock which she had placed on the seat beside her. Did it contain old Josiah's mysterious notebook as she suspected?

"Oh, I must find out!" She got her flashlight.

Since the clock was too unwieldy to open inside the car, Nancy stepped out and laid it on the ground. She unfastened the glass door and ran her hand around the walls. There was nothing in-side. She tried the back. Only the mechanism of the timepiece was there.

"Gone!" Nancy groaned. "Oh dear! Has my luck run out?"

Could it be, she wondered, that the Tophams had discovered the notebook only to destroy it? Nancy discarded this thought as quickly as it came to mind, for she recalled the conversation she had overheard between Ada and Isabel. No, the Top-hams were as ignorant as herself concerning the location of a later will.

It was more likely that Abby Rowen had been confused in her story. After all, she had not de-clared that the notebook would be found inside the clock. Nancy herself had made the deduction.

"I was almost certain I'd find the notebook," she murmured in disappointment. But a moment later she took heart again. "It *must* be here some-where," she told herself.

Turning the clock upside down, Nancy gave it a hard shake. Something inside moved. Hope-fully she repeated the action.

"Unless I'm wrong," Nancy thought excitedly, "there's something inside this clock besides the works!" She examined it more closely. "An ex-tra piece of cardboard back of the face! And some-thing in between the two! The notebook maybe!"

After a vain attempt to remove the heavy card-board face with her fingers, Nancy took a small screw driver from the glove compartment. With the tool it required but an instant to remove the two hands of the clock and jerk off the face.

As the cardboard fell to the floor, Nancy peered inside and gave a low cry of joy.

There, at one side of the clock, attached to a hook in the top, dangled a tiny dark-blue notebook!

CHAPTER XVI

The Capture

EAGERLY Nancy removed the little notebook from the hook. By holding the book directly under the beam of her flashlight, she could make out the words on the cover:

Property of Josiah Crowley.

"I've found it at last!" she thought excitedly.

Quickly turning the first few pages, she saw that they were yellowed with age. The writing was fine and cramped, and the ink had faded. The pages were crowded with business notations, and it was difficult to make out the words.

Nancy was thrilled, for she was positive that the notebook would disclose what Josiah Crowley had done with his last will. Yet, she realized that she could not hope to read through the book without a considerable loss of precious time. She must not delay another instant in reporting to the police.

"I'll read the notebook later," she decided, and

tucked it into her pocket. Then she put the clock together.

Hurriedly laying the timepiece back on the car seat, Nancy covered it with her coat and slid behind the wheel. Starting the engine, she swung the convertible onto the highway. Nancy cast an anxious glance in the direction the thieves had taken, and watched for side roads down which the men might turn to avoid the main highway.

"Perhaps I'd better phone the State Police from the first service station or store I come to."

Then suddenly she noticed a sign: *Alternate route to Garwin. Main road under repair.*

Reaching the intersection, she stopped to see if the familiar tire marks of the van indicated it had turned onto this dirt road. It had!

"Now what shall I do?"

As Nancy debated, she saw a car coming toward her. Her hopes soared. She could not be mistaken—it was a police prowl car with a red revolving roof light!

Instantly Nancy grabbed her own flashlight and jumped from the car. Standing at the side of the road, she waved her light and in a few minutes the police sedan stopped.

"I'm Nancy Drew," she said hurriedly to the two men inside. "Are you looking for the furniture thieves in the van?"

"Yes, we are. You're the girl who reported them?"

Nancy nodded, then pointed down the side road. "I think those are their tire marks. The men were at the Black Horse Inn, but left."

"You can identify them?" the driver asked.

"Oh, yes."

"Then please follow us. I'll radio for a car to approach the thieves' van from the other end of the road."

The police car sped down the bad road to Garwin, with Nancy following closely behind. They rode for several miles.

"Oh dear," thought Nancy, "I must have been wrong! We should have overtaken the van by this time."

Another ten minutes passed. Then, unexpectedly, she caught a glimpse of a red taillight on the road far ahead.

"It must be the van!" Nancy told herself hopefully. "The light doesn't appear to be moving fast enough for an automobile."

Evidently the police were of the same opinion, for at that moment their car slowed down. Nancy figured they would not stop the van until they saw the other police car arriving from the opposite direction. A few moments later she could see headlights in the distance.

The squad car in front of Nancy now sped ahead and pulled up alongside the van. "Pull over!" one of the officers shouted to the man in the cab.

Instead of doing so, the van put on a burst of

speed. But in order to avoid smashing into the oncoming squad car, the driver pulled too far to the right. The van swerved sharply. Its two right wheels went off into a deep ditch, and the vehicle toppled over.

In an instant the officers were out of the car and had the fugitives covered.

By this time Nancy, who had stopped her car at the side of the road, came running up. One of the officers turned to her and asked, "Can you identify these men?"

As a light was flashed upon each of the thieves in turn, Nancy nodded. "This one is Sid, who locked me in the closet," she declared, pointing to the leader. "The others are Jake and Parky."

The prisoners stared in complete disbelief. They were astounded to see Nancy Drew standing there. When it dawned on Sid that she evidently was responsible for their capture, he started to say something, then changed his mind and remained silent. The prisoners were quickly identified from licenses and other papers as wanted criminals.

One of the other officers opened the rear of the van and asked Nancy if she could identify the stolen furniture.

"Some of it," she replied. "That desk was taken from the room in which I was locked in the closet."

"Good enough," said the trooper. "These men will get long sentences for this. They'll be held on several charges. Are you willing to go with us and prefer charges against them?''

"Yes, if it's necessary," Nancy promised reluctantly. "But I don't live in this county and I'm eager to get home right away. Don't you have enough evidence against them? I think they're the same men who stole several silver heirlooms from the Turner sisters."

Sid and his companions winced, but did not speak.

"I see," said the trooper. "Well, I guess there's no need for you to go to headquarters now," the officer admitted. "I'll take your address, and if your testimony should be required, I'll get in touch with you."

When Nancy showed her driver's license as identification, the policeman glanced at her with new interest. Taking her aside, he said, "So you're the daughter of Carson Drew! I see you're following in his footsteps. Starting rather young, aren't you?"

Nancy laughed. "It was only by accident that I arrived at the Topham bungalow at the critical moment," she protested modestly.

"Not many girls would have used their wits the way you did," the officer observed. "Unless I'm mistaken, these fellows are old hands at this game. They're no doubt the men who have been stealing various things from around Moon Lake for a number of seasons. The residents will be mighty grateful for what you've done. And that Mrs. Topham you spoke of—she ought to give you a liberal reward for saving her household goods."

Nancy shook her head. "I don't want a reward, really I don't."

"Just the same you've earned one," insisted the officer, who said his name was Cowen. "If you'd like, I'll tell my chief the whole story and he'll take the matter up with this Mrs. Topham."

"You don't know her," Nancy remarked, "and I do. She'd never offer a reward. Even if she did, I wouldn't accept it." After a slight pause, she added, "In fact, I prefer that my name not be mentioned to her at all."

Officer Cowen shook his head in disbelief. "Well, all right, then. If you're sure you don't want any credit for capturing the thieves, I won't say anything. You're certain?"

"I am," Nancy replied firmly, "for a particular reason of my own."

The trooper smiled. "It must be a mighty good one."

"There *is* one favor you might do me," said Nancy. "Ask your chief to put in a good word for the caretaker, Jeff Tucker, to the Tophams. Perhaps then he won't lose his job."

"Be glad to," Officer Cowen promised. "And if you're really anxious not to figure in the case, I'll see if we can get along without your testimony."

Nancy thanked him, then suddenly thought of

the old clock. At the moment it was lying on the front seat of her car, less than a dozen yards away. Should she reveal this information? She decided against doing so in front of the thieves, who, though they could not hear what she had been saying, could see everything plainly. "I'll wait until a more opportune time," Nancy concluded.

It was agreed among the state policemen that one of them would stay to guard the van and keep a radio car standing by there. The other three troopers would take the captive thieves to headquarters.

The three prisoners, their faces sullen, were crowded into the car. One of the troopers took the wheel, while the one beside him kept the handcuffed trio closely covered.

Officer Cowen, a strapping, husky man, turned to Nancy. "I'll ride with you," he said. "You're going past headquarters on the main road?"

"I'm on my way to River Heights," she responded.

"Then the station is on your route. You can drop me off if you will."

"Why—why, of course," Nancy stammered. "I'll be glad to."

At once she had thought of the Crowley clock. What if Officer Cowen should not accept her explanation as to why she had helped herself to the heirloom and its strange contents? If this happened, her progress in solving the mystery might

receive a serious setback! Even as these disturbing ideas raced through her mind, the trooper
started toward the blue convertible.

Nancy braced herself. "I'll just have to 'fess
up," she said to herself, "and take the conse-
quences!"

CHAPTER XVII

Strange Instructions

FOR THE next few seconds Nancy's mind worked like lightning as she rehearsed what she would say to Officer Cowen. One idea stood out clearly: the police were concerned in the theft of the furniture, so she would hand over the clock. But they were not involved in locating Mr. Crowley's missing will. For this reason the young sleuth felt justified in keeping the notebook. She would turn it over to her father, and let him decide what disposition should be made of it.

"After all," Nancy told herself, "Dad is handling the Crowley case for the Hoovers, and even the Turners and Mrs. Rowen, in a way."

By this time she and the trooper had reached her car. "Would you like me to drive?" he asked.

"Why—er—yes, if you wish," Nancy replied. "But first I want to show you something," she added, as he opened the door for her. "I have some stolen property here."

"What!"

Quickly Nancy explained that she had taken the responsibility of trying to learn whether or not the van held the stolen furniture. "I recognized a few of the pieces, and possibly this clock which the Tophams had told me about. I took that out to examine it. Then I never had a chance to get it back without being caught. I'm sure the Tophams will identify the old clock as their property."

Nancy's explanation seemed to satisfy the officer. "I'll take it to headquarters," he said. "Let's go!"

He laid the clock on the rear seat, then slid behind the wheel and drove off.

It was nearly midnight when Nancy, tired and worn from her long ride, reached the Drew home in River Heights. As she drove into the double garage, she noticed that her father's car was gone. A glance at the house disclosed that the windows were dark, with the exception of a light in the hall. Hannah Gruen must be in bed.

"Of course she's not expecting me," Nancy reasoned. "I wonder where Dad can be? Oh, I hope he'll get home soon. I want to tell him about my discovery right away."

After locking the garage door, she went to the kitchen entrance and let herself in.

Her eyes lighted on the refrigerator and suddenly Nancy realized she was very hungry. Many hours had passed since she had eaten. "Um, food!" she thought.

Just as Nancy opened the refrigerator door, she heard steps on the stairs and Hannah Gruen, wearing a sleepy look, appeared in robe and slippers.

"Nancy!" cried the housekeeper, instantly wide awake.

"Surprise, Hannah darling!" Nancy gave the housekeeper an affectionate hug and kiss. "I'm simply starved. Haven't had a bite since lunchtime."

"Why, you poor dear!" the housekeeper exclaimed in concern. "What happened? I'll fix you something right away."

As the two prepared a chicken sandwich, some cocoa, and Hannah cut a large slice of cinnamon cake over which she poured hot applesauce, Nancy told of her adventures.

The housekeeper's eyes widened. "Nancy, you might have been killed by those awful men. Well, I'm certainly glad they've been captured."

"So am I!" declared Nancy fervently as she finished the last crumb of cake. "And I hope the Turners get back their silver heirlooms."

"How about the Tophams?" Hannah Gruen questioned teasingly.

"Somehow," said Nancy with a wink, "that doesn't seem to worry me." Then she asked, "Where's Dad?"

"Working at his office," Hannah Gruen replied. "He phoned earlier that something unexpected had come up in connection with one of his cases."

"Then I'll wait for him," said Nancy. "You go back to bed. And thanks a million." The sleepy housekeeper did not demur.

Left alone, Nancy tidied the kitchen, then went to the living room.

"Now to find out what became of Josiah Crowley's last will," she thought excitedly, as she curled up in a comfortable chair near a reading lamp.

Carefully she thumbed the yellowed pages, for she was afraid they might tear. Evidently Josiah Crowley had used the same notebook for many years.

"He certainly knew how to save money," she mused.

Nancy read page after page, perusing various kinds of memoranda and many notations of property owned by Mr. Crowley. There were also figures on numerous business transactions in which he had been involved. Nancy was surprised at the long list of stocks, bonds, and notes which apparently belonged to the estate.

"I had no idea Josiah Crowley was worth so much," she murmured.

After a time Nancy grew impatient at the seemingly endless list of figures. She skipped several pages of the little notebook, and turned toward the end where Mr. Crowley had listed his possessions.

"Why, what's this?" she asked herself. Fastened to one page was a very thin, flat key with a tag marked 148.

Suddenly a phrase on the opposite page, "My last will and testament," caught and held Nancy's attention. Eagerly she began to read the whole section.

"I've found it!" she exclaimed excitedly. "I'm glad I didn't give up the search!"

The notation concerning the will was brief. Nancy assumed the cramped writing was Josiah Crowley's. It read:

To whom it may concern: My last will and test-ament will be found in safe-deposit box number 148 in the Merchants Trust Company. The box is under the name of Josiah Johnston.

"And this is the key to the box!" Nancy told herself.

For several moments the young sleuth sat staring ahead of her. It seemed unbelievable that she had solved the mystery. But surely there could no mistake. The date of the entry in the notebook was recent and the ink had not faded as it had on the earlier pages.

"There *is* a later will!" Nancy exclaimed aloud. "Oh, if only it leaves something to the Turners, and the Mathews, and Abby Rowen, and the Hoover girls! Then Allison could take voice lessons and little Judy would be taken care of, and—"

Nancy hurriedly read on, hoping to learn something definite. But although she carefully examined every page in the book, there was no other mention of the will, nor any clue to its contents.

"No wonder the document didn't come to light," Nancy mused. "Who would have thought of looking for it in a safe-deposit box under the name of Josiah Johnston? In his desire for safe-keeping, Josiah Crowley nearly defeated his own purpose."

Her thoughts were interrupted as she heard a car turn into the driveway. Rushing to the window, Nancy saw her father pull into the garage. She ran to meet him at the kitchen door.

"Why, hello, Nancy," he greeted her in surprise. "If I had known you were here, I'd have come home sooner. I was doing some special work on a case. Back from Moon Lake ahead of schedule, aren't you?"

"Yes," Nancy admitted, trying to hide her excitement. "But for a good reason."

Before her father could hang up his hat in the hall closet, she plunged into the story of her adventures and ended by showing him the notebook which she had found inside the mantel clock. When she had finished, Carson Drew stared at his daughter with mingled pride and amazement.

"You're a good detective, Nancy. You've picked up an excellent clue," he said.

"Dad, I thought it best not tell the police about

the notebook. We don't want to reveal the secret of another will to the executor mentioned in the old one."

"You mean Mr. Topham. I agree," the lawyer replied. "The new will may name someone else as executor." He smiled. "I think you and I should try to see this will. But," he added, "which Merchants Trust Company is it in? There must be dozens of banks by that name."

Nancy suddenly snapped her fingers. "Dad, I believe I know. You recall that Judge Hart and his wife told me they had seen Josiah Crowley in Masonville a couple of times. And there's a Merchants Trust Company there."

Mr. Drew looked at his daughter admiringly. "I believe you have the answer, Nancy. And Judge Hart is just the man to help us. I'll phone him in the morning. Well, I guess we both need some sleep."

As the lawyer kissed his daughter good night, he added, "My dear, you were in serious danger when you encountered those thieves. I don't like to have you take such risks. I am very grateful indeed that you are back home safe."

"The Tophams aren't going to thank me when they find out what I have done," Nancy said, as she went up the stairs ahead of her father. "In fact, we may have a battle on our hands, Dad."

"That's right, Nancy. And it will be just as well that they don't learn the details of how the will was found until the matter is settled beyond a doubt."

"I'm certainly curious to find out if the new will left anything to the Tophams," said Nancy.

"If not," her father put in, "your discovery will strike them at an especially awkward time."

Nancy paused on the stairs and turned to face her father. "What do you mean?"

"Well, there's talk about town that Richard Topham has been losing heavily in the stock market this past month. He has been getting credit at a number of places on the strength of the inheritance, and I suspect he is depending on Crowley's money to pull him through a tight spot. He's making every effort to speed up the settlement of the estate."

"Then we'd better hurry," said Nancy, resuming the climb.

"Don't build your hopes too high," Mr. Drew advised her wisely. "There may be a slip, you know."

"How?"

"We may fail to find the will in the safe-deposit box."

"Oh, I can't believe it, Dad. The notebook says it's there!"

"Then," the lawyer continued, "there is a chance that Josiah Crowley didn't dispose of the fortune as the Turners and the Hoovers and others expected he would."

"But he promised all those people—"

"I know, Nancy. But there's just the possibility that the notation in the notebook was wishful thinking and Mr. Crowley never got around to making the new will."

"You can discourage me all you want to, Dad, but I'm not going to stop hoping!" Nancy said. "Oh, I can scarcely wait for morning to come!"

Her father laughed. "You're an incurable optimist! Now put Josiah Crowley out of your mind and get a good night's sleep."

At the door of her bedroom Nancy hesitated, then turned back toward the stairs.

"What's up?" Mr. Drew asked.

Without answering Nancy ran down to the living room, picked up the notebook which lay on the table, and hurried back up the carpeted steps.

"After all I've gone through to get my hands on this," she told her father, "I'm not going to take any chances!" Nancy laughed. "Tonight I'll sleep with it under my pillow!"

CHAPTER XVIII

A Suspenseful Search

WHEN Nancy awoke the following morning, bright sunlight was streaming through her open bedroom window. As her eyes turned toward the clock on her dresser, she was alarmed to see that it was a little after nine o'clock.

"How could I have overslept on a morning like this?" she chided herself.

Quickly running her hand under the pillow, she brought out the Crowley notebook and surveyed it with satisfaction.

"What a surprise the Tophams are going to get!" she murmured softly.

After hastily bathing and dressing, Nancy hurried downstairs looking very attractive in a blue summer sweater suit. She kissed Hannah Gruen, who said a cheery good morning and told Nancy that Mr. Drew had already left for his office.

"Oh dear," Nancy said, "I wonder if he forgot our date?"

"No indeed," the housekeeper replied. "He phoned Judge Hart and expects word from him by ten o'clock. He'll let you know the result. My goodness, Nancy, you've really made a big discovery. I do hope everything turns out for the best."

She went into the kitchen but returned in a moment with a plate of crisp, golden waffles.

"Better eat your breakfast," she advised. "Your dad may call any minute."

Nancy ate a dish of strawberries, then started on the waffles. "These are yummy," she stated, pouring maple syrup over a second one.

She had just finished eating when the phone rang. Mr. Drew was calling to say Judge Hart had made arrangements at the bank. "Come to my office with the notebook and key, Nancy. We'll start from here."

"I'll be right down, Dad."

Nancy went upstairs for her purse, then drove to her father's office.

"I have the notebook with me," she told the lawyer. "Do you want it?"

"We'll take the book along. I want to show it to the head of the trust department at the bank," Mr. Drew said. "It's our proof we have good reason for taking a look in Mr. Crowley's box."

After leaving a number of instructions with his private secretary, Carson Drew followed his daugh-

ter from the office.   He took his place beside her
in the convertible.

"I'll never get over it if we don't find a newer
will," Nancy declared, as they drove along.   A
flush of excitement had tinted her cheeks and her
eyes were bright.

"You must remember one thing, Nancy," returned her father calmly.   "Crowley was an odd
person and did things in an odd way.   A will may
be there, and again it may not.   Perhaps he only
left further directions to finding it.

"I remember one case in Canada years ago.   An
eccentric Frenchman died and left directions to
look in a trunk of old clothes for a will.   In the
pocket of a coat were found further instructions
to look in a closet of his home.   There his family
found a note telling them to look in a copper
boiler.

"The boiler had disappeared but was finally located in a curiosity shop.   Inside, pasted on the
bottom, was what proved to be a word puzzle in
Chinese.   The old Frenchman's heirs were about
to give up in despair when a Chinese solved the
puzzle and the old man's fortune was found—a bag
of gold under a board in his bedroom floor!"

"At least they found it," said Nancy.

The trip to Masonville was quickly accomplished, and Nancy parked the car in front of the
Merchants Trust Company.

Father and daughter alighted and entered the

bank.   Mr. Drew gave his name and asked to see
the president.   After a few minutes' wait they
were ushered into a private conference room.   An
elderly man, Mr. Jensen, arose to greet them.

The introductions over, Mr. Drew hastened to
state his mission.   Before he could finish the story,
the bank president broke in.

"Judge Hart has told me the story.   I'll call Mr.
Warren, our trust officer."

He picked up his desk phone and in a few minutes Mr. Warren appeared and was introduced.
Nancy now brought out the notebook, opened it
to the important page, and handed it to the men
to read.

When they finished, Mr. Jensen said, "What a
mystery!"

Mr. Warren pulled from his pocket the file card
which the owner of Box 148 had filled out in the
name of Josiah Johnston.   The two samples of
cramped handwritings were compared.

"I would say," Mr. Drew spoke up, "that there
is no doubt but that Crowley and Johnston were
the same person."

"I agree," asserted Mr. Jensen, and his trust officer nodded.

"Then there's no reason why we shouldn't open
the box?" Mr. Drew asked.

"None," Mr. Warren replied.   "Of course nothing may be removed, you understand."

"All I want to see," Nancy spoke up, "is whether

there is a will in the box, the date on it, who the
executor is, and who the heirs are."

The bankers smiled and Mr. Jensen said,
"You're hoping to solve four mysteries all at once!
Well, let's get started."

With Mr. Warren in the lead, the four walked
toward the rear of the bank to the vault of the
trust department. A guard opened the door and
they went through. Mr. Jensen took the key
from Mr. Crowley's notebook, while Mr. Warren
opened the first part of the double safety lock with
the bank key. Then he inserted the key from the
notebook. It fitted!

In a moment he lifted out Deposit Box Number
148. It was a small one and not heavy, he said.

"We'll take this into a private room," Mr. Jensen stated. He, Nancy, and Mr. Drew followed
the trust officer down a corridor of cubbyhole
rooms until they reached one not in use.

"Now," said Mr. Jensen, when the door was
closed behind them, "we shall see how many—if
any—of the mysteries are solved."

Nancy held her breath as he raised the lid of the
box. All peered inside. The box was empty, except for one bulky document in the bottom.

"Oh, it must be the will!" Nancy exclaimed.

"It is a will," Mr. Jensen announced, after a
hasty glance at the first page. "Josiah Crowley's
last will and testament."

"When was it written?" Nancy asked quickly.

"In March of this year," Mr. Jensen told her.

"Oh, Dad," Nancy cried, "this was later than the will the Tophams submitted for probate!"

"That's right."

"Let's read it right away," Nancy begged.

Mr. Jensen handed the sheets to Mr. Drew. "Maybe you can decipher this. The handwriting is too much for me."

The lawyer took the will. Then, as Nancy looked over his shoulder, he haltingly read aloud, giving an interpretation rather than a word by word account.

"Mr. Jensen—Mr. Warren, your bank has been named as executor," he said.

"Very good." The president smiled. "But I expect Mr. Topham won't be happy to hear this."

Mr. Drew had turned to the last page. "The signature of Josiah is in order," he remarked, "and there are two witnesses—Dr. Nesbitt and Thomas Wackley. No wonder this will didn't come to light. Both those men died in April."

As Nancy tried to decipher the handwriting, she noticed to her delight that the Hoover girls and Abby Rowen were mentioned.

At this moment the president said, "Mr. Drew, the bank's regular lawyer had just left for Europe on an extended vacation. Since you and your daughter have solved the mystery and are so vitally interested in it, would you handle this case for us?"

*Nancy held her breath as Mr. Jensen opened the
safe-deposit box*

Nancy's eyes sparkled and Mr. Drew smiled. "I'd certainly be very glad to," he said.

"What instructions have you for us?" Mr. Warren asked.

Mr. Drew thought a moment, then said, "Because of the unusual aspects of this case, I believe that first of all I'd like you to have photostats of the will made, so I can study the contents carefully."

"We'll be happy to do that," Mr. Jensen replied. "And then?"

"After I'm sure everything is legal," Mr. Drew went on, "I'll deliver the original will for probate and notify the people who will benefit from Mr. Crowley's estate."

"Fine," said Mr. Jensen. "We have photostating equipment right here. I'll have a couple of copies made while you wait. Or shall I send them to your office?"

Mr. Drew glanced at his daughter. "We'll wait," he said, smiling.

While the photostats were being made, Nancy's mind was racing. "Oh, I hope Allison receives enough money to pay for singing lessons, and the other deserving people get nice amounts," she whispered to her father, who nodded.

The wait seemed interminable to Nancy, who could not sit still. She walked back and forth until finally her father remarked teasingly, "You're like a caged lion."

Nancy pretended to pout. "At least I'm not growling," she said, and Mr. Drew grinned.

Soon a messenger brought back the will, together with two photostats of the document.

"Thank you," said Mr. Jensen, who handed the photostatic copies to Mr. Drew.

"I'll work on this at once," the lawyer promised as he put the papers in his brief case. Then he and his daughter left the bank.

Mr. Drew insisted that he and Nancy stop for lunch and refused to let her look at the will while they were waiting to be served. "Relax, young lady," he warned. "There's no point in letting any prying eyes know our secret."

As he saw his daughter's animation fading, Mr. Drew said, "Suppose you come to my office with me and we'll work on the problem together. I'll have the will typed. In this way its full meaning can be understood more easily."

"Oh, thanks, Dad," said Nancy.

In the lawyer's office the young sleuth sat down beside his typist, Miss Lamby. As each page came from the machine, Nancy read it avidly.

"Mr. Crowley certainly seemed to know the correct phraseology for drawing up a will," she remarked.

Finally, when the typing had been completed, Nancy said to the secretary, "I have a lot of questions to ask Dad."

Miss Lamby smiled. "If they're legal ones, he'll

know all the answers," she said. "There's no better lawyer in River Heights than your father."

Nancy smiled as she dashed into her father's office. The two Drews sat down to study Josiah Crowley's last will and testament.

"If this does prove to be legal," said Nancy, "it will certainly be a blow to the Tophams."

"I'm afraid so."

"Dad, when you call a meeting of all the relatives and read the will aloud," Nancy said, "please may I be there?"

Mr. Drew laughed. "I'll humor you this time, Nancy. You may be present when the Tophams get the surprise of their lives!"

CHAPTER XIX

Startling Revelations

"DAD, it's nearly two o'clock now. Mr. Crowley's relatives should be here in a few minutes! I'm so excited!"

Carson Drew, who stood in the living room of the Drew home with Mr. Warren from the bank, smiled at his daughter as she fluttered about, arranging chairs.

"I believe you're more thrilled than if you were inheriting the fortune yourself," he remarked.

"I am thrilled," Nancy admitted. "I can scarcely wait until the will is read aloud. Won't everyone be surprised? Especially the Tophams. Do you think they will come?"

"Oh, yes, the Tophams will be here. And, unless I am mistaken, they will bring a lawyer with them. Just as soon as they learned that another will had come to light, they began to worry. They will certainly want to hear what is in this one."

"Are you certain the will we found can't be broken?" Nancy inquired anxiously.

"Of course I can't be certain, Nancy. But I have gone over it carefully, and so far as I can tell, it is technically perfect. I also asked a couple of lawyer friends and they agree. Josiah Crowley was peculiar in some ways, but he was a very smart man. I'll promise you the Tophams will have a difficult time if they try to contest this will."

"The bank will help you fight," Mr. Warren put in.

With the exception of Abby Rowen, who was still confined to bed, all the old gentleman's relatives had promised to be present. Grace and Allison Hoover, although not relatives, had also been invited.

"It's too bad Mrs. Rowen can't come," said Nancy. "But I'll take the news to her this very afternoon."

"The size of the fortune will probably be a great surprise to everyone but the Tophams," said her father with a smile. "Nancy, you did a remarkable piece of detective work."

"It was fun," she said modestly. "And I can hardly wait to have it all cleared up."

"We may have some trying minutes with the Tophams, Nancy," her father warned.

"Yes, I suppose so. I expect anybody would be sorry to see a fortune slip away. . . . Dad, I see

Grace and Allison coming up the walk now,"
Nancy announced, glancing out the window.

She greeted them with kisses and escorted the
sisters into the living room, where she introduced
them to Mr. Warren. As Allison sat down, she
whispered to Nancy:

"Is it true a later will has been found?"

"You and Grace have no cause to worry," Nancy
assured her with a mysterious smile.

The doorbell rang. This time Nancy admitted
Edna and Mary Turner, who were dressed as if for
a party. With them was little Judy, who threw
herself into Nancy's arms. A few minutes later
the Mathews brothers, William and Fred, arrived.

"I guess everyone is here except the Tophams,"
Mr. Drew commented. "We had better wait for
them a few minutes."

There was no need to wait, for at that moment
the bell rang sharply. Nancy opened the door and
the four members of the Topham family walked
in haughtily, merely nodding to the others in the
room. As Mr. Drew had predicted, they were ac-
companied by a lawyer.

"Why have we been called here?" Mrs. Topham
demanded, addressing Mr. Drew. "Have you the
audacity to claim that another will has been
found?"

"I have a will written only this past March, Mrs.
Topham," Carson Drew replied evenly. "And I'd

like to introduce to all of you Mr. John Warren, trust officer of the Merchants Trust Company, of Masonville, which has been named as executor."

"It's preposterous!" Mrs. Topham stormed. "Josiah Crowley made only one will and in that he left everything to us with my husband as executor."

"It looks like a conspiracy to me," Ada added tartly, as she gazed coldly upon the relatives and friends who were seated about the room.

Isabel did not speak, but tossed her head contemptuously. Richard Topham likewise did not offer a comment, but uneasily seated himself beside his own attorney.

"If you will please be seated, Mrs. Topham, I will read the will," Mr. Drew suggested.

Reluctantly Mrs. Topham sat down.

"As I have said," Mr. Drew began, "a recent will of the late Josiah Crowley was found in a safe-deposit box in the Masonville bank. The will is unusually long, and with your permission I will read from a typed copy only the portions which have to do with the disposal of the property. But first I want to ask Mr. Topham what value he puts on the estate."

"A hundred thousand after taxes," the man replied.

"Oh!" the Turners exclaimed, and Mary said, "I had no idea Josiah had that much money."

"Nor I," Edna agreed.

Mr. Drew picked up several typewritten sheets from the table, and began to read in a clear voice:

" 'I, Josiah Crowley, do make this my last will and testament, hereby revoking all former wills by me at any time made. I give and bequeath all my property, real and personal, as follows:

" 'To my beloved friends and neighbors, Grace and Allison Hoover, a sum equal to twenty per cent of my estate, share and share alike.' "

"I must be dreaming!" Grace gasped.

"You mean I'm going to get ten thousand dollars?" Allison cried out. She burst into tears. "Oh, Nancy, you did this for me! Now I can have my voice lessons."

Isabel Topham eyed her disdainfully. "It would take more than ten thousand dollars to make a singer out of you!" she said maliciously.

"Quiet!" commanded her father. "Let's hear what else this will says."

His daughter subsided, but his wife exclaimed spitefully, "The will is a fraud. The Hoovers aren't even relatives."

"It is no fraud," Mr. Drew told her quietly. Again he picked up the will and began to read:

" 'To Abby Rowen, my late wife's cousin, in consideration of her kindness to me, a sum equal to ten per cent of my estate.' "

"Oh, I'm so glad," Grace murmured. "Now she'll be able to get the medical and other attention she needs."

"And have someone live at her house to take care of her," said Nancy.

"That old lady gets ten thousand dollars?" Ada Topham said harshly. "What did she ever do for Cousin Josiah?" Angrily she turned to her mother. "We took care of him for years—she didn't!"

"I'll say not," Isabel echoed, her voice tart.

" 'To my cousins, Fred and William Mathews, a sum equal to twenty per cent of my estate, share and share alike,' " Mr. Drew read.

"We didn't expect that much," Fred Mathews declared in genuine surprise. "Josiah was very kind." Fred smiled. "Now we can take a trip like we've always wanted to do, William."

"That's right. I just can't believe it. A long trip on an ocean liner or a plane."

" 'To my cousins, Edna and Mary Turner, twenty per cent of my estate, share and share alike.' "

"Oh, how generous!" Edna murmured. "Now little Judy can have the things we've always wanted to give her."

"Yes," said Mary Turner. "Oh, I feel so relieved."

"Aren't we mentioned at all?" Mrs. Topham broke in sharply.

Mr. Drew smiled. "Yes, you are mentioned. I'm coming to that now. 'To Richard Topham,

five thousand dollars.   To Grace and Allison Hoover—' "

"Hold on!" cried Mrs. Topham.   "What about
me and the girls?"

"No money was left to you," the lawyer stated
simply.

Isabel gave a shriek.   "Oh, no!   Oh, no!   Oh,
Mother, all those bills!   What'll we do?"

Ada too had cried out.   "I'll have to go to work!
Oh, I can't bear the thought of it!"

When the furor died down, Mr. Drew read on,
" 'To Grace and Allison Hoover my household
furniture now in the possession of Mrs. Richard
Topham.' "

There was a gasp of surprise from everyone in
the room, and Mrs. Topham half arose from her
chair.   It was generally known in River Heights
that she had practically confiscated Josiah Crowley's furniture at the time he had been induced to
make his home with the Tophams.

"How insulting!" the woman cried.   "Does Josiah Crowley dare hint that I took his furniture?"

"I'm sure I don't know what was in his mind at
the time he wrote the will," Mr. Drew told her
with a smile.

Grace Hoover interposed quickly, "We have
enough furniture without Josiah Crowley's."

Allison nodded.   "We'll not take any of it from
you, Mrs. Topham."

Mr. Drew carefully folded the document he had been reading, and after placing it in his pocket, he said to the people in the room:

"That is all, except that there is a proviso for the executor to pay all Mr. Crowley's just debts, including his funeral expenses, and that what balance is left in the estate goes to the Manningham Old Men's Home. I understand Josiah Crowley kept his assets in a liquid state. It will not be difficult to convert the estate into cash. For that reason I should think it would be possible to draw on your inheritances at once."

Ada wheeled upon Nancy, her face convulsed with anger. "You engineered this whole thing, Nancy Drew!" she accused bitterly.

"Any good I've done I'm happy about," Nancy answered.

"We'll break the will!" Mrs. Topham announced firmly.

CHAPTER XX

A Happy Finale

"OF COURSE you may take the matter into court if you like," Mr. Drew responded to Mrs. Topham's threat. "But I warn you it will be a waste of your time and money. If you don't wish to accept my judgment, ask your own lawyer."

"Mr. Drew is right," the other lawyer said, after arising and looking carefully at the legal document which Mr. Drew took from his pocket.

"Oh, he is, is he?" Mrs. Topham retorted. "If that's all you know about law, you're discharged! We'll get another lawyer and we'll fight to the last ditch!"

With that she arose and stalked from the room. Isabel and Ada followed, after bestowing a withering glance upon Nancy. Mr. Topham brought up the rear. As soon as the door had closed behind them, their lawyer arose and picked up his brief case.

"Well, I can't say I'm sorry to be taken off the case," he remarked as he, too, took his leave. "But I advise you to be on your guard. That woman is certainly belligerent."

At once the atmosphere in the Drew living room became less strained, though each person was fearful Mrs. Topham would make trouble. Everyone began to talk at once.

"Oh, Nancy, I can hardly believe it yet!" Allison declared happily. "The money means so much to Grace and me! And we owe it all to you, Nancy Drew! You haven't told us how you came to find the will, but I know you were responsible."

When the Hoover girls and Mr. Crowley's relatives begged her for the details, Nancy told of her adventure with the thieves at Moon Lake. After she had finished the story, they praised her highly for what she had done.

"We'll never be able to thank you enough," Grace said quietly. "But after the estate has been settled, we'll try to show our appreciation."

It was on the tip of Nancy's tongue to say that she did not want a reward, when Mr. Drew turned the conversation into a different channel.

"Mrs. Topham will not give up the money without a fight," he warned. "My advice would be to go along as you have until the court has decided to accept this will as the final one. However, if Mrs. Topham and her daughters bring the matter into court, I'll give them a battle they'll never forget!"

After thanking Mr. Drew and Nancy for everything they had done, the relatives and friends departed. Allison and Grace were the last to leave. On the porch, Allison paused to hug Nancy and say, "Please let us know what develops. I'm so eager to start taking voice lessons."

Nancy wanted to set off at once to see Abby Rowen and tell her the good news. But upon second thought she decided to wait. Suppose the Tophams succeeded in upsetting the whole case!

For a week Nancy waited impatiently to hear the result of the battle over the will. As she and her father had anticipated, Mrs. Topham was fighting bitterly for the Crowley estate. She had put forth the claim that the will Nancy had unearthed was a forged document.

"This suspense is just awful," Nancy told her father one morning. "When are we going to get final word?"

"I can't answer that, Nancy. But apparently Mr. Topham thinks it's a losing battle. I suppose you've heard about the family."

"Why, no, what about them?"

"They're practically bankrupt. Richard Topham has been losing steadily on the stock market of late. After his failure to recover the Crowley fortune, the banks reduced his credit. He's been forced to give up his beautiful home."

"No, really? How that must hurt Mrs. Topham and the two girls!"

"Yes, it's undoubtedly a bitter pill to swallow. They are moving into a small house this week, and from now on they'll have to give up their extravagant way of living.   Both girls are working. Personally, I think it will be good for them."

Word came that the three furniture thieves had finally confessed to many robberies and their unsold loot was recovered.   Among the pieces were all the heirlooms they had stolen from the Turners.

One evening Mr. Drew came home wearing a broad smile.   Facing Nancy and laying both hands on her shoulders, he said:

"We've won, my dear.   The will you located has been accepted as the last one Mr. Crowley wrote."

"Oh, Dad, how wonderful!" she cried, whirling her father about in a little dance.   "First thing tomorrow morning, may I go and tell Allison and Grace and the others?"

"I think that would be a fine idea.   Of course the bank and I will formally notify them later."

The following morning Nancy was the first one downstairs and started breakfast before Hannah Gruen appeared.

"My goodness, you're an early bird, Nancy," the housekeeper said with a smile.   "Big day, eh?"

"*Very* big," Nancy replied.

As soon as the family had eaten, Hannah said,

"Never mind helping me today. You run along and make those people happy as soon as possible."

"Oh, thank you, Hannah. I'll leave right away."

Nancy, dressed in a simple green linen sports dress with a matching sweater, kissed her little family good-by and drove off. Her first stop was at the Mathews brothers. They greeted her affably, then waited for Nancy to speak.

"I have good news," she said, her eyes dancing. "Mrs. Topham lost her case. The will Dad and I found has been accepted for probate. You will receive the inheritance Mr. Crowley left you!"

"Praise be!" Fred cried. "And we never would have received it if it hadn't been for you." His brother nodded in agreement.

To cover her embarrassment at their praise, Nancy reached into a pocket and pulled out a handful of travel folders and airline schedules. "I thought you might like to look at these. Now I must hurry off and tell the other heirs."

As she drove away, the two men smiled, waved, then immediately began to look at the folders. "I hope they have a grand trip," Nancy thought.

Half an hour later she pulled into the driveway of the Turner home. Before the car stopped, Judy came racing from the front door. As Nancy stepped out, the little girl threw herself into the young sleuth's arms. "Nancy, guess what! My aunties found an old, old doll that belonged to my mommy and they gave it to me. Come and see her. She's pretty as can be."

Judy pulled Nancy by the hand up the steps and into the house. "There she is," the child said proudly, pointing to a blond, curly-haired doll seated in a tiny rocking chair.

"Why, she's darling," Nancy commented. "And, Judy, she looks like you, dimples and all."

Judy nodded. "And Aunt Mary says she looks like my mommy did when she was a little girl, so I'm always going to take very good care of my dolly."

At this moment her great-aunts came from the rear of the house to greet their caller.

"I see," said Nancy, "that you have made Judy very happy. Now it's my turn to pass along good news to you," and she told about their inheritance.

The women smiled happily and tears came to their eyes. Then suddenly Edna Turner gave Nancy an impulsive hug. "You dear, dear girl!" she half sobbed with joy. "Now Judy will always be well taken care of and receive the kind of schooling we think she should have!"

Mary kissed Nancy and thanked the young sleuth for her untiring efforts to see justice done. Judy, meanwhile, looked on in puzzlement at the scene. But sensing that it called for her participation, she grabbed up her new doll and began to dance around with it.

"Now you can go to school too, Carol," she told her doll.

It was hard for Nancy to break away from the Turners, but she reminded them that she still had two calls to make.

"But come back soon," Judy said.

When Nancy arrived at Abby Rowen's she was delighted to find her seated by the window in a chair. Her kind neighbor, Mrs. Jones, was there preparing food for the invalid. To this Nancy added a jar of homemade beef broth and a casserole of rice and chicken which Hannah Gruen had insisted upon sending.

"Can you stay a little while?" Mrs. Jones asked. "I ought to run home for half an hour, then I'll come back."

"She's been so kind," Abby Rowen spoke up. "Today she took my laundry home to wash and iron." After the woman had left, Abby went on, "The folks around here have been very thoughtful of me, but I just can't impose on them any longer. Yet I haven't any money—"

Nancy took the invalid's hand in hers and smiled. "I came to tell you that now you have lots of money, left to you by Josiah Crowley."

"What! You mean I won't have to depend on just my little pension any longer? Bless Josiah! Nancy, I never could believe that my cousin would go back on his word."

Nancy ate some broth and crackers with Abby

Rowen and told the whole story. The old woman's eyes began to sparkle and color came into her cheeks. "Oh, this is so wonderful!" she said. Then she chuckled. "It does my heart good to know you outwitted those uppity Topham women!"

Nancy grinned, then said soberly, "If I hadn't become involved in this mystery, I might never have met several wonderful people—and their names aren't Topham!"

Abby Rowen laughed aloud—the first time Nancy had heard her do this. She laughed again just as the neighbor returned. Mrs. Jones, amazed, had no chance to exclaim over the elderly woman's high spirits. Abby launched into an account of her inheritance.

As soon as Mrs. Rowen finished the story, Nancy said good-by and left. She now headed straight for the Hoover farm. The two sisters were working in a flower bed.

"Hi!" Nancy called.

"Hi, yourself. How's everything?" Allison asked, as she brushed some dirt off her hands and came forward with Grace.

"Hurry and change your clothes," Nancy said. "I have a surprise for you."

"You mean we're going somewhere?" Grace inquired.

"That's right. To Signor Mascagni's so Allison can sign up for lessons."

"Oh, Nancy, you mean—?"

"Yes. The inheritance is yours!"

"I can't believe it! I can't believe it!" Allison cried out ecstatically. She grabbed the other two girls and whirled them around.

"It's simply marvelous," said Grace. "Marvelous. Oh, Nancy, you and Mr. Crowley are just the dearest friends we've ever had." Then, seeing Nancy's deep blush, she added, "Come on, Allison. Let's get dressed."

Nancy waited in the garden. Fifteen minutes later the sisters were ready to leave for River Heights. "But before we go," said Grace, "Allison and I want to give you something—it's sort of a reward."

"Something very special," her sister broke in.

"Oh, I don't want any reward," Nancy objected quickly.

"Please take this one," Allison spoke up.

She led the way to the living-room mantel. There stood the Crowley clock. "We received it this morning from the Tophams," Grace explained.

Allison added, "We think you earned this heirloom, Nancy, and somehow Grace and I feel Mr. Crowley would want you to have it."

"Why, thank you," said Nancy.

She was thrilled, and gazed meditatively at the old clock. Though quaint, it was not handsome, she thought. But for her it certainly held a special significance. She was too modest to explain to Allison and Grace why she would prize the heirloom, and besides, her feeling was something she could not put into words. Actually she had become attached to the clock because of its association with her recent adventure.

"This is the first mystery I've solved alone," she thought. "I wonder if I'll ever have another one half so thrilling."

As Nancy stood looking wistfully at the old clock she little dreamed that in the near future she would be involved in *The Hidden Staircase* mystery, a far more baffling case than the one she had just solved. But somehow, as Nancy gazed at the timepiece, she sensed that exciting days were soon to come.

Nancy ceased daydreaming as the clock was handed to her and looked at the Hoover girls. "I'll always prize this clock as a trophy of my first venture as a detective," she said with a broad smile.

The Hidden Staircase

Both girls froze in their tracks

NANCY DREW MYSTERY STORIES

The Hidden Staircase

BY CAROLYN KEENE

PUBLISHERS *Grosset & Dunlap* NEW YORK

A NATIONAL GENERAL COMPANY

*This new story for today's readers is based
on the original of the same title.*

Contents

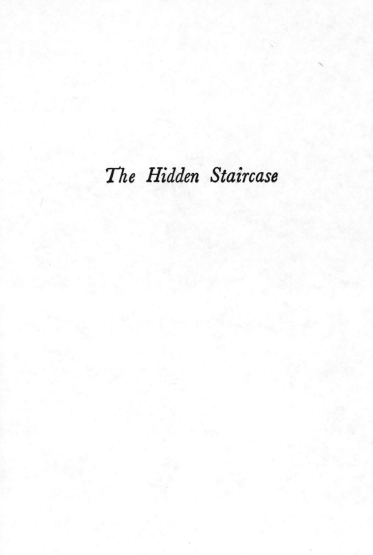

The Hidden Staircase

CHAPTER I

The Haunted House

NANCY DREW began peeling off her garden gloves as she ran up the porch steps and into the hall to answer the ringing telephone. She picked it up and said, "Hello!"

"Hi, Nancy! This is Helen." Although Helen Corning was nearly three years older than Nancy, the two girls were close friends.

"Are you tied up on a case?" Helen asked.

"No. What's up? A mystery?"

"Yes—a haunted house."

Nancy sat down on the chair by the telephone. "Tell me more!" the eighteen-year-old detective begged excitedly.

"You've heard me speak of my Aunt Rosemary," Helen began. "Since becoming a widow, she has lived with her mother at Twin Elms, the old family mansion out in Cliffwood. Well, I went to see them yesterday. They said that many strange,

1

mysterious things have been happening there recently. I told them how good you are at solving mysteries, and they'd like you to come out to Twin Elms and help them." Helen paused, out of breath.

"It certainly sounds intriguing," Nancy replied, her eyes dancing.

"If you're not busy, Aunt Rosemary and I would like to come over in about an hour and talk to you about the ghost."

"I can't wait."

After Nancy had put down the phone, she sat lost in thought for several minutes. Since solving *The Secret of the Old Clock,* she had longed for another case. Here was her chance!

Attractive, blond-haired Nancy was brought out of her daydreaming by the sound of the doorbell. At the same moment the Drews' housekeeper, Hannah Gruen, came down the front stairs.

"I'll answer it," she offered.

Mrs. Gruen had lived with the Drews since Nancy was three years old. At that time Mrs. Drew had passed away and Hannah had become like a second mother to Nancy. There was a deep affection between the two, and Nancy confided all her secrets to the understanding housekeeper.

Mrs. Gruen opened the door and instantly a man stepped into the hall. He was short, thin, and rather stooped. Nancy guessed his age to be about forty.

"Is Mr. Drew at home?" he asked brusquely. "My name is Gomber—Nathan Gomber."

"No, he's not here just now," the housekeeper replied.

The caller looked over Hannah Gruen's shoulder and stared at Nancy. "Are you Nancy Drew?"

"Yes, I am. Is there anything I can do for you?"

The man's shifty gaze moved from Nancy to Hannah. "I've come out of the goodness of my heart to warn you and your father," he said pompously.

"Warn us? About what?" Nancy asked quickly.

Nathan Gomber straightened up importantly and said, "Your father is in great danger, Miss Drew!"

Both Nancy and Hannah Gruen gasped. "You mean this very minute?" the housekeeper questioned.

"All the time," was the startling answer. "I understand you're a pretty bright girl, Miss Drew —that you even solve mysteries. Well, right now I advise you to stick close to your father. Don't leave him for a minute."

Hannah Gruen looked as if she were ready to collapse and suggested that they all go into the living room, sit down, and talk the matter over. When they were seated, Nancy asked Nathan Gomber to explain further.

"The story in a nutshell is this," he began. "You know that your father was brought in to do legal work for the railroad when it was buying property for the new bridge here."

As Nancy nodded, he continued, "Well, a lot of the folks who sold their property think they were gypped."

Nancy's face reddened. "I understood from my father that everyone was well paid."

"That's not true," said Gomber. "Besides, the railroad is in a real mess now. One of the property owners, whose deed and signature they claim to have, says that he never signed the contract of sale."

"What's his name?" Nancy asked.

"Willie Wharton."

Nancy had not heard her father mention this name. She asked Gomber to go on with his story.

"I'm acting as agent for Willie Wharton and several of the land owners who were his neighbors," he said, "and they can make it pretty tough for the railroad. Willie Wharton's signature was never witnessed and the attached certificate of acknowledgment was not notarized. That's good proof the signature was a forgery. Well, if the railroad thinks they're going to get away with this, they're not!"

Nancy frowned. Such a procedure on the part of the property owners meant trouble for her father! She said evenly, "But all Willie Wharton has to do is swear before a notary that he did sign the contract of sale."

Gomber chuckled. "It's not that easy, Miss Drew. Willie Wharton is not available. Some of us have a good idea where he is and we'll produce him at the right time. But that time won't be until the railroad promises to give the sellers more money. Then he'll sign. You see, Willie is a real kind man and he wants to help his friends out whenever he can. Now he's got a chance."

Nancy had taken an instant dislike to Gomber and now it was quadrupled. She judged him to be the kind of person who stays within the boundaries of the law but whose ethics are questionable. This was indeed a tough problem for Mr. Drew!

"Who are the people who are apt to harm my father?" she asked.

"I'm not saying who they are," Nathan Gomber retorted. "You don't seem very appreciative of my coming here to warn you. Fine kind of a daughter you are. You don't care what happens to your father!"

Annoyed by the man's insolence, both Nancy and Mrs. Gruen angrily stood up. The housekeeper, pointing toward the front door, said, "Good day, Mr. Gomber!"

The caller shrugged as he too arose. "Have it your own way, but don't say I didn't warn you!"

He walked to the front door, opened it, and as he went outside, closed it with a tremendous bang.

"Well, of all the insulting people!" Hannah snorted.

Nancy nodded. "But that's not the worst of it, Hannah darling. I think there's more to Gomber's warning than he is telling. It seems to me to imply a threat. And he almost has me convinced. Maybe I should stay close to Dad until he and the other lawyers have straightened out this railroad tangle."

She said this would mean giving up a case she had been asked to take. Hastily Nancy gave Hannah the highlights of her conversation with Helen about the haunted mansion. "Helen and her aunt will be here in a little while to tell us the whole story."

"Oh, maybe things aren't so serious for your father as that horrible man made out," Hannah said encouragingly. "If I were you I'd listen to the details about the haunted house and then decide what you want to do about the mystery."

In a short time a sports car pulled into the winding, tree-shaded driveway of the Drew home. The large brick house was set some distance back from the street.

Helen was at the wheel and stopped just beyond the front entrance. She helped her aunt from the car and they came up the steps together. Mrs. Rosemary Hayes was tall and slender and had graying hair. Her face had a gentle expression but she looked tired.

Helen introduced her aunt to Nancy and to Hannah, and the group went into the living room to sit down. Hannah offered to prepare tea and left the room.

"Oh, Nancy," said Helen, "I do hope you can take Aunt Rosemary and Miss Flora's case." Quickly she explained that Miss Flora was her aunt's mother. "Aunt Rosemary is really my great-aunt and Miss Flora is my great-grandmother. From the time she was a little girl everybody has called her Miss Flora."

"The name may seem odd to people the first time they hear it," Mrs. Hayes remarked, "but we're all so used to it, we never think anything about it."

"Please tell me more about your house," Nancy requested, smiling.

"Mother and I are almost nervous wrecks," Mrs. Hayes replied. "I have urged her to leave Twin Elms, but she won't. You see, Mother has lived there ever since she married my father, Everett Turnbull."

Mrs. Hayes went on to say that all kinds of strange happenings had occurred during the past couple of weeks. They had heard untraceable music, thumps and creaking noises at night, and had seen eerie, indescribable shadows on walls.

"Have you notified the police?" Nancy asked.

"Oh, yes," Mrs. Hayes answered. "But after talking with my mother, they came to the conclusion that most of what she saw and heard could be explained by natural causes. The rest, they said, probably was imagination on her part. You see, she's over eighty years old, and while I know her mind is sound and alert, I'm afraid that the police don't think so."

After a pause Mrs. Hayes went on, "I had almost talked myself into thinking the ghostly noises could be attributed to natural causes, when something else happened."

"What was that?" Nancy questioned eagerly.

"We were robbed! During the night several pieces of old jewelry were taken. I did telephone the police about this and they came to the house for a description of the pieces. But they still would not admit that a 'ghost' visitor had taken them."

Nancy was thoughtful for several seconds before making a comment. Then she said, "Do the police have any idea who the thief might be?"

Aunt Rosemary shook her head. "No. And I'm afraid we might have more burglaries."

Many ideas were running through Nancy's head. One was that the thief apparently had no intention of harming anyone—that his only motive had been burglary. Was he or was he not the person who was "haunting" the house? Or could the strange happenings have some natural explanations, as the police had suggested?

At this moment Hannah returned with a large silver tray on which was a tea service and some dainty sandwiches. She set the tray on a table and asked Nancy to pour the tea. She herself passed the cups of tea and sandwiches to the callers.

As they ate, Helen said, "Aunt Rosemary hasn't told you half the things that have happened. Once Miss Flora thought she saw someone sliding out of a fireplace at midnight, and another time a chair moved from one side of the room to the other while her back was turned. But no one was there!"

"How extraordinary!" Hannah Gruen exclaimed. "I've often read about such things, but I never thought I'd meet anyone who lived in a haunted house."

Helen turned to Nancy and gazed pleadingly at her friend. "You see how much you're needed at Twin Elms? Won't you please go out there with me and solve the mystery of the ghost?"

CHAPTER II

The Mysterious Mishap

SIPPING their tea, Helen Corning and her aunt waited for Nancy's decision. The young sleuth was in a dilemma. She wanted to start at once solving the mystery of the "ghost" of Twin Elms. But Nathan Gomber's warning still rang in her ears and she felt that her first duty was to stay with her father.

At last she spoke. "Mrs. Hayes—" she began.

"Please call me Aunt Rosemary," the caller requested. "All Helen's friends do."

Nancy smiled. "I'd love to. Aunt Rosemary, may I please let you know tonight or tomorrow? I really must speak to my father about the case. And something else came up just this afternoon which may keep me at home for a while at least."

"I understand," Mrs. Hayes answered, trying to conceal her disappointment.

Helen Corning did not take Nancy's announce-

ment so calmly. "Oh, Nancy, you just must come.
I'm sure your dad would want you to help us.
Can't you postpone the other thing until you get
back?"

"I'm afraid not," said Nancy. "I can't tell you
all the details, but Dad has been threatened and I
feel that I ought to stay close to him."

Hannah Gruen added her fears. "Goodness
only knows what they may do to Mr. Drew," she
said. "Somebody could come up and hit him on
the head, or poison his food in a restaurant, or—"

Helen and her aunt gasped. "It's that bad?"
Helen asked, her eyes growing wide.

Nancy explained that she would talk to her
father when he returned home. "I hate to disap-
point you," she said, "but you can see what a quan-
dary I'm in."

"You poor girl!" said Mrs. Hayes sympathetically. "Now don't you worry about us."

Nancy smiled. "I'll worry whether I come or
not," she said. "Anyway, I'll talk to my dad tonight."

The callers left shortly. When the door had
closed behind them, Hannah put an arm around
Nancy's shoulders. "I'm sure everything will
come out all right for everybody," she said. "I'm
sorry I talked about those dreadful things that
might happen to your father. I let my imagination run away with me, just like they say Miss
Flora's does with her."

"You're a great comfort, Hannah dear," said Nancy. "To tell the truth, I have thought of all kinds of horrible things myself." She began to pace the floor. "I wish Dad would get home."

During the next hour she went to the window at least a dozen times, hoping to see her father's car coming up the street. It was not until six o'clock that she heard the crunch of wheels on the driveway and saw Mr. Drew's sedan pull into the garage.

"He's safe!" she cried out to Hannah, who was testing potatoes that were baking in the oven.

In a flash Nancy was out the back door and running to meet her father. "Oh, Dad, I'm so glad to see you!" she exclaimed.

She gave him a tremendous hug and a resounding kiss. He responded affectionately, but gave a little chuckle. "What have I done to rate this extra bit of attention?" he teased. With a wink he added, "I know. Your date for tonight is off and you want me to substitute."

"Oh, Dad," Nancy replied. "Of course my date's not off. But I'm just about to call it off."

"Why?" Mr. Drew questioned. "Isn't Dirk going to stay on your list?"

"It's not that," Nancy replied. "It's because—because you're in terrible danger, Dad. I've been warned not to leave you."

Instead of looking alarmed, the lawyer burst out laughing. "In terrible danger of what? Are you going to make a raid on my wallet?"

"Dad, be serious! I really mean what I'm saying. Nathan Gomber was here and told me that you're in great danger and I'd better stay with you at all times."

The lawyer sobered at once. "That pest again!" he exclaimed. "There are times when I'd like to thrash the man till he begged for mercy!"

Mr. Drew suggested that they postpone their discussion about Nathan Gomber until dinner was over. Then he would tell his daughter the true facts in the case. After they had finished dinner, Hannah insisted upon tidying up alone while father and daughter talked.

"I will admit that there is a bit of a muddle about the railroad bridge," Mr. Drew began. "What happened was that the lawyer who went to get Willie Wharton's signature was very ill at the time. Unfortunately, he failed to have the signature witnessed or have the attached certificate of acknowledgment executed. The poor man passed away a few hours later."

"And the other railroad lawyers failed to notice that the signature hadn't been witnessed or the certificate notarized?" Nancy asked.

"Not right away. The matter did not come to light until the man's widow turned his brief case over to the railroad. The old deed to Wharton's property was there, so the lawyers assumed that the signature on the contract was genuine. The contract for the railroad bridge was awarded and work began. Suddenly Nathan Gomber appeared, saying he represented Willie Wharton and others who had owned property which the railroad had bought on either side of the Muskoka River."

"I understood from Mr. Gomber," said Nancy, "that Willie Wharton is trying to get more money for his neighbors by holding out for a higher price himself."

"That's the story. Personally, I think it's a sharp deal on Gomber's part. The more people he can get money for, the higher his commission," Mr. Drew stated.

"What a mess!" Nancy exclaimed. "And what can be done?"

"To tell the truth, there is little anyone can do until Willie Wharton is found. Gomber knows this, of course, and has probably advised Wharton to stay in hiding until the railroad agrees to give everybody more money."

Nancy had been watching her father intently. Now she saw an expression of eagerness come over his face. He leaned forward in his chair and said, "But I think I'm about to outwit Mr. Nathan Gomber. I've had a tip that Willie Wharton is in Chicago and I'm leaving Monday morning to find out."

Mr. Drew went on, "I believe that Wharton will say he did sign the contract of sale which the railroad company has and will readily consent to having the certificate of acknowledgment notarized.

Then, of course, the railroad won't pay him or any of the other property owners another cent."

"But, Dad, you still haven't convinced me you're not in danger," Nancy reminded him.

"Nancy dear," her father replied, "I feel that I am not in danger. Gomber is nothing but a blowhard. I doubt that he or Willie Wharton or any of the other property owners would resort to violence to keep me from working on this case. He's just trying to scare me into persuading the railroad to accede to his demands."

Nancy looked skeptical. "But don't forget that you're about to go to Chicago and produce the very man Gomber and those property owners don't want around here just now."

"I know." Mr. Drew nodded. "But I still doubt if anyone would use force to keep me from going." Laughingly the lawyer added, "So I won't need you as a bodyguard, Nancy."

His daughter gave a sigh of resignation. "All right, Dad, you know best." She then proceeded to tell her father about the Twin Elms mystery, which she had been asked to solve. "If you approve," Nancy said in conclusion, "I'd like to go over there with Helen."

Mr. Drew had listened with great interest. Now, after a few moments of thought, he smiled. "Go by all means, Nancy. I realize you've been itching to work on a new case—and this sounds like a real challenge. But please be careful."

"Oh, I will, Dad!" Nancy promised, her face lighting up. "Thanks a million." She jumped from her chair, gave her father a kiss, then went to phone Helen the good news. It was arranged that the girls would go to Twin Elms on Monday morning.

Nancy returned to the living room, eager to discuss the mystery further. Her father, however, glanced at his wrist watch. "Say, young lady, you'd better go dress for that date of yours." He winked. "I happen to know that Dirk doesn't like to be kept waiting."

"Especially by any of my mysteries." She laughed and hurried upstairs to change into a dance dress.

Half an hour later Dirk Jackson arrived. Nancy and the red-haired, former high-school tennis champion drove off to pick up another couple and attend an amateur play and dance given by the local Little Theater group.

Nancy thoroughly enjoyed herself and was sorry when the affair ended. With the promise of another date as soon as she returned from Twin Elms, Nancy said good night and waved from her doorway to the departing boy. As she prepared for bed, she thought of the play, the excellent orchestra, how lucky she was to have Dirk for a date, and what fun it had all been. But then her thoughts turned to Helen Corning and her relatives in the haunted house, Twin Elms.

"I can hardly wait for Monday to come," she murmured to herself as she fell asleep.

The following morning she and her father attended church together. Hannah said she was going to a special service that afternoon and therefore would stay at home during the morning.

"I'll have a good dinner waiting for you," she announced, as the Drews left.

After the service was over, Mr. Drew said he would like to drive down to the waterfront and see what progress had been made on the new bridge. "The railroad is going ahead with construction on the far side of the river," he told Nancy.

"Is the Wharton property on this side?" Nancy asked.

"Yes. And I must get to the truth of this mixed-up situation, so that work can be started on this side too."

Mr. Drew wound among the many streets leading down to the Muskoka River, then took the vehicular bridge across. He turned toward the construction area and presently parked his car. As he and Nancy stepped from the sedan, he looked ruefully at her pumps.

"It's going to be rough walking down to the waterfront," he said. "Perhaps you had better wait here."

"Oh, I'll be all right," Nancy assured him. "I'd like to see what's being done."

Various pieces of large machinery stood about on the high ground—a crane, a derrick, and hydraulic shovels. As the Drews walked toward the river, they passed a large truck. It faced the river and stood at the top of an incline just above two of the four enormous concrete piers which had already been built.

"I suppose there will be matching piers on the opposite side," Nancy mused, as she and her father reached the riverbank. They paused in the space between the two huge abutments. Mr. Drew glanced from side to side as if he had heard something. Suddenly Nancy detected a noise behind them.

Turning, she was horrified to see that the big truck was moving toward them. No one was at the wheel and the great vehicle was gathering speed at every moment.

"Dad!" she screamed.

In the brief second of warning, the truck almost seemed to leap toward the water. Nancy and her father, hemmed in by the concrete piers, had no way to escape being run down.

"Dive!" Mr. Drew ordered.

Without hesitation, he and Nancy made running flat dives into the water, and with arms flailing and legs kicking, swam furiously out of harm's way.

The truck thundered into the water and sank

The truck seemed to leap toward them

immediately up to the cab.   The Drews turned
and came back to the shore.

"Whew!   That was a narrow escape!" the lawyer exclaimed, as he helped his daughter retrieve
her pumps which had come off in the oozy bank.
"And what sights we are!" Nancy remarked.

"Indeed we are," her father agreed, as they
trudged up the incline.   "I'd like to get hold of the
workman who was careless enough to leave that
heavy truck on the slope without the brake on
properly."

Nancy was not so sure that the near accident was
the fault of a careless workman.   Nathan Gomber
had warned her that Mr. Drew's life was in danger.
The threat might already have been put into action!

CHAPTER III

A Stolen Necklace

"WE'D better get home in a hurry and change our clothes," said Mr. Drew. "And I'll call the contracting company to tell them what happened."

"And notify the police?" Nancy suggested.

She dropped behind her father and gazed over the surrounding ground for telltale footprints. Presently she saw several at the edge of the spot where the truck had stood.

"Dad!" the young sleuth called out. "I may have found a clue to explain how that truck started downhill."

Her father came back and looked at the footprints. They definitely had not been made by a workman's boots.

"You may think me an old worrier, Dad," Nancy spoke up, "but these footprints, made by a man's business shoes, convince me that somebody deliberately tried to injure us with that truck."

The lawyer stared at his daughter. Then he looked down at the ground. From the size of the shoe and the length of the stride one could easily perceive that the wearer of the shoes was not tall. Nancy asked her father if he thought one of the workmen on the project could be responsible.

"I just can't believe anyone associated with the contracting company would want to injure us," Mr. Drew said.

Nancy reminded her father of Nathan Gomber's warning. "It might be one of the property owners, or even Willie Wharton himself."

"Wharton is short and has a small foot," the lawyer conceded. "And I must admit that these look like fresh footprints. As a matter of fact, they show that whoever was here ran off in a hurry. He may have released the brake on the truck, then jumped out and run away."

"Yes," said Nancy. "And that means the attack *was* deliberate."

Mr. Drew did not reply. He continued walking up the hill, lost in thought. Nancy followed and they climbed into the car. They drove home in silence, each puzzling over the strange incident of the runaway truck. Upon reaching the house, they were greeted by a loud exclamation of astonishment.

"My goodness!" Hannah Gruen cried out. "Whatever in the world happened to you?"

They explained hastily, then hurried upstairs

to bathe and change into dry clothes. By the time they reached the first floor again, Hannah had placed sherbet glasses filled with orange and grapefruit slices on the table. All during the delicious dinner of spring lamb, rice and mushrooms, fresh peas and chocolate angel cake with vanilla ice cream, the conversation revolved around the railroad bridge mystery and then the haunted Twin Elms mansion.

"I knew things wouldn't be quiet around here for long," Hannah Gruen remarked with a smile. "Tomorrow you'll both be off on big adventures. I certainly wish you both success."

"Thank you, Hannah," said Nancy. She laughed. "I'd better get a good night's sleep. From now on I may be kept awake by ghosts and strange noises."

"I'm a little uneasy about your going to Twin Elms," the housekeeper told her. "Please promise me that you'll be careful."

"Of course," Nancy replied. Turning to her father, she said, "Pretend I've said the same thing to you about being careful."

The lawyer chuckled and pounded his chest. "You know me. I can be pretty tough when the need arises."

Early the next morning Nancy drove her father to the airport in her blue convertible. Just before she kissed him good-by at the turnstile, he said, "I expect to return on Wednesday, Nancy. Suppose

I stop off at Cliffwood and see how you're making out?"

"Wonderful, Dad! I'll be looking for you."

As soon as her father left, Nancy drove directly to Helen Corning's home. The pretty, brunette girl came from the front door of the white cottage, swinging a suitcase. She tossed it into the rear of Nancy's convertible and climbed in.

"I ought to be scared," said Helen. "Goodness only knows what's ahead of us. But right now I'm so happy nothing could upset me."

"What happened?" Nancy asked as she started the car. "Did you inherit a million?"

"Something better than that," Helen replied. "Nancy, I want to tell you a big, big secret. I'm going to be married!"

Nancy slowed the car and pulled to the side of the street. Leaning over to hug her friend, she said, "Why, Helen, how wonderful! Who is he? And tell me all about it. This is rather sudden, isn't it?"

"Yes, it is," Helen confessed. "His name is Jim Archer and he's simply out of this world. I'm a pretty lucky girl. I met him a couple of months ago when he was home on a short vacation. He works for the Tristam Oil Company and has spent two years abroad. Jim will be away a while longer, and then be given a position here in the States."

As Nancy started the car up once more, her eyes

twinkled. "Helen Corning, have you been engaged for two months and didn't tell me?"

Helen shook her head. "Jim and I have been corresponding ever since he left. Last night he telephoned from overseas and asked me to marry him." Helen giggled. "I said yes in a big hurry. Then he asked to speak to Dad. My father gave his consent but insisted that our engagement not be announced until Jim's return to this country."

The two girls discussed all sorts of delightful plans for Helen's wedding and before they knew it they had reached the town of Cliffwood.

"My great-grandmother's estate is about two miles out of town," Helen said. "Go down Main Street and turn right at the fork."

Ten minutes later she pointed out Twin Elms. From the road one could see little of the house. A high stone wall ran along the front of the estate and beyond it were many tall trees. Nancy turned into the driveway which twisted and wound among elms, oaks, and maples.

Presently the old Colonial home came into view. Helen said it had been built in 1785 and had been given its name because of the two elm trees which stood at opposite ends of the long building. They had grown to be giants and their foliage was beautiful. The mansion was of red brick and nearly all the walls were covered with ivy. There was a ten-foot porch with tall white pillars at the huge front door.

"It's charming!" Nancy commented as she pulled up to the porch.

"Wait until you see the grounds," said Helen. "There are several old, old buildings. An icehouse, a smokehouse, a kitchen, and servants' cottages."

"The mansion certainly doesn't look spooky from the outside," Nancy commented.

At that moment the great door opened and Aunt Rosemary came outside. "Hello, girls," she greeted them. "I'm so glad to see you."

Nancy felt the warmness of the welcome but thought that it was tinged with worry. She wondered if another "ghost" incident had taken place at the mansion.

The girls took their suitcases from the car and followed Mrs. Hayes inside. Although the furnishings looked rather worn, they were still very beautiful. The high-ceilinged rooms opened off a center hall and in a quick glance Nancy saw lovely damask draperies, satin-covered sofas and chairs, and on the walls, family portraits in large gilt frames of scrollwork design.

Aunt Rosemary went to the foot of the shabbily carpeted stairway, took hold of the handsome mahogany balustrade, and called, "Mother, the girls are here!"

In a moment a slender, frail-looking woman with snow-white hair started to descend the steps. Her face, though older in appearance than Rosemary's, had the same gentle smile. As Miss Flora reached the foot of the stairs, she held out her hands to both girls.

At once Helen said, "I'd like to present Nancy Drew, Miss Flora."

"I'm so glad you could come, my dear," the elderly woman said. "I know that you're going to solve this mystery which has been bothering Rosemary and me. I'm sorry not to be able to entertain you more auspiciously, but a haunted house hardly lends itself to gaiety."

The dainty, yet stately, Miss Flora swept toward a room which she referred to as the parlor. It was opposite the library. She sat down in a high-backed chair and asked everyone else to be seated.

"Mother," said Aunt Rosemary, "we don't have to be so formal with Nancy and Helen. I'm sure they'll understand that we've just been badly frightened." She turned toward the girls. "Something happened a little while ago that has made us very jittery."

"Yes," Miss Flora said. "A pearl necklace of mine was stolen!"

"You don't mean the lovely one that has been in the family so many years!" Helen cried out.

The two women nodded. Then Miss Flora said, "Oh, I probably was very foolish. It's my own fault. While I was in my room, I took the necklace from the hiding place where I usually keep it. The catch had not worked well the last time I wore the pearls and I wanted to examine it. While I was doing this, Rosemary called to me to come downstairs. The gardener was here and wanted to talk about some work. I put the necklace in my dresser drawer. When I returned ten minutes later the necklace wasn't there!"

"How dreadful!" said Nancy sympathetically. "Had anybody come into the house during that time?"

"Not to our knowledge," Aunt Rosemary replied. "Ever since we've had this ghost visiting us we've kept every door and window on the first floor locked all the time."

Nancy asked if the two women had gone out into the garden to speak to their helper. "Mother did," said Mrs. Hayes. "But I was in the kitchen the entire time. If anyone came in the back door, I certainly would have seen the person."

"Is there a back stairway to the second floor?" Nancy asked.

"Yes," Miss Flora answered. "But there are doors at both top and bottom and we keep them locked. No one could have gone up that way."

"Then anyone who came into the house had to go up by way of the front stairs?"

"Yes." Aunt Rosemary smiled a little. "But if anyone had, I would have noticed. You probably heard how those stairs creak when Mother came down. This can be avoided if you hug the wall, but practically no one knows that."

"May I go upstairs and look around?" Nancy questioned.

"Of course, dear. And I'll show you and Helen to your room," Aunt Rosemary said.

The girls picked up their suitcases and followed the two women up the stairs. Nancy and Helen were given a large, quaint room at the front of the old house over the library. They quickly deposited their luggage, then Miss Flora led the way across the hall to her room, which was directly above the parlor. It was large and very attractive with its canopied mahogany bed and an old-fashioned candlewick spread. The dresser, dressing table, and chairs also were mahogany. Long chintz draperies hung at the windows.

An eerie feeling began to take possession of Nancy. She could almost feel the presence of a ghostly burglar on the premises. Though she tried to shake off the mood, it persisted. Finally she told herself that it was possible the thief was still around. If so, he must be hiding.

Against one wall stood a large walnut wardrobe. Helen saw Nancy gazing at it intently. She went over and whispered, "Do you think there might be someone inside?"

"Who knows?" Nancy replied in a low voice. "Let's find out!"

She walked across the room, and taking hold of the two knobs on the double doors, opened them wide.

CHAPTER IV

Strange Music

THE ANXIOUS group stared inside the wardrobe. No one stood there. Dresses, suits, and coats hung in an orderly row.

Nancy took a step forward and began separating them. Someone, she thought, might be hiding behind the clothes. The others in the room held their breaths as she made a thorough search.

"No one here!" she finally announced, and a sigh of relief escaped the lips of Miss Flora and Aunt Rosemary.

The young sleuth said she would like to make a thorough inspection of all possible hiding places on the second floor. With Helen helping her, they went from room to room, opening wardrobe doors and looking under beds. They did not find the thief.

Nancy suggested that Miss Flora and Aunt Rosemary report the theft to the police, but the older woman shook her head. Mrs. Hayes, although she agreed this might be wise, added softly, "Mother just *might* be mistaken. She's a little forgetful at times about where she puts things."

With this possibility in mind, she and the girls looked in every drawer in the room, under the mattress and pillows, and even in the pockets of Miss Flora's clothes. The pearl necklace was not found. Nancy suggested that she and Helen try to find out how the thief had made his entrance.

Helen led the way outdoors. At once Nancy began to look for footprints. No tracks were visible on the front or back porches, or on any of the walks, which were made of finely crushed stone.

"We'll look in the soft earth beneath the windows," Nancy said. "Maybe the thief climbed in."

"But Aunt Rosemary said all the windows on the first floor are kept locked," Helen objected.

"No doubt," Nancy said. "But I think we should look for footprints just the same."

The girls went from window to window, but there were no footprints beneath any. Finally Nancy stopped and looked thoughtfully at the ivy on the walls.

"Do you think the thief climbed up to the second floor that way?" Helen asked her. "But there'd still be footprints on the ground."

Nancy said that the thief could have carried a plank with him, laid it down, and stepped from the walk to the wall of the house. "Then he could have climbed up the ivy and down again, and gotten back to the walk without leaving any footprints."

Once more Nancy went around the entire house, examining every bit of ivy which wound up from the foundation. Finally she said, "No, the thief didn't get into the house this way."

"Well, he certainly didn't fly in," said Helen. "So *how* did he enter?"

Nancy laughed. "If I could tell you that I'd have the mystery half solved."

She said that she would like to look around the grounds of Twin Elms. "It may give us a clue as to how the thief got into the house."

As they strolled along, Nancy kept a sharp lookout but saw nothing suspicious. At last they came to a half-crumbled brick walk laid out in an interesting crisscross pattern.

"Where does this walk lead?" Nancy asked.

"Well, I guess originally it went over to Riverview Manor, the next property," Helen replied. "I'll show you that mansion later. The first owner was a brother of the man who built this place."

Helen went on to say that Riverview Manor was a duplicate of Twin Elms mansion. The two brothers had been inseparable companions, but their sons who later lived there had had a violent quarrel and had become lifelong enemies.

"Riverview Manor has been sold several times during the years but has been vacant for a long time."

"You mean no one lives there now?" Nancy asked. As Helen nodded, she added with a laugh, "Then maybe that's the ghost's home!"

"In that case he really must be a ghost," said Helen lightly. "There's not a piece of furniture in the house."

The two girls returned to the Twin Elms mansion and reported their lack of success in picking up a clue to the intruder. Nancy, recalling that many Colonial houses had secret entrances and passageways, asked Miss Flora, "Do you know of any secret entrance to your home that the thief could use?"

She said no, and explained that her husband had been a rather reticent person and had passed away when Rosemary was only a baby. "It's just possible he knew of a secret entrance, but did not want to worry me by telling me about it," Mrs. Turnbull said.

Aunt Rosemary, sensing that her mother was becoming alarmed by the questions, suggested that they all have lunch. The two girls went with her to the kitchen and helped prepare a tasty meal of chicken salad, biscuits, and fruit gelatin.

During the meal the conversation covered several subjects, but always came back to the topic of the mystery. They had just finished eating when suddenly Nancy sat straight up in her chair.

"What's the matter?" Helen asked her.

Nancy was staring out the dining-room door toward the stairway in the hall. Then she turned to Miss Flora. "Did you leave a radio on in your bedroom?"

"Why, no."

"Did you, Aunt Rosemary?"

"No. Neither Mother nor I turned our radios on this morning. Why do—" She stopped speaking, for now all of them could distinctly hear music coming from the second floor.

Helen and Nancy were out of their chairs instantly. They dashed into the hall and up the stairway. The music was coming from Miss Flora's room, and when the girls rushed in, they knew indeed that it was from her radio.

Nancy went over to examine the set. It was an old one and did not have a clock attachment with an automatic control.

"Someone came into this room and turned on the radio!" she stated.

A look of alarm came over Helen's face, but she tried to shake off her nervousness and asked, "Nancy, do you think the radio could have been turned on by remote control? I've heard of such things."

Nancy said she doubted this. "I'm afraid, Helen, that the thief has been in the house all the time. He and the ghost are one and the same person. Oh, I wish we had looked before in the cellar and the attic. Maybe it's not too late. Come on!"

Helen, instead of moving from the room, stared at the fireplace. "Nancy," she said, "do you suppose someone is hiding up there?"

Without hesitation she crossed the room, got down on her knees, and tried to look up the chimney. The damper was closed. Reaching her arm up, Helen pulled the handle to open it.

The next moment she cried out, "Ugh!"

"Oh, Helen, you poor thing!" Nancy exclaimed, running to her friend's side.

A shower of soot had come down, covering Helen's hair, face, shoulders, and arms.

"Get me a towel, will you, Nancy?" she requested.

Nancy dashed to the bathroom and grabbed two large towels. She wrapped them around her friend, then went with Helen to help her with a shampoo and general cleanup job. Finally Nancy brought her another sports dress.

"I guess my idea about chimneys wasn't so good," Helen stated ruefully. "And we're probably too late to catch the thief."

Nevertheless, she and Nancy climbed the stairs to the attic and looked behind trunks and boxes to see if anyone were hiding. Next, the girls went to the cellar and inspected the various rooms there. Still there was no sign of the thief who had entered Twin Elms.

After Miss Flora had heard the whole story, she gave a nervous sigh. "It's the ghost—there's no other explanation."

"But why," Aunt Rosemary asked, "has a ghost suddenly started performing here? This house has been occupied since 1785 and no ghost was ever reported haunting the place."

"Well, apparently robbery is the motive," Nancy replied. "But why the thief bothers to frighten you is something I haven't figured out yet."

"The main thing," Helen spoke up, "is to catch him!"

"Oh, if we only could!" Miss Flora said, her voice a bit shaky.

The girls were about to pick up the luncheon dishes from the table, to carry them to the kitchen, when the front door knocker sounded loudly.

"Oh, dear," said Miss Flora, "who can that be? Maybe it's the thief and he's come to harm us!"

Aunt Rosemary put an arm around her mother's shoulders. "Please don't worry," she begged. "I think our caller is probably the man who wants to buy Twin Elms." She turned to Nancy and Helen. "But Mother doesn't want to sell for the low price that he is offering."

Nancy said she would go to the door. She set the dishes down and walked out to the hall. Reaching the great door, she flung it open.

Nathan Gomber stood there!

CHAPTER V

A Puzzling Interview

FOR SEVERAL seconds Nathan Gomber stared at Nancy in disbelief. "You!" he cried out finally.

"You didn't expect to find me here, did you?" she asked coolly.

"I certainly didn't. I thought you'd taken my advice and stayed with your father. Young people today are so hardhearted!" Gomber wagged his head in disgust.

Nancy ignored Gomber's remarks. Shrugging, the man pushed his way into the hall. "I know this. If anything happens to your father, you'll never forgive yourself. But you can't blame Nathan Gomber! I warned you!"

Still Nancy made no reply. She kept looking at him steadily, trying to figure out what was really in his mind. She was convinced it was not solicitude for her father.

Nathan Gomber changed the subject abruptly.

"I'd like to see Mrs. Turnbull and Mrs. Hayes,"
he said. "Go call them."

Nancy was annoyed by Gomber's crudeness, but
she turned around and went down the hall to the
dining room.

"We heard every word," Miss Flora said in a
whisper. "I shan't see Mr. Gomber. I don't want
to sell this house."

Nancy was amazed to hear this. "You mean
he's the person who wants to buy it?"

"Yes."

Instantly Nancy was on the alert. Because of
the nature of the railroad deal in which Nathan
Gomber was involved, she was distrustful of his
motives in wanting to buy Twin Elms. It flashed
through her mind that perhaps he was trying to
buy it at a very low price and planned to sell it off
in building lots at a huge profit.

"Suppose I go tell him you don't want to sell,"
Nancy suggested in a low voice.

But her caution was futile. Hearing footsteps
behind her, she turned to see Gomber standing in
the doorway.

"Howdy, everybody!" he said.

Miss Flora, Aunt Rosemary, and Helen showed
annoyance. It was plain that all of them thought
the man completely lacking in good manners.

Aunt Rosemary's jaw was set in a grim line, but
she said politely, "Helen, this is Mr. Gomber. Mr.
Gomber, my niece, Miss Corning."

"Pleased to meet you," said their caller, extending a hand to shake Helen's.

"Nancy, I guess you've met Mr. Gomber," Aunt Rosemary went on.

"Oh, sure!" Nathan Gomber said with a somewhat raucous laugh. "Nancy and me, we've met!"

"Only once," Nancy said pointedly.

Ignoring her rebuff, he went on, "Nancy Drew is a very strange young lady. Her father's in great danger and I tried to warn her to stick close to him. Instead of that, she's out here visiting you folks."

"Her father's in danger?" Miss Flora said worriedly.

"Dad says he's not," Nancy replied. "And besides, I'm sure my father would know how to take care of any enemies." She looked straight at Nathan Gomber, as if to let him know that the Drews were not easily frightened.

"Well," the caller said, "let's get down to business." He pulled an envelope full of papers from his pocket. "Everything's here—all ready for you to sign, Mrs. Turnbull."

"I don't wish to sell at such a low figure," Miss Flora told him firmly. "In fact, I don't know that I want to sell at all."

Nathan Gomber tossed his head. "You'll sell all right," he prophesied. "I've been talking to some of the folks downtown. Everybody knows this old place is haunted and nobody would give you five cents for it—that is, nobody but me."

As he waited for his words to sink in, Nancy spoke up, "If the house is haunted, why do you want it?"

"Well," Gomber answered, "I guess I'm a gambler at heart. I'd be willing to put some money into this place, even if there is a ghost parading around." He laughed loudly, then went on, "I declare it might be a real pleasure to meet a ghost and get the better of it!"

Nancy thought with disgust, "Nathan Gomber, you're about the most conceited, obnoxious person I've met in a long time."

Suddenly the expression of cunning on the man's face changed completely. An almost wistful look came into his eyes. He sat down on one of the dining-room chairs and rested his chin in his hand.

"I guess you think I'm just a hardheaded business man with no feelings," he said. "The truth is I'm a real softy. I'll tell you why I want this old house so bad. I've always dreamed of owning a Colonial mansion, and having a kinship with early America. You see, my family were poor folks in Europe. Now that I've made a little money, I'd like to have a home like this to roam around in and enjoy its traditions."

Miss Flora seemed to be touched by Gomber's story. "I had no idea you wanted the place so much," she said kindly. "Maybe I ought to give it up. It's really too big for us."

As Aunt Rosemary saw her mother weakening, she said quickly, "You don't have to sell this house, Mother. You know you love it. So far as the ghost is concerned, I'm sure that mystery is going to be cleared up. Then you'd be sorry you had parted with Twin Elms. Please don't say yes!"

As Gomber gave Mrs. Hayes a dark look, Nancy asked him, "Why don't you buy Riverview Manor? It's a duplicate of this place and is for sale. You probably could purchase it at a lower price than you could this one."

"I've seen that place," the man returned. "It's in a bad state. It would cost me a mint of money to fix it up. No sir. I want this place and I'm going to have it!"

This bold remark was too much for Aunt Rosemary. Her eyes blazing, she said, "Mr. Gomber, this interview is at an end. Good-by!"

To Nancy's delight and somewhat to her amusement, Nathan Gomber obeyed the "order" to leave. He seemed to be almost meek as he walked through the hall and let himself out the front door.

"Of all the nerve!" Helen burst out.

"Perhaps we shouldn't be too hard on the man," Miss Flora said timidly. "His story is a pathetic one and I can see how he might want to pretend he had an old American family background."

"I'd like to bet a cooky Mr. Gomber didn't mean one word of what he was saying," Helen remarked.

"Oh dear, I'm so confused," said Miss Flora, her voice trembling. "Let's all sit down in the parlor and talk about it a little more."

The two girls stepped back as Miss Flora, then Aunt Rosemary, left the dining room. They followed to the parlor and sat down together on the recessed couch by the fireplace. Nancy, on a sudden hunch, ran to a front window to see which direction Gomber had taken. To her surprise he was walking down the winding driveway.

"That's strange. Evidently he didn't drive," Nancy told herself. "It's quite a walk into town to get a train or bus to River Heights."

As Nancy mulled over this idea, trying to figure out the answer, she became conscious of creaking sounds. Helen suddenly gave a shriek. Nancy turned quickly.

"Look!" Helen cried, pointing toward the ceiling, and everyone stared upward.

The crystal chandelier had suddenly started swaying from side to side!

"The ghost again!" Miss Flora cried out. She looked as if she were about to faint.

Nancy's eyes quickly swept the room. Nothing else in it was moving, so vibration was not causing the chandelier to sway. As it swung back and forth, a sudden thought came to the young sleuth. Maybe someone in Miss Flora's room above was causing the shaking.

The chandelier suddenly started to sway

"I'm going upstairs to investigate," Nancy told the others.

Racing noiselessly on tiptoe out of the room and through the hall, she began climbing the stairs, hugging the wall so the steps would not creak. As she neared the top, Nancy was sure she heard a door close. Hurrying along the hall, she burst into Miss Flora's bedroom. No one was in sight!

"Maybe this time the ghost couldn't get away and is in that wardrobe!" Nancy thought.

Helen and her relatives had come up the stairs behind Nancy. They reached the bedroom just as she flung open the wardrobe doors. But for the second time she found no one hiding there.

Nancy bit her lip in vexation. The ghost was clever indeed. Where *had* he gone? She had given him no time to go down the hall or run into another room. Yet there was no denying the fact that he had been in Miss Flora's room!

"Tell us why you came up," Helen begged her. Nancy told her theory, but suddenly she realized that maybe she was letting her imagination run wild. It was possible, she admitted to the others, that no one had caused the chandelier to shake.

"There's only one way to find out," she said. "I'll make a test."

Nancy asked Helen to go back to the first floor and watch the chandelier. She would try to make it sway by rocking from side to side on the floor above it.

"If this works, then I'm sure we've picked up a clue to the ghost," she said hopefully.

Helen readily agreed and left the room. When Nancy thought her friend had had time to reach the parlor below, she began to rock hard from side to side on the spot above the chandelier.

She had barely started the test when from the first floor Helen Corning gave a piercing scream!

CHAPTER VI

The Gorilla Face

"SOMETHING has happened to Helen!" Aunt Rosemary cried out fearfully.

Nancy was already racing through the second-floor hallway. Reaching the stairs, she leaped down them two steps at a time. Helen Corning had collapsed in a wing chair in the parlor, her hands over her face.

"Helen! What happened?" Nancy asked, reaching her friend's side.

"Out there! Looking in that window!" Helen pointed to the front window of the parlor next to the hall. "The most horrible face I ever saw!"

"Was it a man's face?" Nancy questioned.

"Oh, I don't know. It looked just like a gorilla!" Helen closed her eyes as if to shut out the memory of the sight.

Nancy did not wait to hear any more. In another second she was at the front door and had yanked it open. Stepping outside, she looked all around. She could see no animal near the house, nor any sign under the window that one had stood there.

Puzzled, the young sleuth hurried down the steps and began a search of the grounds. By this time Helen had collected her wits and come outside. She joined Nancy and together they looked in every outbuilding and behind every clump of bushes on the grounds of Twin Elms. They did not find one footprint or any other evidence to prove that a gorilla or other creature had been on the grounds of the estate.

"I saw it! I know I saw it!" Helen insisted.

"I don't doubt you," Nancy replied.

"Then what explanation is there?" Helen demanded. "You know I never did believe in spooks. But if we have many more of these weird happenings around here, I declare I'm going to start believing in ghosts."

Nancy laughed. "Don't worry, Helen," she said. "There'll be a logical explanation for the face at the window."

The girls walked back to the front door of the mansion. Miss Flora and Aunt Rosemary stood there and immediately insisted upon knowing what had happened. As Helen told them, Nancy once more surveyed the outside of the window at which Helen had seen the terrifying face.

"I have a theory," she spoke up. "Our ghost simply leaned across from the end of the porch and held a mask in front of the window." Nancy stretched her arm out to demonstrate how this was possible.

"So that's why he didn't leave any footprints under the window," Helen said. "But he certainly got away from here fast." She suddenly laughed. "He must be on some ghosts' track team."

Her humor, Nancy was glad to see, relieved the tense situation. She had noticed Miss Flora leaning wearily on her daughter's arm.

"You'd better lie down and rest, Mother," Mrs. Hayes advised.

"I guess I will," Aunt Flora agreed.

It was suggested that the elderly woman use Aunt Rosemary's room, while the others continued the experiment with the chandelier.

Helen and Aunt Rosemary went into the parlor and waited as Nancy ascended the front stairway and went to Miss Flora's bedroom. Once more she began to rock from side to side. Downstairs, Aunt Rosemary and her niece were gazing intently at the ceiling.

"Look!" Helen exclaimed, pointing to the crystal chandelier. "It's moving!" In a moment it swung to the left, then back to the right.

"Nancy has proved that the ghost was up in my mother's room!" Aunt Rosemary said excitedly.

After a few minutes the rocking motion of the chandelier slackened and finally stopped. Nancy came hurrying down the steps.

"Did it work?" she called.

"Yes, it did," Aunt Rosemary replied. "Oh, Nancy, we must have two ghosts!"

"Why do you say that?" Helen asked.

"One rocking the chandelier, the other holding the horrible face up to the window. No one could have gone from Miss Flora's room to the front porch in such a short time. Oh, this complicates everything!"

"It certainly does," Nancy agreed. "The question is, are the two ghosts in cahoots? Or, it's just possible, there is only one. He could have disappeared from Miss Flora's room without our seeing him and somehow hurried to the first floor and let himself out the front door while we were upstairs. I'm convinced there is at least one secret entrance into this house, and maybe more. I think our next step should be to try to find it—or them."

"We'd better wash the luncheon dishes first," Aunt Rosemary suggested.

As she and the girls worked, they discussed the mystery, and Mrs. Hayes revealed that she had talked to her mother about leaving the house, whether or not she sold it.

"I thought we might at least go away for a little vacation, but Mother refuses to leave. She says she intends to remain right here until this ghost business is settled."

Helen smiled. "Nancy, my great-grandmother

is a wonderful woman. She has taught me a lot
about courage and perseverance. I hope if I ever
reach her age, I'll have half as much."

"Yes, she's an example to all of us," Aunt Rosemary concurred.

Nancy nodded. "I agree. I haven't known your
mother long, Aunt Rosemary, but I think she is
one of the dearest persons I've ever met."

"If Miss Flora won't leave," said Helen, "I guess
that means we all stay."

"That's settled," said Nancy with a smile.

After the dishes were put away, the girls were
ready to begin their search for a secret entrance
into the mansion.

"Let's start with Miss Flora's room," Helen
suggested.

"That's a logical place," Nancy replied, and took
the lead up the stairway.

Every inch of the wall, which was paneled in
maple halfway to the ceiling, was tapped. No
hollow sound came from any section of it to indicate an open space behind. The bureau, dressing
table, and bed were pulled away from the walls
and Nancy carefully inspected every inch of the
paneling for cracks or wide seams to indicate a concealed door.

"Nothing yet," she announced, and then decided to inspect the sides of the fireplace.

The paneled sides and brick front revealed nothing. Next, Nancy looked at the sides and rear of

the stone interior. She could see nothing unusual, and the blackened stones did not look as if they had ever been disturbed.

She closed the damper which Helen had left open, and then suggested that the searchers transfer to another room on the second floor. But no trace of any secret entrance to the mansion could be found.

"I think we've had enough investigation for one day," Aunt Rosemary remarked.

Nancy was about to say that she was not tired and would like to continue. But she realized that Mrs. Hayes had made this suggestion because her mother was once more showing signs of fatigue and strain.

Helen, who also realized the situation, said, "Let's have an early supper. I'm starved!"

"I am, too," Nancy replied, laughing gaily.

The mood was contagious and soon Miss Flora seemed to have forgotten about her mansion being haunted. She sat in the kitchen while Aunt Rosemary and the girls cooked the meal.

"*Um*, steak and French fried potatoes, fresh peas, and yummy floating island for dessert," said Helen. "I can hardly wait."

"Fruit cup first," Aunt Rosemary announced, taking a bowl of fruit from the refrigerator.

Soon the group was seated at the table. Tactfully steering the conversation away from the mystery, Nancy asked Miss Flora to tell the group about parties and dances which had been held in the mansion long ago.

The elderly woman smiled in recollection. "I remember one story my husband told me of something that happened when he was a little boy," Miss Flora began. "His parents were holding a masquerade and he was supposed to be in bed fast asleep. His nurse had gone downstairs to talk to some of the servants. The music awakened my husband and he decided it would be great fun to join the guests.

" 'I'll put on a costume myself,' he said to himself. He knew there were some packed in a trunk in the attic." Miss Flora paused. "By the way, girls, I think that sometime while you are here you ought to see them. They're beautiful.

"Well, Everett went to the attic, opened the trunk, and searched until he found a soldier's outfit. It was very fancy—red coat and white trousers. He had quite a struggle getting it on and had to turn the coat sleeves way up. The knee britches came to his ankles, and the hat was so large it came down over his ears."

By this time Miss Flora's audience was laughing and Aunt Rosemary remarked, "My father really must have looked funny. Please go on, Mother."

"Little Everett came down the stairs and mingled with the masqueraders at the dance. For a while he wasn't noticed, then suddenly his mother discovered the queer-looking figure."

"And," Aunt Rosemary interrupted, "quickly put him back to bed, I'm sure."

Miss Flora laughed. "That's where you're wrong. The guests thought the whole thing was such fun that they insisted Everett stay. Some of the women danced with him—he went to dancing school and was an excellent dancer. Then they gave him some strawberries and cream and cake."

Helen remarked, "And then put him to bed."

Again Miss Flora laughed. "The poor little fellow never knew that he had fallen asleep while he was eating, and his father had to carry him upstairs. He was put into his little four-poster, costume and all. Of course his nurse was horrified, and I'm afraid that during the rest of the night the poor woman thought she would lose her position. But she didn't. In fact, she stayed with the family until all the children were grown up."

"Oh, that's a wonderful story!" said Nancy.

She was about to urge Miss Flora to tell another story when the telephone rang. Aunt Rosemary answered it, and then called to Nancy, "It's for you."

Nancy hurried to the hall, grabbed up the phone, and said, "Hello." A moment later she cried out, "Dad! How wonderful to hear from you!"

Mr. Drew said that he had not found Willie Wharton and certain clues seemed to indicate that he was not in Chicago, but in some other city.

"I have a few other matters to take care of that will keep me here until tomorrow night. How are you getting along?"

"I haven't solved the mystery yet," his daughter reported. "We've had some more strange happenings. I'll certainly be glad to see you here at Cliffwood. I know you can help me."

"All right, I'll come. But don't try to meet me. The time is too uncertain, and as a matter of fact, I may find that I'll have to stay here in Chicago."

Mr. Drew said he would come out to the mansion by taxi. Briefly Nancy related her experiences at Twin Elms, and after a little more conversation, hung up. When she rejoined the others at the table, she told them about Mr. Drew's promised visit.

"Oh, I'll be so happy to meet your father," said Miss Flora. "We may need legal advice in this mystery."

There was a pause after this remark, with everyone silent for a few moments. Suddenly each one in the group looked at the others, startled. From somewhere upstairs came the plaintive strains of violin music. Had the radio been turned on again by the ghost?

Nancy dashed from the table to find out.

CHAPTER VII

Frightening Eyes

WITHIN five seconds Nancy had reached the second floor. The violin playing suddenly ceased.

She raced into Miss Flora's room, from which the sounds had seemed to come. The radio was not on. Quickly Nancy felt the instrument to see if it were even slightly warm to prove it had been in use.

"The music wasn't being played on this," she told herself, finding the radio cool.

As Nancy dashed from the room, she almost ran into Helen. "What did you find out?" her friend asked breathlessly.

"Nothing so far," Nancy replied, as she raced into Aunt Rosemary's bedroom to check the bedside radio in there.

This instrument, too, felt cool to the touch.

She and Helen stood in the center of the room, puzzled frowns creasing their foreheads. "There *was* music, wasn't there?" Helen questioned.

"I distinctly heard it," Nancy replied. "But *where* is the person who played the violin? Or put a disk on a record player, or turned on a hidden radio? Helen, I'm positive an intruder comes into this mansion by some secret entrance and tries to frighten us all."

"And succeeds," Helen answered. "It's positively eerie."

"And dangerous," Nancy thought.

"Let's continue our search right after breakfast tomorrow," Helen proposed.

"We will," Nancy responded. "But in the meantime I believe Miss Flora and Aunt Rosemary, to say nothing of ourselves, need some police protection."

"I think you're right," Helen agreed. "Let's go downstairs and suggest it to the others."

The girls returned to the first floor and Nancy told Mrs. Hayes and her mother of the failure to find the cause of the violin playing, and what she had in mind.

"Oh dear, the police will only laugh at us," Miss Flora objected.

"Mother dear," said her daughter, "the captain and his men didn't believe us before because they thought we were imagining things. But Nancy and Helen heard music at two different times and they saw the chandelier rock. I'm sure that Captain Rossland will believe Nancy and send a guard out here."

Nancy smiled at Miss Flora. "I shan't ask the captain to believe in a ghost or even hunt for one. I think all we should request at the moment is that he have a man patrol the grounds here at night. I'm sure that we're perfectly safe while we're all awake, but I must admit I'd feel a little uneasy about going to bed wondering what that ghost may do next."

Mrs. Turnbull finally agreed to the plan and Nancy went to the telephone. Captain Rossland readily agreed to send a man out a little later.

"He'll return each night as long as you need him," the officer stated. "And I'll tell him not to ring the bell to tell you when he comes. If there is anyone who breaks into the mansion by a secret entrance, it would be much better if he does not know a guard is on duty."

"I understand," said Nancy.

When Miss Flora, her daughter, and the two girls went to bed, they were confident they would have a restful night. Nancy felt that if there was no disturbance, then it would indicate that the ghost's means of entry into Twin Elms was directly from the outside. "In which case," she thought, "it will mean he saw the guard and didn't dare come inside the house."

The young sleuth's desire for a good night's sleep was rudely thwarted as she awakened about midnight with a start. Nancy was sure she had heard a noise nearby. But now the house was

quiet. Nancy listened intently, then finally got
out of bed.

"Perhaps the noise I heard came from outdoors," she told herself.

Tiptoeing to a window, so that she would not
awaken Helen, Nancy peered out at the moonlit
grounds. Shadows made by tree branches, which
swayed in a gentle breeze, moved back and forth
across the lawn. The scent from a rose garden in
full bloom was wafted to Nancy.

"What a heavenly night!" she thought.

Suddenly Nancy gave a start. A furtive figure
had darted from behind a tree toward a clump of
bushes. Was he the guard or the ghost? she wondered. As Nancy watched intently to see if she
could detect any further movements of the mysterious figure, she heard padding footsteps in the hall.
In a moment there was a loud knock on her door.

"Nancy! Wake up! Nancy! Come quick!"

The voice was Miss Flora's, and she sounded extremely frightened. Nancy sped across the room,
unlocked her door, and opened it wide. By this
time Helen was awake and out of bed.

"What happened?" she asked sleepily.

Aunt Rosemary had come into the hall also.
Her mother did not say a word; just started back
toward her own bedroom. The others followed,
wondering what they would find. Moonlight
brightened part of the room, but the area near the
hall was dark.

"There! Up there!" Miss Flora pointed to a corner of the room near the hall.

Two burning eyes looked down on the watchers!

Instantly Nancy snapped on the wall light and the group gazed upward at a large brown owl perched on the old-fashioned, ornamental picture molding.

"Oh!" Aunt Rosemary cried out. "How did that bird ever get in here?"

The others did not answer at once. Then Nancy, not wishing to frighten Miss Flora, remarked as casually as she could, "It probably came down the chimney."

"But—" Helen started to say.

Nancy gave her friend a warning wink and Helen did not finish the sentence. Nancy was sure she was going to say that the damper had been closed and the bird could not possibly have flown into the room from the chimney. Turning to Miss Flora, Nancy asked whether or not her bedroom door had been locked.

"Oh, yes," the elderly woman insisted. "I wouldn't leave it unlocked for anything."

Nancy did not comment. Knowing that Miss Flora was a bit forgetful, she thought it quite possible that the door had not been locked. An intruder had entered, let the owl fly to the picture molding, then made just enough noise to awaken the sleeping woman.

To satisfy her own memory about the damper,
Nancy went over to the fireplace and looked inside. The damper was closed.

"But if the door to the hall was locked," she
reasoned, "then the ghost has some other way of
getting into this room. And he escaped the detection of the guard."

"I don't want that owl in here all night," Miss
Flora broke into Nancy's reverie. "We'll have to
get it out."

"That's not going to be easy," Aunt Rosemary
spoke up. "Owls have very sharp claws and beaks
and they use them viciously on anybody who
tries to disturb them. Mother, you come and
sleep in my room the rest of the night. We'll
chase the owl out in the morning."

Nancy urged Miss Flora to go with her daughter.
"I'll stay here and try getting Mr. Owl out of
the house. Have you a pair of old heavy gloves?"

"I have some in my room," Aunt Rosemary replied. "They're thick leather. I use them for
gardening."

She brought them to Nancy, who put the gloves
on at once. Then she suggested that Aunt Rosemary and her mother leave. Nancy smiled.
"Helen and I will take over Operation Owl."

As the door closed behind the two women,
Nancy dragged a chair to the corner of the room
beneath the bird. She was counting on the fact
that the bright overhead light had dulled the owl's

vision and she would be able to grab it without too much trouble.

"Helen, will you open one of the screens, please?" she requested. "And wish me luck!"

"Don't let that thing get loose," Helen warned as she unfastened the screen and held it far out.

Nancy reached up and by stretching was just able to grasp the bird. In a lightning movement she had put her two hands around its body and imprisoned its claws. At once the owl began to bob its head and peck at her arms above the gloves. Wincing with pain, she stepped down from the chair and ran across the room.

The bird squirmed, darting its beak in first one direction, then another. But Nancy managed to hold the owl in such a position that most of the pecking missed its goal. She held the bird out the window, released it, and stepped back. Helen closed the screen and quickly fastened it.

"Oh!" Nancy said, gazing ruefully at her wrists which now showed several bloody digs from the owl's beak. "I'm glad that's over."

"And I am too," said Helen. "Let's lock Miss Flora's door from the outside, so that ghost can't bring in any owls to the rest of us."

Suddenly Helen grabbed Nancy's arm. "I just thought of something," she said. "There's supposed to be a police guard outside. Yet the ghost got in here without being seen."

"Either that, or there's a secret entrance to this

mansion which runs underground, probably to one of the outbuildings on the property."

Nancy now told about the furtive figure she had seen dart from behind a tree. "I must find out right away if he was the ghost or the guard. I'll do a little snooping around. It's possible the guard didn't show up." Nancy smiled. "But if he did, and he's any good, he'll find me!"

"All right," said Helen. "But, Nancy, do be careful. You're really taking awful chances to solve the mystery of Twin Elms."

Nancy laughed softly as she walked back to the girls' bedroom. She dressed quickly, then went downstairs, put the back-door key in her pocket, and let herself out of the house. Stealthily she went down the steps and glided to a spot back of some bushes.

Seeing no one around, she came from behind them and ran across the lawn to a large maple tree. She stood among the shadows for several moments, then darted out toward a building which in Colonial times had been used as the kitchen.

Halfway there, she heard a sound behind her and turned. A man stood in the shadows not ten feet away. Quick as a wink one hand flew to a holster on his hip.

"Halt!" he commanded.

CHAPTER VIII

A Startling Plunge

NANCY halted as directed and stood facing the man. "Who are you?" she asked.

"I'm a police guard, miss," the man replied. "Just call me Patrick. And who are you?"

Quickly Nancy explained and then asked to see his identification. He opened his coat, pulled out a leather case, and showed her his shield proving that he was a plain-clothes man. His name was Tom Patrick.

"Have you seen anyone prowling around the grounds?" Nancy asked him.

"Not a soul, miss. This place has been quieter than a cemetery tonight."

When the young sleuth told him about the furtive figure she had seen from the window, the detective laughed. "I believe you saw me," he said. "I guess I'm not so good at hiding as I thought I was."

Nancy laughed lightly. "Anyway, you soon nabbed me," she told him.

The two chatted for several minutes. Tom Patrick told Nancy that people in Cliffwood regarded Mrs. Turnbull as being a little queer. They said that if she thought her house was haunted, it was all in line with the stories of the odd people who had lived there from time to time during the past hundred years or so.

"Would this rumor make the property difficult to sell?" Nancy questioned the detective.

"It certainly would."

Nancy said she thought the whole thing was a shame. "Mrs. Turnbull is one of the loveliest women I've ever met and there's not a thing the matter with her, except that once in a while she is forgetful."

"You don't think that some of these happenings we've heard about are just pure imagination?" Tom Patrick asked.

"No, I don't."

Nancy now told him about the owl in Miss Flora's bedroom. "The door was locked, every screen was fastened, and the damper in the chimney closed. You tell me how the owl got in there."

Tom Patrick's eyes opened wide. "You say this happened only a little while ago?" he queried. When Nancy nodded, he added, "Of course I can't be everywhere on these grounds at once, but I've been round and round the building. I've never stopped walking since I arrived. I don't see how anyone could have gotten inside that mansion without my seeing him."

"I'll tell you my theory," said Nancy. "I believe there's a secret underground entrance from some other place on the grounds. It may be in one of these outbuildings. Anyway, tomorrow morning I'm going on a search for it."

"Well, I wish you luck," Tom Patrick said. "And if anything happens during the night, I'll let you know."

Nancy pointed to a window on the second floor. "That's my room," she said. "If you don't have a chance to use the door knocker, just throw a stone up against the screen to alert me. I'll wake up instantly, I know."

The guard promised to do this and Nancy went back into the mansion. She climbed the stairs and for a second time that night undressed. Helen had already gone back to sleep, so Nancy crawled into the big double bed noiselessly.

The two girls awoke the next morning about the same time and immediately Helen asked for full details of what Nancy had learned outdoors the night before. After hearing how her friend had been stopped by the guard, she shivered.

"You might have been in real danger, Nancy, not knowing who he was. You *must* be more careful. Suppose that man had been the ghost?"

Nancy laughed but made no reply. The girls

went downstairs and started to prepare breakfast. In a few minutes Aunt Rosemary and her mother joined them.

"Did you find out anything more last night?" Mrs. Hayes asked Nancy.

"Only that a police guard named Tom Patrick is on duty," Nancy answered.

As soon as breakfast was over, the young sleuth announced that she was about to investigate all the outbuildings on the estate.

"I'm going to search for an underground passage leading to the mansion. It's just possible that we hear no hollow sounds when we tap the walls, because of double doors or walls where the entrance is."

Aunt Rosemary looked at Nancy intently. "You are a real detective, Nancy. I see now why Helen wanted us to ask you to find our ghost."

Nancy's eyes twinkled. "I may have some instinct for sleuthing," she said, "but unless I can solve this mystery, it won't do any of us much good."

Turning to Helen, she suggested that they put on the old clothes they had brought with them.

Attired in sport shirts and jeans, the girls left the house. Nancy led the way first to the old icehouse. She rolled back the creaking, sliding door and gazed within. The tall, narrow building was about ten feet square. On one side were a series of sliding doors, one above the other.

"I've heard Miss Flora say," Helen spoke up, "that in days gone by huge blocks of ice were cut from the river when it was frozen over and dragged here on a sledge. The blocks were stored here and taken off from the top down through these various sliding doors."

"That story rather rules out the possibility of any underground passage leading from this building," said Nancy. "I presume there was ice in here most of the year."

The floor was covered with dank sawdust, and although Nancy was sure she would find nothing of interest beneath it, still she decided to take a look. Seeing an old, rusted shovel in one corner, she picked it up and began to dig. There was only dirt beneath the sawdust.

"Well, that clue fizzled out," Helen remarked, as she and Nancy started for the next building.

This had once been used as a smokehouse. It, too, had an earthen floor. In one corner was a small fireplace, where smoldering fires of hickory wood had once burned. The smoke had curled up a narrow chimney to the second floor, which was windowless.

"Rows and rows of huge chunks of pork hung up there on hooks to be smoked," Helen explained, "and days later turned into luscious hams and bacon."

There was no indication of a secret opening and Nancy went outside the small, two-story, peak-roofed structure and walked around. Up one side of the brick building and leading to a door above were the remnants of a ladder. Now only the sidepieces which had held the rungs remained.

"Give me a boost, will you, Helen?" Nancy requested. "I want to take a look inside."

Helen squatted on the ground and Nancy climbed to her shoulders. Then Helen, bracing her hands against the wall, straightened up. Nancy opened the half-rotted wooden door.

"No ghost here!" she announced.

Nancy jumped to the ground and started for the servants' quarters. But a thorough inspection of this brick-and-wood structure failed to reveal a clue to a secret passageway.

There was only one outbuilding left to investigate, which Helen said was the old carriage house. This was built of brick and was fairly large. No carriages stood on its wooden floor, but around the walls hung old harnesses and reins. Nancy paused a moment to examine one of the bridles. It was set with two hand-painted medallions of women's portraits.

Suddenly her reflection was interrupted by a scream. Turning, she was just in time to see Helen plunge through a hole in the floor. In a flash Nancy was across the carriage house and looking down into a gaping hole where the rotted floor had given way.

"Helen!" she cried out in alarm.

"I'm all right," came a voice from below. "Nice and soft down here. Please throw me your flash."

Nancy removed the flashlight from the pocket of her jeans and tossed it down.

"I thought maybe I'd discovered something," Helen said. "But this is just a plain old hole. Give me a hand, will you, so I can climb up?"

Nancy lay flat on the floor and with one arm grabbed a supporting beam that stood in the center of the carriage house. Reaching down with the other arm, she assisted Helen in her ascent.

"We'd better watch our step around here," Nancy said as her friend once more stood beside her.

"You're so right," Helen agreed, brushing dirt off her jeans. Helen's plunge had given Nancy an idea that there might be other openings in the floor and that one of them could be an entrance to a subterranean passage. But though she flashed her light over every inch of the carriage-house floor, she could discover nothing suspicious.

"Let's quit!" Helen suggested. "I'm a mess, and besides, I'm hungry."

"All right," Nancy agreed. "Are you game to search the cellar this afternoon?"

"Oh, sure."

After lunch they started to investigate the store-rooms in the cellar. There was a cool stone room where barrels of apples had once been kept. There was another, formerly filled with bags of whole-wheat flour, barley, buckwheat, and oat-meal.

"And everything was grown on the estate," said Helen.

"Oh, it must have been perfectly wonderful," Nancy said. "I wish we could go back in time and see how life was in those days!"

"Maybe if we could, we'd know how to find that ghost," Helen remarked. Nancy thought so too.

As the girls went from room to room in the cellar, Nancy beamed her flashlight over every inch of wall and floor. At times, the young sleuth's pulse would quicken when she thought she had discovered a trap door or secret opening. But each time she had to admit failure—there was no evidence of either one in the cellar.

"This has been a discouraging day," Nancy remarked, sighing. "But I'm not giving up."

Helen felt sorry for her friend. To cheer Nancy, she said with a laugh, "Storeroom after storeroom but no room to store a ghost!"

Nancy had to laugh, and together the two girls ascended the stairway to the kitchen. After changing their clothes, they helped Aunt Rosemary prepare the evening dinner. When the group had eaten and later gathered in the parlor, Nancy reminded the others that she expected her father to arrive the next day.

"Dad didn't want me to bother meeting him,

but I just can't wait to see him.   I think I'll meet all the trains from Chicago that stop here."

"I hope your father will stay with us for two or three days," Miss Flora spoke up.   "Surely he'll have some ideas about our ghost."

"And good ones, too," Nancy said.   "If he's on the early train, he'll have breakfast with us.   I'll meet it at eight o'clock."

But later that evening Nancy's plans were suddenly changed.   Hannah Gruen telephoned her to say that a man at the telegraph office had called the house a short time before to read a message from Mr. Drew.   He had been unavoidably detained and would not arrive Wednesday.

"In the telegram your father said that he will let us know when he will arrive," the housekeeper added.

"I'm disappointed," Nancy remarked, "but I hope this delay means that Dad is on the trail of Willie Wharton!"

"Speaking of Willie Wharton," said Hannah, "I heard something about him today."

"What was that?" Nancy asked.

"That he was seen down by the river right here in River Heights a couple of days ago!"

CHAPTER IX

A Worrisome Delay

"You say Willie Wharton was seen in River Heights down by the river?" Nancy asked unbelievingly.

"Yes," Hannah replied. "I learned it from our postman, Mr. Ritter, who is one of the people that sold property to the railroad. As you know, Nancy, Mr. Ritter is very honest and reliable. Well, he said he'd heard that some of the property owners were trying to horn in on this deal of Willie Wharton's for getting more money. But Mr. Ritter wouldn't have a thing to do with it—calls it a holdup "

"Did Mr. Ritter himself see Willie Wharton?" Nancy asked eagerly.

"No," the housekeeper replied. "One of the other property owners told him Willie was around."

"That man *could* be mistaken," Nancy suggested.

"Of course he might," Hannah agreed. "And I'm inclined to think he is. If your father is staying over in Chicago, it must be because of Willie Wharton."

Nancy did not tell Hannah what was racing through her mind. She said good night cheerfully, but actually she was very much worried.

"Maybe Willie Wharton *was* seen down by the river," she mused. "And maybe Dad was 'unavoidably detained' by an enemy of his in connection with the railroad bridge project. One of the dissatisfied property owners might have followed him to Chicago."

Or, she reflected further, it was not inconceivable that Mr. Drew had found Willie Wharton, only to have Willie hold the lawyer a prisoner.

As Nancy sat lost in anxious thought, Helen came into the hall. "Something the matter?" she asked.

"I don't know," Nancy replied, "but I have a feeling there is. Dad telegraphed to say that he wouldn't be here tomorrow. Instead of wiring, he always phones me or Hannah or his office when he is away and it seems strange that he didn't do so this time."

"You told me a few days ago that your father had been threatened," said Helen. "Are you afraid it has something to do with that?"

"Yes, I am."

"Is there anything I can do?" Helen offered.

"Thank you, Helen, but I think not. There isn't anything I can do either. We'll just have to wait and see what happens. Maybe I'll hear from Dad again."

Nancy looked so downcast that Helen searched her mind to find something which would cheer her friend. Suddenly Helen had an idea and went to speak to Miss Flora and Aunt Rosemary about it.

"I think it's a wonderful plan if Nancy will do it," Aunt Rosemary said.

Helen called Nancy from the hall and proposed that they all go to the attic to look in the big trunk containing the old costumes.

"We might even put them on," Miss Flora proposed, smiling girlishly.

"And you girls could dance the minuet," said Aunt Rosemary enthusiastically. "Mother plays the old spinet very well. Maybe she would play a minuet for you."

"I love your idea," said Nancy. She knew that the three were trying to boost her spirits and she appreciated it. Besides, what they had proposed sounded like fun.

All of them trooped up the creaky attic stairs. In their haste, none of the group had remembered to bring flashlights.

"I'll go downstairs and get a couple," Nancy offered.

"Never mind," Aunt Rosemary spoke up.

"There are some candles and holders right here. We keep them for emergencies."

She lighted two white candles which stood in old-fashioned, saucer-type brass holders and led the way to the costume trunk.

As Helen lifted the heavy lid, Nancy exclaimed in delight, "How beautiful the clothes are!"

She could see silks, satins, and laces at one side. At the other was a folded-up rose velvet robe. She and Helen lifted out the garments and held them up.

"They're really lovelier than our formal dance clothes today," Helen remarked. "Especially the men's!"

Miss Flora smiled. "And a lot more flattering!"

The entire trunk was unpacked, before the group selected what they would wear.

"This pale-green silk gown with the panniers would look lovely on you, Nancy," Miss Flora said. "And I'm sure it's just the right size, too."

Nancy surveyed the tiny waist of the ball gown. "I'll try it on," she said. Then laughingly she added, "But I'll probably have to hold my breath to close it in the middle. My, but the women in olden times certainly had slim waistlines!"

Helen was holding up a man's purple velvet suit. It had knee breeches and the waistcoat had a lace-ruffled front. There were a tricorn hat, long white stockings, and buckled slippers to complete the costume.

"I think I'll wear this and be your partner, Nancy," Helen said.

Taking off her pumps, she slid her feet into the buckled slippers. The others laughed aloud. A man with a foot twice the size of Helen's had once worn the slippers!

"Never mind. I'll stuff the empty space with paper," Helen announced gaily.

Miss Flora and Aunt Rosemary selected gowns for themselves, then opened a good-sized box at the bottom of the trunk. It contained various kinds of wigs worn in Colonial times. All were pure white and fluffy.

Carrying the costumes and wigs, the group descended to their bedrooms, where they changed into the fancy clothes, then went to the first floor. Miss Flora led the way into the room across the hall from the parlor. She said it once had been the drawing room. Later it had become a library, but the old spinet still stood in a corner.

Miss Flora sat down at the instrument and began to play Beethoven's "Minuet." Aunt Rosemary sat down beside her.

Nancy and Helen, dubbed by the latter, Master and Mistress Colonial America, began to dance. They clasped their right hands high in the air, then took two steps backward and made little bows. They circled, then strutted, and even put in a few steps with which no dancers in Colonial times would have been familiar.

Aunt Rosemary giggled and clapped. "I wish President Washington would come to see you," she said, acting out her part in the entertainment. "Mistress Nancy, prithee do an encore and Master Corning, wilt thou accompany thy fair lady?"

The girls could barely keep from giggling. Helen made a low bow to her aunt, her tricorn in her hand, and said, "At your service, my lady. Your every wish is my command!"

The minuet was repeated, then as Miss Flora stopped playing, the girls sat down.

"Oh, that was such fun!" said Nancy. "Some time I'd like to— Listen!" she commanded suddenly.

From outside the house they could hear loud shouting. "Come here! You in the house! Come here!"

Nancy and Helen dashed from their chairs to the front door. Nancy snapped on the porch light and the two girls raced outside.

"Over here!" a man's voice urged.

Nancy and Helen ran down the steps and out onto the lawn. Just ahead of them stood Tom Patrick, the police detective. In a viselike grip he was holding a thin, bent-over man whom the girls judged to be about fifty years of age.

"Is this your ghost?" the guard asked.

His prisoner was struggling to free himself but was unable to get loose. The girls hurried forward to look at the man.

"Is this your ghost?" the police guard asked

"I caught him sneaking along the edge of the grounds," Tom Patrick announced.

"Let me go!" the man cried out angrily. "I'm no ghost. What are you talking about?"

"You may not be a ghost," the detective said, "but you could be the thief who has been robbing this house."

"What!" his prisoner exclaimed. "I'm no thief! I live around here. Anyone will tell you I'm okay."

"What's your name and where do you live?" the detective prodded. He let the man stand up straight but held one of his arms firmly.

"My name's Albert Watson and I live over on Tuttle Road."

"What were you doing on this property?"

Albert Watson said he had been taking a short cut home. His wife had taken their car for the evening.

"I'd been to a friend's house. You can call him and verify what I'm saying. And you can call my wife, too. Maybe she's home now and she'll come and get me."

The guard reminded Albert Watson that he had not revealed why he was sneaking along the ground.

"Well," the prisoner said, "it was because of you. I heard downtown that there was a detective patrolling this place and I didn't want to bump into you. I was afraid of just what did happen."

The man relaxed a little. "I guess you're a pretty good guard at that."

Detective Patrick let go of Albert Watson's arm. "Your story sounds okay, but we'll go in the house and do some telephoning to find out if you're telling the truth."

"You'll find out all right. Why, I'm even a notary public! They don't give a notary's license to dishonest folks!" the trespasser insisted. Then he stared at Nancy and Helen, "What are you doing in those funny clothes?"

"We—are—we were having a little costume party," Helen responded. In the excitement she and Nancy had forgotten what they were wearing!

The two girls started for the house, with the men following. When Mr. Watson and the guard saw Miss Flora and Aunt Rosemary also in costume they gazed at the women in amusement.

Nancy introduced Mr. Watson. Miss Flora said she knew of him, although she had never met the man. Two phone calls by the guard confirmed Watson's story. In a little while his wife arrived at Twin Elms to drive her husband home, and Detective Patrick went back to his guard duty.

Aunt Rosemary then turned out all the lights on the first floor and she, Miss Flora, and the girls went upstairs. Bedroom doors were locked, and everyone hoped there would be no disturbance during the night.

"It was a good day, Nancy," said Helen, yawning, as she climbed into bed.

"Yes, it was," said Nancy. "Of course, I'm a little disappointed that we aren't farther along solving the mystery but maybe by this time tomorrow—" She looked toward Helen who did not answer. She was already sound asleep.

Nancy herself was under the covers a few minutes later. She lay staring at the ceiling, going over the various events of the past two days. As her mind recalled the scene in the attic when they were pulling costumes from the old trunk, she suddenly gave a start.

"That section of wall back of the trunk!" she told herself. "The paneling looked different somehow from the rest of the attic wall. Maybe it's movable and leads to a secret exit! Tomorrow I'll find out!"

CHAPTER X

The Midnight Watch

As soon as the two girls awoke the next morning, Nancy told Helen her plan.

"I'm with you," said Helen. "Oh, I do wish we could solve the mystery of the ghost! I'm afraid that it's beginning to affect Miss Flora's health and yet she won't leave Twin Elms."

"Maybe we can get Aunt Rosemary to keep her in the garden most of the day," Nancy suggested. "It's perfectly beautiful outside. We might even serve lunch under the trees."

"I'm sure they'd love that," said Helen. "As soon as we get downstairs, let's propose it."

Both women liked the suggestion. Aunt Rosemary had guessed their strategy and was appreciative of it.

"I'll wash and dry the dishes," Nancy offered when breakfast was over. "Miss Flora, why don't you and Aunt Rosemary go outside right now and take advantage of this lovely sunshine?"

The frail, elderly woman smiled. There were deep circles under her eyes, indicating that she had had a sleepless night.

"And I'll run the vacuum cleaner around and dust this first floor in less than half an hour," Helen said merrily.

Her relatives caught the spirit of her enthusiasm and Miss Flora remarked, "I wish you girls lived here all the time. Despite our troubles, you have brought a feeling of gaiety back into our lives."

Both girls smiled at the compliment. As soon as the two women had gone outdoors, the girls set to work with a will. At the end of the allotted half hour, the first floor of the mansion was spotless. Nancy and Helen next went to the second floor, quickly made the beds, and tidied the bathrooms.

"And now for that ghost!" said Helen, brandishing her flashlight.

Nancy took her own from a bureau drawer.

"Let's see if we can figure out how to climb these attic stairs without making them creak," Nancy suggested. "Knowing how may come in handy some time."

This presented a real challenge. Every inch of each step was tried before the girls finally worked out a pattern to follow in ascending the stairway noiselessly.

Helen laughed. "This will certainly be a

memory test, Nancy. I'll rehearse our directions. First step, put your foot to the left near the wall. Second step, right center. Third step, against the right wall. I'll need three feet to do that!"

Nancy laughed too. "For myself, I think I'll skip the second step. Let's see. On the fourth and fifth it's all right to step in the center, but on the sixth you hug the left wall, on the seventh, the right wall—"

Helen interrupted. "But if you step on the eighth any place, it will creak. So you skip it."

"Nine, ten, and eleven are okay," Nancy recalled. "But from there to fifteen at the top we're in trouble."

"Let's see if I remember," said Helen. "On twelve, you go left, then right, then right again. How can you do that without a jump and losing your balance and tumbling down?"

"How about skipping fourteen and then stretching as far as you can to reach the top one at the left where it doesn't squeak," Nancy replied. "Let's go!"

She and Helen went back to the second floor and began what was meant to be a silent ascent. But both of them made so many mistakes at first the creaking was terrific. Finally, however, the girls had the silent spots memorized perfectly and went up noiselessly.

Nancy clicked on her flashlight and swung it onto the nearest wood-paneled wall. Helen stared at it, then remarked, "This isn't made of long panels from ceiling to floor. It's built of small pieces."

"That's right," said Nancy. "But see if you don't agree with me that the spot back of the costume trunk near the chimney looks a little different. The grain doesn't match the other wood."

The girls crossed the attic and Nancy beamed her flashlight over the suspected paneling.

"It does look different," Helen said. "This could be a door, I suppose. But there's no knob or other hardware on it." She ran her finger over a section just above the floor, following the cracks at the edge of a four-by-two-and-a-half-foot space.

"If it's a secret door," said Nancy, "the knob is on the other side."

"How are we going to open it?" Helen questioned.

"We might try prying the door open," Nancy proposed. "But first I want to test it."

She tapped the entire panel with her knuckles. A look of disappointment came over her face. "There's certainly no hollow space behind it," she said.

"Let's make sure," said Helen. "Suppose I go downstairs and get a screw driver and hammer? We'll see what happens when we drive the screw driver through this crack."

"Good idea, Helen."

While she was gone, Nancy inspected the rest

of the attic walls and floor. She did not find another spot which seemed suspicious. By this time Helen had returned with the tools. Inserting the screw driver into one of the cracks, she began to pound on the handle of it with the hammer.

Nancy watched hopefully. The screw driver went through the crack very easily but immediately met an obstruction on the other side. Helen pulled the screw driver out. "Nancy, you try your luck."

The young sleuth picked a different spot, but the results were the same. There was no open space behind that portion of the attic wall.

"My hunch wasn't so good," said Nancy.

Helen suggested that they give up and go downstairs. "Anyway, I think the postman will be here soon." She smiled. "I'm expecting a letter from Jim. Mother said she would forward all my mail."

Nancy did not want to give up the search yet. But she nodded in agreement and waved her friend toward the stairs. Then the young detective sat down on the floor and cupped her chin in her hands. As she stared ahead, Nancy noticed that Helen, in her eagerness to meet the postman, had not bothered to go quietly down the attic steps. It sounded as if Helen had picked the squeakiest spot on each step!

Nancy heard Helen go out the front door and suddenly realized that she was in the big mansion all alone. "That may bring the ghost on a visit," she thought. "If he is around, he may think I went outside with Helen! And I may learn where the secret opening is!"

Nancy sat perfectly still, listening intently. Suddenly she flung her head up. Was it her imagination, or did she hear the creak of steps? She was not mistaken. Nancy strained her ears, trying to determine from where the sounds were coming.

"I'm sure they're not from the attic stairs or the main staircase. And not the back stairway. Even if the ghost was in the kitchen and unlocked the door to the second floor, he'd know that the one at the top of the stairs was locked from the other side."

Nancy's heart suddenly gave a leap. She was positive that the creaking sounds were coming from somewhere behind the attic wall!

"A secret staircase!" she thought excitedly. "Maybe the ghost is entering the second floor!"

Nancy waited until the sounds stopped, then she got to her feet, tiptoed noiselessly down the attic steps and looked around. She could hear nothing. Was the ghost standing quietly in one of the bedrooms? Probably Miss Flora's?

Treading so lightly that she did not make a sound, Nancy peered into each room as she reached it. But no one was in any of them.

"Maybe he's on the first floor!" Nancy thought.
She descended the main stairway, hugging the

wall so she would not make a sound. Reaching the first floor, Nancy peered into the parlor. No one was there. She looked in the library, the dining room, and the kitchen. She saw no one.

"Well, the ghost didn't come into the house after all," Nancy concluded. "He may have intended to, but changed his mind."

She felt more certain than at any time, however, that there was a secret entrance to Twin Elms Mansion from a hidden stairway. But how to find it? Suddenly the young sleuth snapped her fingers. "I know what I'll do! I'll set a trap for that ghost!"

She reflected that he had taken jewelry, but those thefts had stopped. Apparently he was afraid to go to the second floor.

"I wonder if anything is missing from the first floor," she mused. "Maybe he has taken silverware or helped himself to some food."

Going to the back door, Nancy opened it and called to Helen, who was now seated in the garden with Miss Flora and Aunt Rosemary. "What say we start lunch?" she called, not wishing to distress Miss Flora by bringing up the subject of the mystery.

"Okay," said Helen. In a few moments she joined Nancy, who asked if her friend had received a letter.

Helen's eyes sparkled. "I sure did. Oh, Nancy, I can hardly wait for Jim to get home!"

Nancy smiled. "The way you describe him, I can hardly wait to see him myself." Then she told Helen the real reason she had called her into the kitchen. She described the footsteps on what she was sure was a hidden, creaking stairway, then added, "If we discover that food or something else is missing we'll know he's been here again."

Helen offered to inspect the flat silver. "I know approximately how many pieces should be in the buffet drawer," she said.

"And I'll look over the food supplies," Nancy suggested. "I have a pretty good idea what was in the refrigerator and on the pantry shelf."

It was not many minutes before each of the girls discovered articles missing. Helen said that nearly a dozen teaspoons were gone and Nancy figured that several cans of food, some eggs, and a quart of milk had been taken.

"It just seems impossible to catch that thief," Helen said with a sigh.

On a sudden hunch Nancy took down from the wall a memo pad and pencil which hung there. Putting a finger to her lips to indicate that Helen was not to comment, Nancy wrote on the sheet:

"I think the only way to catch the ghost is to trap him. I believe he has one or more microphones hidden some place and that he hears all our plans."

Nancy looked up at Helen, who nodded silently. Nancy continued to write, "I don't want to worry

Miss Flora or Aunt Rosemary, so let's keep our plans a secret. I suggest that we go to bed tonight as usual and carry on a conversation about our plans for tomorrow. But actually we won't take off our clothes. Then about midnight let's tiptoe downstairs to watch. I'll wait in the kitchen. Do you want to stay in the living room?"

Again Helen nodded. Nancy, thinking that they had been quiet too long, and that if there was an eavesdropper nearby he might become suspicious, said aloud, "What would Miss Flora and Aunt Rosemary like for lunch, Helen?"

"Why, uh—" Helen found it hard to transfer to the new subject. "They—uh—both love soup."

"Then I'll make cream of chicken soup," said Nancy. "Hand me a can of chicken and rice, will you? And I'll get the milk."

As Helen was doing this, Nancy lighted a match, held her recently written note over the sink, and set fire to the paper.

Helen smiled. "Nancy thinks of everything," she said to herself.

The girls chatted gaily as they prepared the food and finally carried four trays out to the garden. They did not mention their midnight plan. The day in the garden was proving to be most beneficial to Miss Flora, and the girls were sure she would sleep well that night.

Nancy's plan was followed to the letter. Just

as the grandfather clock in the hall was striking midnight, Nancy arrived in the kitchen and sat down to await developments. Helen was posted in a living-room chair near the hall doorway. Moonlight streamed into both rooms but the girls had taken seats in the shadows.

Helen was mentally rehearsing the further instructions which Nancy had written to her during the afternoon. The young sleuth had suggested that if Helen should see anyone, she was to run to the front door, open it, and yell "Police!" At the same time she was to try to watch where the intruder disappeared.

The minutes ticked by. There was not a sound in the house. Then suddenly Nancy heard the front door open with a bang and Helen's voice yell loudly and clearly:

"Police! Help! Police!"

CHAPTER XI

An Elusive Ghost

By the time Nancy reached the front hall, Tom Patrick, the police guard, had rushed into the house. "Here I am!" he called. "What's the matter?"

Helen led the way into the living room, and switched on the chandelier light.

"That sofa next to the fireplace!" she said in a trembling voice. "It moved! I saw it move!"

"You mean somebody moved it?" the detective asked.

"I—I don't know," Helen replied. "I couldn't see anybody."

Nancy walked over to the old-fashioned sofa, set in the niche alongside the fireplace. Certainly the piece was in place now. If the ghost had moved it, he had returned the sofa to its original position.

"Let's pull it out and see what we can find," Nancy suggested.

She tugged at one end, while the guard pulled the other. It occurred to Nancy that a person who moved it alone would have to be very strong.

"Do you think your ghost came up through a trap door or something?" the detective asked.

Neither of the girls replied. They had previously searched the area, and even now as they looked over every inch of the floor and the three walls surrounding the high sides of the couch, they could detect nothing that looked like an opening.

By this time Helen looked sheepish. "I—I guess I was wrong," she said finally. Turning to the police guard, she said, "I'm sorry to have taken you away from your work."

"Don't feel too badly about it. But I'd better get back to my guard duty," the man said, and left the house.

"Oh, Nancy!" Helen cried out. "I'm so sorry!"

She was about to say more but Nancy put a finger to her lips. They could use the same strategy for trapping the thief at another time. In case the thief might be listening, Nancy did not want to give away their secret.

Nancy felt that after all the uproar the ghost would not appear again that night. She motioned to Helen that they would go quietly upstairs and get some sleep. Hugging the walls of the stairway once more, they ascended noiselessly, tiptoed to their room, and got into bed.

"I'm certainly glad I didn't wake up Miss Flora and Aunt Rosemary," said Helen sleepily as she whispered good night.

Though Nancy had been sure the ghost would not enter the mansion again that night, she discovered in the morning that she had been mistaken. More food had been stolen sometime between midnight and eight o'clock when she and Helen started breakfast. Had the ghost taken it for personal use or only to worry the occupants of Twin Elms?

"I missed my chance this time," Nancy murmured to her friend. "After this, I'd better not trust what that ghost's next move may be!"

At nine o'clock Hannah Gruen telephoned the house. Nancy happened to answer the ring and after the usual greetings was amazed to hear Hannah say, "I'd like to speak to your father."

"Why, Dad isn't here!" Nancy told her. "Don't you remember—the telegram said he wasn't coming?"

"He's not there!" Hannah exclaimed. "Oh, this is bad, Nancy—very bad."

"What do you mean, Hannah?" Nancy asked fearfully.

The housekeeper explained that soon after receiving the telegram on Tuesday evening, Mr. Drew himself had phoned. "He wanted to know if you were still in Cliffwood, Nancy. When I told him yes, he said he would stop off there on his way home Wednesday."

Nancy was frightened, but she asked steadily, "Hannah, did you happen to mention the telegram to him?"

"No, I didn't," the housekeeper replied. "I didn't think it was necessary."

"Hannah darling," said Nancy, almost on the verge of tears, "I'm afraid that telegram was a hoax!"

"A hoax!" Mrs. Gruen cried out.

"Yes. Dad's enemies sent it to keep me from meeting him!"

"Oh, Nancy," Hannah wailed, "you don't suppose those enemies that Mr. Gomber warned you about have waylaid your father and are keeping him prisoner?"

"I'm afraid so," said Nancy. Her knees began to quake and she sank into the chair alongside the telephone table.

"What'll we do?" Hannah asked. "Do you want me to notify the police?"

"Not yet. Let me do a little checking first."

"All right, Nancy. But let me know what happens."

"I will."

Nancy put the phone down, then looked at the various telephone directories which lay on the table. Finding one which contained River

Heights numbers, she looked for the number of the telegraph office and put in a call. She asked the clerk who answered to verify that there had been a telegram from Mr. Drew on Tuesday.

After a few minutes wait, the reply came. "We have no record of such a telegram."

Nancy thanked the clerk and hung up. By this time her hands were shaking with fright. What had happened to her father?

Getting control of herself, Nancy telephoned in turn to the airport, the railroad station, and the bus lines which served Cliffwood. She inquired about any accidents which might have occurred on trips from Chicago the previous day or on Tuesday night. In each case she was told there had been none.

"Oh, what shall I do?" Nancy thought in dismay.

Immediately an idea came to her and she put in a call to the Chicago hotel where her father had registered. Although she thought it unlikely, it was just possible that he had changed his mind again and was still there. But a conversation with the desk clerk dashed this hope.

"No, Mr. Drew is not here. He checked out Tuesday evening. I don't know his plans, but I'll connect you with the head porter. He may be able to help you."

In a few seconds Nancy was asking the porter what he could tell her to help clear up the mystery of her father's disappearance. "All I know, miss, is that your father told me he was taking a sleeper train and getting off somewhere Wednesday morning to meet his daughter."

"Thank you. Oh, thank you very much," said Nancy. "You've helped me a great deal."

So her father had taken the train home and probably had reached the Cliffwood station! Next she must find out what had happened to him after that!

Nancy told Aunt Rosemary and Helen what she had learned, then got in her convertible and drove directly to the Cliffwood station. There she spoke to the ticket agent. Unfortunately, he could not identify Mr. Drew from Nancy's description as having been among the passengers who got off either of the two trains arriving from Chicago on Wednesday.

Nancy went to speak to the taximen. Judging by the line of cabs, she decided that all the drivers who served the station were on hand at the moment. There had been no outgoing trains for nearly an hour and an incoming express was due in about fifteen minutes.

"I'm in luck," the young detective told herself. "Surely one of these men must have driven Dad."

She went from one to another, but each of them denied having carried a passenger of Mr. Drew's description the day before.

By this time Nancy was in a panic. She hurried inside the station to a telephone booth and called the local police station. Nancy asked to speak to the captain and in a moment he came on the line.

"Captain Rossland speaking," he said crisply.

Nancy poured out her story. She told of the warning her father had received in River Heights and her fear that some enemy of his was now detaining the lawyer against his will.

"This is very serious, Miss Drew," Captain Rossland stated. "I will put men on the case at once," he said.

As Nancy left the phone booth, a large, gray-haired woman walked up to her. "Pardon me, miss, but I couldn't help overhearing what you said. I believe maybe I can help you."

Nancy was surprised and slightly suspicious. Maybe this woman was connected with the abductors and planned to make Nancy a prisoner too by promising to take her to her father!

"Don't look so frightened," the woman said, smiling. "All I wanted to tell you is that I'm down here at the station every day to take a train to the next town. I'm a nurse and I'm on a case over there right now."

"I see," Nancy said.

"Well, yesterday I was here when the Chicago train came in. I noticed a tall, handsome man—such as you describe your father to be—step off the train. He got into the taxi driven by a man named Harry. I have a feeling that for some reason the cabbie isn't telling the truth. Let's talk to him."

Nancy followed the woman, her heart beating furiously. She was ready to grab at any straw to get a clue to her father's whereabouts!

"Hello, Miss Skade," the taximan said. "How are you today?"

"Oh, I'm all right," the nurse responded. "Listen, Harry. You told this young lady that you didn't carry any passenger yesterday that looked like her father. Now I saw one get into your cab. What about it?"

Harry hung his head. "Listen, miss," he said to Nancy, "I got three kids and I don't want nothin' to happen to 'em. See?"

"What do you mean?" Nancy asked, puzzled.

When the man did not reply, Miss Skade said, "Now look, Harry. This girl's afraid that her father has been kidnaped. It's up to you to tell her all you know."

"Kidnaped!" the taximan shouted. "Oh, goodnight! Now I don't know what to do."

Nancy had a sudden thought. "Has somebody been threatening you, Harry?" she asked.

The cab driver's eyes nearly popped from his head. "Well," he said, "since you've guessed it, I'd better tell you everything I know."

He went on to say that he had taken a passenger who fitted Mr. Drew's description toward Twin

Elms where he had said he wanted to go. "Just as we were leaving the station, two other men came up and jumped into my cab. They said they were going a little farther than that and would I take them? Well, about halfway to Twin Elms, one of those men ordered me to pull up to the side of the road and stop. He told me the stranger had blacked out. He and his buddy jumped out of the car and laid the man on the grass."

"How ill was he?" Nancy asked.

"I don't know. He was unconscious. Just then another car came along behind us and stopped. The driver got out and offered to take your father to a hospital. The two men said okay."

Nancy took heart. Maybe her father was in a hospital and had not been abducted at all! But a moment later her hopes were again dashed when Harry said:

"I told those guys I'd be glad to drive the sick man to a hospital, but one of them turned on me, shook his fist, and yelled, 'You just forget everything that's happened or it'll be too bad for you and your kids!'"

"Oh!" Nancy cried out, and for a second everything seemed to swim before her eyes. She clutched the door handle of the taxi for support.

There was no question now but that her father had been drugged, then kidnaped!

CHAPTER XII

The Newspaper Clue

MISS SKADE grabbed Nancy. "Do you feel ill?" the nurse asked quickly.

"Oh, I'll be all right," Nancy replied. "This news has been a great shock to me."

"Is there any way I can help you?" the woman questioned. "I'd be very happy to."

"Thank you, but I guess not," the young sleuth said. Smiling ruefully, she added, "But I must get busy and do something about this."

The nurse suggested that perhaps Mr. Drew was in one of the local hospitals. She gave Nancy the names of the three in town.

"I'll get in touch with them at once," the young detective said. "You've been most kind. And here comes your train, Miss Skade. Good-by and again thanks a million for your help!"

Harry climbed out of his taxi and went to stand at the platform to signal passengers for his cab. Nancy hurried after him, and before the train came in, asked if he would please give her a description of the two men who had been with her father.

"Well, both of them were dark and kind of athletic-looking. Not what I'd call handsome. One of 'em had an upper tooth missing. And the other fellow—his left ear was kind of crinkled, if you know what I mean."

"I understand," said Nancy. "I'll give a description of the two men to the police."

She went back to the telephone booth and called each of the three hospitals, asking if anyone by the name of Carson Drew had been admitted or possibly a patient who was not conscious and had no identification. Only Mercy Hospital had a patient who had been unconscious since the day before. He definitely was not Mr. Drew— he was Chinese!

Sure now that her father was being held in some secret hiding place, Nancy went at once to police headquarters and related the taximan's story.

Captain Rossland looked extremely concerned. "This is alarming, Miss Drew," he said, "but I feel sure we can trace that fellow with the crinkly ear and we'll make him tell us where your father is! I doubt, though, that there is anything you can do. You'd better leave it to the police."

Nancy said nothing. She was reluctant to give up even trying to do something, but she acquiesced.

"In the meantime," said the officer, "I'd advise you to remain at Twin Elms and concentrate on solving the mystery there. From what you tell me about your father, I'm sure he'll be able to get out of the difficulty himself, even before the police find him."

Aloud, Nancy promised to stay on call in case Captain Rossland might need her. But in her own mind the young sleuth determined that if she got any kind of a lead concerning her father, she was most certainly going to follow it up.

Nancy left police headquarters and strolled up the street, deep in thought. "Instead of things getting better, all my problems seem to be getting worse. Maybe I'd better call Hannah."

Since she had been a little girl, Nancy had found solace in talking to Hannah Gruen. The housekeeper had always been able to give her such good advice!

Nancy went into a drugstore and entered one of the telephone booths. She called the Drew home in River Heights and was pleased when Mrs. Gruen answered. The housekeeper was aghast to learn Nancy's news but said she thought Captain Rossland's advice was sound.

"You've given the police the best leads in the world and I believe that's all you can do. But wait—" the housekeeper suddenly said. "If I were you, Nancy, I'd call up those railroad lawyers and tell them exactly what has happened. Your father's disappearance is directly concerned with that bridge project, I'm sure, and the lawyers may have some ideas about where to find him."

"That's a wonderful suggestion, Hannah," said Nancy. "I'll call them right away."

But when the young detective phoned the railroad lawyers, she was disappointed to learn that all the men were out to lunch and none of them would return before two o'clock.

"Oh dear!" Nancy sighed. "Well, I guess I'd better get a snack while waiting for them to come back." But in her worried state she did not feel like eating.

There was a food counter at the rear of the drugstore and Nancy made her way to it. Perching on a high-backed stool, she read the menu over and over. Nothing appealed to her. When the counterman asked her what she wanted, Nancy said frankly she did not know—she was not very hungry.

"Then I recommend our split-pea soup," he told her. "It's homemade and out of this world."

Nancy smiled at him. "I'll take your advice and try it."

The hot soup was delicious. By the time she had finished it, Nancy's spirits had risen considerably.

"And how about some custard pie?" the counterman inquired. "It's just like Mother used to make."

"All right," Nancy answered, smiling at the solicitous young man. The pie was ice cold and proved to be delicious. When Nancy finished eating it, she glanced at her wrist watch. It was only one-thirty. Seeing a rack of magazines, she decided to while away the time reading in her car.

She purchased a magazine of detective stories, one of which proved to be so intriguing that the half hour went by quickly. Promptly at two o'clock Nancy returned to the phone booth and called the offices of the railroad lawyers. The switchboard operator connected her with Mr. Anthony Barradale and Nancy judged from his voice that he was fairly young. Quickly she told her story.

"Mr. Drew being held a prisoner!" Mr. Barradale cried out. "Well, those underhanded property owners are certainly going to great lengths to gain a few dollars."

"The police are working on the case, but I thought perhaps your firm would like to take a hand also," Nancy told the lawyer.

"We certainly will," the young man replied. "I'll speak to our senior partner about it. I know he will want to start work at once on the case."

"Thank you," said Nancy. She gave the address and telephone number of Twin Elms and asked that the lawyers get in touch with her there if any news should break.

"We'll do that," Mr. Barradale promised.

Nancy left the drugstore and walked back to her car. Climbing in, she wondered what her next move ought to be.

"One thing is sure," she thought. "Work is the best antidote for worry. I'll get back to Twin Elms and do some more sleuthing there."

As she drove along, Nancy reflected about the ghost entering Twin Elms mansion by a subterranean passage. Since she had found no sign of one in any of the outbuildings on the estate, it occurred to her that possibly it led from an obscure cave, either natural or man-made. Such a device would be a clever artifice for an architect to use.

Taking a little-used road that ran along one side of the estate, Nancy recalled having seen a long, grassed-over hillock which she had assumed to be an old aqueduct. Perhaps this was actually the hidden entrance to Twin Elms!

She parked her car at the side of the road and took a flashlight from the glove compartment. In anticipation of finding the answer to the riddle, Nancy crossed the field, and as she came closer to the beginning of the huge mound, she could see stones piled up. Getting nearer, she realized that it was indeed the entrance to a rocky cave.

"Well, maybe this time I've found it!" she thought, hurrying forward.

The wind was blowing strongly and tossed her hair about her face. Suddenly a freakish gust swept a newspaper from among the rocks and scattered the pages helter-skelter.

Nancy was more excited than ever. The newspaper meant a human being had been there not too long ago! The front page sailed toward her. As she grabbed it up, she saw to her complete astonishment that the paper was a copy of the *River Heights Gazette.* The date was the Tuesday before.

"Someone interested in River Heights has been here very recently!" the young sleuth said to herself excitedly.

Who was the person? Her father? Gomber? Who?

Wondering if the paper might contain any clue, Nancy dashed around to pick up all the sheets. As she spread them out on the ground, she noticed a hole in the page where classified ads appeared.

"This may be a very good clue!" Nancy thought. "As soon as I get back to the house, I'll call Hannah and have her look up Tuesday's paper to see what was in that ad."

It suddenly occurred to Nancy that the person who had brought the paper to the cave might be inside at this very moment. She must watch her step; he might prove to be an enemy!

"This may be where Dad is being held a prisoner!" Nancy thought wildly.

Flashlight in hand, and her eyes darting intently

about, Nancy proceeded cautiously into the cave. Five feet, ten. She saw no one. Fifteen more. Twenty. Then Nancy met a dead end. The empty cave was almost completely round and had no other opening.

"Oh dear, another failure," Nancy told herself disappointedly, as she retraced her steps. "My only hope now is to learn something important from the ad in the paper."

Nancy walked back across the field. Her eyes were down, as she automatically looked for footprints. But presently she looked up and stared in disbelief.

A man was standing alongside her car, examining it. His back was half turned toward Nancy, so she could not see his face very well. But he had an athletic build and his left ear was definitely crinkly!

CHAPTER XIII

The Crash

THE STRANGER inspecting Nancy's car must have heard her coming. Without turning around, he dodged back of the automobile and started off across the field in the opposite direction.

"He certainly acts suspiciously. He must be the man with the crinkly ear who helped abduct my father!" Nancy thought excitedly.

Quickly she crossed the road and ran after him as fast as she could, hoping to overtake him. But the man had had a good head start. Also, his stride was longer than Nancy's and he could cover more ground in the same amount of time.

The far corner of the irregular-shaped field ended at the road on which Riverview Manor stood. When Nancy reached the highway, she was just in time to see the stranger leap into a parked car and drive off.

The young detective was exasperated. She had

had only a glimpse of the man's profile. If only she could have seen him full face or caught the license number of his car!

"I wonder if he's the one who dropped the newspaper?" she asked herself. "Maybe he's from River Heights!" She surmised that the man himself was not one of the property owners but he might have been hired by Willie Wharton or one of the owners to help abduct Mr. Drew.

"I'd better hurry to a phone and report this," Nancy thought.

She ran all the way back across the field, stepped into her own car, turned it around, and headed for Twin Elms. When Nancy arrived, she sped to the telephone in the hall and dialed Cliffwood Police Headquarters. In a moment she was talking to the captain and gave him her latest information.

"It certainly looks as if you picked up a good clue, Miss Drew," the officer remarked. "I'll send out an alarm immediately to have this man picked up."

"I suppose there is no news of my father," Nancy said.

"I'm afraid not. But a couple of our men talked to the taxi driver Harry and he gave us a pretty good description of the man who came along the road while your father was lying unconscious on the grass—the one who offered to take him to the hospital."

"What did he look like?" Nancy asked.

The officer described the man as being in his early fifties, short, and rather heavy-set. He had shifty pale-blue eyes.

"Well," Nancy replied, "I can think of several men who would fit that description. Did he have any outstanding characteristics?"

"Harry didn't notice anything, except that the fellow's hands didn't look as if he did any kind of physical work. The taximan said they were kind of soft and pudgy."

"Well, that eliminates all the men I know who are short, heavy-set and have pale-blue eyes. None of them has hands like that."

"It'll be a good identifying feature," the police officer remarked. "Well, I guess I'd better get that alarm out."

Nancy said good-by and put down the phone. She waited several seconds for the line to clear, then picked up the instrument again and called Hannah Gruen. Before Nancy lay the sheet of newspaper from which the advertisement had been torn.

"The Drew residence," said a voice on the phone.

"Hello, Hannah. This is Nancy."

"How are you, dear? Any news?" Mrs. Gruen asked quickly.

"I haven't found Dad yet," the young detective replied. "And the police haven't either. But I've picked up a couple of clues."

"Tell me about them," the housekeeper requested excitedly.

Nancy told her about the man with the crinkly ear and said she was sure that the police would soon capture him. "If he'll only talk, we may find out where Dad is being held."

"Oh, I hope so!" Hannah sighed. "Don't get discouraged, Nancy."

At this point Helen came into the hall, and as she passed Nancy on her way to the stairs, smiled at her friend. The young sleuth was about to ask Hannah to get the Drews' Tuesday copy of the *River Heights Gazette* when she heard a cracking noise overhead. Immediately she decided the ghost might be at work again.

"Hannah, I'll call you back later," Nancy said and put down the phone.

She had no sooner done this than Helen screamed, "Nancy, run! The ceiling!" She herself started for the front door.

Nancy, looking up, saw a tremendous crack in the ceiling just above the girls' heads. The next instant the whole ceiling crashed down on them! They were thrown to the floor.

"Oh!" Helen moaned. She was covered with lath and plaster, and had been hit hard on the head. But she managed to call out from under the debris, "Nancy, are you all right?" There was no answer.

The whole ceiling crashed down on them!

The tremendous noise had brought Miss Flora and Aunt Rosemary on a run from the kitchen. They stared in horror at the scene before them. Nancy lay unconscious and Helen seemed too dazed to move.

"Oh my! Oh my!" Miss Flora exclaimed.

She and Aunt Rosemary began stepping over the lath and plaster, which by now had filled the air with dust. They sneezed again and again but made their way forward nevertheless.

Miss Flora, reaching Helen's side, started pulling aside chunks of broken plaster and lath. Finally, she helped her great-granddaughter to her feet.

"Oh, my dear, you're hurt!" she said solicitously.

"I'll—be—all right—in a minute," Helen insisted, choking with the dust. "But Nancy—"

Aunt Rosemary had already reached the unconscious girl. With lightning speed, she threw aside the debris which almost covered Nancy. Whipping a handkerchief from her pocket, she gently laid it over Nancy's face, so that she would not breathe in any more of the dust.

"Helen, do you feel strong enough to help me carry Nancy into the library?" she asked. "I'd like to lay her on the couch there."

"Oh, yes, Aunt Rosemary. Do you think Nancy is badly hurt?" she asked worriedly.

"I hope not."

At this moment Nancy stirred. Then her arm

moved upward and she pulled the handkerchief from her face. She blinked several times as if unable to recall where she was.

"You'll be all right, Nancy," said Aunt Rosemary kindly. "But I don't want you to breathe this dust. Please keep the handkerchief over your nose." She took it from Nancy's hand and once more laid it across the girl's nostrils and mouth.

In a moment Nancy smiled wanly. "I remember now. The ceiling fell down."

"Yes," said Helen. "It knocked you out for a few moments. I hope you're not hurt."

Miss Flora, who was still sneezing violently, insisted that they all get out of the dust at once. She began stepping across the piles of debris, with Helen helping her. When they reached the library door, the elderly woman went inside.

Helen returned to help Nancy. But by this time her friend was standing up, leaning on Aunt Rosemary's arm. She was able to make her way across the hall to the library. Aunt Rosemary suggested calling a doctor, but Nancy said this would not be necessary.

"I'm so thankful you girls weren't seriously hurt," Miss Flora said. "What a dreadful thing this is! Do you think the ghost is responsible?"

Her daughter replied at once. "No, I don't. Mother, you will recall that for some time we have had a leak in the hall whenever it rained. And the last time we had a storm, the whole ceiling was soaked. I think that weakened the plaster and it fell of its own accord."

Miss Flora remarked that a new ceiling would be a heavy expense for them. "Oh dear, more troubles all the time. But I still don't want to part with my home."

Nancy, whose faculties by now were completely restored, said with a hint of a smile, "Well, there's one worry you might not have any more, Miss Flora."

"What's that?"

"Mr. Gomber," said Nancy, "may not be so interested in buying this property when he sees what happened."

"Oh, I don't know," Aunt Rosemary spoke up. "He's pretty persistent."

Nancy said she felt all right now and suggested that she and Helen start cleaning up the hall.

Miss Flora would not hear of this. "Rosemary and I are going to help," she said determinedly.

Cartons were brought from the cellar and one after the other was filled with the debris. After it had all been carried outdoors, mops and dust cloths were brought into use. Within an hour all the gritty plaster dust had been removed.

The weary workers had just finished their job when the telephone rang. Nancy, being closest to the instrument, answered it. Hannah Gruen was calling.

"Nancy! What happened?" she asked. "I've

been waiting over an hour for you to call me back. What's the matter?"

Nancy gave her all the details.

"What's going to happen to you next?" the housekeeper exclaimed.

The young sleuth laughed. "Something good, I hope."

She asked Hannah to look for her copy of the *River Heights Gazette* of the Tuesday before. In a few minutes the housekeeper brought it to the phone and Nancy asked her to turn to page fourteen. "That has the classified ads," she said. "Now tell me what the ad is right in the center of the page."

"Do you mean the one about used cars?"

"That must be it," Nancy replied. "That's not in my paper."

Hannah Gruen said it was an ad for Aken's, a used-car dealer. "He's at 24 Main Street in Hancock."

"And now turn the page and tell me what ad is on the back of it," Nancy requested.

"It's a story about a school picnic," Hannah told her. "Does either one of them help you?"

"Yes, Hannah, I believe you've given me just the information I wanted. This may prove to be valuable. Thanks a lot."

After Nancy had finished the call, she started to dial police headquarters, then changed her mind. The ghost might be hiding somewhere in the

house to listen—or if he had installed microphones at various points, any conversations could
be picked up and recorded on a machine a distance
away.

"It would be wiser for me to discuss the whole
matter in person with the police, I'm sure," Nancy
decided.

Divulging her destination only to Helen, she
told the others she was going to drive downtown
but would not be gone long.

"You're sure you feel able?" Aunt Rosemary
asked her.

"I'm perfectly fine," Nancy insisted.

She set off in the convertible, hopeful that
through the clue of the used-car dealer, the police
might be able to pick up the name of one of the
suspects.

"They can track him down and through the man
locate my father!"

CHAPTER XIV

An Urgent Message

"EXCELLENT!" Captain Rossland said after Nancy had told her story. He smiled. "The way you're building up clues, if you were on my force, I'd recommend a citation for you!"

The young sleuth smiled and thanked him. "I must find my father," she said earnestly.

"I'll call Captain McGinnis of the River Heights force at once," the officer told her. "Why don't you sit down here and wait? It shouldn't take long for them to get information from Aken's used-car lot."

Nancy agreed and took a chair in a corner of the captain's office. Presently he called to her.

"I have your answer, Miss Drew."

She jumped up and went over to his desk. The officer told her that Captain McGinnis in River Heights had been most co-operative. He had sent two men at once to Aken's used-car lot. They had just returned with a report.

"Day before yesterday an athletic-looking man with a crinkly ear came there and purchased a car. He showed a driver's license stating that he was Samuel Greenman from Huntsville."

Nancy was excited over the information. "Then it will be easy to pick him up, won't it?" she asked.

"I'm afraid not," Captain Rossland replied. "McGinnis learned from the Huntsville police that although Greenman is supposed to live at the address he gave, he is reported to have been out of town for some time."

"Then no one knows where he is?"

"Not any of his neighbors."

The officer also reported that Samuel Greenman was a person of questionable character. He was wanted on a couple of robbery charges, and police in several states had been alerted to be on the lookout for him.

"Well, if the man I saw at my car is Samuel Greenman, then maybe he's hiding in this area."

Captain Rossland smiled. "Are you going to suggest next that he is the ghost at Twin Elms?"

"Who knows?" Nancy countered.

"In any case," Captain Rossland said, "your idea that he may be hiding out around here is a good one."

Nancy was about to ask the officer another question when his phone rang. A moment later he said, "It's for you, Miss Drew."

The girl detective picked up the receiver and said, "Hello." The caller was Helen Corning and her voice sounded frantic.

"Oh, Nancy, something dreadful has happened here! You must come home at once!"

"What it it?" Nancy cried out, but Helen had already put down the instrument at her end.

Nancy told Captain Rossland of the urgent request and said she must leave at once.

"Let me know if you need the police," the officer called after her.

"Thank you, I will."

Nancy drove to Twin Elms as fast as the law allowed. As she pulled up in front of the house, she was startled to see a doctor's car there. Someone had been taken ill!

Helen met her friend at the front door. "Nancy," she said in a whisper, "Miss Flora may have had a heart attack!"

"How terrible!" Nancy said, shocked. "Tell me all about it."

"Dr. Morrison wants Miss Flora to go to the hospital right away, but she refuses. She says she won't leave here."

Helen said that the physician was still upstairs attending her great-grandmother.

"When did she become ill?" Nancy asked. "Did something in particular bring on the attack?"

Helen nodded. "Yes. It was very frightening. Miss Flora, Aunt Rosemary, and I were in the kitchen talking about supper. They wanted to have a special dish to surprise you, because they knew you were dreadfully upset."

"That was sweet of them," Nancy remarked. "Please go on, Helen."

"Miss Flora became rather tired and Aunt Rosemary suggested that she go upstairs and lie down. She had just started up the stairway, when, for some unknown reason, she turned to look back. There, in the parlor, stood a man!"

"A caller?" Nancy questioned.

"Oh, no!" Helen replied. "Miss Flora said he was an ugly, horrible-looking person. He was unshaven and his hair was kind of long."

"Do you think he was the ghost?" Nancy inquired.

"Miss Flora thought so. Well, she didn't scream. You know, she's really terribly brave. She just decided to go down and meet him herself. And then, what do you think?"

"I could guess any number of things," Nancy replied. "What did happen?"

Helen said that when Mrs. Turnbull had reached the parlor, no one was in it! "And there was no secret door open."

"What did Miss Flora do then?" Nancy asked.
"She fainted."

At this moment a tall, slender, gray-haired man, carrying a physician's bag, walked down the stairs to the front hall. Helen introduced Nancy to him, then asked about the patient.

"Well, fortunately, Miss Flora is going to be all right," said Dr. Morrison. "She is an amazing woman. With complete rest and nothing more to worry her, I believe she will be all right. In fact, she may be able to be up for short periods by this time tomorrow."

"Oh, I'm so relieved," said Helen. "I'm terribly fond of my great-grandmother and I don't want anything to happen to her."

The physician smiled. "I'll do all I can, but you people will have to help."

"How can we do that?" Nancy asked quickly.

The physician said that no one was to talk about the ghost. "Miss Flora says that she saw a man in the parlor and that he must have come in by some secret entrance. Now you know, as well as I do, that such a thing is not plausible."

"But the man couldn't have entered this house any other way," Helen told him quickly. "Every window and door on this first floor is kept locked."

The doctor raised his eyebrows. "You've heard of hallucinations?" he asked.

Nancy and Helen frowned, but remained silent.

They were sure that Miss Flora had not had an hallucination. If she had said there was a man in the parlor, then one had been there!

"Call me if you need me before tomorrow morning," the doctor said as he moved toward the front door. "Otherwise I'll drop in some time before twelve."

After the medic had left, the two girls exchanged glances. Nancy said, "Are you game to search the parlor again?"

"You bet I am," Helen responded. "Shall we start now or wait until after supper?"

Although Nancy was eager to begin at once, she thought that first she should go upstairs and extend her sympathy to Miss Flora. She also felt that a delay in serving her supper while the search went on might upset the ill woman. Helen offered to go into the kitchen at once and start preparing the meal. Nancy nodded and went up the steps.

Miss Flora had been put to bed in her daughter's room to avoid any further scares from the ghost, who seemed to operate in the elderly woman's own room.

"Miss Flora, I'm so sorry you have to stay in bed," said Nancy, walking up and smiling at the patient.

"Well, I am too," Mrs. Turnbull replied. "And I think it's a lot of nonsense. Everybody faints once in a while. If you'd ever seen what I did—that horrible face!"

"Mother!" pleaded Aunt Rosemary, who was seated in a chair on the other side of the bed. "You know what the doctor said."

"Oh, these doctors!" her mother said pettishly. "Anyway, Nancy, I'm sure I saw the ghost. Now you just look for a man who hasn't shaved in goodness knows how long and has an ugly face and kind of longish hair."

It was on the tip of Nancy's tongue to ask for information on the man's height and size, but recalling the doctor's warning, she said nothing about this. Instead, she smiled and taking one of Miss Flora's hands in her own, said:

"Let's not talk any more about this until you're up and well. Then I'll put you on the Drew and Company detective squad!"

The amusing remark made the elderly woman smile and she promised to try getting some rest.

"But first I want something to eat," she demanded. "Do you think you girls can manage alone? I'd like Rosemary to stay here with me."

"Of course we can manage, and we'll bring you exactly what you should have to eat."

Nancy went downstairs and set up a tray for Miss Flora. On it was a cup of steaming chicken bouillon, a thin slice of well-toasted bread, and a saucer of plain gelatin.

A few minutes later Helen took another tray upstairs with a more substantial meal on it for Aunt Rosemary. Then the two girls sat down in the dining room to have their own supper. After finishing it, they quickly washed and dried all the dishes, then started for the parlor.

"Where do you think we should look?" Helen whispered.

During the past half hour Nancy had been going over in her mind what spot in the parlor they might have overlooked—one which could possibly have an opening behind it. She had decided on a large cabinet built into the wall. It contained a beautiful collection of figurines, souvenirs from many places, and knickknacks of various kinds.

"I'm going to look for a hidden spring that may move the cabinet away from the wall," Nancy told Helen in a low voice.

For the first time she noticed that each of the figurines and knickknacks were set in small depressions on the shelves. Nancy wondered excitedly if this had been done so that the figurines would not fall over in case the cabinet were moved.

Eagerly she began to look on the back wall of the interior of the cabinet for a spring. She and Helen together searched every inch of the upper part but found no spring to move the great built-in piece of furniture.

On the lower part of the cabinet were two doors which Nancy had already opened many times. But then she had been looking for a large opening.

Now she was hoping to locate a tiny spring or movable panel.

Helen searched the left side, while Nancy took the right. Suddenly her pulse quickened in anticipation. She had felt a spot slightly higher than the rest.

Nancy ran her fingers back and forth across the area which was about half an inch high and three inches long.

"It may conceal something," she thought, and pushed gently against the wood.

Nancy felt a vibration in the whole cabinet.

"Helen! I've found something!" she whispered hoarsely. "Better stand back!"

Nancy pressed harder. This time the right side of the cabinet began to move forward. Nancy jumped up from her knees and stood back with Helen. Slowly, very slowly, one end of the cabinet began to move into the parlor, the other into an open space behind it.

Helen grabbed Nancy's hand in fright. What were they going to find in the secret passageway?

CHAPTER XV

A New Suspect

THE GREAT crystal chandelier illuminated the narrow passageway behind the cabinet. It was not very long. No one was in it and the place was dusty and filled with cobwebs.

"There's probably an exit at the other end of this," said Nancy. "Let's see where it goes."

"I think I'd better wait here, Nancy," Helen suggested. "This old cabinet might suddenly start to close itself. If it does, I'll yell so you can get out in time."

Nancy laughed. "You're a real pal, Helen."

As Nancy walked along the passageway, she looked carefully at the two walls which lined it. There was no visible exit from either of the solid, plastered walls. The far end, too, was solid, but this wall had been built of wood.

Nancy felt it might have some significance. At the moment she could not figure it out and started to return to the parlor. Halfway along the narrow corridor, she saw a folded piece of paper lying on the floor.

"This may prove something," she told herself eagerly, picking it up.

Just as Nancy stepped back into the parlor, Aunt Rosemary appeared. She stared in astonishment at the opening in the wall and at the cabinet which now stood at right angles to it.

"You found something?" she asked.

"Only this," Nancy replied, and handed Aunt Rosemary the folded paper.

As the girls looked over her shoulder, Mrs. Hayes opened it. "This is an unfinished letter," she commented, then started to decipher the old-fashioned handwriting. "Why, this was written way back in 1785—not long after the house was built."

The note read:

My honorable friend Benjamin:

The disloyalty of two of my servants has just come to my attention. I am afraid they plan to harm the cause of the Colonies. I will have them properly punished. My good fortune in learning about this disloyalty came while I was at my listening post. Every word spoken in the servants' sitting room can be overheard by me.

I will watch for further—

The letter ended at this point. Instantly Helen said, "Listening post?"

"It must be at the end of this passageway," Nancy guessed. "Aunt Rosemary, what room would connect with it?"

"I presume the kitchen," Mrs. Hayes replied. "And it seems to me that I once heard that the present kitchen was a sitting room for the servants long ago. You recall that back in Colonial days food was never cooked in a mansion. It was always prepared in another building and brought in on great trays."

Helen smiled. "With a listening post the poor servants here didn't have a chance for a good chit-chat together. Their conversations were never a secret from their master!"

Nancy and Aunt Rosemary smiled too and nodded, then the young sleuth said, "Let's see if this listening post still works."

It was arranged that Helen would go into the kitchen and start talking. Nancy would stand at the end of the corridor to listen. Aunt Rosemary, who was shown how to work the hidden spring on the cabinet, would act as guard if the great piece of furniture suddenly started to move and close the opening.

"All ready?" Helen asked. She moved out of the room.

When she thought Nancy was at her post, she

began to talk about her forthcoming wedding and asked Nancy to be in the bridal party.

"I can hear Helen very plainly!" Nancy called excitedly to Aunt Rosemary. "The listening post is as good as ever!"

When the test was over, and the cabinet manually closed by Nancy, she and Helen and Aunt Rosemary held a whispered conversation. They all decided that the ghost knew about the passage-way and had overheard plans which those in the house were making. Probably this was where the ghost disappeared after Miss Flora spotted him.

"Funny that we seem to do more planning while we're in the kitchen than in any other room," Aunt Rosemary remarked.

Helen said she wondered if this listening post was unique with the owner and architect of Twin Elms mansion.

"No, indeed," Aunt Rosemary told her. "Many old homes where there were servants had such places. Don't forget that our country has been involved in several wars, during which traitors and spies found it easy to get information while posing as servants."

"Very clever," Helen remarked. "And I suppose a lot of the people who were caught never knew how they had been found out."

"No doubt," said Aunt Rosemary.

At that moment they heard Miss Flora's feeble

voice calling from the bedroom and hurried up the steps to be sure that she was all right. They found her smiling, but she complained that she did not like to stay alone so long.

"I won't leave you again tonight, Mother," Aunt Rosemary promised. "I'm going to sleep on the couch in this room so as not to disturb you. Now try to get a little sleep."

The following morning Nancy had a phone call from Hannah Gruen, whose voice sounded very irate. "I've just heard from Mr. Barradale, the railroad lawyer, Nancy. He lost your address and phone number, so he called here. I'm furious at what he had to say. He hinted that your father might be staying away on purpose because he wasn't able to produce Willie Wharton!"

Nancy was angry too. "Why, that's absolutely unfair and untrue," she cried.

"Well, I just wouldn't stand for it if I were you," Hannah Gruen stated flatly. "And that's only half of it."

"You mean he had more to say about Dad?" Nancy questioned quickly.

"No, not that," the housekeeper answered. "He was calling to say that the railroad can't hold up the bridge project any longer. If some new evidence isn't produced by Monday, the railroad will be forced to accede to the demands of Willie Wharton and all those other property owners!"

"Oh, that would be a great blow to Dad!" said

Nancy. "He wouldn't want this to happen. He's
sure that the signature on that contract of sale is
Willie Wharton's. All he has to do is find him
and prove it."

"Everything is such a mess," said Mrs. Gruen.
"I was talking to the police just before I called you
and they have no leads at all to where your father
might be."

"Hannah, this is dreadful!" said Nancy. "I
don't know how, but I intend to find Dad—and
quickly, too!"

After the conversation between herself and the
housekeeper was over, Nancy walked up and down
the hall, as she tried to formulate a plan. Something must be done!

Suddenly Nancy went to the front door, opened
it, and walked outside. She breathed deeply of
the lovely morning air and headed for the rose
garden. She let the full beauty of the estate sink
into her consciousness, before permitting herself
to think further about the knotty problem before
her.

Long ago Mr. Drew had taught Nancy that the
best way to clear one's brain is to commune with
Nature for a time. Nancy went up one walk and
down another, listening to the twittering of the
birds and now and then the song of the meadow
lark. Again she smelled deeply of the roses and
the sweet wisteria which hung over a sagging
arbor.

Ten minutes later she returned to the house and sat down on the porch steps. Almost at once a mental image of Nathan Gomber came to her as clearly as if the man had been standing in front of her. The young sleuth's mind began to put together the various pieces of the puzzle regarding him and the railroad property.

"Maybe Nathan Gomber is keeping Willie Wharton away!" she said to herself. "Willie may even be a prisoner! And if Gomber is that kind of a person, maybe he engineered the abduction of my father!"

The very thought frightened Nancy. Leaping up, she decided to ask the police to have Nathan Gomber shadowed.

"I'll go down to headquarters and talk to Captain Rossland," she decided. "And I'll ask Helen to go along. The cleaning woman is here, so she can help Aunt Rosemary in case of an emergency."

Without explaining her real purpose in wanting to go downtown, Nancy merely asked Helen to accompany her there for some necessary marketing. The two girls drove off, and on the way to town Nancy gave Helen full details of her latest theories about Nathan Gomber.

Helen was amazed. "And here he was acting so worried about your father's safety!"

When the girls reached police headquarters, they had to wait a few minutes to see Captain Rossland. Nancy fidgeted under the delay. Every moment seemed doubly precious now. But finally the girls were ushered inside and the officer greeted them warmly.

"Another clue, Miss Drew?" he asked with a smile.

Nancy told her story quickly.

"I think you're on the right track," the officer stated. "I'll be very glad to get in touch with your Captain McGinnis in River Heights and relay your message. And I'll notify all the men on my force to be on the lookout for this Nathan Gomber."

"Thank you," said Nancy gratefully. "Every hour that goes by I become more and more worried about my father."

"A break should come soon," the officer told her kindly. "The minute I hear anything I'll let you know."

Nancy thanked him and the girls went on their way. It took every bit of Nancy's stamina not to show her inmost feelings. She rolled the cart through the supermarket almost automatically, picking out needed food items. Her mind would say, "We need more canned peas because the ghost took what we had," and at the meat counter she reflected, "Dad loves thick, juicy steaks."

Finally the marketing was finished and the packages stowed in the rear of the convertible. On the way home, Helen asked Nancy what plans she had for pursuing the mystery.

"To tell the truth, I've been thinking about it continuously, but so far I haven't come up with any new ideas," Nancy answered. "I'm sure, though, that something will pop up."

When the girls were a little distance from the entrance to the Twin Elms estate, they saw a car suddenly pull out of the driveway and make a right turn. The driver leaned out his window and looked back. He wore a smug grin.

"Why, it's Nathan Gomber!" Nancy cried out.

"And did you see that smirk on his face?" Helen asked. "Oh, Nancy, maybe that means he's finally persuaded Miss Flora to sell the property to him!"

"Yes," Nancy replied grimly. "And also, here I've just asked the police to shadow him and I'm the first person to see him!"

With that Nancy put on speed and shot ahead. As she passed the driveway to the estate, Helen asked, "Where are you going?"

"I'm following Nathan Gomber until I catch him!"

CHAPTER XVI

Sold!

"OH, NANCY, I hope we meet a police officer!" said Helen Corning. "If Gomber is a kidnaper, he may try to harm us if we do catch up to him!"

"We'll have to be cautious," Nancy admitted. "But I'm afraid we're not going to meet any police-man. I haven't seen one on these roads in all the time I've been here."

Both girls watched the car ahead of them intently. It was near enough for Nancy to be able to read the license number. She wondered if the car was registered under Gomber's name or someone else's. If it belonged to a friend of his, this fact might lead the police to another suspect.

"Where do you think Gomber's going?" Helen asked presently. "To meet somebody?"

"Perhaps. And he may be on his way back to River Heights."

"Not yet," Helen said, for at that moment Gomber had reached a crossroads and turned sharp right. "That road leads away from River Heights."

"But it does lead past Riverview Manor," Nancy replied tensely as she neared the crossroads.

Turning right, the girls saw Gomber ahead, tearing along at a terrific speed. He passed the vacant mansion. A short distance beyond it he began to turn his car lights off and on.

"What's he doing that for?" Helen queried. "Is he just testing his lights?"

Nancy was not inclined to think so. "I believe he's signaling to someone. Look all around, Helen, and see if you can spot anybody." She herself was driving so fast that she did not dare take her eyes from the road.

Helen gazed right and left, and then turned to gaze through the back window. "I don't see a soul," she reported.

Nancy began to feel uneasy. It was possible that Gomber might have been signaling to someone to follow the girls. "Helen, keep looking out the rear window and see if a car appears and starts to follow us."

"Maybe we ought to give up the chase and just tell the police about Gomber," Helen said a bit fearfully.

But Nancy did not want to do this. "I think it will help us a lot to know where he's heading."

She continued the pursuit and several miles farther on came to the town of Hancock.

"Isn't this where that crinkly-eared fellow lives?" Helen inquired.

"Yes."

"Then it's my guess Gomber is going to see him."

Nancy reminded her friend that the man was reported to be out of town, presumably because he was wanted by the police on a couple of robbery charges.

Though Hancock was small, there was a great deal of traffic on the main street. In the center of town at an intersection, there was a signal light. Gomber shot through the green, but by the time Nancy reached the spot, the light had turned red.

"Oh dear!" she fumed. "Now I'll probably lose him!"

In a few seconds the light changed to green and Nancy again took up her pursuit. But she felt that at this point it was futile. Gomber could have turned down any of a number of side streets, or if he had gone straight through the town he would now be so far ahead of her that it was doubtful she could catch him. Nancy went on, nevertheless, for another three miles. Then, catching no sight of her quarry, she decided to give up the chase.

"I guess it's hopeless, Helen," she said. "I'm going back to Hancock and report everything to the police there. I'll ask them to get in touch with Captain Rossland and Captain McGinnis."

"Oh, I hope they capture Gomber!" Helen

said. "He's such a horrible man! He ought to
be put in jail just for his bad manners!"

Smiling, Nancy turned the car and headed back
for Hancock. A woman passer-by gave her directions to police headquarters and a few moments
later Nancy parked in front of it. The girls went
inside the building. Nancy told the officer in
charge who they were, then gave him full details
of the recent chase.

The officer listened attentively, then said, "I'll
telephone your River Heights captain first."

"And please alert your own men and the State
Police," Nancy requested.

He nodded. "Don't worry, Miss Drew, I'll
follow through from here." He picked up his
phone.

Helen urged Nancy to leave immediately.
"While you were talking, I kept thinking about
Gomber's visit to Twin Elms. I have a feeling
something may have happened there. You remember what a self-satisfied look Gomber had on
his face when we saw him come out of the driveway."

"You're right," Nancy agreed. "We'd better
hurry back there."

It was a long drive back to Twin Elms and the
closer the girls go to it, the more worried they
became. "Miss Flora was already ill," Helen said
tensely, "and Gomber's visit may have made her
worse."

On reaching the house, the front door was opened by Aunt Rosemary, who looked pale.

"I'm so glad you've returned," she said. "My mother is much worse. She has had a bad shock. I'm waiting for Dr. Morrison."

Mrs. Hayes' voice was trembling and she found it hard to go on. Nancy said sympathetically, "We know Nathan Gomber was here. We've been chasing his car, but lost it. Did he upset Miss Flora?"

"Yes. I was out of the house about twenty minutes talking with the gardener and didn't happen to see Gomber drive up. The cleaning woman, Lillie, let him in. Of course she didn't know who he was and thought he was all right. When she finally came outside to tell me, I had walked way over to the wisteria arbor at the far end of the grounds.

"In the meantime, Gomber went upstairs. He began talking to Mother about selling the mansion. When she refused, he threatened her, saying that if she did not sign, all kinds of dreadful things would happen to me and to both you girls.

"Poor mother couldn't hold out any longer. At this moment Lillie, who couldn't find me, returned and went upstairs. She actually witnessed Mother's signature on the contract of sale and signed her own name to it. So Gomber has won!"

Aunt Rosemary sank into the chair by the telephone and began to cry. Nancy and Helen put their arms around her, but before either could say a word of comfort, they heard a car drive up in front of the mansion. At once Mrs. Hayes dried her eyes and said, "It must be Dr. Morrison."

Nancy opened the door and admitted the physician. The whole group went upstairs where Miss Flora lay staring at the ceiling like someone in a trance. She was murmuring:

"I shouldn't have signed! I shouldn't have sold Twin Elms!"

Dr. Morrison took the patient's pulse and listened to her heartbeat with a stethoscope. A few moments later he said, "Mrs. Turnbull, won't you please let me take you to the hospital?"

"Not yet," said Miss Flora stubbornly. She smiled wanly. "I know I'm ill. But I'm not going to get better any quicker in the hospital than I am right here. I'll be moving out of Twin Elms soon enough and I want to stay here as long as I can. Oh, why did I ever sign my name to that paper?"

As an expression of defeat came over the physician's face, Nancy moved to the bedside. "Miss Flora," she said gently, "maybe the deal will never go through. In the first place, perhaps we can prove that you signed under coercion. If that doesn't work, you know it takes a long time to have a title search made on property. By then, maybe Gomber will change his mind."

"Oh, I hope you're right," the elderly woman replied, squeezing Nancy's hand affectionately.

The girls left the room, so that Dr. Morrison could examine the patient further and prescribe for her. They decided to say nothing of their morning's adventure to Miss Flora, but at luncheon they gave Aunt Rosemary a full account.

"I'm almost glad you didn't catch Gomber." Mrs. Hayes exclaimed. "He might have harmed you both."

Nancy said she felt sure that the police of one town or the other would soon capture him, and then perhaps many things could be explained. "For one, we can find out why he was turning his lights off and on. I have a hunch he was signaling to someone and that the person was hidden in Riverview Manor!"

"You may be right," Aunt Rosemary replied.

Helen suddenly leaned across the table. "Do you suppose our ghost thief hides out there?"

"I think it's very probable," Nancy answered. "I'd like to do some sleuthing in that old mansion."

"You're not going to break in?" Helen asked, horrified.

Her friend smiled. "No, Helen, I'm not going to evade the law. I'll go to the realtor who is handling the property and ask him to show me the place. Want to come along?"

Helen shivered a little but said she was game. "Let's do it this afternoon."

"Oh dear." Aunt Rosemary gave an anxious

sigh. "I don't know whether or not I should let you. It sounds very dangerous to me."

"If the realtor is with us, we should be safe," Helen spoke up. Her aunt then gave her consent, and added that the realtor, Mr. Dodd, had an office on Main Street.

Conversation ceased for a few moments as the threesome finished luncheon. They had just left the table when they heard a loud thump upstairs.

"Oh, goodness!" Aunt Rosemary cried out. "I hope Mother hasn't fallen!"

She and the girls dashed up the stairs. Miss Flora was in bed, but she was trembling like a leaf in the wind. She pointed a thin, white hand toward the ceiling.

"It was up in the attic! Sombody's there!"

CHAPTER XVII

Through the Trap Door

"LET's find out who's in the attic!" Nancy urged as she ran from the room, Helen at her heels.

"Mother, will you be all right if I leave you a few moments?" Aunt Rosemary asked. "I'd like to go with the girls."

"Of course. Run along."

Nancy and Helen were already on their way to the third floor. They did not bother to go noiselessly, but raced up the center of the creaking stairs. Reaching the attic, they lighted two of the candles and looked around. They saw no one, and began to look behind trunks and pieces of furniture. Nobody was hiding.

"And there's no evidence," said Nancy, "that the alarming thump was caused by a falling box or carton."

"There's only one answer," Helen decided. "The ghost *was* here. But how did he get in?"

The words were scarcely out of her mouth when the group heard a man's spine-chilling laugh. It had not come from downstairs.

"He—he's back of the wall!" Helen gasped fearfully. Nancy agreed, but Aunt Rosemary said, "That laugh could have come from the roof."

Helen looked at her aunt questioningly. "You —you mean that the ghost swings onto the roof from a tree and climbs in here somehow?"

"I think it very likely," her aunt replied. "My father once told my mother that there's a trap door to the roof. I never saw it and I forgot having heard of it until this minute."

Holding their candles high, the girls examined every inch of the peaked, beamed ceiling. The rafters were set close together with wood panels between them.

"I see something that might be a trap door!" Nancy called out presently from near one end of the attic. She showed the others where some short panels formed an almost perfect square.

"But how does it open?" Helen asked. "There's no knob or hook or any kind of gadget to grab hold of."

"It might have been removed, or rusted off," Nancy said.

She asked Helen to help her drag a high wooden box across the floor until it was directly under the suspected section and Nancy stepped up onto it. Focusing her light on the four edges of the panels, the young sleuth finally discovered a piece of metal wedged between two of the planks.

"I think I see a way to open this," Nancy said, "but I'll need some tools."

"I'll get the ones I found before," Helen offered. She hurried downstairs and procured them. Nancy tried one tool after another, but none would work; they were either too wide to fit into the crack or they would not budge the piece of metal either up or down.

Nancy looked down at Aunt Rosemary. "Do you happen to have an old-fashioned buttonhook?" she asked. "That might be just the thing for this job."

"Indeed I have—in fact, Mother has several of them. I'll get one."

Aunt Rosemary was gone only a few minutes. Upon her return, she handed Nancy a long, silver-handled buttonhook inscribed with Mrs. Turnbull's initials. "Mother used this to fasten her high button shoes. She has a smaller matching one for glove buttons. In olden days," she told the girls, "no lady's gloves were the pull-on type. They all had buttons."

Nancy inserted the long buttonhook into the ceiling crack and almost at once was able to grasp the piece of metal and pull it down. Now she began tugging on it. When nothing happened, Helen climbed up on the box beside her friend and helped pull.

Presently there was a groaning, rasping noise and the square section of the ceiling began to move downward. The girls continued to yank on the metal piece and slowly a folded ladder attached to the wood became visible.

"The trap door's up there!" Helen cried gleefully, looking at the roof. "Nancy, you shall have the honor of being the first one to look out."

Nancy smiled. "And, you mean, capture the ghost?"

As the ladder was straightened out, creaking with each pull, and set against the roof, Nancy felt sure, however, that the ghost did not use it. The ladder made entirely too much noise! She also doubted that he was on the roof, but it would do no harm to look. She might pick up a clue of some sort!

"Well, here I go," Nancy said, and started to ascend the rungs.

When she reached the top, Nancy unfastened the trap door and shoved it upward. She poked her head outdoors and looked around. No one was in sight on the roof, but in the center stood a circular wooden lookout. It occurred to Nancy that possibly the ghost might be hiding in it!

She called down to Aunt Rosemary and Helen to look up at the attic ceiling for evidence of an opening into the tower. They returned to Nancy in half a minute to report that they could find no sign of another trap door.

"There probably was one in olden days," said Aunt Rosemary, "but it was closed up."

A sudden daring idea came to the girl detective. "I'm going to crawl over to that lookout and see if anybody's in it!" she told the two below.

Before either of them could object, she started to crawl along the ridgepole above the wooden shingled sides of the deeply slanting roof. Helen had raced up the ladder, and now watched her friend fearfully.

"Be careful, Nancy!" she warned.

Nancy was doing just that. She must keep a perfect balance or tumble down to almost certain death. Halfway to the tower, the daring girl began to feel that she had been foolhardy, but she was determined to reach her goal.

"Only five more feet to go," Nancy told herself presently.

With a sigh of relief, she reached the tower and pulled herself up. It was circular and had openings on each side. She looked in. No "ghost"!

Nancy decided to step inside the opening and examine the floor. She set one foot down, but immediately the boards, rotted from the weather, gave way beneath her.

"It's a good thing I didn't put my whole weight on it," she thought thankfully.

"Do you see anything?" Helen called.

"Not a thing. This floor hasn't been in use for a long time."

"Then the ghost didn't come in by way of the roof," Helen stated.

Nancy nodded in agreement. "The only places left to look are the chimneys," the young sleuth told her friend. "I'll check them."

There were four of these and Nancy crawled to each one in turn. She looked inside but found nothing to suggest that the ghost used any of them for entry.

Balancing herself against the last chimney, Nancy surveyed the countryside around her. What a beautiful and picturesque panorama it was,

she thought! Not far away was a lazy little river, whose waters sparkled in the sunlight. The surrounding fields were green and sprinkled with patches of white daisies.

Nancy looked down on the grounds of Twin Elms and tried in her mind to reconstruct the original landscaping.

"That brick walk to the next property must

have had a lovely boxwood hedge at one time," she said to herself.

Her gaze now turned to Riverview Manor. The grounds there were overgrown with weeds and several shutters were missing from the house. Suddenly Nancy's attention was drawn to one of the uncovered windowpanes. Did she see a light moving inside?

It disappeared a moment later and Nancy could not be sure. Perhaps the sun shining on the glass had created an optical illusion.

"Still, somebody just might be in that house," the young sleuth thought. "The sooner I get over there and see what I can find out, the better! If the ghost is hiding out there, maybe he uses some underground passage from one of the outbuildings on the property."

She crawled cautiously back to the trap door and together the girls closed it. Aunt Rosemary had already gone downstairs to take care of her mother.

Nancy told Helen what she thought she had just seen in the neighboring mansion. "I'll change my clothes right away. Then let's go see Mr. Dodd, the realtor broker for Riverview Manor."

A half hour later the two girls walked into the real-estate office. Mr. Dodd himself was there and Nancy asked him about looking at Riverview Manor.

"I'm sorry, miss," he said, "but the house has just been sold."

Nancy was stunned. She could see all her plans crumbling into nothingness. Then a thought came to her. Perhaps the new owner would not object if she looked around, anyway.

"Would you mind telling me, Mr. Dodd, who purchased Riverview Manor?"

"Not at all," the realtor replied. "A man named Nathan Gomber."

CHAPTER XVIII

A Confession

NANCY DREW's face wore such a disappointed look that Mr. Dodd, the realtor, said kindly, "Don't take it so hard, miss. I don't think you'd be particularly interested in Riverview Manor. It's really not in very good condition. Besides, you'd need a pile of money to fix that place up."

Without commenting on his statement, Nancy asked, "Couldn't you possibly arrange for me to see the inside of the mansion?"

Mr. Dodd shook his head. "I'm afraid Mr. Gomber wouldn't like that."

Nancy was reluctant to give up. Why, her father might even be a prisoner in that very house! "Of course I can report my suspicion to the police," the young sleuth thought.

She decided to wait until morning. Then, if there was still no news of Mr. Drew, she would pass along the word to Captain Rossland.

Mr. Dodd's telephone rang. As he answered it, Nancy and Helen started to leave his office. But he immediately waved them back.

"The call is from Chief Rossland, Miss Drew," he said. "He phoned Twin Elms and learned you were here. He wants to see you at once."

"Thank you," said Nancy, and the girls left.

They hurried to police headquarters, wondering why the officer wanted to speak to Nancy.

"Oh, if only it's news of Dad," she exclaimed fervently. "But why didn't he get in touch with me himself?"

"I don't want to be a killjoy," Helen spoke up. "But maybe it's not about your father at all. Perhaps they've caught Nathan Gomber."

Nancy parked in front of headquarters and the two girls hurried inside the building. Captain Rossland was expecting them and they were immediately ushered into his office. Nancy introduced Helen Corning.

"I won't keep you in suspense," the officer said, watching Nancy's eager face. "We have arrested Samuel Greenman!"

"The crinkly-eared man?" Helen asked.

"That's right," Captain Rossland replied. "Thanks to your tip about the used car, Miss Drew, our men had no trouble at all locating him."

The officer went on to say, however, that the prisoner refused to confess that he had had anything to do with Mr. Drew's disappearance.

"Furthermore, Harry the taxi driver—we have him here—insists that he cannot positively identify Greenman as one of the passengers in his cab. We believe Harry is scared that Greenman's pals will beat him up or attack members of his family."

"Harry did tell me," Nancy put in, "that his passenger had threatened harm to his family unless he forgot all about what he had seen."

"That proves our theory," Captain Rossland stated with conviction. "Miss Drew, we think you can help the police."

"I'll be glad to. How?"

Captain Rossland smiled. "You may not know it, but you're a very persuasive young lady. I believe that you might be able to get information out of both Harry and Greenman, where we have failed."

After a moment's thought, Nancy replied modestly, "I'll be happy to try, but on one condition." She grinned at the officer. "I must talk to these men alone."

"Request granted." Captain Rossland smiled. He added that he and Helen would wait outside and he would have Harry brought in.

"Good luck," said Helen as she and the captain left the room.

A few moments later Harry walked in alone. "Oh hello, miss," he said to Nancy, barely raising his eyes from the floor.

"Won't you sit down, Harry," Nancy asked, indicating a chair alongside hers. "It was nice of the captain to let me talk to you."

Harry seated himself, but said nothing. He twisted his driver's cap nervously in his hands and kept his gaze downward.

"Harry," Nancy began, "I guess your children would feel terrible if you were kidnaped."

"It would cut 'em to pieces," the cabman stated emphatically.

"Then you know how I feel," Nancy went on. "Not a word from my father for two whole days. If your children knew somebody who'd seen the person who kidnaped you, wouldn't they feel bad if the man wouldn't talk?"

Harry at last raised his eyes and looked straight at Nancy. "I get you, miss. When somethin' comes home to you, it makes all the difference in the world. You win! I *can* identify that scoundrel Greenman, and I will. Call the captain in."

Nancy did not wait a second. She opened the door and summoned the officer.

"Harry has something to tell you," Nancy said to Captain Rossland.

"Yeah," said Harry, "I'm not goin' to hold out any longer. I admit Greenman had me scared, but he's the guy who rode in my cab, then ordered me to keep my mouth shut after that other passenger blacked out."

Captain Rossland looked astounded. It was evident he could hardly believe that Nancy in only a few minutes had persuaded the man to talk!

"And now," Nancy asked, "may I talk to your prisoner?"

"I'll have you taken to his cell," the captain responded, and rang for a guard.

Nancy was led down a corridor, past a row of cells until they came to one where the man with the crinkled ear sat on a cot.

"Greenman," said the guard, "step up here. This is Miss Nancy Drew, daughter of the kidnaped man. She wants to talk to you."

The prisoner shuffled forward, but mumbled, "I ain't goin' to answer no questions."

Nancy waited until the guard had moved off, then she smiled at the prisoner. "We all make mistakes at times," she said. "We're often misled by people who urge us to do things we shouldn't. Maybe you're afraid you'll receive the death sentence for helping to kidnap my father. But if you didn't realize the seriousness of the whole thing, the complaint against you may turn out just to be conspiracy."

To Nancy's astonishment, Greenman suddenly burst out, "You've got me exactly right, miss. I had almost nothing to do with takin' your father away. The guy I was with—*he's* the old-timer. He's got a long prison record. I haven't. Honest, miss, this is my first offense.

"I'll tell you the whole story. I met this guy

only Monday night. He sure sold me a bill of goods. But all I did was see that your pop didn't run away. The old-timer's the one that drugged him."

"Where is my father now?" Nancy interrupted.

"I don't know. Honest I don't," Greenman insisted. "Part of the plan was for somebody to follow the taxi. After a while Mr. Drew was to be given a whiff of somethin'. It didn't have no smell. That's why our taxi driver didn't catch on. And it didn't knock the rest of us out, 'cause you have to put the stuff right under a fellow's nose to make it work."

"And the person who was following in a car and took my father away, who is he?"

"I don't know," the prisoner answered, and Nancy felt that he was telling the truth.

"Did you get any money for doing this?" Nancy asked him.

"A little. Not as much as it was worth, especially if I have to go to prison. The guy who paid us for our work was the one in the car who took your father away."

"Will you describe him?" Nancy requested.

"Sure. Hope the police catch him soon. He's in his early fifties—short and heavy-set, pale, and has kind of watery blue eyes."

Nancy asked the prisoner if he would dictate the same confession for the police and the man nodded. "And I'm awful sorry I caused all this

worry, miss. I hope you find your father soon and
I wish I could help you more. I guess I am a
coward. I'm too scared to tell the name of the
guy who talked me into this whole thing. He's
really a bad actor—no tellin' what'd happen to
me if I gave his name."

The young sleuth felt that she had obtained all
the information she possibly could from the man.
She went back to Captain Rossland, who for the
second time was amazed by the girl's success. He
called a stenographer. Then he said good-by to
Nancy and Helen and went off toward Greenman's
cell.

On the way back to Twin Elms, Helen con-
gratulated her friend. "Now that one of the kid-
napers has been caught, I'm sure that your father
will be found soon, Nancy. Who do you suppose
the man was who took your father from Greenman
and his friend?"

Nancy looked puzzled, then answered, "We
know from his description that he wasn't Gomber.
But, Helen, a hunch of mine is growing stronger
all the time that he's back of this whole thing.
And putting two and two together, I believe it
was Willie Wharton who drove that car.

"And I also believe Wharton's the one who's
been playing ghost, using masks at times—like the
gorilla and the unshaven, long-haired man.

"Somehow he gets into the mansion and listens
to conversations. He heard that I was going to be

asked to solve the mystery at Twin Elms and told Gomber. That's why Gomber came to our home and tried to keep me from coming here by saying I should stick close to Dad."

"That's right," said Helen. "And when he found that didn't work, he had Willie and Green-man and that other man kidnap your dad. He fig-ured it would surely get you away from Twin Elms. He wanted to scare Miss Flora into selling the property, and he thought if you were around you might dissuade her."

"But in that I didn't succeed," said Nancy a bit forlornly. "Besides, they knew Dad could stop those greedy land owners from forcing the rail-road to pay them more for their property. That's why I'm sure Gomber and Wharton won't release him until after they get what they want."

Helen laid a hand on Nancy's shoulder. "I'm so terribly sorry about this. What can we do next?"

"Somehow I have a feeling, Helen," her friend replied, "that you and I are going to find Willie Wharton before very long. And if we do, and I find out he really signed that contract of sale, I want certain people to be around."

"Who?" Helen asked, puzzled.

"Mr. Barradale, the lawyer, and Mr. Watson, the notary public."

The young sleuth put her thought into action. Knowing that Monday was the deadline set by the railroad, she determined to do her utmost before that time to solve the complicated mystery. Back at Twin Elms, Nancy went to the telephone and put in a call to Mr. Barradale's office. She did not dare mention Gomber's or Willie Wharton's name for fear one or the other of them might be listening. She merely asked the young lawyer if he could possibly come to Cliffwood and bring with him whatever he felt was necessary for him to win his case.

"I think I understand what you really mean to say," he replied. "I take it you can't talk freely. Is that correct?"

"Yes."

"Then I'll ask the questions. You want me to come to the address that you gave us the other day?"

"Yes. About noon."

"And you'd like me to bring along the contract of sale with Willie Wharton's signature?"

"Yes. That will be fine." Nancy thanked him and hung up.

Turning from the telephone, she went to find Helen and said, "There's still lots of daylight. Even though we can't get inside Riverview Manor, we can hunt through the outbuildings over there for the entrance to an underground passage to this house."

"All right," her friend agreed. "But this time you do the searching. I'll be the lookout."

Nancy chose the old smokehouse of Riverview Manor first, since this was closest to the Twin Elms property line. It yielded no clue and she moved on to the carriage house. But neither in this building, nor any of the others, did the girl detective find any indication of entrances to an underground passageway. Finally she gave up and rejoined Helen.

"If there is an opening, it must be from inside Riverview Manor," Nancy stated. "Oh, Helen, it's exasperating not to be able to get in there!"

"I wouldn't go in there now in any case," Helen remarked. "It's way past suppertime and I'm starved. Besides, pretty soon it'll be dark."

The girls returned to Twin Elms and ate supper. A short time later someone banged the front-door knocker. Both girls went to the door. They were amazed to find that the caller was Mr. Dodd, the realtor. He held out a large brass key toward Nancy.

"What's this for?" she asked, mystified.

Mr. Dodd smiled.

"It's the front-door key to Riverview Manor. I've decided that you can look around the mansion tomorrow morning all you please."

CHAPTER XIX

The Hidden Staircase

SEEING the look of delight on Nancy's face, Mr. Dodd laughed. "Do you think that house is haunted as well as this one?" he asked. "I hear you like to solve mysteries."

"Yes, I do." Not wishing to reveal her real purpose to the realtor, the young sleuth also laughed. "Do you think I might find a ghost over there?" she countered.

"Well, I never saw one, but you never can tell," the man responded with a chuckle. He said he would leave the key with Nancy until Saturday evening and then pick it up. "If Mr. Gomber should show up in the meantime, I have a key to the kitchen door that he can use."

Nancy thanked Mr. Dodd and with a grin said she would let him know if she found a ghost at Riverview Manor.

She could hardly wait for the next morning to

arrive. Miss Flora was not told of the girls' plan to visit the neighboring house.

Immediately after breakfast, they set off for Riverview Manor. Aunt Rosemary went with them to the back door and wished the two good luck. "Promise me you won't take any chances," she begged.

"Promise," they said in unison.

With flashlights in their skirt pockets, Nancy and Helen hurried through the garden and into the grounds of Riverview Manor estate.

As they approached the front porch, Helen showed signs of nervousness. "Nancy, what will we do if we meet the ghost?" she asked.

"Just tell him we've found him out," her friend answered determinedly.

Helen said no more and watched as Nancy inserted the enormous brass key in the lock. It turned easily and the girls let themselves into the hall. Architecturally it was the same as Twin Elms mansion, but how different it looked now! The blinds were closed, lending an eerie atmosphere to the dusky interior. Dust lay everywhere, and cobwebs festooned the corners of the ceiling and spindles of the staircase.

"It certainly doesn't look as if anybody lives here," Helen remarked. "Where do we start hunting?"

"I want to take a look in the kitchen," said Nancy.

When they walked into it, Helen gasped. "I guess I was wrong. Someone has been eating here." Eggshells, several empty milk bottles, some chicken bones and pieces of waxed paper cluttered the sink.

Nancy, realizing that Helen was very uneasy, whispered to her with a giggle, "If the ghost lives here, he has a good appetite!"

The young sleuth took out her flashlight and beamed it around the floors and walls of the kitchen. There was no sign of a secret opening. As she went from room to room on the first floor, Helen followed and together they searched every inch of the place for a clue to a concealed door. At last they came to the conclusion there was none.

"You know, it could be in the cellar," Nancy suggested.

"Well, you're not going down there," Helen said firmly. "That is, not without a policeman. It's too dangerous. As for myself, I want to live to get married and not be hit over the head in the dark by that ghost, so Jim won't have a bride!"

Nancy laughed. "You win. But I'll tell you why. At the moment I am more interested in finding my father than in hunting for a secret passageway. He may be a prisoner in one of the rooms upstairs. I'm going to find out."

The door to the back stairway was unlocked and the one at the top stood open. Nancy asked

Helen to stand at the foot of the main staircase, while she herself went up the back steps. "If that ghost is up there and tries to escape, he won't be able to slip out that way," she explained.

Helen took her post in the front hall and Nancy crept up the back steps. No one tried to come down either stairs. Helen now went to the second floor and together she and Nancy began a search of the rooms. They found nothing suspicious. Mr. Drew was not there. There was no sign of a ghost. None of the walls revealed a possible secret opening. But the bedroom which corresponded to Miss Flora's had a clothes closet built in at the end next to the fireplace.

"In Colonial times closets were a rarity," Nancy remarked to Helen. "I wonder if this closet was added at that time and has any special significance."

Quickly she opened one of the large double doors and looked inside. The rear wall was formed of two very wide wooden planks. In the center was a round knob, sunk in the wood.

"This is strange," Nancy remarked excitedly.

She pulled on the knob but the wall did not move. Next, she pushed the knob down hard, leaning her full weight against the panel.

Suddenly the wall pushed inward. Nancy lost her balance and disappeared into a gaping hole below!

Helen screamed. "Nancy!"

Trembling with fright, Helen stepped into the closet and beamed her flashlight below. She could see a long flight of stone steps.

"Nancy! Nancy!" Helen called down.

A muffled answer came from below. Helen's heart gave a leap of relief. "Nancy's alive!" she told herself, then called, "Where are you?"

"I've found the secret passageway," came faintly to Helen's ears. "Come on down."

Helen did not hesitate. She wanted to be certain that Nancy was all right. Just as she started down the steps, the door began to close. Helen, in a panic that the girls might be trapped in some subterranean passageway, made a wild grab for the door. Holding it ajar, she removed the sweater she was wearing and wedged it into the opening.

Finding a rail on one side of the stone steps, Helen grasped it and hurried below. Nancy arose from the dank earthen floor to meet her.

"Are you sure you're all right?" Helen asked solicitously.

"I admit I got a good bang," Nancy replied, "but I feel fine now. Let's see where this passageway goes."

The flashlight had been thrown from her hand, but with the aid of Helen's light, she soon found it. Fortunately, it had not been damaged and she turned it on.

The passageway was very narrow and barely high enough for the girls to walk without bending over. The sides were built of crumbling brick and stone.

"This may tumble on us at any moment," Helen said worriedly.

"Oh, I don't believe so," Nancy answered. "It must have been here for a long time."

The subterranean corridor was unpleasantly damp and had an earthy smell. Moisture clung to the walls. They felt clammy and repulsive to the touch.

Presently the passageway began to twist and turn, as if its builders had found obstructions too difficult to dig through.

"Where do you think this leads?" Helen whispered.

"I don't know. I only hope we're not going in circles."

Presently the girls reached another set of stone steps not unlike the ones down which Nancy had tumbled. But these had solid stone sides. By their lights, the girls could see a door at the top with a heavy wooden bar across it.

"Shall we go up?" Helen asked.

Nancy was undecided what to do. The tunnel did not end here but yawned ahead in blackness. Should they follow it before trying to find out what was at the top of the stairs?

She voiced her thoughts aloud, but Helen urged that they climb the stairs. "I'll be frank with you. I'd like to get out of here."

Nancy acceded to her friend's wish and led the way up the steps.

Suddenly both girls froze in their tracks.

A man's voice from the far end of the tunnel commanded, "Stop! You can't go up there!"

CHAPTER XX

Nancy's Victory

THEIR initial fright over, both girls turned and beamed their flashlights toward the foot of the stone stairway. Below them stood a short, unshaven, pudgy man with watery blue eyes.

"You're the ghost!" Helen stammered.

"And you're Mr. Willie Wharton," Nancy added.

Astounded, the man blinked in the glaring lights, then said, "Ye-yes, I am. But how did you know?"

"You live in the old Riverview Manor," Helen went on, "and you've been stealing food and silver and jewelry from Twin Elms!"

"No, no. I'm not a thief!" Willie Wharton cried out. "I took some food and I've been trying to scare the old ladies, so they would sell their property. Sometimes I wore false faces, but I

never took any jewelry or silver. Honest I didn't.
It must have been Mr. Gomber."

Nancy and Helen were amazed—Willie Wharton, with little urging from them, was confessing
more than they had dared to hope.

"Did you know that Nathan Gomber is a thief?"
Nancy asked the man.

Wharton shook his head. "I know he's sharp—
that's why he's going to get me more money for
my property from the railroad."

"Mr. Wharton, did you sign the original contract of sale?" Nancy queried.

"Yes, I did, but Mr. Gomber said that if I disappeared for a while, he'd fix everything up so I'd
get more money. He said he had a couple of other
jobs which I could help him with. One of them
was coming here to play ghost—it was a good place
to disappear to. But I wish I had never seen
Nathan Gomber or Riverview Manor or Twin
Elms or had anything to do with ghosts."

"I'm glad to hear you say that," said Nancy.
Then suddenly she asked, "Where's my father?"

Willie Wharton shifted his weight and looked
about wildly. "I don't know, really I don't."

"But you kidnaped him in your car," the young
sleuth prodded him. "We got a description of
you from the taximan."

Several seconds went by before Willie Wharton
answered. "I didn't know it was kidnaping. Mr.
Gomber said your father was ill and that he was

going to take him to a special doctor. He said Mr. Drew was coming on a train from Chicago and was going to meet Mr. Gomber on the road half-way between here and the station. But Gomber said he couldn't meet him—had other business to attend to. So I was to follow your father's taxi and bring him to Riverview Manor."

"Yes, yes, go on," Nancy urged, as Willie Wharton stopped speaking and covered his face with his hands.

"I didn't expect your father to be unconscious when I picked him up," Wharton went on. "Well, those men in the taxi put Mr. Drew in the back of my car and I brought him here. Mr. Gomber drove up from the other direction and said he would take over. He told me to come right here to Twin Elms and do some ghosting."

"And you have no idea where Mr. Gomber took my father?" Nancy asked, with a sinking feeling.

"Nope."

In a few words she pointed out Nathan Gomber's real character to Willie Wharton, hoping that if the man before her did know anything about Mr. Drew's whereabouts which he was not telling, he would confess. But from Wharton's emphatic answers and sincere offers to be of all the help he could in finding the missing lawyer, Nancy concluded that Wharton was not withholding any information.

"How did you find out about this passageway and the secret staircases?" Nancy questioned him.

"Gomber found an old notebook under a heap of rubbish in the attic of Riverview Manor," Wharton answered. "He said it told everything about the secret entrances to the two houses. The passageways, with openings on each floor, were built when the houses were. They were used by the original Turnbulls in bad weather to get from one building to the other. This stairway was for the servants. The other two stairways were for the family. One of these led to Mr. Turnbull's bedroom in this house. The notebook also said that he often secretly entertained government agents and sometimes he had to hurry them out of the parlor and hide them in the passageway when callers came."

"Where does this stairway lead?" Helen spoke up.

"To the attic of Twin Elms." Willie Wharton gave a little chuckle. "I know, Miss Drew, that you almost found the entrance. But the guys that built the place were pretty clever. Every opening has heavy double doors. When you poked that screw driver through the crack, you thought you were hitting another wall but it was really a door."

"Did you play the violin and turn on the radio —and make that thumping noise in the attic— and were you the one who laughed when we were up there?"

"Yes, and I moved the sofa to scare you and I even knew about the listening post. That's how I found out all your plans and could report them to Mr. Gomber."

Suddenly it occurred to Nancy that Nathan Gomber might appear on the scene at any moment. She must get Willie Wharton away and have him swear to his signature before he changed his mind!

"Mr. Wharton, would you please go ahead of us up this stairway and open the doors?" she asked. "And go into Twin Elms with us and talk to Mrs. Turnbull and Mrs. Hayes? I want you to tell them that you've been playing ghost but aren't going to any longer. Miss Flora has been so frightened that she's ill and in bed."

"I'm sorry about that," Willie Wharton replied. "Sure I'll go with you. I never want to see Nathan Gomber again!"

He went ahead of the girls and took down the heavy wooden bar from across the door. He swung it wide, pulled a metal ring in the back of the adjoining door, then quickly stepped downward. The narrow panel opening which Nancy had suspected of leading to the secret stairway now was pulled inward. There was barely room alongside it to go up the top steps and into the attic. To keep Gomber from becoming suspicious if he should arrive, Nancy asked Willie Wharton to close the secret door again.

"Helen," said Nancy, "will you please run downstairs ahead of Mr. Wharton and me and tell Miss Flora and Aunt Rosemary the good news."

She gave Helen a three-minute start, then she and Willie Wharton followed. The amazed women were delighted to have the mystery solved. But there was no time for celebration.

"Mr. Barradale is downstairs to see you, Nancy," Aunt Rosemary announced.

Nancy turned to Willie Wharton. "Will you come down with me, please?"

She introduced both herself and the missing property owner to Mr. Barradale, then went on, "Mr. Wharton says the signature on the contract of sale is his own."

"And you'll swear to that?" the lawyer asked, turning to Willie.

"I sure will. I don't want anything more to do with this underhanded business," Willie Wharton declared.

"I know where I can find a notary public right away," Nancy spoke up. "Do you want me to phone him, Mr. Barradale?" she asked.

"Please do. At once."

Nancy dashed to the telephone and dialed the number of Albert Watson on Tuttle Road. When he answered, she told him the urgency of the situation and he promised to come over at once. Mr. Watson arrived within five minutes, with his notary equipment. Mr. Barradale showed him the contract of sale containing Willie Wharton's name and signature. Attached to it was the certificate of acknowledgment.

Mr. Watson asked Willie Wharton to raise his right hand and swear that he was the person named in the contract of sale. After this was done, the notary public filled in the proper places on the certificate, signed it, stamped the paper, and affixed his seal.

"Well, this is really a wonderful job, Miss Drew," Mr. Barradale praised her.

Nancy smiled, but her happiness at having accomplished a task for her father was dampened by the fact that she still did not know where he was. Mr. Barradale and Willie Wharton also were extremely concerned.

"I'm going to call Captain Rossland and ask him to send some policemen out here at once," Nancy stated. "What better place for Mr. Gomber to hide my father than somewhere along that passageway? How far does it go, Mr. Wharton?"

"Mr. Gomber says it goes all the way to the river, but the end of it is completely stoned up now. I never went any farther than the stairways."

The young lawyer thought Nancy's idea a good one, because if Nathan Gomber should return to Riverview Manor and find that Willie was gone, he would try to escape.

The police promised to come at once. Nancy had just finished talking with Captain Rossland when Helen Corning called from the second floor.

"Nancy, can you come up here? Miss Flora insists upon seeing the hidden staircase."

The young sleuth decided that she would just about have time to do this before the arrival of the police. Excusing herself to Mr. Barradale, she ran up the stairs. Aunt Rosemary had put on a rose-colored dressing gown while attending her mother. To Nancy's amazement, Mrs. Turnbull was fully dressed and wore a white blouse with a high collar and a black skirt.

Nancy and Helen led the way to the attic. There, the girl detective, crouching on her knees, opened the secret door.

"And all these years I never knew it was here!" Miss Flora exclaimed.

"And I doubt that my father did or he would have mentioned it," Aunt Rosemary added.

Nancy closed the secret door and they all went downstairs. She could hear the front-door bell ringing and assumed that it was the police. She and Helen hurried below. Captain Rossland and another officer stood there. They said other men had surrounded Riverview Manor, hoping to catch Nathan Gomber if he did arrive there.

With Willie Wharton leading the way, the girls, Mr. Barradale, and the police trooped to the attic and went down the hidden staircase to the dank passageway below.

"I have a hunch from reading about old passage-ways that there may be one or more rooms off this tunnel," Nancy told Captain Rossland.

There were so many powerful flashlights in play now that the place was almost as bright as daylight. As the group moved along, they suddenly came to a short stairway. Willie Wharton explained that this led to an opening back of the sofa in the parlor. There was still another stone stairway which went up to Miss Flora's bedroom with an opening alongside the fireplace.

The searchers went on. Nancy, who was ahead of the others, discovered a padlocked iron door in the wall. Was it a dungeon? She had heard of such places being used for prisoners in Colonial times.

By this time Captain Rossland had caught up to her. "Do you think your father may be in there?" he asked.

"I'm terribly afraid so," said Nancy, shivering at the thought of what she might find.

The officer found that the lock was very rusty. Pulling from his pocket a penknife with various tool attachments, he soon had the door unlocked and flung it wide. He beamed his light into the blackness beyond. It was indeed a room without windows.

Suddenly Nancy cried out, "Dad!" and sprang ahead.

Lying on blankets on the floor, and covered with others, was Mr. Drew. He was murmuring faintly.

"He's alive!" Nancy exclaimed, kneeling down to pat his face and kiss him.

"He's been drugged," Captain Rossland observed. "I'd say Nathan Gomber has been giving your father just enough food to keep him alive and mixing sleeping powders in with it."

From his trousers pocket the officer brought out a small vial of restorative and held it to Mr. Drew's nose. In a few moments the lawyer shook his head, and a few seconds later, opened his eyes.

"Keep talking to your dad," the captain ordered Nancy.

"Dad! Wake up! You're all right! We've rescued you!"

Within a very short time Mr. Drew realized that his daughter was kneeling beside him. Reaching out his arms from beneath the blankets, he tried to hug her.

"We'll take him upstairs," said Captain Rossland. "Willie, open that secret entrance to the parlor."

"Glad to be of help." Wharton hurried ahead and up the short flight of steps.

In the meantime, the other three men lifted Mr. Drew and carried him along the passageway. By the time they reached the stairway, Willie

Wharton had opened the secret door behind the
sofa in the parlor. Mr. Drew was placed on the
couch. He blinked, looked around, and then
said in astonishment:

"Willie Wharton! How did you get here?
Nancy, tell me the whole story."

The lawyer's robust health and sturdy constitu-
tion had stood him in good stead. He recovered
with amazing rapidity from his ordeal and listened
in rapt attention as one after another of those in
the room related the events of the past few days.

As the story ended, there was a knock on the
front door and another police officer was admitted. He had come to report to Captain Rossland that not only had Nathan Gomber been captured outside of Riverview Manor, and all the loot
recovered, but also that the final member of the
group who had abducted Mr. Drew had been
taken into custody. Gomber had admitted everything, even to having attempted to injure Nancy
and her father with the truck at the River Heights'
bridge project. He had tried to frighten Miss
Flora into selling Twin Elms because he had
planned to start a housing project on the two Turnbull properties.

"It's a real victory for you!" Nancy's father
praised his daughter proudly.

The young sleuth smiled. Although she was
glad it was all over, she could not help but look for-

ward to another mystery to solve. One soon came her way when, quite accidentally, she found herself involved in *The Bungalow Mystery*.

Miss Flora and Aunt Rosemary had come downstairs to meet Mr. Drew. While they were talking to him, the police officer left, taking Willie Wharton with him as a prisoner. Mr. Barradale also said good-by. Nancy and Helen slipped out of the room and went to the kitchen.

"We'll prepare a super-duper lunch to celebrate this occasion!" said Helen happily.

"And we can make all the plans we want," Nancy replied with a grin. "There won't be anyone at the listening post!"

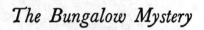

The Bungalow Mystery

The man chained to the bench was Jacob Aborn!

The Bungalow
Mystery

BY CAROLYN KEENE

PUBLISHERS *Grosset & Dunlap* NEW YORK

A NATIONAL GENERAL COMPANY

*This new story for today's readers is based
on the original of the same title.*

Contents

The Bungalow Mystery

CHAPTER I

A Blinding Storm

"Look at those black storm clouds!" Nancy Drew pointed out to her friend, Helen Corning, who was seated beside her in the bow of the small red motorboat.

Nancy, blue-eyed, and with reddish-gold glints in her blond hair, was at the wheel. She gazed anxiously across a long expanse of water to the distant shores of Twin Lakes. The Pinecrest Motel, where the eighteen-year-old girl and her older friend were staying, was almost two miles away on the smaller of the two lakes.

Helen Corning, dark-haired and petite, looked at Nancy with concern. "I think we're in for a cloudburst," she said, "and Twin Lakes becomes as rough as the ocean in a storm."

A few minutes later angry waves began to beat against the sides of the boat.

"Are there life preservers aboard, Helen?" Nancy asked.

"No," Helen answered fearfully.

Nancy set her chin grimly. Although it was only four o'clock in the afternoon, the sky was becoming increasingly dark. The pleasant summer breeze, which had been blowing earlier, was turning into a stiff wind.

"It's getting harder to keep on course," Nancy remarked, gripping the wheel more tightly.

As she increased the boat's speed to the maximum, the craft fairly leaped through the water, dashing spray into the girls' faces.

"I wonder if there are any raincoats in the lockers," said Helen.

"Please look," Nancy requested. "We'll be drenched by the time we reach the motel dock."

Luckily Helen found two plastic coats. She slipped into one, then helped Nancy into the other.

A streak of forked lightning cut across the sky, momentarily disclosing a thick mass of ugly clouds. The lightning was followed by an ominous crack of thunder, which caused the girls to jump.

"This is terrible!" Helen wailed.

A moment later the wind began to howl. It struck the boat with a force which made Helen grasp the railing next to her for support. Another dazzling flash of lightning illuminated the sky, and simultaneously a deluge of rain began to descend.

Nancy peered ahead into the dimness. The shore line had vanished and the blinding rain made it impossible for her to see more than a few feet beyond the bow of the boat.

"At least we have half a tank of fuel," Nancy announced, trying to sound optimistic. "We'll reach shore soon, I'm sure."

"I wouldn't bet on that," Helen said nervously.

A worried expression furrowed the young pilot's brow. The boat was making little progress against the wind. If anything happened to the motor they would be at the mercy of the waves.

A few minutes later the rain came down even harder. The wind continued to blow a raging gale and the waves seemed higher.

The girls leaned forward, trying to get their bearings. As a jagged ribbon of lightning illuminated the path ahead, Helen screamed, "About!"

Nancy froze with horror. A tremendous log was floating directly into the path of the motorboat!

Her heart pounding, the young skipper gave the wheel a vicious turn, but not quickly enough. With a splintering crash, the bow of the boat struck the log!

The impact sent Helen sprawling to the deck. Nancy clung to the steering wheel, but was thrown forward violently.

"Helen, are you hurt?" she asked.

"I— I'm all right. Are you?" she stammered, as Nancy helped Helen to her feet. Both girls were breathing heavily.

By now the small boat was listing sharply to starboard. Nancy saw instantly that the log had torn a jagged hole in the side of the craft. Water was pouring in rapidly.

"Quick, Helen!" Nancy ordered tersely. "You bail and I'll try to stop the leak!"

She sprang forward, tore off her raincoat, and stuffed it into the hole. Helen, meanwhile, found a rusty can and began to bail. Despite their efforts, water continued to pour through the opening.

"Let's shout for help!" Nancy cried above the wind, but she doubted that there was any other craft on the lake.

The girls cupped their hands to their lips and shouted frantically. Their only answer was the howl of the gale and the steady beat of rain.

"Louder!" Helen urged, and they screamed until they were hoarse.

"It's no use," Nancy said at last. "We'll have to think of something else."

Just then Nancy saw a giant wave bearing down on them. She met it head on, hoping to ride the crest, but a deluge of water almost inundated the girls. They were flung overboard and the motorboat sank to the bottom of the lake!

An excellent swimmer, Nancy managed to get her head above water almost immediately. Her first thought was for Helen. What had become of her?

Treading water, Nancy glanced about. Helen was not in sight.

"I must find her!" Nancy thought desperately. "She may have been injured!"

Then, several yards away, Nancy saw a white hand flash above the water. With powerful crawl strokes she plowed through the waves to the spot. The hand had vanished!

Nancy made a neat surface dive. Opening her eyes, she tried to see through the clouded water but to no avail. At last, she surfaced and drew in a deep breath.

Clearing her eyes, Nancy was relieved to spot her friend several feet ahead. Helen was floating on her back. Strong strokes brought Nancy directly behind her friend.

"My arms feel numb," Helen said weakly. "Guess I hit them on the boat."

"Don't worry," said Nancy. "Just lie still and I'll tow you to shore."

Nancy, however, had grave misgivings regarding her ability to accomplish this in the turbulent water. She needed every ounce of strength to swim the distance alone. *Could* she manage to save Helen? The storm had made the water very cold. Nancy prayed that she would not get a cramp and both girls go down.

"Hold your breath when you see a wave coming," she instructed Helen, as they started off.

At frequent intervals Nancy shouted for help, although she felt it was wasted energy. On and on they went.

Helen noticed finally that Nancy's breathing showed the great strain on her. "Save yourself," she begged. "Go on to shore without me."

"Never!" said Nancy, as a huge wave bore down upon the two girls, smothering them in its impact.

Feebly, Nancy struggled back to the surface with her burden. "One more like that and I'll be through," she said to herself.

Just then Nancy thought she detected a voice above the roar of the wind. Was it her imagination or had she really heard someone call?

"Help!" she screamed.

This time there could be no mistake, for she distinguished the words:

"Hold on! I'm coming!"

Through the blinding rain Nancy caught a glimpse of a dark object. A rowboat! If only she could hold out until it reached her!

"Over here!" Nancy cried loudly, waving.

As the boat approached, she fully expected to see it swamped. The boat swept safely toward the two girls, barely avoiding a crash, however. To Nancy's surprise, there was only one occupant in the boat—a slender, auburn-haired girl of about sixteen.

Twice she tried to bring the boat alongside the swimmers, but failed. The third time, as the craft swept past, Nancy lunged forward and caught the side of it. She dragged Helen along, supporting her with one hand until she, too, secured a hold.

"Can you climb aboard?" their rescuer asked. "I'll balance the boat while you get in."

Nancy explained about the submerged motorboat and Helen's useless arms.

With the strange girl and Nancy working together, they managed to get Helen into the craft. Then Nancy pulled herself over the side.

"Safe!" Helen said in relief. "I don't know how to thank you," she told their rescuer.

"Are you both all right?" asked the strange girl. "We're not far from the beach—otherwise, I couldn't have heard your cries for help in this wind."

"You were very brave to come for us," said Nancy. "I'm Nancy Drew and this is Helen Corning."

The girl at the oars stared at Nancy with keen interest. "I'm Laura Pendleton," she said. "I read in a newspaper about one of the mysteries you solved. I may need your help some day soon, Nancy."

Without another word Laura bent over her oars again.

"I'll help you row," Nancy offered, snatching up an extra oar from the bottom of the rowboat, and wondering what Laura Pendleton's mystery was.

Using the oar like a paddle, Nancy attempted to keep the boat on course. As she and Laura made some progress against the wind and waves, Helen took new hope.

"I think we're going to make it!" she said in relief. "Oh!"

A vivid flash of lightning illuminated the water. Directly ahead, through the rain, she and Nancy caught a glimpse of the rocky shore line.

"The rocks, Laura! Be careful or we'll be dashed against them!" Helen cried out, as the rowboat was tossed and slapped by the crashing waves.

Another zigzag streak of lightning disclosed the shore line more distinctly. A short distance out from the land and directly in front of their boat stood the ugly protruding nose of a jagged boulder!

CHAPTER II

Uninvited Guests

FOR an instant Nancy panicked. Would the girls be able to steer clear of the menacing rocks? A collision seemed unavoidable!

"We'll be killed!" gasped Helen.

"Row to the left, Laura!" Nancy commanded. "It's our only chance."

With a burst of energy the rowers turned the boat and deftly avoided the jagged boulder. An oncoming wave pushed them farther out of danger.

"There's a cove ahead!" Laura shouted above the wind. "We'll try to make it."

In another five minutes they reached the cove. Here the water was comparatively quiet.

"Thank goodness!" Helen murmured. "Oh, you girls are wonderful!"

As Nancy's oar struck a sand bar, she dropped it and quickly stepped out into water up to her knees. Laura followed and the two girls pulled the boat up onto the beach. Then they helped Helen Corning step onto firm sand.

"How do your arms feel now?" Nancy asked her.

"Better," Helen replied. "But I'm freezing." Her teeth were chattering.

Nancy herself was cold. She squinted through the darkness and rain, trying to see where they were. It seemed to be a desolate spot.

"Where are we?" she asked Laura. "Is there some place nearby where we can sit out the storm and get warm?"

"The only place I know," Laura replied, "is a bungalow I passed a while ago as I was walking along the beach. It's to our right, secluded among the trees."

"Sounds fine," Nancy said. "Let's hurry!"

The three bedraggled girls stumbled along the beach. Water oozed from Laura's sandals. Nancy and Helen had kicked theirs off in the lake and now slipped and slid in their soggy socks.

Presently the girls reached a small, concealed building, a one-and-a-half-storied weather-beaten bungalow which stood a short distance from the water's edge. The upper level nestled into the steep, wooded hillside. Since there was no light inside, Nancy assumed no one was there. She knocked. No answer. Nancy tried to open the door. It was locked.

"Looks as if we're out of luck," said Helen.

But Nancy was not easily discouraged, and she knew it was imperative for the girls to get warm. Her father, a well-known lawyer, had trained her to be self-reliant. He frequently handled mystery cases, and Nancy had often helped him in unearthing valuable clues.

In addition, Nancy had solved some mystery cases on her own—one involving an old clock and another a haunted house. There, Nancy had aided its owners to discover a hidden staircase which led to the capture of the mansion's "ghost."

"I'm sure that the owner of this bungalow will forgive us for going in," Nancy said.

There was a small window to the right of the door. She tried it and found to her relief that it was unlocked.

"That's a lucky break," said Helen, as Nancy opened the window.

Fortunately, it was low enough to the ground for the girls to hoist themselves through easily.

"Whew!" Laura exclaimed, as the wind almost blew them inside. She helped Nancy close the window.

It was pitch dark inside the building. Nancy groped around for a light switch, finally found

one, and flicked it on. A small bulb in the ceiling
disclosed nothing except two canoes and a wooden
bench which stood against one wall.

"Maybe it's only a boathouse," said Helen, flop-
ping wearily onto the bench.

The girls noticed a narrow flight of stairs
leading to the second floor.

"I wonder," Nancy mused, "if we might find
something up there to wrap around us. Or maybe
even some towels to dry ourselves off with. Let's
see."

Laura followed Nancy to the rear of the building. Seeing a light switch for the upper story,
Nancy turned it and the two girls climbed the
steps. To their surprise, the second floor of the
bungalow was furnished with two cots and blankets, a table and chairs, tiny refrigerator, a sink,
and a two-burner electric stove.

"We're in luck!" Nancy exclaimed happily.
"Come on up, Helen," she called.

Laura spotted an open closet in a corner of the
room. It was well stocked with food. She held up a
can of prepared cocoa.

"Under the circumstances," she said, "I doubt
that the owner of this place would object if we
made something warm to drink."

Helen and Nancy agreed. Within a short time
the three girls had taken off their wet clothing and
were wrapped in blankets. Laura had turned on

one burner of the stove and made hot chocolate.

"Umm, this is good," Nancy said contentedly.

Both she and Helen again thanked Laura profusely for coming to their rescue, and said they had been trying to get back to the Pinecrest Motel.

"Are you staying there?" Laura questioned.

"For a week," Helen replied. "My Aunt June is coming tomorrow. She was supposed to ride up with us Thursday from River Heights where we live, but was detained. She's going to help design my dress for my marriage to Jim Archer. He's in Europe now on business for an oil company. When he returns to the States, we'll be married."

Nancy Drew asked Laura if she, too, was a summer visitor at the resort. When her question met with silence, Nancy was surprised to see tears gathering in Laura's eyes.

"I'm sorry, Laura," Nancy said instantly. "You've been through a terrible ordeal. You should be resting instead of talking."

"Of course," Helen agreed.

Laura blinked her eyes, then said soberly, "You don't understand. You see, my mother passed away a month ago and—" She could not continue.

Nancy impulsively put an arm around Laura's shoulders. "I do understand," she said, and told of losing her own mother at the age of three.

Helen added, "Nancy lives with her father, a lawyer, and Hannah Gruen, their housekeeper."

"I'm an orphan," Laura stated simply. "My father was in a boat accident nearly six years ago." She explained that Mr. Pendleton's sailboat had capsized during a storm. He had been alone and no one had been near enough to save him.

"That's why," Laura added, "I knew I had to save whoever was crying for help on the lake today. I love to walk in a storm."

Nancy and Helen felt their hearts go out to the parentless girl. Not only was Laura brave, but also she showed great strength of character.

"With whom are you staying now?" Nancy asked Laura.

The girl looked troubled. "I'm alone at the moment. I checked in at the Montewago Hotel just this morning. But my guardian Jacob Aborn and his wife Marian are to arrive some time this evening. They're taking me to their summer home at Melrose Lake. I believe it's near here."

"Yes, it is," Nancy said.

"Do you know the Aborns?" Helen asked.

Laura said that she did not remember the couple. Her mother had frequently spoken of them, however.

"Mr. Aborn is distantly related to my mother, and it was her request that he become my legal guardian in case of her death."

Laura gave a slight sob, then went on, "But no answer came from our lawyer's letter to Mr. Aborn, who was traveling."

"How strange!" Nancy remarked.

"Finally I wrote to Mr. and Mrs. Aborn myself at the Melrose Lake address," Laura said. "The truth was I needed some money as a down payment on tuition at the boarding school I attend."

"And they replied?" Nancy asked.

"Yes. Mr. Aborn told me to come here and he and his wife would meet me."

Helen interrupted. "Then everything's settled, so you should be happy."

The girl shook her head. "I feel I'm not wanted. The letter wasn't cordial. Oh dear, what shall I do?"

Nancy gave Laura a hug. "You'll be at school and during vacations you can visit friends. And you have a new friend named Nancy Drew!"

"Oh, Nancy, you're sweet." Laura smiled for the first time, but in a moment her mood became sad again. "Living that way isn't like having your own home. Mother and I had such wonderful times together." She brushed away a few tears.

Nancy wanted to learn more but saw by her waterproof watch that it was six o'clock. Laura would have to hurry off to meet her guardian. The sky was getting lighter and the rain had almost stopped.

"We'd better leave," she suggested to Helen and Laura.

The girls washed the cups and saucepan, dressed, and put the blankets where they had found them. Before leaving the bungalow, Nancy wrote a note of thanks to the owner, signing it "Three grateful girls."

As they were parting, Laura said, "If my guardians don't arrive I'll call you and arrange a date for tomorrow."

"Please do!" Nancy and Helen urged, and waved good-by.

When they reached the Pinecrest Motel, the two girls went at once to talk to Mr. Franklin, the manager. They told him about the sunken motorboat, expressing extreme regret, and assured him that their parents would pay for the craft.

"Don't worry about that," the manager said. "We have insurance which takes care of such accidents. I'm just glad you girls are all right."

At that moment a short, thin woman swaggered into the office. Her print dress was mud-splattered and she had lost the heel to one shoe. Her wet, bleached hair clung to her head in an unbecoming fashion.

Ignoring Nancy and Helen, who were still conversing with Mr. Franklin, the woman said bluntly, "Is there anyone here who can change a tire for me? I just had a flat half a mile away."

"I'm afraid not," Mr. Franklin apologized. "I'm busy in the office and most of the help are off this evening."

"That's great!" the woman said angrily. "What am I supposed to do—walk to the Montewago Hotel? I'm late already!"

Although Nancy thought the stranded motorist was being extremely rude, she, nevertheless, suggested that the woman telephone a nearby service station. "I'm sure they'll send someone out to help you."

This idea was received with a snort as sparks of annoyance flashed in the woman's pale-blue eyes. "I'll think about that!" she said sarcastically, and, turning, limped toward the telephone booth. She banged the door shut behind her.

The three spectators looked after her with disgust and Helen said, "Some people don't deserve a helping hand."

The irate stranger was still in the booth when Nancy and Helen went off to their room on the ground floor. After a bath and change of clothes the girls felt better. A tasty dinner in the restaurant restored their energy and they played shuffleboard under the floodlights.

The next morning, as the two friends dressed, Helen asked, "Do you think Laura Pendleton will call us?" Helen was putting on Bermuda shorts and a candy-striped blouse.

"I imagine so," said Nancy, "unless her guardian and his wife took her to Melrose Lake last night."

"How far is that from here?" Helen inquired.

Nancy consulted a road map. "About twenty-five miles," she replied. Then, as she was putting on loafers, someone knocked on the door. Nancy went to see who it was.

Laura Pendleton stood in the doorway. She looked very pretty in a becoming pink cotton dress. But the girl's eyes were shadowed and she seemed highly distressed.

"Oh, Nancy—Helen!" Laura exclaimed. "I just had to come see you as soon as I could!"

"We're glad you did," Nancy said. "Come in." Before she could continue, Laura flung herself on Helen's bed and started to sob.

"What's wrong, Laura?" Nancy asked in concern, going over to her.

Slowly the girl sat up and wiped away her tears with a handkerchief. She apologized for her behavior, then said, "I don't think I'm going to be happy living with the Aborns—at least not with Mrs. Aborn!"

Troubled, Nancy asked Laura whether the guardian and his wife had arrived the evening before.

"Only Mrs. Aborn," Laura replied. "She came to my room about an hour after I left you girls.

She was wet and in a very nasty mood. Apparently she'd had a flat tire on the road and was delayed in getting help from some gasoline station."

Nancy and Helen exchanged significant glances. Mrs. Aborn sounded like the woman they had met in Mr. Franklin's office!

"What does your guardian's wife look like, Laura?" Helen asked with interest.

"She's blond, small, and thin. And I guess she was terribly upset about all the trouble she'd had. I understood this and tried to make her comfortable in the extra bedroom, but—"

Laura went on to say that Mrs. Aborn, instead of calming down, had become even more unpleasant, blaming the girl for making it necessary for her to drive to Twin Lakes in the bad storm.

"She said that Mary, my mother, had spoiled me and that I was going to have to toe the mark in her home— Oh, what will I do?" Laura asked.

Nancy did not know, but said Mrs. Aborn's behavior was inexcusable. Then she asked whether Laura's mother had known the guardian's wife well.

Instead of replying to the question, Laura said absently, "Mrs. Aborn called my mother 'Mary.' But, Nancy, Mother's name was Marie!"

CHAPTER III

Strange Guardians

NANCY was almost certain now that she and Helen had met the unpleasant Mrs. Aborn the night before. The woman's quarrelsome mood had extended to Laura.

Aloud Helen said, "But don't forget it's no fun to have car trouble on a bad night. That is apt to make anyone cross."

"I suppose so," Laura conceded.

"How was Mrs. Aborn this morning?" Nancy asked.

Laura's face brightened somewhat as she admitted that the woman had been pleasant and charming. "Mrs. Aborn apologized for her actions last night and said both she and her husband could hardly wait for me to come and live with them."

"I see," said Nancy, but with inward reservations.

"I guess I'm being foolish to worry." Laura smiled. "Mrs. Aborn did say she had met Mother only once, so that could explain the name mix-up."

"Where is Mr. Aborn?" Helen asked.

"He's arriving after lunch today. He was detained on business."

Nancy was puzzled. The Aborns' behavior was unusual and thoughtless, she felt.

"Mrs. Aborn is having her hair set at the beauty parlor in the hotel," Laura explained. "She suggested that I take a taxi here this morning if I felt I had to see you two—which I insisted I did," Laura said, grinning cheerfully.

Suddenly Nancy smiled. "I'm starved." She asked Laura to have a second breakfast with her and Helen in the motel restaurant.

"And afterward," Helen went on, "let's ask Marty Malone—the girl we met yesterday, Nancy —to make a foursome in tennis."

"Great!" said Laura to both suggestions.

When the three girls stepped outside, Nancy took a deep breath of air. She loved the earthy smell of the forests surrounding the lake resort, particularly the scent of the tall pines.

"What a day!" she exclaimed. Only a few fleecy white clouds broke the clear blue sky.

"The weatherman must be on our side." Helen chuckled.

A little later Nancy lent Laura tennis clothes, and the girls went to meet Marty Malone. Soon the four were playing a lively set on the courts located behind the motel. Laura and Nancy, who were partners, won. Helen and Marty took the second set.

"You're a terrific player, Nancy!" Laura exclaimed, as she scored a point during set three.

"Thanks," Nancy said, as they changed courts for service. "Where did you learn to play so well?"

"Private lessons." Laura grimaced. "At boarding school. Mother insisted. Before her illness she was a great sportswoman."

When Nancy and Laura had won the third set, Laura called for time out. "I must go back to the hotel now," she said. "It's almost noon."

After Laura had changed her clothes, Nancy offered to drive her to the hotel. The three girls piled into Nancy's blue convertible. Ten minutes later they drew up in front of the spacious Montewago Hotel. It was several stories high and stood a long distance back from the main road. In front stretched a green lawn bordered by beds of multicolored gladioli, dahlias, and giant asters.

"It's beautiful!" Nancy commented, as Laura stepped from the car.

Helen pointed to an attractive outdoor swim-

ming pool to the right of the hotel. It was filled
with bathers. Laura said that there was also a
riding stable behind the Montewago.

"There are a lot of families here," Laura said
wistfully. "I wish I could stay." Then hastily she
thanked Nancy for driving her over.

"I loved doing it," Nancy replied. "I hope we
see each other again, Laura."

"So do I," Helen added.

Laura snapped her fingers. "I have a wonderful
idea! Why don't you girls come back around three
o'clock? You can meet my guardians. And if
there's time, we can join the other young people
at a tea dance scheduled for four."

"Fine!" Nancy said at once.

"Come directly to my room." Laura waved
good-by.

Nancy detected a worried expression on Laura's
face, and knew she hated the thought of meeting
her strange new guardian.

The young sleuth was so quiet on the return
trip that Helen said, "Penny for your thoughts,
Nancy."

Her friend smiled. "I've concluded that the
Pendletons must have been wealthy."

"What gives you that idea?"

"It's very expensive to live year round in New
York hotels where Laura lived and she also mentioned boarding school. In addition," Nancy enu-

merated, "Laura's clothes have that simple but expensive look—you know what I mean."

"Yes," said Helen. "Well, if you're right, Mr. Aborn will control a great deal of money while he's managing Laura's affairs."

"In the case of a minor," said Nancy, "an inheritance is held in trust until she is twenty-one, Dad says. That's five years for Mr. Aborn. I hope he'll be a wise guardian."

She turned onto Lakeview Lane, a long, straight road bordered by woods. There were no homes along the way but a sign ahead advertised Sterling's real-estate office. Suddenly Nancy stopped.

"I think I'll run in here for a minute," she said, "and ask who owns that bungalow we helped ourselves to."

She walked into the office, introduced herself to Mr. Sterling, an elderly man, and told him the purpose of her call. The realtor grinned. "Any port in a storm is all right, I'm sure."

He said that the bungalow was owned by one of his clients. He had rented it a week before to a Mrs. Frank Marshall from Pittsburgh.

"I guess she fixed up the second floor," Mr. Sterling added. "She and her husband plan to use the place week ends. I'll pass the word along to Mrs. Marshall that you were there."

"I left a note but didn't sign it," Nancy said.

"Perhaps some time I'll stop in person and thank the Marshalls."

Returning to the car, she told Helen what she had learned. "Just for fun let's go out to the bungalow now."

A quarter of a mile farther on Nancy made a right-hand turn which brought them out on the lake drive. Below them, the girls could see the bungalow they had visited.

Suddenly a black foreign car pulled out of the lane that led down to the bungalow. Gaining speed, the automobile came toward Nancy's convertible.

"Watch out!" Helen yelled, jerking to attention as the vehicle passed and nearly sideswiped them.

Nancy slowed down and stopped. She looked back at the car which was almost out of sight. "Some drivers don't deserve a license," she said. "Do you suppose that was Mr. Marshall?"

Helen shrugged. "He wore a straw hat pulled low over his forehead. All I could see was the sleeve of his tan-and-white jacket."

"That's quite a bit," Nancy teased, "in so short a time."

Helen laughed. "Close association with you is making me more observant," she said.

When the girls reached the Pinecrest Motel, Helen exclaimed, "There's Aunt June!" While

Nancy parked, the dark-haired girl slipped from the convertible and hurried to the porch outside the room they occupied.

"Hello, Helen dear." The slim, stylishly dressed woman, with softly waved black hair, smiled at her niece.

Helen returned the greeting and gave her father's younger sister a kiss. "When did you arrive?" she asked. "Have you been waiting long?"

"No. I got here half an hour ago."

The attractive-looking woman was a buyer for a River Heights department store. She told Helen of a retailing problem which had prevented her departure with the girls, then turned to greet Nancy with enthusiasm.

"Isn't this a lovely spot?" Nancy remarked, and Aunt June Corning agreed that the view of the lake was superb.

After learning that Aunt June had not had lunch, the three went into the tearoom. When they had given their order, Miss Corning said, "I have some slightly bad news for you, Nancy."

"What's happened?"

"Well, just before I left River Heights, I phoned your housekeeper to see if she had any messages for you. To my surprise Dr. Darby answered. He said that Mrs. Gruen had sprained her ankle early this morning, and she must not walk for a couple of days."

"I'll call Dad right away and talk to him," said Nancy with concern.

"Wait!" Aunt June said. "Dr. Darby mentioned that your father left on a business trip today before the accident occurred."

"That means Hannah is all alone," Nancy said, rising. "I'll have to go home at once. Will you both excuse me for a minute, please?"

She went to a telephone booth and dialed the Drews' next-door neighbor, Mrs. Gleason. Nancy was relieved to hear that the woman's sister was taking care of Hannah for the afternoon. The housekeeper was in no pain and resting comfortably.

The young sleuth did some rapid thinking. If she left for River Heights late that afternoon she could still fulfill her promise to Laura to meet her guardian and arrive home in time to cook Hannah's supper.

"Will you please tell Mrs. Gruen I'll see her at six o'clock," Nancy requested, and Mrs. Gleason agreed to do this.

When Nancy returned to the others, Helen was telling her aunt of the adventure on the lake and Laura Pendleton's story.

"How dreadful for the girl!" exlaimed Miss Corning. "I feel very sorry for her."

Nancy now told of her plans to return home, and although Helen and her aunt were disappointed, they agreed that it was the right thing to do.

"But before I leave," said Nancy, "I want to meet Mr. and Mrs. Aborn."

After lunch Nancy packed her suitcase, put it in the car, and paid her motel bill. Soon it was time for her and Helen to leave for the Montewago Hotel.

"Are you sure you won't accompany us, Aunt June?" asked Helen.

Miss Corning shook her head. "I'm a little tired," she said, "and besides, I must unpack."

A short while later the two girls entered the Montewago lobby. Nancy made her way directly to the desk and after a brief wait was informed that Miss Pendleton would receive the girls in her suite. An elevator took them to the third floor.

Scarcely had they knocked on the door when Laura opened it. "Oh, I'm so glad you came," she cried out, smiling with relief.

Laura led the girls into a well-appointed living room with a bedroom on either side. As Nancy stepped inside, she saw a man and a woman seated in chairs near a picture window. In a glance Nancy realized that she and Helen had been right about Mrs. Aborn being the woman they had met the night before. Right now she looked more friendly.

Jacob Aborn arose and smiled graciously. He

was a well-built, somewhat stocky man in his early fifties. His face was square, and his small brown eyes were shifty.

When Laura introduced the girls, Mrs. Aborn rushed toward them. "Darlings!" she said, giving Helen and Nancy a butterfly peck on their cheeks. "You've been so good to poor Laura."

"Perfect bricks!" Mr. Aborn said gruffly. He extended a hand first to Nancy, then to Helen. "The reason I'm late in getting Laura is that I want everything to be perfect for her arrival at our Melrose Lake house."

Nancy was sure Mrs. Aborn recognized the callers and was embarrassed to admit it. They said nothing. There was an awkward silence until Laura said, "Well, let's all sit down."

For a few minutes everyone chatted generally, then Helen asked, "When are you leaving, Mr. Aborn?"

"In half an hour," was the reply. "Laura is tired and I want to get her settled before supper-time."

Mrs. Aborn broke in, "Yes, the poor child needs a lot of rest and good care."

Laura Pendleton seemed annoyed to be treated as a child and an invalid. "I'm fine," she stated defiantly. Turning to Nancy, she said quietly, "I'm afraid that we can't attend the hotel tea dance."

"That's all right," Nancy replied. She told of Hannah's accident and the fact that she must soon head for home.

"Are you all packed, Laura?" Mr. Aborn asked.

"Yes, except to get Mother's jewelry from the hotel safe."

"I'll do that for you, dear," Mrs. Aborn volunteered, rising. She smoothed her skirt restlessly.

Laura said, "Thank you, but I must present the receipt in person." She excused herself, saying she would be right back.

As Laura left the suite, Mr. Aborn turned to the two guests. "I wish Marie Pendleton had been a little more cautious with her inheritance from her husband," he confided.

"What do you mean?" Nancy asked.

"Laura is practically penniless," her guardian explained. "Mrs. Pendleton's illness and the way she lived took almost all her funds."

Nancy and Helen were surprised and dismayed to hear this.

"It doesn't matter, though," Mrs. Aborn said. "We have ample means to provide for Laura. She'll have everything she needs."

Nancy was confused by the woman's seemingly dual personality. She could be crude as on the evening before, or sweet as she appeared now. Perhaps, at heart, she meant well. Nancy hoped so for Laura's sake, but a strange feeling of distrust persisted.

When Laura returned, Helen and Nancy said they must be on their way. The friends shook hands.

"We never can thank you enough, Laura, for coming to our rescue yesterday," Helen said gratefully.

"That's right," Nancy agreed. "If you hadn't come along at that moment we'd probably be at the bottom of the lake!"

Laura shuddered. "Oh, I'm sure you would have reached shore some way! But I am glad I could help and it's been such fun knowing you. I hope you'll come to see me while I'm at Melrose Lake."

"We will," Nancy promised. "What is your address there?"

"Anyone can direct you to my house," Mr. Aborn said heartily. "It's well known in that section."

His wife tapped her foot on the floor. "Jacob, it's getting late," she hinted.

Nancy and Helen hastily bade the Aborns good-by and walked toward the door of the suite with Laura. Suddenly Helen turned around.

"It's lucky you brought two cars!" she called back. "Laura has a lot of luggage."

Without another word, Helen gave Laura a quick kiss and walked into the corridor. Nancy followed a moment later.

"Why did you say that?" Nancy questioned Helen as they rode down in the elevator.

The dark-haired girl signaled for silence. There were several other people in the car. When they stepped out into the lobby Nancy repeated her question.

Helen grabbed her chum's arm excitedly. "I couldn't resist it!" she exclaimed. "Jacob Aborn was the driver in the tan-and-white sports jacket I saw coming out of the road by the bungalow this morning! The driver of the black foreign car!"

CHAPTER IV

The Tree Crash

IF HELEN was right about Mr. Aborn's being the driver of the foreign car, then it should be in the hotel parking lot, Nancy thought.

"Let's take a look," she suggested.

The girls walked to the rear of the hotel where Nancy had left her own convertible. They scouted the lot. There was no sign of a black foreign car. Helen asked the attendant if one had been driven in that day. The man said no.

Helen was puzzled. "I was so sure I was right."

"You still could be," said Nancy. "The car may be parked somewhere else. Mrs. Aborn may have picked up her husband at some other point."

Puzzled, she and Helen climbed into the convertible and Nancy started the engine. As she drove back to the Pinecrest Motel, Helen remarked:

"I don't care for either Mr. or Mrs. Aborn. Their friendliness seems forced, and their promises don't ring true."

"I agree." Nancy nodded. "By the way, did you notice how Laura's guardian went out of his way to tell us she was penniless? And we were total strangers."

"I certainly did," Helen replied. "It was in very bad taste, I'd say."

"As soon as Hannah's ankle is better," Nancy declared, "I'm coming back here. Let's pay Laura a visit together at Melrose Lake. I feel very uneasy about her."

"A wonderful idea!" Helen exclaimed.

When they reached the motel, she got out. "I hope Hannah's foot improves quickly," she said, and waved Nancy out of sight.

A minute later Nancy was on the main highway which paralleled Twin Lakes for some distance. Presently, as she left the lake area, Nancy cast a speculative glance toward the sky. Did she imagine it or was it beginning to cloud over?

Nancy glanced at the speedometer. She was nearly halfway to River Heights. "Maybe I can get home before the storm breaks," she told herself.

A quarter of a mile farther on Nancy saw an obstruction in the road and brought the convertible to a halt. A huge sign read:

Detour. Bridge out. Take Melrose Lake Road. An arrow pointed to the left.

"Just when I'm in a hurry!" Nancy fumed, knowing she would have to go miles out of her way before reaching the River Heights road.

Another anxious glance at the sky told her there was no time to be lost. Already huge storm clouds were appearing.

"I'll be caught in another cloudburst like the one on the lake," she thought.

Hastily she headed the car down the Melrose Lake detour, a narrow, rutty road bordered with tall pines and thick shrubbery. Nancy was forced to reduce her speed to ten miles an hour, and even then it seemed as though the car would shake to pieces.

Within a few minutes it grew so dark that Nancy snapped on the headlights. Giant raindrops began to strike the windshield. In a short time they were followed by a blinding downpour, and the deep ruts in the road filled up like miniature streams.

"I'm in for it now," Nancy groaned, as the car crept up a hill.

Before she could reach a level stretch on the other side of the hill, the storm broke in all its fury. Trees along the roadside twisted and bent before the onslaughts of the rushing wind.

It was difficult for Nancy to see the road ahead.

She crawled along, endeavoring to keep the convertible's wheels out of deep ruts. As she swerved to avoid a particularly large puddle, a blinding tongue of lightning streaked directly in front of the car.

There was a flash of fire and simultaneously a deafening roar. For an instant, Nancy thought the car had been struck.

Almost blinded, the girl jammed on the brakes in time to hear a splintering, ripping noise. Before her horrified eyes a pine tree fell earthward. The convertible seemed to be directly in its line of fall!

"Oh!" Nancy gasped, as the tree missed her car by inches, landing directly in front of it.

Nancy felt as though she were frozen in her seat. How closely she had escaped possible death! When she was breathing normally again, Nancy ruefully surveyed the tree which blocked the road. What was she to do?

"I can't go back because the bridge is out," she told herself. "And there probably isn't anyone within miles of this place." She suddenly realized she had not seen another car going in either direction.

As Nancy continued to gaze at the fallen tree, she decided it could be moved by two people.

"Too bad I'm not twins," she thought. "I wonder how long it will be before someone comes past here."

Finally Nancy decided to try pulling the tree aside. She reached in the back seat for plastic boots and a raincoat with a hood. After putting these on, she stepped outside.

Gingerly picking her way through the mud and heavy rain, she walked to the fallen pine. She grasped the branches and tugged with all her might. The tree did not budge. Nancy next tried rolling it. This, too, she found was impossible.

"Oh, this is maddening," she thought, feeling completely frustrated.

As another low roll of thunder broke the quietness of the woods, Nancy was delighted to see headlights approaching. A moment later a small jeep pulled up behind her car.

The driver's door opened and a young man's voice said, "Hello there! Having trouble?"

"I sure am," said Nancy, as he walked toward her and stood outlined in the convertible's headlights. He appeared to be about seventeen, had dark hair, and twinkling eyes. Quickly Nancy explained about the fallen tree.

"Wow! You were lucky that it missed you!" the boy cried, then added, "It will be easy for the three of us to move the tree."

"Three?" Nancy questioned.

He laughed. "My sister's in the jeep," he explained, then called out, "Come on out, Cath!"

They were joined by a pretty girl, whom Nancy guessed to be fourteen years old. Introductions were exchanged. The brother and sister were Jim and Cathy Donnell. They lived off the next main highway and were returning home from visiting friends.

"I'm glad we came by," Cathy said. "There's only one house on this road and the people haven't moved in yet for the summer."

After Jim had pulled some tangled pine branches away from the convertible, he and the two girls were able to lift the trunk. Little by little they moved the tree far enough aside so that the cars could drive ahead.

"I'll report this to the highway patrol when we get home," said Jim.

"Thanks so much for your help," Nancy told the brother and sister. "By the way, do you know a Mr. and Mrs. Aborn who live at Melrose Lake?"

"We certainly do," said Cathy. "They're the ones whose house is on this route. It's a lovely place, with a lane leading to the house. You passed it about a mile back. The Aborns just bought the place."

"It's a small world," Nancy observed. She told the Donnells, however, that they were wrong

Nancy tried to pull the fallen tree aside

about the Aborns not being at their home, and explained about meeting the couple and Laura Pendleton at Twin Lakes.

"That's funny," said Jim. He explained that his parents had known the Aborns for years. "They used to have a place on the other side of the larger lake, and bought this new house only a month ago. They mentioned that Laura Pendleton was coming to visit them, but said they were taking an extensive trip first."

"I see," said Nancy, thinking, "Another strange angle to this thing!" Aloud she asked, "Is Mrs. Aborn a blond-haired woman, rather small and slight, Cathy?"

"Yes."

Jim said that he and Cathy must say good-by. Their parents would be worried if they did not arrive home soon.

"We'll tell Mother and Dad about the Aborns and Laura," said Jim. "We're all keen to meet Laura. The Aborns think she must be tops!"

"And we want to introduce Laura to our friends here at the lake," Cathy added.

"Grand!" Nancy said enthusiastically. "Laura has had a pretty sad time recently. She needs friends."

The three said good-by and got into their own cars. As Nancy drove on, she kept mulling over the Aborn-Pendleton enigma. She inferred from the Donnells' remarks that the man and his wife were very acceptable people. But Nancy certainly had not received this impression of them.

"I can't wait to meet them again," she thought, "and see how they're treating Laura."

By the time Nancy reached the end of the detour, the storm was over. A little later she turned into the Drews' driveway and parked near the front porch of the large red-brick house. She climbed from the car and made a dash for the porch with her suitcase.

As she inserted her key in the lock and pushed the front door open, a voice called out from the living room, "Nancy? Is that you?"

"Yes, Hannah. Be right in."

Nancy took off her raincoat and boots and put them in the vestibule closet. Then she hurried into the living room and hugged the motherly-looking woman, who was reclining on the sofa.

"Hannah! I'm so sorry about your ankle. How are you feeling?"

A worried expression faded from the house-keeper's face as she said, "I'm fine, now that you're home. This storm has been dreadful and I was concerned about you being on the road. Helen phoned that you were on your way."

Nancy told of the fallen tree at Melrose Lake, and how it had taken her longer than she had planned to make the trip.

"Goodness!" the housekeeper exclaimed. Then she smiled. "Nancy, you're like a cat with nine lives, the way you so often just miss being injured."

Nancy laughed. Then, becoming serious, she asked, "Where did Dad go?"

"To the state capital," Hannah replied, "and that reminds me, dear—you're to call Mr. Drew at eight tonight—" She gave Nancy a slip of paper with a telephone number on it.

"Did he say what he wanted?" Nancy inquired.

A look of concern appeared on Hannah's face as she said, "Mr. Drew wishes you to help him with an embezzlement case he's investigating!"

CHAPTER V

The Unexpected Prowler

An EMBEZZLEMENT case! Nancy was excited. What, she wondered, did her father want her to do? The young detective longed to place a call to him immediately, but knew she must wait until eight o'clock.

"Where is Mrs. Gleason's sister?" she asked.

Hannah said that the woman had left a short while before, after hearing that Nancy would be home by suppertime.

"But first she fixed a chicken casserole dish for us," Hannah added. "It's all ready to pop in the oven. My dear, I hate to bother you—"

Nancy grinned mischievously and teased, "You mean you hate to have anyone else but you reign in your kitchen. Don't worry, Hannah, I'll be neat."

"Oh posh!" said Hannah. She blushed and gave Nancy a loving glance.

Humming softly, Nancy went to the modern pink-and-white kitchen. The casserole, which looked tempting, stood on one of the gleaming counter tops. After lighting the oven, Nancy placed the dish inside to heat.

She set two wooden trays with doilies, napkins, and silver. Then, after placing bread and butter on each, Nancy poured two glasses of milk. Lastly, she made a crisp salad of lettuce and tomatoes and marinated it with a tangy French dressing.

While waiting for the casserole, Nancy went back to the living room. Hannah was reading the evening paper.

"You're a wonderful help, dear," the house-keeper said gratefully, looking up. "Tell me, did you enjoy your vacation?"

"It was lovely," said Nancy, and described the resort. She then told Hannah of the adventure on Twin Lakes and of Laura Pendleton and the Aborns.

"Hannah, wouldn't it be nice if Laura could visit us sometime soon?"

"It certainly would."

By now their supper was ready and Nancy brought it in on the trays. After they had eaten, she put the dishes in the washer, then helped Hannah, who was using crutches, upstairs to bed.

Nancy then went out to put her car in the garage, and returned to the house just as the clock was striking eight. She went to place the call to Carson Drew.

Nancy looked at the series of numbers on the slip of paper Hannah had given her:

942 HA 5-4727

She dialed the long-distance number, and after one brief ring the phone on the other end was picked up.

"Hotel Williamston," the switchboard operator answered.

"May I speak with Mr. Carson Drew?" his daughter requested.

"One moment, please."

There was a pause, then the operator's voice said, "I'm sorry but Mr. Drew checked out this evening."

"Did he say where he was going?" Nancy inquired in amazement.

The desk clerk said no. Nancy thanked him and hung up, feeling oddly upset. It was unlike her father to change his plans without calling home to tell where he would be. Could anything have happened to him? she wondered.

Since Hannah was asleep, Nancy did not awaken her to discuss the matter. Leaving on a light in the lower hall, she went to her own room and unpacked, deep in thought. As she hung up her dresses in the closet the young sleuth wondered if her father might be following a new clue in another city.

Deciding that this probably was what had happened and that she would hear from her father the next morning, Nancy felt reassured, took a bath, and went to bed. She fell asleep almost immediately.

Several hours later Nancy was awakened by the sound of a dull thud. She sat up and groped for the bedside light. Turning it on, she got out of bed and slipped into her robe and slippers.

"I hope Hannah hasn't fallen out of bed," Nancy thought worriedly, and hurried down the carpeted hall to the housekeeper's room.

Peering in the bedroom door, Nancy saw that Hannah was sound asleep. Puzzled, Nancy went back to her own room. The girl detective had almost decided she had been dreaming, then she heard an even louder noise.

The creaky window in the ground-floor library was being opened! Someone was entering the house!

Alarmed, Nancy decided to call the police and tiptoed to the bedside telephone in Mr. Drew's room. When the sergeant answered, she told him she would unlock the front door.

Nancy tiptoed quietly down the stairs. Upon reaching the ground floor, she eyed the closed door of the library, located at the far end of the living room. Not a sound came from the library which Mr. Drew used as a study.

With bated breath Nancy moved toward the front door and opened it. At that instant the library door was flung open. A man's dark figure was outlined in the doorway. Nancy's heart skipped three beats.

As Nancy debated whether to run outdoors or upstairs, she heard a loud chuckle. At the same time, a table lamp was turned on.

"Dad!" cried Nancy in disbelief, as color flooded back into her face. "Is it really you?"

"Of course!" said Carson Drew, a tall, distinguished-looking man who right now seemed a little sheepish.

He placed the brief case he was carrying on a table, then walked toward Nancy with outstretched arms. His daughter rushed into them and gave Mr. Drew a loving kiss.

"You're the best-looking burglar I've ever seen!" Nancy declared, and told her father of fearing the house was being entered. Then she clapped a hand to her face. "The police! I notified the police when I heard the window creaking open."

At that very moment father and daughter heard a car stop outside. Two policemen rushed in.

"Where's the burglar?"

"Right here," Mr. Drew confessed. "I forgot my house key. Sorry to put you to this trouble."

The policemen grinned and one said, "I wish all our burglary cases were solved this easy!" A few minutes later the officers left.

Mr. Drew explained to Nancy that he had hesitated about ringing the doorbell and disturbing Mrs. Gruen and Nancy. Recalling that one of the windows in the library did not close completely and needed repair, he removed the screen and opened the window.

"I'm sorry I scared you. I flew home tonight rather unexpectedly and didn't have a chance to let you know, Nancy."

"Has there been a new development in your embezzlement case, Dad?" she inquired.

Mr. Drew nodded. "Yes, but since it's late I suggest we both go to bed. We can talk about it in the morning."

Nancy stifled a yawn. "Good idea," she agreed.

Father and daughter turned off the lights and went upstairs. Both slept soundly until eight o'clock the following morning when Nancy was awakened by Hannah.

"Get up, sleepyhead!" said the housekeeper. Teasingly she prodded Nancy's foot with the tip of a wooden crutch while leaning on another one. "It's a beautiful day!"

Nancy jerked awake, rubbing her eyes. "Hannah!" she gasped. "What are you doing up?"

The housekeeper smiled. "One day of staying off my feet will keep me well for a year," she declared. "Besides, I feel fine this morning."

"But Dr. Darby said—" Nancy began.

"Stuff and nonsense!" Hannah replied tartly. "He left me these crutches to use and that's what I intend to do with them. Nancy, is your father home? I noticed his door is closed."

"Yes, Hannah." Nancy related the burglar scare.

The housekeeper smiled in amusement. Then, with a swish of her skirt, she turned and clumped out of the room. She paused at the door, winked at Nancy, and said:

"Pancakes and sausage at eight-thirty—and you tell your dad that I'm going to squeeze some extra-juicy oranges."

Mr. Drew was awake also. Nancy could hear the buzz of his electric razor! It was good, she thought, for the little family to be home again.

In half an hour they were seated in the cheerful breakfast room. As they began to eat, Mr. Drew caught up on the latest news and listened with concern to the story of Nancy's two storm adventures.

"I'm grateful that you're here safely beside me," he said gravely.

When the lawyer heard about Laura Pendleton and the Aborns, he frowned. "I agree with you, Nancy, it does sound strange," he said. "But you should not interfere with Laura and her guardians unless she asks you to. They may turn out to be very nice people."

"I agree," said Hannah, then added pointedly, "But if things should prove otherwise, Mr. Drew?"

"Then I'd be happy to help Laura have another guardian appointed by the court," the lawyer replied. "In the meantime, Nancy, let's invite Laura to spend a few days with us very soon."

Nancy beamed. "Thanks, Dad. That's just what I wanted to do."

When the meal was finished and the dishes had been put in the washer, Mr. Drew and Nancy went to his study, a comfortable room with book-lined shelves, deep-seated leather chairs, and a wide, highly polished mahogany desk.

Nancy sat down in a yellow club chair, then said eagerly, "Come on, Dad, don't hold out on me any longer about this case of yours."

Mr. Drew smiled, and absently fingered a glass paperweight. Sitting down, he began to talk.

Mr. Drew's client, a Mr. Seward, was the president of the Monroe National Bank in Monroe. It had branches throughout the country, including one in River Heights. During a recent audit, many valuable securities had been discovered missing from the main bank's vault. Most of the securities were bonds which read "Payable to Bearer."

"How dreadful!" said Nancy. "It means that whoever has the bonds can cash them."

"That's right." Mr. Drew said that the bonds belonged to various bank clients throughout the country. In all cases the clients had inherited money and had asked the bank as custodian to invest it for them. A Mr. Hamilton was put in charge. This was a very common bank procedure: the bank made the investments and paid the dividends to the individual, thus relieving the person of handling his own transactions.

"I was called in on the case," Carson Drew said, "by Mr. Sill, manager of our River Heights branch, when Mr. Seward advised him that a number of the missing securities belong to residents in our community. Mr. Seward felt this was an odd coincidence."

"It is," Nancy agreed. "Have you any idea who might have taken the property?"

Mr. Drew said no. So far the evidence pointed to Mr. Hamilton, although the man was a highly trusted officer.

"What about the people who work in the vault?" Nancy asked, wrinkling her forehead.

"They're being checked on now. Most of these

employees have worked for the bank a long time,
however. At present two of them are on vacation,
so the investigation may take some time."

"Couldn't you find out where they went?"
Nancy asked.

"We've tried that," her father replied, "but
they're not at their homes and the neighbors don't
know where they're vacationing. We'll just have
to wait until the men get home."

"I see," Nancy agreed.

"The main thing is," said Mr. Drew, "that Mr.
Seward doesn't want any publicity about the
theft. The bank will continue to pay dividends to
the security holders, of course. My assignment is
to find the missing property and the guilty person."

"A big order," said Nancy. "How are you going
to do this?"

Carson Drew said he was presently checking on
employees other than Hamilton who worked in
the custodian department. Also, he was trying to
find out if there might be a tie-in between the
thief and one or more of the persons whose property was missing.

"There must be several people behind this
theft," the lawyer explained. "It's pretty difficult
in these times to rob a bank, with all the security
measures they employ. Nothing is impossible,
however, if a plan is well worked out."

"Sounds like an exciting case, Dad," said Nancy. "What can I do to help?"

In reply Mr. Drew gave Nancy a slip of paper with four names on it and their corresponding River Heights addresses. They were: Mrs. William Farley, Mr. Herbert Brown, Mrs. John Stewart, Mr. Stephen Dowd. None of the names was familiar to the young detective.

"These are the local people whose securities are missing," Mr. Drew said. "Think of some reason to meet these people," he directed. "See what kind of homes they have, and try to get an insight into their characters. This is a very vague assignment, but I feel you may find out something incriminating about one of them—you see, we have to be very careful not to arouse suspicion in a case of this type."

"I'll do my best," Nancy assured him.

"The out-of-town names I'll check myself," her father explained. "They live in various large cities around the country, so I'll have to be away a good bit during the next few weeks."

"I'll get busy on these names right away," Nancy said. She gave her father a quick hug. "You're an old dear to let me help you!"

"Promise me you'll be careful," the lawyer warned. "An embezzler can be a dangerous person. And in this case whoever is behind the thefts is playing for big stakes."

The young sleuth said she would take every precaution. As Nancy stood up, the telephone rang.

"I'll get it, Dad," she offered, and hurried to pick up the receiver of the hall phone.

A low-pitched feminine voice said tersely, "Nancy? Nancy Drew?"

"Yes. This is Nancy speaking."

As she held on, waiting for the caller's identification, she heard sounds of a scuffle on the other end of the receiver. This was followed by a cry of pain and a loud *crash!*

CHAPTER VI

An Invitation to Sleuth

"WHO is this?" Nancy asked.

But the caller had cut off the connection. What had happened to her? Nancy wondered. Certainly she had sounded very distressed. Nancy hung up and waited for a second call, but the phone did not ring.

"Who was it?" Mr. Drew asked, coming into the hall.

Nancy told what had occurred.

"You didn't recognize the voice?" he remarked.

"No, so I can't call back. Oh dear, someone is in trouble, I just know it. And here I stand helpless to do a thing! It's maddening!"

"It certainly is," her father said. "Well, dear, I must run down to the office." Presently he left the house.

After seeing that Hannah was comfortable, Nancy went to her bedroom and thoughtfully opened the closet door.

"This is as good a day as any to start Dad's investigation," she thought.

Nancy took out a two-piece navy-blue dress which made her look older than her eighteen years. Next, she found a pair of comfortable low-heeled pumps.

For several minutes Nancy experimented with various hair styles. She finally chose a simple off-the-face arrangement. Nancy put on tiny pearl earrings, dusted her nose lightly with powder, and finally added a dash of lipstick.

After she had changed her clothes and given herself a final appraisal, Nancy went to Hannah's room to tell her she was going out for a while.

"Gracious, Nancy," said the housekeeper, giving the girl a sharp glance, "you look awfully businesslike today. Where are you going?"

"Dad asked me to look up something for him," she said. "I'll be back in time for lunch."

"Don't worry about that," said Hannah. "I can get around. Have a good time, dear."

When Nancy left the house she consulted the list Mr. Drew had given her. Mrs. William Farley, the first name on the paper, lived on Acorn Street, seven blocks from the Drew residence.

Nancy set out at a brisk pace, rehearsing in her

mind the approach on which she had decided. One of the girl's favorite community projects was a recreational youth center located in downtown River Heights. The center always needed volunteer helpers as well as entertainers for the children.

"A good way to find out something about Dad's suspects," Nancy decided, "is to see how they will respond to a needy cause. And I'll be telling the truth when I say that I'm working for the organization."

This resolved, Nancy soon reached a modest white house which was set back from the street a short distance. The front walk was outlined with pink and white petunias and the grass was well tended.

Nancy rang the bell. The door was opened almost immediately by an elderly woman with wavy white hair and the greenest, most alert, eyes Nancy had ever seen.

"Yes?" she inquired pleasantly.

Nancy introduced herself, then explained the purpose of her call. She was invited inside.

"Please be seated," said the woman, sitting down herself. Nancy chose a Duncan Phyfe rocking chair covered with a black floral print.

The hostess smiled. "I'd be glad to help you with your project, my dear," she said, "although I have no talent. Also, I don't leave this house very much. I'm a recent widow, you see, and I haven't been too well lately."

Nancy expressed sympathy and said she understood completely. She liked this friendly little woman on first sight.

"Would a small check help your cause?" the widow asked. "Perhaps you could buy some equipment for the children."

"That would be wonderful," Nancy said. "But I'm not soliciting funds."

Mrs. Farley smiled shyly. "I realize this," she said. "But there's so little I can do to help others. Mr. Farley left most of his estate, which was modest, in trust. And I have only a tiny income to live on."

The woman arose, and despite Nancy's protests, went to the desk where she wrote out a check.

Nancy thanked her profusely, for she realized that this was a sacrifice on the widow's part.

"I'm glad I can help," said Mrs. Farley. "Please come see me again and tell me how the youth center is coming along."

Nancy promised to do this. After a few more minutes of conversation, she bade Mrs. Farley good-by and left the house.

"If I'm a judge of human nature," thought Nancy, "that woman never did a mean thing in her life!"

When she reached the sidewalk, Nancy took out Mr. Drew's list from her handbag. Thoughtfully she crossed out Mrs. Farley's name.

Herbert Brown, the next suspect, lived in River Heights Estates, a rather exclusive housing area located on the outskirts of the city.

"It's kind of a long walk," Nancy told herself. "But it will do me good."

As Nancy strolled along, she was so engrossed with her thoughts that she failed to notice a tan sedan whose driver cruised by, honked the horn, then pulled over to the curb.

As the door opened, a good-looking young man about eighteen called, "Hi, Nancy!"

To her surprise, she saw Don Cameron, who had been a fellow student in River Heights High School. Nancy had, in fact, gone to the Spring Prom with the tall, black-haired boy.

"Hello, Don," she said. "What are you doing home? I thought you were working on your uncle's farm this summer before going to college."

Don grinned engagingly. "I've been picking string beans and berries and hoeing potatoes for nearly a month," he replied. "But I have a leave of absence to attend my sister's wedding this Friday."

Nancy had read of Janet Cameron's wedding plans in the *River Heights Gazette* two weeks before. "Jan must be excited!" she exclaimed.

"Everyone at home is going 'round in circles," Don stated, laughing. "Bill Bent, my brother-in-law-to-be, is no better.

"By the way, Nancy," Don continued, "I intended calling you later today. If you're free Thursday afternoon and evening I'd like to have you go to a barbecue party with me. It's being given in honor of Jan and Bill."

"I'd love to," said Nancy. "Where will it be?"

"At the Herbert Browns' home in River Heights Estates," Don said. "Their daughter, Lynn, is Jan's maid of honor."

Herbert Brown! One of the possible suspects in the bank security theft! Nancy could scarcely conceal her excitement. Although she did not like the idea of spying on a host, here was an excellent chance for her to find out what Mr. Brown was like.

"What time does the barbecue begin?" Nancy asked.

"I'll call for you at four," said Don.

He offered to drive Nancy home, and she hopped in beside him. When the young sleuth entered the house, she found Hannah in the living room.

"My goodness," the housekeeper exclaimed, "you haven't solved the mystery already!"

"I gave up," Nancy teased.

"What!"

With a grin Nancy told why she had postponed her trip. "I'll get some lunch for us," Nancy offered, "and then drive to the other two places on the list."

Hannah chuckled. "Since you said you'd be home," she said, "I prepared a fresh fruit salad— it's in the refrigerator. And rolls ready to pop into the oven."

"You're a fine patient!" Nancy scolded.

"I feel better keeping busy," Hannah countered.

Nancy asked whether there had been any telephone calls in her absence.

"No. But you did get a post card in the mail."

Nancy went to the mail tray in the hall and recognized Helen Corning's writing. The message read:

Dear Nancy:

Aunt June and I have decided to take a week's automobile trip up North. Will return directly to River Heights. Plan to stop and see Laura Pendleton on our way. Hope Hannah is better.

Love,
Helen

Nancy read the card aloud and commented, "I hope Helen lets me know how everything is at the Aborns' home. Anyway, I'm going to call

Laura myself in a few days to find out how she is
and make a date with her to come here."

"Do you think her guardian will let her leave
his care so soon?" the housekeeper asked, as she
reached for her crutches.

When there was no reply, Hannah looked out
toward the hall. Nancy's normally rosy complex-
ion was deadly white. She looked as if she were
about to faint!

CHAPTER VII

A Startling Assignment

"NANCY! Nancy! What's wrong with you?" Hannah cried out, as she tried to hurry to the girl's side.

As the housekeeper limped toward her, Nancy snapped to attention. "I'm all right, Hannah," she said. "But Helen's post card—it brought back the phone call I had this morning—"

Nancy told Mrs. Gruen about the call which had ended so abruptly with a cry of pain. "The caller's voice sounded vaguely familiar, but I couldn't place it," she explained. "Now I think I know who it was."

"Who?" said Hannah.

"Laura Pendleton! I believe someone was trying to stop her from talking to me!"

"Mercy!" Hannah exclaimed, sinking weakly into a soft chair. "Do you think it was one of the

Aborns, Nancy? And why would they do such a thing?"

Nancy shrugged. "I'm going to call the Aborn home right now."

While Hannah listened nervously, Nancy picked up the phone and dialed Information. When the operator replied, Nancy asked for Jacob Aborn's number.

The operator cut off for a minute, then reported, "I'm sorry, miss, but that number has been temporarily disconnected!"

"Can you tell me when this was done?" Nancy requested tersely.

"I'm sorry. I have no further information."

Nancy thanked the operator and hung up.

"It sounds suspicious," Hannah remarked, "but, Nancy, the Aborns may have changed their plans and gone away with Laura for a vacation somewhere else."

"I know one way to find out," said Nancy with determination. She reminded Hannah of the young couple, Cathy and Jim Donnell, who had helped move the fallen tree at Melrose Lake.

"I'll ask them if they've seen Laura or the Aborns," Nancy explained.

Hannah sighed. "You're just like your father," she said, "and he certainly is astute. But I'm worried that you're becoming involved in another complicated mystery."

Nancy tweaked Hannah's cheek. "The more there are, the better I like them!"

The housekeeper smiled. She said that while Nancy was calling Cathy and Jim she would put lunch on the table.

"Fine. I'll help you in a moment."

As Hannah hobbled to the kitchen, Nancy got the Donnells' number and dialed it. After two rings a girl's voice said, "Hello!"

"Cathy?" Nancy inquired.

"Yes."

Nancy gave her name. "Do you remember me?" she asked.

"Of course," said Cathy. "My family and I were talking about you just a short while ago. Jim and I told them about the Aborns' being home and we all went over this morning to say hello and meet Laura. But the house was closed. Nobody's staying there."

"Oh!" said Nancy, disappointed. She explained that this was her reason for calling, and told of the Aborns' telephone having been disconnected.

Cathy already knew this, and added, "Dad found a note on the back porch telling the milk-man to discontinue deliveries until further notice."

"Cathy, does Mr. Aborn own a foreign make of car?" Nancy queried.

"Why, no," Cathy replied. She added that her

parents thought the Aborns might have planned suddenly to take a short trip somewhere. "I'm sure that we'll hear from them in a few days. If we do, I'll call you, Nancy."

"Fine," said the young detective. "Remember me to Jim. Good-by."

Deeply troubled, Nancy went to the kitchen and told Hannah what Cathy had said.

"Chances are," said the housekeeper, "the call you received this morning was not from Laura at all. You know a lot of people, dear."

Nancy replied that usually when someone had to break a telephone conversation in an abrupt manner the person called back as soon as possible to explain what had happened.

"That's true," Hannah admitted. "It's very strange."

After lunch Hannah said she was going next door to visit with Mrs. Gleason. Nancy helped her to the neighbor's front porch. Then Nancy backed her convertible from the garage and headed for Mr. Drew's downtown office.

"I'll report my progress so far regarding his suspects."

Nancy parked the car in a lot adjoining a large building where lawyers, doctors, and other professional people had offices. Mr. Drew's suite was on the fifth floor. A few minutes later Nancy greeted her father's secretary, Miss Hanson.

"My, how pretty you look, Nancy!" said the efficient young woman, who had been with Carson Drew for the past five years.

"Thank you." Nancy blushed a trifle. "You look lovely yourself."

When the lawyer learned that his daughter had arrived, Carson Drew at once asked Nancy to come into his office.

"I can see by the gleam in your eyes, Nancy, that you have some information for me."

Nancy told him of her interview with Mrs. Farley. "In my opinion, she's a woman of very fine character." Then Nancy mentioned the invitation to the barbecue party at Mr. Herbert Brown's home.

Mr. Drew raised his eyes and chuckled. "Better than I expected."

"My main reason for coming was to tell you something else," Nancy said.

She quickly reviewed the latest developments in the Laura Pendleton case. Mr. Drew listened quietly. Finally he said:

"There's something odd about all this. Nancy, I must leave River Heights on the three-o'clock plane this afternoon for Cincinnati, but I'll be home by Sunday. Why don't we plan to drive to the Aborns' home later that afternoon and see for ourselves what the story is? They may have returned by then."

"That's a grand idea!" Nancy exclaimed. Then, knowing that he was busy, she kissed her father good-by and wished him a successful trip.

"I'll call you every night at eight!" Mr. Drew promised, and Nancy left the office.

On the way down in the elevator, Nancy asked Hank, the operator, if he knew where Hilo Street was located. Mrs. John Stewart, the third suspect, lived in an apartment at this address.

"I know the general area," Nancy added. "It's about three miles from here on the eastern side of the city."

"That's right," Hank said. "It's a classy neighborhood! All high-priced apartment buildings. I believe Hilo Street runs off East Main."

Nancy thanked him, then went to her convertible. She drove carefully through the city traffic and finally reached Hilo Street. Mrs. Stewart's apartment house was Number 76.

Nancy scanned the buildings and found that this one was the largest on the street. It was ultra-modern in design and about twenty stories high. After parking her car, she smoothed her hair and got out.

A red-coated doorman nodded pleasantly to the young detective as she entered the building a minute later. Nancy checked the directory and saw that Mrs. Stewart was in Apartment Three on the fourth floor. She rang the elevator button.

Almost instantly, aluminum doors slid open noiselessly, and Nancy stepped inside the carpeted elevator. It was self-operated, and Nancy pushed the fourth-floor control.

Her heart was pounding with excitement. Would Mrs. Stewart prove to be a link in the embezzlement case? Nancy hoped to find a clue this time!

When the elevator stopped at the fourth floor, Nancy got out and easily located Apartment Three. She pressed the doorbell.

A trim-looking maid, a rather harassed expression on her pretty face, opened the door immediately. "Oh, hello!" she said. "You must be the walker."

"Why, no—" Nancy began, but before she could explain, the maid went into the living room, leaving the door ajar.

As Nancy, speechless, glanced hastily into the apartment beyond, the maid reappeared. She was leading a pair of frisky black-and-white French poodles by a gold-linked leash.

"Here!" she said abruptly, thrusting the leash into Nancy's hand. "Their names are Irene and Frederika. Mrs. Stewart says to take them for a nice, long walk!"

Before Nancy could utter a word, the door was closed with an emphatic bang!

CHAPTER VIII

The Frightened Runaway

NANCY DREW, dog tender! This was a new title, the young detective thought. As she burst into laughter, the two poodles began to yap excitedly and dance around in little circles.

"Hello, girls," Nancy said to them, and bent down to pat the friendly animals. She then rang the doorbell with determination.

This time the door was opened by a tremendously stout woman whose chubby face was framed by a mass of fuzzy brown curls.

"Yes?" she inquired coyly. "Have you had some trouble with the babies? I told Collette to give you explicit instructions."

Nancy smothered a giggle. "Are you Mrs. Stewart?" she asked briskly.

"Of course," the woman said impatiently.

Nancy introduced herself and said that a mistake had been made. She was not the dog walker, but had come to solicit Mrs. Stewart's aid for the River Heights Youth Center.

"Oh dear!" Mrs. Stewart blushed, obviously flustered. "Collette's made a mistake. I'm sorry." She jerked the leash from Nancy and gave the poodles a loving glance. "Mama will give you both cookies while we wait for your real walker."

Nancy cleared her throat and Mrs. Stewart's glance returned to the caller. "Oh, yes—your project. I'm afraid that we'll have to discuss it another time. I'm having an afternoon musicale featuring the most divine violinist—Professor Le Bojo. He is expected any moment—"

"I understand," Nancy nodded. "Perhaps I can return later when Mr. Stewart is home?"

"He left today for a fishing trip in Maine," Mrs. Stewart replied. She added somewhat angrily, "I simply don't understand Gerald—he doesn't appreciate our home life here with the children!" Her glance swept toward the poodles.

Nancy managed to keep a straight face, said good-by to Mrs. Stewart, and left. When she returned to her car Nancy reached the conclusion that Mrs. Stewart was hardly the type to plan a bank swindle!

"Her poor husband," Nancy thought with a laugh.

There was only one more name for Nancy to check today—Mr. Stephen Dowd. She drove out Hilo Street and headed across the city. The man's address was in a business zone which was partly residential, although most of the homes were two-family dwellings.

After a little difficulty, Nancy found the house she sought—a brown duplex situated between a gasoline station and a tailor shop. She parked and went up the walk. Mr. Dowd's half of the house was on the right-hand side.

The young sleuth rang the bell and waited. No answer. She pushed the button again. Still no one came to the door.

"Maybe I can find out something from his next-door neighbor," Nancy thought hopefully.

As she was about to ring the bell on the left, the door was opened by a young woman, a shopping bag in her hand. She appeared startled to see Nancy.

The young sleuth smiled pleasantly. "I came to call on Mr. Dowd," she explained. "He's probably at work?"

"No. Mr. and Mrs. Dowd are both away now—on tour with a show, they said. They board here. I'm Mrs. Wyman."

"Are they entertainers?" Nancy inquired with interest, and explained about the youth center.

Mrs. Wyman said the couple were actors, but

she did not know what parts they played. "Since moving here two months ago, they've been away a great deal of the time."

Nancy thanked Mrs. Wyman and said she would call again. "They sound like the type of people I'm looking for to help amuse the children," she explained.

Nancy drove away, but told herself they would bear further investigation. It seemed unnatural that they would not have told what parts they were playing.

Nancy felt a little discouraged about her findings so far. She realized that she could do nothing else until she met Herbert Brown the next afternoon.

"I think I'll go home, get my bathing suit, and head for the club," she decided. The day was becoming very warm.

Fifteen minutes later Nancy parked in her driveway. As she was about to insert her key in the front lock, the door was opened from inside. *Laura Pendleton, wan and disheveled, stared at the young detective!*

"Laura!" Nancy gasped. She could hardly believe her eyes.

"Hello, Nancy," her friend said, as Hannah Gruen came into view, walking slowly on her crutches.

"Come in, Nancy," the housekeeper invited

urgently. "Laura's been waiting for you over an hour. She's terribly upset—"

The three went into the living room and Nancy sat down on the couch beside the visitor. Before Nancy could ask why she was in River Heights, Laura burst into tears.

"Oh, I'm so unhappy!" she sobbed. "That's why I ran away!"

Nancy gently stroked Laura's hair and waited for the hysterical girl to calm down. Then she said quietly, "Tell me everything that has happened since I saw you last."

Slowly Laura started to speak. After Nancy and Helen had left the hotel suite, Mr. Aborn said he had to attend to some business for a short while. He had left the hotel. Meanwhile, Laura and Mrs. Aborn had checked out and waited for the guardian in his blue sedan, which was parked in the hotel lot.

"Where did Mr. Aborn go?" asked Nancy.

"I don't know, but when he met us a short while later he was carrying a brief case. As we started toward Melrose Lake, Mrs. Aborn asked what I had done with Mother's jewelry. When I said it was in my handbag she asked me to give it to her for safekeeping. I said I would when we got home."

"Then you *did* go directly to Melrose Lake?" Nancy questioned.

"Yes," Laura replied. She hesitated, then went on with her story. "The Aborns showed me to my room and I started to unpack.

"I found I needed more hangers," the girl went on, "but when I went to the door to ask Mrs. Aborn for them, I discovered it was locked on the outside."

"Locked!" Hannah gasped and Nancy was shocked.

Laura nodded. "I was so frightened," she said, "that at first I didn't know what to do. Then I heard voices coming from the Aborns' room. I lay down on the floor so I could hear them better and listened.

"Marian Aborn said, 'What did you lock her in for—she doesn't know anything!' and my guardian replied, 'Not yet, but she's a smart kid. See if you can gain her confidence and get hold of the jewels.' "

As Laura paused, a terrible thought came to Nancy. Were the Aborns *thieves?* But they could not be, she argued, if Marie Pendleton had trusted the couple to take care of her daughter. "And besides, I gather the Donnells think they are nice people." Aloud she asked, "What happened next?"

"I thought I must have heard them wrong," the auburn-haired girl said slowly, "but I suddenly remembered Mother telling me always to take good care of her jewelry. So I took it from my handbag and hid it underneath the mattress of the bed.

"Just as I finished doing this, the door to my room opened. Mrs. Aborn stood there, looking very friendly. She offered to help unpack my bags, and admired several dresses as I hung them in the closet—"

"And then—" Nancy pressed.

Laura said that she and Mrs. Aborn had prepared a tasty dinner, then she and the couple had watched television for a while.

"Just before we went upstairs to bed, Mrs. Aborn said it would be a good idea for me to put my mother's jewels in the wall safe in the living room. I agreed and said that I would give them to her in the morning."

"What was Mrs. Aborn's reaction to this?" Hannah asked.

"Oh, both she and her husband became very angry. They said that apparently I didn't trust them to take care of a few insignificant gems, while they in turn had the responsibility of caring for a penniless orphan! Oh, Nancy, I thought Mother had a lot of money! Mrs. Aborn yelled at me and said I was ungrateful and a big burden to them. They were sorry they had ever agreed to take me!

"I can't explain how I felt," Laura went on, her

hands shaking with nervousness. "I was just numb. Then I burst into tears and rushed to my room."

Laura said that finally she had fallen asleep and awakened this morning to find she was again locked in.

"At eight o'clock Mrs. Aborn opened the door, acting very friendly, and said breakfast was ready in the kitchen."

"Was anything said about last night?" Nancy asked.

Laura said no, that the Aborns had acted as though nothing had happened. "But a strange thing occurred after breakfast," Laura stated. "Mr. Aborn took a small package from the refrigerator and left the house, saying he would be back later. Before he went he said I would be sorry if I didn't co-operate with them!"

"I presume he meant to hand over the jewels," Hannah guessed, and Laura nodded.

"I knew then that I had to leave their house and also get word to Nancy. While Mrs. Aborn was emptying the rubbish I tried to use the phone, but she caught me and twisted my arm, then hung up the receiver!"

"You see, I was right, Hannah!" Nancy exclaimed, and told Laura her theory about the call.

"Were you locked up again?" Hannah asked.

Laura explained that before Mrs. Aborn could do this she had run past her and barricaded herself inside the bedroom, not wanting the jewels to be unguarded. At that moment the doorbell had rung. Apparently Mrs. Aborn had not answered it, for the woman had kept quiet for a long while on the first floor.

"So I quickly took my handbag and the jewels, and climbed down a trellis outside my window," Laura said. "Once I was on the detour I was lucky enough to get a ride to the highway and there I caught a bus to River Heights. I took a taxi to your house."

As Laura sat back with an exhausted sigh, Hannah stood up. "You're worn out, dear," the housekeeper said. "I'm going to get you a cup of hot tea and you're not to say another word until you've drunk it!"

With that, she bustled out of the room and returned shortly with a small tray on which was a cup of hot tea and a piece of toast. By the time Laura had finished the snack, color had returned to her cheeks and she looked more relaxed.

"I wonder if we should report your experience to the police," Nancy mused.

"What could we tell them?" Laura quavered.

"That's the point," Nancy continued. "We could tell them that the Aborns tried to get your jewels, but of course they would deny it all. It would be their word against yours."

"And I don't have definite proof!" Laura said dejectedly.

Nancy patted the girl's hand. "We'll do everything we can to help you, Laura. You've really had a terrible experience, you poor girl."

"Nancy, you're a real friend," Laura said. Tears came into her eyes. "Mr. Aborn is my legal guardian—I saw the papers—but what am I going to do?"

"You'll stay with us," Hannah said quickly, "and when Mr. Drew comes home he'll know how to handle the situation."

Nancy was quiet, but she was doing a lot of figuring. Something mysterious was going on at Melrose Lake. She intended to find out for herself what it was.

CHAPTER IX

A Valuable Inheritance

IF IT had been possible Nancy would have started out for Melrose Lake at once, but she felt that Laura needed her. Besides, there was a job to do for her father at the Browns' barbecue next day.

"Helping Dad comes first," Nancy decided.

Laura spoke again of her mother's affairs. "She used to say I'd always be financially independent if anything happened to her."

"We'll find out," Nancy said, and then took Laura upstairs so she might shower and rest.

In the meantime, Nancy selected some of her own clothes for the visitor. When she appeared at the dinner table, Hannah declared that Laura looked pretty as a picture and much more relaxed.

"I am—thanks to both of you," their guest said gratefully.

When the meal was finished the two girls sat out on the Drews' porch. To cheer up her guest, Nancy told Laura of her funny experience with the French poodles, while trying to get volunteers for the youth center. The young detective did not mention her real reason for calling at the apartment.

Laura giggled. "I wish I could have been with you," she said. "Tell me, Nancy, have you any souvenirs of the mysteries you've solved?"

"Two trophies." Nancy displayed a mantel clock and a valuable silver urn. Laughingly she told Laura that her father often said she would have the house cluttered before she finished her career!

Just then the telephone rang and Hannah called from upstairs that Mr. Drew was on the line. Nancy hurried to talk with him.

"Nancy, I've come across some evidence that indicates Mr. Hamilton, or some person working for him in the trust department, was behind the security thefts. A detective is tailing Hamilton, and if he tries to leave town, the Monroe police will be notified."

"How about the others in his department?" Nancy asked.

"They're being watched, too, but not so steadily. Of course we don't want to arrest an innocent man."

Nancy said she hoped the guilty person would make a misstep soon so the case might be solved, and told her father what she had learned of the River Heights suspects since she had seen him.

He suggested that she keep trying to contact the Dowds. "And that reminds me," the lawyer said. "You can forget about Mr. Herbert Brown being suspicious." He explained that Brown was a personal friend of the bank president's and had been cleared.

Nancy was relieved to hear this. "I'll keep trying to get in touch with the Dowds," she promised.

Next, she told her father about Laura Pendleton's flight from the Aborns' home. "Do you think we should report her experience with them to the police?" she asked.

Mr. Drew said no, that so far the two girls had only their suspicions of the couple's dishonesty, even though Laura had overheard them talking about her jewels. "You need some concrete evidence before calling in the authorities," he stated.

"I thought I'd run up to Melrose Lake and do some sleuthing," she said.

"All right, but keep out of danger," he warned. "I'll be eager to hear what you find out. We'll have a conference when I get home and decide what we can do for Laura."

"Thanks, Dad." A moment later they bade each other good night and hung up.

As the teen-aged detective started for the porch, she had an inspiration. It was not essential now for her to meet Herbert Brown. If Don Cameron would agree to take Laura as a substitute to the barbecue party, it would leave Nancy free to go to Melrose Lake the next day!

"I'll ask Don if he'd mind. If he does—well, that's that."

Hopefully Nancy dialed the Cameron house. Don answered and the girl detective told him the problem.

"Wow! A real mystery!" he remarked. "If I didn't know what sleuthing means to you, Nancy, I'd say you were just trying to brush me off. But you have me feeling sorry for this Laura Pendleton, too. Okay. If she's willing to go with me, I'll be glad to take her. But I'm sure sorry you can't make it. See you another time."

"Thanks, Don. I shan't forget this. Of course if Laura won't go, I'll keep the date. 'By now."

As Nancy walked toward the porch, she smilingly crossed her fingers, hoping that Laura would agree to the plan. Stepping outside, Nancy asked, "How would you like to go to a barbecue tomorrow, Laura?"

The girl's face glowed with anticipation. "It would be fun!" she exclaimed. "Where, Nancy?"

When the plan was explained, Laura said, "Oh, but I don't want to take your date away from you."

"Don and I have already arranged everything," Nancy assured her. Then she told of her desire to do some sleuthing at Melrose Lake.

At once Laura said she was afraid to have Nancy go to the Aborns' home. "There's no telling what my guardian might do to you," she said fearfully. "He has a terrible temper, and if he learns you're helping me—"

"He won't learn that," Nancy said determinedly.

Reluctantly Laura agreed to Nancy's whole scheme. "But if anything should happen to you, I— I'd just want to die!" she declared.

Before the girls went to bed, Hannah suggested that Laura's jewelry be put into the wall safe in Mr. Drew's study.

"Dad, Hannah, and I are the only persons who know the combination," Nancy told Laura.

"It would be a good idea," the brown-eyed girl replied. "First, I'd like to show you some of Mother's treasures. She gave them to me before her last illness."

"Do you have this in writing?" Hannah asked.

"Yes, I do. Why?"

"Then the jewelry wouldn't be part of your

mother's estate," Mrs. Gruen answered, "and there'd be no tax on it."

Laura took a package from her handbag and opened it. She displayed a string of priceless matched pearls, a gorgeous diamond clip and earrings, several jeweled pins set with rubies, pearls, and emeralds, and six rings, including one with a brilliant star sapphire.

Nancy and Hannah were astounded. "Why, this is the most beautiful collection I've ever seen!" Nancy exclaimed. She pointed to a ring set with a perfect aquamarine. "I love this!"

Laura smiled. "That was Mother's favorite," she said. "My father gave it to her on their first wedding anniversary."

"Thank goodness your guardian didn't find these things!" Hannah declared.

Finally the jewels were put into the safe and everyone went to bed.

Nancy awoke at seven o'clock the next morning. After taking a shower, she decided to wear a forest-green cotton dress and flat-heeled brown play shoes.

Laura was still sleeping when Nancy joined Mrs. Gruen at breakfast. The housekeeper was using a cane.

"My ankle feels almost as good as new," Hannah announced. "I've discarded the crutches."

Nancy was delighted to hear this. As they ate, she and the housekeeper talked about the young sleuth's trip.

"I'll worry about you every second until you return home," Mrs. Gruen declared. "If you're not here by ten thirty, I'll notify the police."

Nancy grinned. "I'll try to be here by suppertime. If not, I'll call you."

A short while later Nancy battled the early-morning traffic through the city. Reaching the outskirts, she took the road to Melrose Lake.

"Poor Laura," she thought, wondering what the day would disclose about the girl's strange guardian and his wife.

If Laura were really penniless, maybe the man thought he had a legitimate right to take and sell the jewelry for the girl's support. But his wife had bragged about having plenty of money to take care of their ward.

After a time Nancy came to the Melrose Lake detour. Laura had told her there was a sign marked "Eagle Rock" in front of the lane leading to her guardian's property.

Presently Nancy approached the spot where the pine tree had fallen. Fortunately, it had been removed.

She drove more slowly, afraid of inadvertently missing the Eagle Rock sign. Then, sighting the turnoff, Nancy left the detour.

"This ring was Mother's favorite," Laura said

She had gone but a few hundred feet along the Aborns' road when she decided it might be safer to walk. After parking along the side of the roadway, she started off. In a few minutes Nancy suddenly caught sight of a man walking rapidly through the woods. He carried a small bundle under his arm.

"Jacob Aborn!" she thought, recognizing his profile and the peculiar stoop of his shoulders.

Nancy recalled Laura's story of her guardian taking a small package from the refrigerator and leaving the house with it. What was in the bundle and where was he taking it?

"I'm going to find out!" Nancy declared. Without hesitation, she quietly plunged into the thicket. Following at a safe distance she managed to keep the man in sight.

"He doesn't seem to be worried about being followed," Nancy thought. "He must not have heard my car when I turned into the lane." She continued her musing. "I'm glad I wore this green dress. It's good camouflage!"

Just then a twig crackled under her foot, breaking the stillness of the woods. Jacob Aborn turned and looked back, frowning. He stood a minute, listening intently. Only by ducking quickly behind a large bush had Nancy avoided detection.

"I'd better be more careful if I don't want to get caught," she warned herself.

As the man continued through the forest Nancy followed, painstakingly avoiding twigs or loose stones. She kept well behind him.

"Wouldn't it be a joke on me if he's just a bird watcher!" She giggled at the thought. "And maybe that package has his lunch in it!"

Laughing to herself, Nancy picked her way through the woods as she trailed Laura Pendleton's guardian. Suddenly he disappeared behind a clump of high blueberry bushes. Nancy hurried forward. When she reached the spot the girl detective looked about in all directions.

"Which way did he go?" she asked herself.

Jacob Aborn seemed to have vanished into thin air!

CHAPTER X

The Danger Sign

ALERT for possible danger, Nancy moved forward with the utmost caution. It occurred to her that possibly Aborn had become aware he was being followed and had hidden in the bushes to watch the pursuer.

"I'll walk into a trap!" Nancy thought with alarm. "Mr. Aborn will learn I'm spying on him and everything will be ruined!"

With great caution she moved from one bush and tree to another. Laura's guardian was not hiding behind any of them.

"That's funny," Nancy said to herself.

She examined the ground, almost expecting there would be a cave or secret tunnel in the vicinity. But the earth was firm and in many places very rocky.

Finally Nancy came to a tiny clearing. On the far side attached to a large oak was a crudely printed wooden sign which read:

PRIVATE PROPERTY. KEEP OUT. DANGER!

"I wonder if that's where Mr. Aborn went and why?" the young detective asked herself.

She waited several minutes, then decided to cross the clearing. She was not stopped. Entering the woods again, she saw a dilapidated shack. The windows had been boarded up, and the roof sagged.

"One good gust of wind would blow the place over," Nancy said to herself.

She stepped from among the bushes and stood in the shadow of the trees, curiously surveying the building. Was it possible that Jacob Aborn had entered it?

Nancy's eyes searched the ground for footprints. Directly ahead, in the soft earth, she saw the fresh mark of a man's shoe. Instantly her suspicions were confirmed.

Jacob Aborn had come this way!

"I'll just have a look at this shack," the young sleuth decided.

After quickly glancing about to make certain she was not being watched, Nancy hurried forward. Tiptoeing across the front porch, she quietly tried the door. It was locked. Nancy walked around to the rear door and found that it likewise was securely fastened.

Although disappointed, Nancy was unwilling to give up. Making a complete circuit of the shack, she saw a window from which several boards had fallen. It was too high for her to peer through. Nancy returned to the rear of the building to get an old box that she had seen. She set it beneath the window and mounted it.

Pressing her face against the glass, she gazed inside. The room, apparently a kitchen, was bare of furniture and covered with dust and cobwebs.

"I wish I could get inside," Nancy thought.

She was about to climb down from the box when a strange feeling came over her. Though she had heard no sound, Nancy sensed that unfriendly eyes were watching her every move.

Before she could turn around and look over her shoulder, a coarse, angry voice barked into her ear:

"What are you doing here, young lady?"

Nancy wheeled and faced Jacob Aborn!

With as much dignity as she could muster, the girl detective stepped to the ground and regarded the man with composure. His eyes burned with rage.

"I was merely curious," Nancy replied. "And may I ask why *you* are here?"

"Yes, I'll tell you. I'm looking for my ward."

"You mean Laura Pendleton?"

"Yes. Who else? I thought maybe she was hiding here. But nobody's in the shack."

"Why in the world would Laura hide in this ramshackle place?" Nancy asked, trying to show as much surprise as possible.

"Search me," Mr. Aborn said, then added angrily, his eyes boring Nancy's, "Laura has run away!"

"*Run away?*" Nancy repeated.

"Yes. Yesterday. I'll tell you something about that ward of mine—" A crafty light came into Jacob Aborn's eyes as he went on, "At times she acts unbalanced—thinks folks don't treat her right."

"Indeed?" said Nancy, pretending to be shocked.

By now Laura's guardian had calmed down. When he spoke again he was once more the pleasant man Nancy had met at the Montewago Hotel.

"It's for Laura's own good that she ought to return home," he said. "Mrs. Aborn is dreadfully upset. She loves Laura just like a mother. Miss Drew, have you heard from Laura by any chance?"

Nancy was on her guard. "Why should I hear from her?" she countered. "We never met until that accident on the lake and she came to rescue my friend Helen and me."

Mr. Aborn did not pursue the subject. Instead, he said, "Laura's a nervous, high-strung girl. Why, do you know she locked herself in her room the entire time she was with us—wouldn't eat, or even let us try to help her?"

"Terrible!" Nancy said, pretending to be shocked. "Laura does need help."

Secretly Nancy felt that Jacob Aborn was telling this version of the locked-door story to cover his own actions, in case they came to light.

"Have you notified the police, Mr. Aborn?" she asked, probing for further information.

"We have a private detective working on the matter," the man stated. "We don't want any bad publicity because of dear Marie Pendleton's memory. She entrusted Laura to my care because she knew how much my wife and I would love the girl."

Nancy suddenly was finding it hard to concentrate on what Mr. Aborn was saying. Was she wrong or had she heard a sound inside the shack?

"This is very strange," she told herself. "But I don't dare pursue the subject or Mr. Aborn will really become suspicious." Aloud she said, "I certainly hope Laura is all right. Well, I must go now. I have some friends here at Melrose Lake I plan to call on." She paused, then added lightly, "In fact, I believe you know them, Mr. Aborn— the Donnell family."

The man looked startled, then recovered himself. "Oh, yes. Fine family. Say hello to them for me, please."

Nancy promised that she would. Since Mr. Aborn made no move to accompany her, she said good-by and walked rapidly back to the spot where her convertible was parked.

As Nancy climbed into it, she cast a glance over her shoulder. There was no sign of Mr. Aborn. Had he gone into the shack? Was someone there? Had he been delivering packages to the person?

Nancy started the car's motor and backed out to the main road. As she drove along, her thoughts were entirely on Mr. Aborn. She had no doubt but that the man had been lying about Laura's behavior.

"I must find out more about that man," Nancy decided.

Reaching the highway, she stopped at a service station, had the gas tank of her car filled, and asked directions to the Donnell home. The attendant told her how to reach the place, and a short while later Nancy drew up before a lovely redwood house located well off the road.

She got out and rang the front doorbell. There was no answer. Nancy walked around to the back of the house. A gardener was there, trimming the flower beds.

"Howdy, miss!" the elderly man hailed her. "Looking for the Donnells?"

"Yes. Are they away?" Nancy inquired.

"Yep. They're visiting relatives in Crescent Gardens 'til tonight. Any message?"

Nancy said no, that she would call again, and thanked the man. As she drove away Nancy was disappointed that she had been unable to pick up any information regarding Mr. Aborn.

"I don't want to leave Melrose Lake until I have learned *something* to help Laura," she thought. "Mr. Aborn may trace her whereabouts to our home and force Laura to return with him before Dad gets back to town. I suppose he has a legal right to do it."

At last an idea came to Nancy. "I'll go to one of the hotels on the lake and engage a room. Then, after it gets dark, I'll do a little more investigating."

Fortunately, Nancy always carried an overnight case in her car trunk. It contained pajamas and robe, two changes of clothing, toilet articles, and, this time of year, a bathing suit.

Presently she saw a large white building ahead of her. Its green lawn sloped down to the sandy beach. On the stone pillar at the side of the driveway was the sign: *Beach Cliff Hotel*.

"I think I'll stop here," Nancy decided. She parked her car and entered the pleasant lobby. In

a few minutes she had registered and been taken
to a comfortable room overlooking the lake.

"I'll telephone home," Nancy said to herself,
"and tell Hannah where I am."

As Nancy placed the call, a chilling thought suddenly popped into her mind. Perhaps the detective whom Aborn had engaged had already traced
the runaway girl, and knew Nancy had not told
all she knew about Laura. If so, Nancy might find
that her guest had already been whisked away
from the Drew home!

CHAPTER XI

Trapped!

WHEN Hannah Gruen answered the telephone at the Drew residence, Nancy at once asked, "Is Laura all right?"

"Why, of course," Hannah answered in surprise. "She's upstairs setting her hair for the party this afternoon."

"Well, tell her to be very careful," Nancy urged. "Mr. Aborn has a detective looking for her!"

"Oh dear!" exclaimed Mrs. Gruen. "And when will you be home, Nancy?"

The young detective explained where she was and that she planned to stay at Melrose Lake and do more sleuthing.

"I think I may be on the trail of something big."

"I don't like the idea of you prowling around the Aborns' home in the dead of night," the housekeeper objected.

"I'll be careful," Nancy promised. "I may even get home tonight."

"Well, all right," Hannah consented reluctantly. "By the way, Nancy, I had a repairman fix the window in Mr. Drew's study this morning, and also requested the police to keep a lookout for anything suspicious going on in this neighborhood."

"Wonderful!" Nancy said, feeling relieved. "Any more news?"

"Everything's quiet here," Hannah reported. "And Laura seems happy."

Laura came to speak to Nancy and was alarmed when she heard that a detective was looking for her. "But I won't go back to those awful Aborns! They can't make me! If they try it, I'll—I'll run right to the police!"

"That's a good idea," said Nancy. "By the way, I'd like to do some sleuthing at the Aborn house. I may want to get inside without ringing the bell." The young sleuth chuckled. "Since it's now your house too, may I have permission to go in and look around?"

"You certainly may," said Laura with a giggle. "If no doors are unlocked, try my bedroom window. I left it open a crack and there's a sturdy rose trellis right alongside it."

"Terrific!" said Nancy elatedly.

After she completed the call, Nancy went to

the hotel coffee shop for a hearty lunch. Since it was now almost one thirty, the room was empty.

After eating, Nancy put on her bathing suit and wandered down to the beach. A boy in attendance gave her a towel and Nancy stretched out on the sand, unaware of the steadfast glance of a couple hidden behind a large green-and-white striped umbrella not far away. They nodded to each other, then when Nancy was not looking, they quickly left the beach.

"Guess we're safe," the woman muttered. "She's here to stay and have a good time."

As the strong rays of the sun beat down on the unsuspecting girl, she rehearsed her plan for the evening. When it was dark she would visit both Jacob Aborn's home and also the shack in the woods, if time permitted.

"I'll miss Dad's call tonight," Nancy reflected.

Standing up half an hour later, Nancy put on her bathing cap and walked to the water. She stuck her toe in. The lake water felt icy cold, and Nancy noticed that there were more people on the beach than in swimming. Nevertheless, she waded out to where it was deep enough to make a surface dive and plunged in. Once she was wet, the water was invigorating.

After swimming for a while, Nancy came back to her beach towel and dried off. Then she returned to her room, showered, and slept for two hours, realizing that the rest would give her more endurance for the evening ahead.

Awakening at six o'clock, Nancy put on the simple black cotton dress from her suitcase and pumps. After brushing her hair until it snapped with electricity, she was ready for supper.

"What will it be this evening, miss?" asked the friendly waitress.

Nancy selected steak, a baked potato, and tossed salad, then sat back to enjoy the soft dinner music playing in the background. The orchestra was in an adjoining lounge.

Nearby diners regarded the lone girl with interest, for the prospect of the daring adventure had brought a becoming flush to her cheeks.

"If I'm wrong in suspecting Jacob Aborn of being dishonest," thought Nancy, "then I guess I'd better give up sleuthing!"

Upon leaving the dining room an hour later, she lingered on the porch for a few minutes, watching couples dance. As a red-haired young man began to walk toward Nancy with an invitation in his eyes for her to dance, she hastily went to her room.

Chuckling to herself, Nancy said aloud, "Romance and detective work won't mix tonight!" Then she changed to walking shoes, sweater, and skirt.

The moment it became dark enough for her

purpose, Nancy left the hotel in her car. As she drew near the Aborns' lane a short while later, she turned the convertible off the road and ran it into a clump of bushes where it would not be seen.

Switching off the engine and locking the doors, Nancy started down the lane leading to the house, holding her flashlight securely. She found the windows of the house dark.

"The Aborns are out, I guess," she told herself. "Well, that means I can do some looking around."

Circling the structure cautiously, Nancy noted that the second-floor wing, where the bedrooms apparently were located, was in the back. She found the trellis easily.

"I'll try the doors first," Nancy decided, and darted to the front. Gently turning the handle, she found the door locked.

An investigation of two other doors revealed that they, too, were securely fastened.

"I guess I'll have to climb after all," Nancy said to herself.

As quietly as possible, she climbed the trellis. It wobbled and creaked a little but did not give way. When Nancy reached the window ledge of Laura's bedroom, she found to her delight that the window raised easily. She crawled through and switched on her flashlight.

As Nancy tiptoed across the room, which was in

disorder, she heard a noise. Halting, she listened. A car was approaching the house. Looking out the window she could barely make out the figures of a man and a woman who alighted. Who were they and what should Nancy do?

"I'll stay right here," she determined.

As Nancy waited tensely she realized someone was walking up the stairs. Quickly Nancy closed the window without a sound. As she looked around for a hiding place she saw a closet, and darted inside it, switching off her flashlight. Crouched in a far corner behind some of Laura's dresses, Nancy scarcely dared to breathe.

The door to the room was opened a moment later and the boudoir lamps switched on. Cautiously Nancy peered out through the keyhole in the closet door. She saw Jacob Aborn!

The man went directly to Laura's dressing table. Apparently he had not heard Nancy, for he did not glance toward the closet.

Ruthlessly he jerked out drawers from the dressing table and emptied their contents upon the bed. As he surveyed the assortment of tiny bottles, boxes, and other paraphernalia, Laura's guardian gave a disgusted grunt.

"Last place to look!" he said, as if addressing someone out in the hall, probably his wife. "Guess Laura really took the jewels with her. Well, I'll soon have them back!"

Nancy's heart leaped. There was no longer any doubt in her mind as to the character of this man. She was now certain that his sole interest in Laura was to get possession of her property! Only the girl's opportune escape from the house had prevented him from seizing the valuable jewelry collection!

"Laura's mother couldn't have known his true character, or she wouldn't have entrusted her daughter to Aborn's care," Nancy pondered.

Her thoughts came to an abrupt end as the man moved toward the closet. Fearfully, Nancy ducked down behind Laura's dresses again and fervently hoped that she would not be discovered.

Suddenly, as Nancy's legs began to grow cramped, the closet door was jerked violently open. Jacob Aborn looked in!

CHAPTER XII

A Black Abyss

As JACOB ABORN stared into the closet where Nancy was hiding, the girl detective wished wildly that she were invisible. There was no telling what harm the man might inflict if he saw her!

"He has such a violent temper," Nancy realized.

But Aborn's glance did not stray to the dress section. Instead, he reached up for two large suitcases which were on a shelf above the clothes. He set them on the floor outside and shut the closet door.

Beads of perspiration trickled down Nancy's neck as she relaxed. Presently she heard the man leave the room and shut the hall door with a loud bang.

Nancy waited a moment, then left her hiding

place. "I suppose I'd better leave while I can," she advised herself.

But running away from a chance to pick up a clue was not in Nancy's nature. As she heard Laura's guardian descending the stairs to the first floor, she became aware of a woman's voice somewhere below. Nancy decided, "I'll stay and see what's going on."

Before leaving Laura's bedroom she gave it a final searching look and shook her head, puzzled. The room was one which Nancy would be happy to call her own. The feminine furnishings and good colonial pieces showed evidence of discerning taste. They did not fit the Aborns' character. Perhaps an interior decorator had planned it!

"One could believe from this room that the Aborns really wanted Laura," Nancy pondered.

It just did not make sense. Many criminals, Nancy knew, laid the groundwork to lull any suspicion on the part of their victim, then cornered him. But Laura had not even been settled in her new home when the Aborns had begun to persecute her.

Soundlessly Nancy opened the bedroom door, and keeping her flashlight low to the floor, tiptoed along the carpeted hall. Step by step, she edged down the stairway to the floor below. Here there was no sign of activity but Nancy saw a light shining through louvered doors to her left.

"That's probably the kitchen. The Aborns are in there," she thought.

A moment later the woman said, "Here's the combination. I'll pack this stuff while you open the safe."

Quickly Nancy stole into the living room and hastily ducked out of sight behind a large sofa. She was just in time. One of the louvered doors opened and Laura's guardian came into the living room carrying a suitcase. He flicked on a table lamp.

Near it hung the small oil painting of a ship. Aborn lifted it from the wall and set the picture against a chair.

Nancy's eyes widened as she saw that the painting had concealed a wall safe. Aborn deftly twirled the dial to the left, then several notches to the right, and back to the left again. He swung the safe door open.

With a grunt of satisfaction, the man removed several packages of bank notes and some papers which looked like stock certificates. Mr. Aborn chortled and called to his wife:

"When we get the rest of these cashed, you and I will be set for life—thanks to Laura and a few others."

Nancy, startled, almost gave herself away. So Laura did have a sizable inheritance other than the jewelry! But how had the securities reached the safe? Had Aborn brought them here or was he stealing them from someone else? Nancy felt more confused by the moment.

As her thoughts raced, Aborn replaced the loose papers in the safe and closed it. Then he put the money and securities into the suitcase. Giving a tired yawn, he switched off the lamp and left the room.

"Guess I'll turn in," he called to his wife. "Got to be up early tomorrow and get Fred. You ready?"

"Yes."

Marian Aborn came from the kitchen carrying the other bag. Together the couple ascended the stairs. Nancy heard a bedroom door above close.

"Now I must get the police," the girl detective thought.

She paused for several seconds, after coming from behind the couch, to stretch her cramped limbs. "I'd better go out the front door," she decided. "The bedrooms don't overlook that."

Noiselessly Nancy slipped outside and started for her hidden car. Then a temptation came to her. "Why don't I investigate that shack in the woods first? I may have an even bigger story to tell the police! I'll do it!"

Taking a deep breath of air, Nancy hurried toward the path leading to the dilapidated building. Had she been right about having heard some-

one inside? Was he a friend or an enemy of
Aborn's? Were the packages being carried there
and what did they contain? Loot?

"Maybe just food," Nancy concluded. "But being taken to whom?"

Beaming her flashlight on the ground, the
young detective soon picked up the trail she had
taken earlier in the day. It was quiet and eerie as
she stumbled along the uneven ground. Nancy became apprehensive once or twice as she heard
scuffling noises of forest creatures in the under-
brush, but went on.

"I wish Dad were here now," she thought fervently.

Nancy reached the shack without mishap and
paused in front of it. A sixth sense seemed to tell
her there was someone inside who needed help.
No person would stay in such a place unless
forced to.

"This is no time for me to hesitate," she told
herself.

As Nancy moved toward the rear of the tumble-
down building, she glanced at her flashlight and
was alarmed to see that it was beginning to grow
dim.

"Just my luck when I need it the most!"

In an attempt to save the battery, Nancy
switched off the light. As her eyes became accustomed to the darkness, she moved toward the

window she had looked through earlier that day. Appraising it, the young sleuth realized that the window ledge was too high from the ground for her to climb through unassisted, even when standing on the box.

Undaunted, she began to examine the other windows. On the south side of the shack she found one which opened from the rickety porch. It was boarded up.

"This is my entry," Nancy determined.

She began searching the yard for something with which to pry off the boards, and finally found a stout stick. Nancy began wedging it between the boards with all her might.

The first board offered stubborn resistance. Then, with a groan and a squeak, it gave way. The remaining boards were removed with less difficulty.

To Nancy's joy, the window was unlocked! Pushing it up, she beamed her flashlight inside. The room beyond was bare and quiet as a tomb.

"Well, here comes Nancy Drew, housebreaker and spy!" Nancy thought with amused determination. "It's certain now no one lives here."

When she was halfway through the window the young sleuth hesitated without knowing just why. She glanced back over her shoulder. A queer sensation made Nancy quiver as she turned searching eyes toward the woods.

"How silly!" she scolded herself. "No one's there. It's just nerves."

Bravely Nancy swung herself through the window. Hastily she moved toward an adjoining room, noting that her flashlight was growing dimmer. Soon she would be left in total darkness! She must hurry!

Her light revealed a small room, also empty, its walls and floor dusty from long lack of any occupant's care. Nancy was disappointed to find nothing of interest.

"I'd better leave and drive to police headquarters," she thought.

Just then Nancy's flashlight revealed a trap door in the floor. Quickly she moved over toward it. But she had taken only a few steps when an unusual sound arrested her attention. Had she heard a board creak behind her, or was it a night sound from the woods?

After hesitating a second, Nancy again started for the trap door. As she reached down to grasp the ring in it, her body became tense.

This time there was no mistake. She had heard a peculiar sound which seemed to come from beneath the floor.

"It sounded like a groan!" Nancy decided. She felt cold all over.

Someone was imprisoned in the cellar! Who? And why?

As Nancy tugged at the ring, another idea came to her. This might be a trap laid for her!

"Oh, what should I do?" she thought, hesitating. There was still time to run away from danger.

But the fear that some person was in distress gave her the courage to open the trap door. As it swung upward, Nancy saw before her a flight of stone steps, leading down into complete darkness. A gust of damp, musty air struck her in the face and momentarily repulsed her.

Nancy glanced nervously at her flashlight. The battery could not last much longer. Already the light was so weak that she could barely see the steps in front of her. Did she dare investigate the cellar?

"It won't take long," she thought.

She descended the steps and came to a landing. The rest of the stairway went toward the left. Nancy peered anxiously into the black abyss below.

To her horror, she saw a man stretched out full length on a bench. His face was turned upward and Nancy caught a full glimpse of the countenance.

He was Jacob Aborn!

CHAPTER XIII

An Actor's Ruse

SPELLBOUND, Nancy stood like a stone image, gazing down into the face of Jacob Aborn. How had the man reached the bungalow ahead of her? What was he doing sleeping in the musty cellar of the old shack?

As these thoughts flashed through Nancy's mind, the beam of her flashlight flickered again. Then it went out, leaving her in total darkness.

Sheer panic took possession of the girl detective. Something very strange was going on! She must not be caught in a trap!

Turning, she gave a low cry and stumbled up the stairway and toward the window through which she had entered. Her flight was abruptly checked as she banged one foot on something metallic that moved ahead of her. In a second she smelled kerosene.

"A lantern!" she decided.

The thought of a light gave her hope. She felt around and discovered an old-time oil lantern.

Collecting her wits, she stopped and listened for any sounds of pursuit. There were none. The shack appeared as deserted and silent as before.

"I'm sure that was Jacob Aborn down in the cellar," Nancy thought in perplexity. "I didn't imagine it. But how did he get here so fast? After I left his house I didn't waste much time."

Suddenly an amazing thought came to Nancy. Was the man she had seen by chance a brother, even a twin, of Jacob Aborn? He might be honest and Jacob had found him in the way!

"I'm going to find out!" Nancy declared excitedly.

Eagerly she reached into the pocket of her dress, recalling that at dinner she had taken a pack of matches from the hotel dining table for her souvenir collection. Good! The pack was still there!

Striking a match she was pleased to discover that the lantern was half full of oil. Someone had used it recently, for the glass was clean. Nancy lighted the wick and a flame spurted up. Carrying the lantern, she returned to the trap door.

Suddenly, from below, Nancy heard a moan of pain. This was followed by a pitiful cry of "Help!"

"That settles it," the worried girl thought.

As she descended the steps, the lantern's flick-

From below came a pitiful cry of "Help!"

ering glow revealed that the cellar was dungeon-like, with solid stone walls and no windows.

She held the light high above the figure on the bench. A man, deathly pale, was lying where she had first seen him.

But he was not Laura's guardian!

"There's certainly a startling resemblance, though," Nancy thought, her heart filled with pity for this unfortunate stranger.

Dropping to her knees, she felt his pulse. It was faint but regular.

"He's just unconscious," she told herself in relief.

At the same time, Nancy saw with horror a large chain around the man's waist. It was attached to the prisoner in such a way that it allowed him some freedom of motion and yet held him captive. Was Jacob Aborn responsible for this atrocity? Nancy wondered angrily.

"I must do something to revive this man," she decided, "and get him away from here."

Picking up the lantern, Nancy mounted the cellar steps two at a time. She headed for a small sink in one corner of the room above, where she had seen a pump.

After a search through the cupboard she at last found a battered tin cup. Quickly pumping water into it, she returned to the cellar.

Nancy wet her handkerchief and applied it

gently to the prisoner's forehead. Then she sprinkled a little of the water on his face and chafed his
wrists. The man stirred slightly and moaned.

As she gazed anxiously into his face, Nancy wondered how she could have mistaken him for Jacob
Aborn. Although the two men were of the same
age, and had similar facial characteristics, the
prisoner was gaunt and thin. His features, con-
trary to Mr. Aborn's, were gentle and relaxed.

Now Nancy saw that the man was slowly regaining consciousness. As his eyes fluttered open he
cried "Help!" feebly, then stared into Nancy's
face, amazed.

"Help has come," Nancy said quietly.

The man attempted to raise himself to a sitting
position with Nancy's aid. "Didn't—think—help
—would—ever come," he murmured. Then he
saw the cup in Nancy's hand and asked for water.

Nancy steadied the cup while he drank. Finally
the man leaned against the wall. "First water I've
had in twenty-four hours," he said more clearly.

The young sleuth was horrified. She introduced
herself, then asked, "Who are you—and who did
this terrible thing to you?"

A bitter expression passed over the prisoner's
face. "I'm Jacob Aborn," he said. "A crook by the
name of Stumpy Dowd took over my house, imprisoned me here, and somehow or other arranged
for my new ward, Laura Pendleton, to come to my

home earlier than she was expected. Yesterday he
told me that he had the girl's inheritance in his
possession—and showed bonds to prove it."

"You're Jacob Aborn!" Nancy repeated, as
the prisoner, exhausted by these words, leaned
against the wall.

Quickly Nancy's mind flashed back to everything that had happened since she had met
Laura. The puzzling questions that had bothered
her about the girl's guardian now became clear.
Most of all, it was a relief to know that the person to whom Marie Pendleton had entrusted her
daughter's care was not a criminal.

Equally important, Nancy realized that Stephen Dowd—alias Stumpy—used his talent as an
actor and skill with make-up to fool other people,
and then probably swindled them. The young
sleuth wondered if there was a tie-in between
Laura's inheritance and the Monroe National
Bank thefts of stocks and bonds. She must find out
from Jacob Aborn, but the police should be notified immediately, as well as her father.

Aloud Nancy said, "I want to hear the whole
story of what has happened to you, Mr. Aborn,
but first—"

Briefly, she told of having met the man who had
impersonated him and of seeing Laura at Twin
Lakes. Nancy was about to add that Laura was
now at her home when Mr. Aborn said:

"If Stumpy caught you here once today we'd better get out right now!" He told Nancy that Dowd kept the key to the padlock on his chains on a hook near the stairway.

"This is a lucky break," said Nancy. She snatched the lantern from the floor and started toward the stairs.

"Please hurry," Mr. Aborn said faintly. "Stumpy Dowd is a dangerous criminal! He boasted to me that he and his accomplices have victimized several people besides Laura!"

Nancy anxiously moved the lantern up and down, illuminating the dingy walls. Just above her head to the left she finally saw the hook, with a key dangling from it.

"I have it!" she exclaimed triumphantly.

As Nancy hurried back to Mr. Aborn's side she speculated on how the Dowds had found out about Mr. Aborn, his wife, and Laura.

"I'll have you free in a minute, Mr. Aborn," Nancy said, as she stooped over the bench.

While she worked on the rusty lock, Nancy asked if he had known the Dowds previously.

"Yes," he replied. "Mrs. Dowd was hired by my wife as a maid to come when we arrived. Soon after I reached the house her husband came. He grew quite loud and abusive and when I objected he knocked me unconscious. When I came to, I was chained in this cellar."

"How dreadful!" Nancy exclaimed. "But where is your wife?" she asked.

"She had to go to Florida unexpectedly. Her mother, who lives there, had an emergency operation. Marian went down to be with her and I moved into our new home." Mr. Aborn sighed. "Of course I haven't heard a word from her since I've been tied up here!"

"You'll be able to find out about her now," Nancy assured him. "Do you know how many people are working with Stumpy Dowd?"

"One or two others besides his wife, I believe. Stumpy Dowd is secretive about some things, although he boasted a lot. I did hear him mention the name Fred, but I don't know who he is."

When the padlock finally snapped open Nancy's spirits soared. Now the suitcase of securities that Stumpy Dowd had packed could be retrieved. The criminals could be apprehended and her father's case perhaps solved!

Meanwhile, neither Nancy nor Mr. Aborn had noticed a dark figure creeping slowly down the steps. Near and nearer the man came, a stout cane gripped tightly in his right hand.

"That's wonderful, Nancy!" Mr. Aborn exclaimed. "Now if I just knew where Laura is." As he spoke Mr. Aborn glanced up. A look of horror froze his face.

"Look out, Nancy!" he shouted.

CHAPTER XIV

A Desperate Situation

THE WARNING came too late. Before Nancy could turn, the end of the cane crashed down on her head. With a low moan of pain, she sagged to the floor and lay still.

How long she remained unconscious, the young sleuth did not know. When at last she opened her eyes Nancy found herself stretched out on the cold floor of the cellar. Bewildered, it was a full minute before she could account for the splitting pain in her head.

Then, with a shudder, the young sleuth remembered what had happened. She had been struck down from behind. Who was her assailant?

Nancy became aware that someone was standing over her, but objects whirled before her eyes and she could not distinguish the face. Then, gradually, her vision cleared. She saw Stumpy Dowd gazing down upon her, a satisfied leer on his face.

"Well, Miss Drew," he said mockingly, "we meet again. You've gotten in my way once too often!"

As Nancy started to speak, Dowd reached down. Catching Nancy by an arm, he jerked her roughly to her feet. Nancy was so weak that she nearly fell over.

Nevertheless, with a show of spirit, she said, "You'll regret this, I promise you!"

"Let the girl go," Jacob Aborn pleaded from the other side of the room. "Do anything you like to me, but set her free." Nancy saw that he was again padlocked.

Stumpy Dowd glared at his other prisoner. "It's quite impossible for me to release either of you," he said calmly. "You see, you both know too much."

Nancy was aware that resistance would be useless. Right now she did not have the strength to make a break for the stairs. But as the criminal began to unwind a long rope, Nancy realized that unless she thought of something the situation would be desperate. There would be no way to escape!

As Stumpy began to bind Nancy's feet together he said sarcastically, "Mr. Aborn will enjoy having company. And you two have so much to talk about."

An idea suddenly came to Nancy. She remembered that a detective who had called on her father a few months before had told her how it was possible to hold one's hands while being bound so as to slip the bonds later. He had given a demonstration.

"If I can only remember the correct position," Nancy prayed fervently.

When Dowd began to bind Nancy's wrists she tried to follow the detective's instructions. As the ropes cut into her flesh it seemed to Nancy that she must have made a mistake. Certainly there was little space between her wrists and the bonds.

"And now, just to make sure you won't get away—" Stumpy muttered with a sneer.

He took the end of the rope and ran it through a ring in the wall, knotting the rope fast.

"I guess that will hold you for a while and teach you not to meddle in affairs that are none of your business!" the man added.

Nancy Drew had never been so angry in her life, but she realized that any argument she might give would only provoke the man to further torture. So she set her jaw grimly and kept still.

"You'll pay for this, Dowd!" Jacob Aborn spoke up in a quavering voice. "When I get free—"

"When you get free!" Stumpy Dowd taunted.

"That's a laugh. Why, you fool, how do you propose to get help? If it hadn't been for this meddlesome Drew girl only the rats would have known you were here!"

Nancy could not help but remark quietly, "The police will catch you in the end."

"I doubt it," Dowd said with confidence. "I've covered my trail thoroughly. I've made plans to leave the country and I'd like to see the police or anyone else catch me!" He turned to Laura's guardian. "First, of course, we'll have to get the jewels away from Laura."

"How do you propose to do that," Nancy asked quickly, "when you don't know where she is?"

Stumpy Dowd laughed. "That's what you think. Laura is at your home in River Heights, Nancy Drew!"

As Nancy blinked, a look of horror came into Mr. Aborn's eyes. Nancy knew he was wondering why she had not mentioned Laura's being at her home. Also, he realized that his last hope of keeping Laura's whereabouts unknown was gone.

Nancy, too, was worried. What did Stumpy plan to do? Right now, he looked pleased at his prisoners' reactions.

"My wife overheard Laura placing a call to Nancy Drew in River Heights yesterday morning. When Laura ran away, we had a hunch she would go there. I asked my detective to find out."

Dowd said the sleuth had seen Laura leaving the house that afternoon with a young man. "I presume she left her jewels behind," he added. "But we'll get them before we leave this area!"

"Don't try anything foolish," Nancy warned.

"All my plans are well made," Dowd said coolly. "Too bad you aren't more cautious, Miss Drew."

He said that his wife had felt a draft in the house and gone downstairs to find the front door part way open. Then she had seen a girl heading into the woods and had awakened him. Dowd had figured out that it might be Nancy.

"That's the end of my story," he said, "except to tell you, Aborn, I sold your blue sedan this morning. The money helped pay for my new foreign car."

Jacob Aborn was so furious he almost choked. "You robber! You kidnaper!" he cried out.

"Tut, tut, none of that!" Dowd said. "You'll get your blood pressure up."

"Laura's not in your clutches, and she won't get there!" Aborn stormed. "And I can support her without any inheritance!"

Dowd shrugged. "It won't do any good to threaten me. You're my prisoner and don't forget it! After the jewels are mine—"

Nancy felt as if she would choke with rage. Mr. Aborn closed his eyes and seemed to have fainted.

Meanwhile, Stumpy Dowd had replaced the key on the wall—the hook supporting it, Nancy saw, was far out of the two prisoners' reach.

"You can think of this in the days ahead," the crook taunted. "And now—good-by!"

Turning, he ambled up the steps. Nancy heard mocking laughter as the trap door was slammed shut. Soon a deathlike quiet fell on the shack.

"Mr. Aborn!" Nancy called.

There was no answer. Nancy's heart beat wildly. Was the man only in a faint or had something worse happened to him?

Holding her breath, she strained her ears to see if she could detect any sign of life. A few seconds later Nancy caught faint sounds of inhaling and exhaling.

"Thank goodness," she thought.

Presently the man stirred, and regaining consciousness, looked about. Seeing Nancy, he exclaimed, "Now I remember! We were so near freedom."

"Yes, we were, Mr. Aborn. And we may get out of here yet. I'm trying to slip this rope off my wrists. In the meantime, I want to tell you why I didn't mention that Laura is at my home. I was about to do so when you urged that we leave the shack as fast as possible."

"I see and I forgive you," said Mr. Aborn. "Never having met you, Dowd's announcement gave me a momentary feeling of distrust in you. But that's gone now."

"Then would you mind telling me about Laura's mother and the estate she left?" Nancy requested, as she worked to free her hands.

"I'll be glad to. Mrs. Pendleton appointed the Monroe National Bank executor of her estate and me as Laura's guardian. During Mrs. Pendleton's long illness she had all her securities taken from her private safe-deposit box and put in care of the bank. They were turned over to the custodian department and kept in the bank's personal vault."

"Then how could Stumpy Dowd get them?" Nancy asked.

"That's the mystery. He didn't say."

Nancy was convinced now that a good portion of Laura's inheritance must be among the securities stolen from the bank. She asked whether Mrs. Pendleton had left a large estate.

Mr. Aborn nodded. "Laura is a very wealthy young woman," he said, then went on to explain that at the time of Mrs. Pendleton's death, the Aborns were abroad. Upon their arrival in New York, Mrs. Aborn had received word of her mother's illness. It was then that Laura had been asked to postpone coming to Melrose Lake until his wife's return.

"Laura was staying on at her boarding school

with the headmistress until our trip to Melrose."

"She never received your letter," Nancy told him. "The Dowds must have intercepted it. Soon they told her to come."

Just then Nancy thought she had found the trick to freeing her hands, but a moment later she sighed in discouragement. The rope still bound her wrists.

"At least we have a light," she said. Fortunately, Stumpy Dowd had forgotten the lantern.

"Yes, but the oil is burning low," Mr. Aborn remarked quietly. "When it's gone we'll be in the dark—as I have been for the past two weeks."

Nancy shuddered. "Did Stumpy bring you food in little packages?"

"Yes, when he thought of it. He kept me alive just to pump me for information, and threatened to harm Laura if I didn't tell him what he wanted to know."

Suddenly Nancy felt the rope which chafed her wrists slacken. At the same time the light went out. The cellar was plunged into darkness.

CHAPTER XV

Plans for Rescue

BACK in River Heights, meanwhile, Hannah Gruen had spent a restless and worried evening, expecting to hear Nancy's convertible pull into the driveway at any moment. Moreover, Mr. Drew had failed to call at the appointed hour and Hannah had no knowledge of how to contact the lawyer.

At ten thirty, when the front doorbell rang, the housekeeper limped hurriedly to answer it. Instantly she felt a sense of keen disappointment.

"Oh, hello, Laura," she said, and turned to greet Don Cameron. "Did you have a good time at the barbecue?"

"It was wonderful!" Laura exclaimed happily, as she and Don entered the house.

"Certainly was fun," Don agreed. "Too bad Nancy wasn't with us. Where is she, Mrs. Gruen?"

At these words tears welled up in Hannah's eyes. She told of not hearing from either Nancy or Mr. Drew that evening. "I'm so upset," she said. "What will we do? Call the police?"

"Probably Nancy decided to stay overnight at the Beach Cliff Hotel," Laura said at once. "Have you called there to find out?"

"No, because Nancy always calls when she changes her plans."

Don, greatly concerned, went at once to the telephone. Impatiently the young man waited for a response to his ring.

The hotel telephone operator answered. When Don asked for Nancy Drew, the girl said, "Just a moment." It was nearly five minutes before she told him:

"We are unable to reach your party. Miss Drew is not in the hotel."

"Then she didn't check out earlier this evening?" Don inquired.

"No. Miss Drew is still registered."

Don Cameron hung up, a drawn expression on his face. He told the others what he had learned.

"Oh, I just know something has happened to Nancy!" Laura cried, her lower lip quivering with nervousness. "And it's all my fault."

Hannah took the girl into her arms. "You must not feel this way," she said gently. "Nancy is trying to help you because she wants to."

Don spoke up, "I don't know whether we should notify the police or drive to Melrose Lake ourselves."

As the three hesitated, they heard an automobile stop in front of the house. Then a door slammed. Don looked out the window.

"It's a man," he said. "He's coming to the door."

Don opened the door to Carson Drew, who came inside immediately. He greeted Hannah and Don. Then, after being introduced to Laura Pendleton and bidding her welcome to his home, the lawyer asked:

"Where's Nancy? Upstairs?"

When told that his daughter had not returned from her investigation at Melrose Lake, the lawyer was gravely concerned.

"I don't like the sound of this at all," he said. "I had no idea that Nancy was planning to sleuth in Mr. Aborn's home at night."

"She mentioned something about wanting to pay another visit to a mysterious shack in the woods, Mr. Drew," Hannah volunteered. "But I don't know where it's located."

Carson Drew's anxiety deepened. "It would be just like Nancy to follow up a good clue," he said, "particularly if she thinks there is something odd about the shack. She never gives up until she figures out the solution to whatever the problem is."

Despite his worry, Nancy's father uttered these words proudly. He had often admired the initiative his daughter displayed when she was trying to unravel a mystery.

"I think you're on the right track, Mr. Drew," Don Cameron said thoughtfully. "Since Nancy hasn't returned to the hotel, there are three possibilities—she's had car trouble, something has happened to her in the woods—"

"Or the Aborns have discovered Nancy prowling about their house," Laura put in fearfully. "And if that is the case, there's no telling what they may do to her!"

The girl quickly mentioned a few of the things which had happened in her brief stay at the Aborns.

"I'll leave for Melrose Lake immediately," Mr. Drew announced. "If I don't find Nancy in a very short time, I'm going to notify the police that she's missing!"

The others begged Mr. Drew to let them accompany him. The lawyer thought it best for Hannah to remain at home in case Nancy should call.

"But I'll be glad to have you accompany me, Laura and Don," he added.

Don hurried to the telephone to notify his parents of the plan, while Laura went for a coat.

Then they went outside and got into Mr. Drew's car.

"Be sure to call me as soon as you've found out something!" Hannah called.

"Don't worry, we will!"

Nancy's father was a skillful driver and right now he was intent upon reaching the lake as soon as possible. He could barely restrain himself from breaking the speed limits.

"This is one time I wish I had a helicopter," he told the two young people.

"It wouldn't do you much good at Melrose Lake, Mr. Drew," said Laura. "It's a pretty thickly wooded area. I doubt that you'd find a landing strip."

Don realized that this remark, although unintentional, heightened Carson Drew's worry about Nancy being lost in the woods. He changed the subject quickly.

"I thought you weren't due home until Sunday, sir," Don said.

"That's right," the lawyer replied, his eyes intent on the highway ahead. "In Cincinnati late this afternoon I had a call from Chief McGinnis of the River Heights police. He thought it was imperative for me to return home immediately."

Mr. Drew proceeded to tell Don and Laura the complete story of the embezzlement case.

Laura looked worried. "The Monroe National Bank had my mother's securities!" she exclaimed. "You don't suppose—"

"Maybe," Don put in, "Nancy learned something in connection with this at the Aborn house and is staying to get more information."

"Oh, she shouldn't have done it!" Laura cried out fearfully.

"Now there may not be anything to your theory," Mr. Drew remarked. "Don't borrow trouble."

Don patted Laura's shoulder. "Sure. We have enough worries as it is. Mr. Drew, you were telling us why you came back early."

"Yes. Although I'm making a private investigation for Mr. Seward, the bank president, Chief McGinnis has been helping me on an unofficial basis. We're old friends, you see.

"When Nancy told me that two of the suspects —the Dowds—were in the acting profession and had been out of town recently, I had a hunch they might tie in with the case. I asked the chief to check on any past records the couple might have, and call me in Cincinnati."

At this point Carson Drew explained that Chief McGinnis had learned that the Dowds both had records for theft and embezzlement. Each had served prison terms. Using various aliases, they had either acted or worked in theaters in several states and among other crimes had robbed the ticket offices.

"When the chief told me this," said Carson Drew, "I asked him to take the list of missing securities to various brokerage offices in the River Heights area. He did this and found that during the past few days all of them had been sold by a woman."

"The same woman?" Don asked.

"Apparently not," Mr. Drew replied. "At least when Chief McGinnis asked for the woman's description it was different every time."

"How odd!" Laura exclaimed. "Could it have been Mrs. Dowd? Since she's an actress she must be good at disguise."

"You may be right," Mr. Drew acknowledged. "Anyway, the chief sent two officers to their house to pick up the Dowds for questioning."

"Did they find them?" Don asked eagerly.

The lawyer shook his head. "When the police got to the house they learned that the actor and actress had had a man caller earlier in the day and that the three had left together. Mr. Dowd said they would not be back."

"How discouraging for you"—Laura sighed in sympathy—"but I'm sure you'll find them."

"There's a state alarm out for the couple," Mr. Drew said. "They shouldn't be able to get very far."

"What do the Dowds look like?" Laura asked.

In reply, the lawyer took two photographs from his breast pocket and handed them to her.

Laura held the pictures toward the light on the dashboard. She shook her head in disbelief. "These are the Dowds?" she repeated.

"Yes, why? Have you seen them before?"

Laura said in a tense voice, "I know them as Mr. and Mrs. Aborn. Oh, Mr. Drew, if they've caught Nancy, she's in real danger!"

CHAPTER XVI

A Speedy Getaway

UNAWARE that help was coming, Nancy worked feverishly to slip her hands out of the ropes in the dark cellar of the shack.

"How are you doing?" Jacob Aborn asked her.

"The bonds are becoming looser," Nancy replied.

Suddenly she recalled Hannah's promise to send the police to the Aborns' home if she had not returned at a reasonable hour. When she told the imprisoned man about this, it seemed to give him courage.

However, to herself Nancy said, "By that time those criminals will have escaped. They may even prevent Hannah from carrying out her plan! And both Laura and Hannah may be harmed!"

As if to offset this alarming possibility, the ropes around Nancy's hands suddenly pulled free.

"I did it!" she exclaimed, and Mr. Aborn sprang from his bench, crying, "We'll be able to escape!"

Nancy did not respond, for she was working grimly at the ropes which bound her feet. "If I could only see!" she muttered.

Then she remembered the packet of matches in her skirt pocket. She took it out and lighted a match, which she stuck in a crack in the wall. As the light burned she worked to untie the knots that bound her ankles. Several more matches were used before she was free.

"Miss Drew, you're the most ingenious girl I've ever met!" Mr. Aborn said admiringly. "I wish I could think that fast. It just occurred to me that there's a can of kerosene under the stairs. You might fill the lantern."

Nancy found the can and in a few seconds the place was aglow with light.

"Now I'll open the padlock again," Nancy told Mr. Aborn.

After getting the key she hurried to the side of Laura's guardian. A minute later the chains fell to the floor with a loud thud.

"At last!" Jacob Aborn cried in relief.

"Our next step," said Nancy, "is to get out of here as fast as we can and then try to alert the police."

"It's my bet," her companion said, "that Dowd has already skipped town."

Nancy was inclined to agree, but since the swindler had not expected his two prisoners to escape, he might still be at the Aborn house with his wife.

"We'll head for my car," Nancy said, "and decide what we'll do when we reach it."

Jacob Aborn moved forward several steps, then his knees began to tremble. "My legs will be all right after I've used them for a few minutes," he apologized.

But try as he would, the man was unable to climb the stairway unassisted. Nancy reached out a strong arm to help him. At last they reached the top of the stairway.

The young sleuth led the way to the door, unbolted it, and the two stepped outside.

"What a relief!" Jacob Aborn gasped, filling his lungs with pure air.

In the east, the moon had risen over the woods and the sky was peppered with stars. The route among the trees would be easy to find in the clear night. Yet Nancy glanced uneasily at her companion, wondering if he would be able to walk to the car.

As if reading her thoughts, Aborn said, "I'm fine now. Let's go!"

Nancy offered her arm again, and at a slow pace they walked across the clearing and entered the woods. They had gone but a short way when Mr. Aborn sank down on a log, breathing heavily.

"You go on without me, Nancy," he said in a voice shaky with fatigue. "I can't do it."

"Just rest here for a moment," Nancy said encouragingly, unwilling to leave the man.

Shortly, Mr. Aborn felt he could continue. Leaning heavily on Nancy, he moved forward, refusing to pause again even for a brief rest.

"You're a very kind girl to help me," he said hoarsely.

Nancy replied modestly, "I'm *so* glad I found you. Think of what it means to Laura to have her real guardian found! I know she will be happy living with you and your wife."

At the mention of his wife's name Mr. Aborn said he was grateful that she had gone away before the Dowds invaded their home. "She might have been made a prisoner too!" he declared.

Presently, with a feeling of relief, Nancy caught sight of her convertible standing among the bushes where she had left it. After she had helped Mr. Aborn into the front seat, Nancy took her place behind the steering wheel.

"Now we'll drive to the nearest police station," she announced. "You direct me."

She inserted the key and tried the starter. To Nancy's surprise, the motor did not turn over.

"That's funny," she said, and tried again. Nothing happened. Next, Nancy glanced at the fuel gauge. It registered half full.

"I wonder if your battery's dead," Mr. Aborn said in a faint voice.

"I think not," Nancy replied, as she reached into the glove compartment and took out an extra flashlight she kept there for emergencies.

She got out of the car, lifted the hood, and flashed her light inside. She had taken a course in automobile mechanics and knew the possible sources of trouble.

"I see what the trouble is," Nancy called. "The distributor has been uncapped and the rotor's missing! This is sabotage!" Without this necessary part the car could not start. "I'm sure that Mr. Dowd is the saboteur," she added angrily.

Mr. Aborn sighed resignedly. "Stumpy Dowd leaves no stones unturned," he said in a tired voice. "Just in case we might escape he wanted to make certain we'd have no transportation. I'm afraid, Nancy, that we'll have to go to the main highway for help."

As Mr. Aborn spoke, Nancy heard a car motor not far away. Eagerly she looked to right and left but saw no approaching headlights.

"Quick! Duck down!" Mr. Aborn whispered, and Nancy crouched in the bushes alongside her car.

A dark foreign sports car emerged from the Eagle Rock lane, then made a left-hand turn in the direction of Twin Lakes!

"It's the Dowds making a getaway!" Mr. Aborn said. "We're too late!"

Nancy was alarmed by this turn of events. She wondered why Stumpy Dowd was not heading toward River Heights. Had he given up the idea of going to the Drews' residence and forcing Laura Pendleton to give him the jewels? Or was he taking an alternative route there?

"Oh dear! I wish there were a telephone nearby!" Nancy moaned. She told Mr. Aborn that his had been disconnected.

Jacob Aborn spoke up. "Nancy, I'm sure that Dowd and his wife have left my house for good. I think the best plan is for us to go there."

"Yes," Nancy agreed. "After you're safely inside I'll go for help."

"I can't let you do that," Jacob Aborn protested. "Few cars come along this road at night. You'll have an extremely long walk before you reach the main highway."

Silently Nancy agreed, but she also noted that the man's strength was almost spent. She helped him from the car, and the two slowly approached the lane that led to Mr. Aborn's house.

"Oh, if I could only get my hands on that scoundrel!" the man muttered.

The thought gave him new strength, and he moved forward again. Cautiously the two crept toward the house, approaching it from the rear.

"We'd better make certain that no one's here," Nancy whispered.

As they drew near the back door she saw that it stood ajar, as though someone had left hurriedly without taking time to shut it.

With Jacob Aborn close behind her, Nancy stepped cautiously into the kitchen. There was profound silence. The place appeared deserted.

Crossing the room on tiptoe, Nancy and Mr. Aborn walked toward the living room. He clicked on a light. Everything was in disorder. A chair had been overturned and papers were scattered about.

"The Dowds certainly made a thorough search," Nancy remarked.

Just then Mr. Aborn's eyes fell upon the wall safe which stood open. With a cry of alarm he tottered across the room to look inside. Everything had been taken out.

Mr. Aborn groaned. He told Nancy that a sizable sum of his own money had been in the safe, along with shares of negotiable stock. Stumpy Dowd had forced him to tell the safe's combination on threat of harming Laura.

Mr. Aborn, white as starch, sank into a nearby chair and buried his head in his hands. "Nearly all my securities were in there," he said. One quick glance at him told Nancy that the man was on the verge of a complete collapse. She could not leave him alone, yet how could she get help without doing so?

A second later she and Mr. Aborn were startled to hear a car driving up the lane. Were the Dowds returning? Had the couple merely gone out for a while, or had they forgotten something in their hasty flight?

Nancy's next thought was far worse than either of these. Had Stumpy Dowd somehow learned that his two prisoners had escaped?

CHAPTER XVII

Two-way Detecting

As THE automobile pulled to a halt, Mr. Aborn slumped to the floor in a faint. Evidently he had shared Nancy's thought that the Dowds were returning, and would force their way in. The terrifying thought that he might become a prisoner again had been too much for the exhausted man.

"Oh!" Nancy cried out.

From the window Nancy saw four people hurriedly alighting from the car. A moment later the bell rang and a woman's voice cried, "Mr. Aborn —Mr. Aborn—please let us in. It's the Donnells!"

Nancy hurried to the front door and flung it open. "Cathy! Jim!" she cried out. "Oh, you don't know how glad I am to see you!"

The two young people introduced Nancy to their parents, a good-looking couple in their forties. Then they stepped inside.

"What are you doing here, Nancy?" Jim Donnell asked, puzzled at the girl's disheveled appearance. "What's going on?"

Nancy replied by saying Mr. Aborn was ill, and there was no time for further explanation right now. She hastily led the family into the living room. When they saw their unconscious friend on the floor, Mrs. Donnell rushed forward with an excited cry.

"How dreadful!" she exclaimed.

As she knelt down, the kindly woman said she was a registered nurse. After a brief examination of the patient she reported that Mr. Aborn appeared to be suffering from malnutrition and shock.

While Jim and his father lifted him onto the couch, Nancy told what had happened to him. The Donnells were stunned.

Before they could discuss it, however, Nancy turned to Jim. "Two phone calls must be made right away," she said. "Would you be able to take care of them for me?"

"Glad to," the boy said. "I suppose you want me to notify the police to pick up Stumpy Dowd—"

"Yes," Nancy said tersely, and described the black foreign car.

She next asked Jim to call Chief McGinnis at River Heights and tell him to have extra men patrol the Drew home. "Find out if Mrs. Gruen and

Laura are all right," she requested, "and see if our housekeeper knows where to get in touch with Dad."

Jim said he would do all of these things. As soon as he returned, he would try to fix Nancy's car.

After Jim left, Nancy turned to the others. Mr. Aborn had regained consciousness and said he felt better and able to talk.

"Lillian," he said, giving Mrs. Donnell a wan smile, "the angels must have sent you. How did you know we were in trouble here?"

"We didn't for sure," Mr. Donnell replied gravely, "until tonight—it's a long story."

The gray-haired man said that he and his wife had been amazed to hear on Tuesday from their children that Marian Aborn had returned from Florida and that she and Jacob had met Laura Pendleton at Twin Lakes.

"We were sure you would have told us of your change of plans, if this were true, Jacob," he said to his old friend. "Anyway, we came over here yesterday morning to say hello and meet Laura. No one answered the bell."

"We concluded," said Mrs. Donnell, "that Nancy Drew had been mistaken in thinking that you were coming back here—anyway, we remembered you saying that due to the illness of Marian's mother you would not be able to come here with Laura until after your wife's return."

"That's right," said Mr. Aborn. He explained to Nancy that first there had been legal technicalities regarding his appointment as the orphan's guardian, since he had been living in another state. That was why his ward had remained at her boarding school.

Mrs. Donnell went on to say that this evening they had received a telephone call from Mrs. Aborn who was still in Florida. "Marian had tried several times to get you and was upset to learn that the phone here was disconnected. She called us to see why."

"My wife hadn't heard from me in over two weeks," Mr. Aborn stated.

Mrs. Donnell said, "But Marian thought she had. Mrs. Aborn sent telegrams here and replies came to her in Florida."

Mr. Donnell said that when the family heard that Marian Aborn was indeed in Florida, they were fearful something was terribly wrong.

"We told Marian what we knew, suggested she come home immediately, and said we would come over here right away to see what we could uncover."

"Thank goodness you did," Nancy sighed, and Mr. Aborn gave his friends a grateful smile. Then he asked, "How is Marian's mother?"

"Getting along very well."

"When will my wife arrive?" Mr. Aborn asked anxiously.

"She's taking a night plane from Miami to the Hamilton airport," Mrs. Donnell replied. "My husband will meet her."

Cathy's mother then went to the kitchen to prepare a light meal for Mr. Aborn. Nancy excused herself and went to wash her face, legs, and grimy hands. Refreshed, she returned to the living room, wondering what was keeping Jim so long.

"He'll be here soon, Nancy," said Cathy.

"I'll feel much better when I know everything's all right at home," Nancy replied.

While Mr. Aborn ate, the pretty detective told the others of Stumpy Dowd's connection with Mr. Drew's case.

"What a story!" Mr. Donnell exclaimed.

Nancy excused herself for a moment and went to the front door to listen for Jim's car. As she stood on the steps her heart suddenly leaped. A tall figure stood up from behind a bush near the front steps.

"Nancy?" a man's voice called softly.

Nancy knew who it was. "Dad!" she cried out.

Carson Drew leaped the steps and gave his daughter a resounding kiss. "Are you all right?" he whispered.

When Nancy said yes, and that it was safe to

talk aloud, Don Cameron and Laura emerged from some shrubbery.

"We saw lights and heard voices," Laura explained. "We thought it was the Aborns. What's going on here, Nancy?"

"Yes, tell us!" Don urged.

Once again Nancy explained what had happened. Carson Drew listened to his daughter's story of her encounter with the thief, a stern expression on his face.

"You were lucky to come out of this so well," he remarked.

"Yes," Laura agreed. "And it's so wonderful to have a guardian whom you say is nice!"

"Mr. Aborn is a fine person, Laura," Nancy said. "I'll take you in to meet him in a minute."

Carson Drew now brought Nancy up to date on his news, and ended by saying, "We were so worried we drove here immediately, not even taking time to call the police."

Don added that they had left Mr. Drew's car at the end of the lane and were scouting the house to see if Nancy were inside when she had appeared on the front steps.

"How many times I wished you were here!" said Nancy. She now suggested that everyone come into the house to meet the others. "Jim Donnell," she added, "should return any minute."

"I'll wait for the young man out here and act

as guard in case the Dowds show up," Carson Drew said, sitting down on a step. "The rest of you run along—"

As Nancy walked inside with Don and Laura she saw that Mr. and Mrs. Donnell were helping Mr. Aborn up the stairs to his bedroom. Hearing voices, the guardian turned, looked at his ward, and exclaimed:

"Laura dear—at last—I'd know you anywhere! You look just like your mother!"

"Mr. Aborn!" Laura cried out. She raced up the steps and gave her guardian a big kiss.

Introductions were quickly made, and when Mr. Aborn was settled in his bed, he had a visit with Laura and Nancy. But after they had chatted for a few minutes the girls could see that the man needed sleep badly.

"We'll say good night now," said Nancy. "Sweet dreams." She turned off the light, and they went downstairs.

When Nancy and Laura reached the first floor, they found Mr. Drew and Jim Donnell talking in the hall with a state trooper. While Cathy took Laura aside, Nancy walked toward the group.

She was introduced to Sergeant Murphy, then Carson Drew explained to her that the state police were putting all available cars on the chase and hoped to round up the Dowds and their accomplice shortly.

"Good!" Nancy exclaimed. "But what about Mrs. Gruen?"

Sergeant Murphy said that he had talked with Chief McGinnis. The River Heights official had immediately sent a patrol car and four men to the Drews' home.

"Your housekeeper was relieved to hear that you, Miss Drew, had been found," he reported. "Nothing unusual has happened at your home tonight. But it will be closely guarded until the Dowds and their accomplice are caught."

"Oh, I'm glad," said Nancy. Sergeant Murphy left, after saying he would check back later.

Nancy and Mr. Drew walked into the living room, and she introduced her father to Mr. and Mrs. Donnell and Cathy. After a few minutes of excited conversation, the young sleuth said:

"Dad, I have a hunch that the man 'Fred' whom Stumpy Dowd mentioned is someone employed at the Monroe National Bank. Tell me, was Mrs. Pendleton's name ever mentioned in connection with the missing securities?"

Mr. Drew shook his head. "No, Nancy, it wasn't."

"Then," said Nancy, "I think we're going to find that Laura's bonds were never deposited in the bank's vault. Whoever took them and passed them on to Stumpy Dowd must be someone who works in the custodian department of the bank."

"That's good reasoning, Nancy," her father agreed, "but we have checked almost all the employees and they've been given a clean bill of health. One man, Mr. Hamilton's assistant, has been on vacation and we won't be able to interview him for another week or so."

"What's the man's name?" Nancy asked.

Mr. Drew consulted a list of names which he took from his pocket. "William Frednich."

Nancy snapped her fingers. "Frednich! Maybe *he's* the 'Fred' the Dowds were talking about. And if he is," she continued excitedly, "I think they're together and I believe I know where the Dowds are hiding out with this man!"

Carson Drew looked at his daughter in amazement. "Where?" he asked.

"Not far from here," Nancy said mysteriously. Then she jumped up from her chair. "Let's find out, Dad!"

CHAPTER XVIII

Night Trail

CARSON DREW, startled, looked at his daughter.

"Where do you think the Dowds and Fred are hiding, Nancy?"

"In a bungalow on Twin Lakes—the one I told you we stayed in after Laura rescued us," she explained. "My main reasons for thinking so are these: I saw a black foreign car come from there, and the place was well-stocked with food. Fred may have been living there."

"Go on. This is interesting," the lawyer said.

Nancy's hunch was that the thieves had first planned the bank theft, then the Dowds had rented the bungalow under an assumed name.

"Makes sense." Carson Drew nodded.

"Fred," Nancy continued, "knew of Laura's large estate and jewelry, and got the idea of having Stumpy Dowd impersonate Mr. Aborn. In order to get the jewelry they had to have Laura with them, so they decided to take her to the Melrose Lake house."

"Good logic," said Mr. Drew. "Then, when the real Mr. Aborn appeared, they had to kidnap him temporarily. Well, we'll follow your hunch. Shall we go?"

The others offered to go, but Mr. Drew thought that the Donnells should stay with Mr. Aborn and Laura.

"Please do," Nancy added. "After all, my hunch could be wrong. The Dowds may return here."

"We'll nab 'em if they do!" Jim said determinedly.

A few minutes later Mr. Drew's car was on the detour again, heading for the Twin Lakes road. When they reached it, there were no other cars in evidence.

"That's odd," said Nancy, knowing that this was the only road which connected the two resorts.

"Oh, oh!" said Don. "Look!"

Mr. Drew had also seen a small red light a few hundred feet distant. He slowed up. Ahead was a gate obstruction across the highway. On it was nailed a sign which read:

ROAD UNDER CONSTRUCTION
Travel at your own risk

"This is great!" Mr. Drew remarked unhappily.

"Maybe it won't be too bad," Nancy said. "I came this way the other day and I think I know all the turns."

"Why don't we try it, sir?" Don spoke up.

"All right."

Don got out of the car and moved the barrier enough so Mr. Drew could drive through. They went slowly, because of the steam shovels, bulldozers, and equipment parked along the road.

To make matters worse, the pavement was gone in places where repairs were being made. The car tires wallowed in soft dirt.

Soon, however, they reached the end of the construction section and Carson Drew stepped on the accelerator. The car responded with a burst of speed.

"We're not far from Twin Lakes now," Nancy said as she spotted a few familiar landmarks.

Don wanted to know what the plan would be when they reached the bungalow. Mr. Drew said they would first check to see if the foreign car were in the vicinity. "Of course it will be hidden."

"Next," Nancy added, "we'll have to make sure Fred and the Dowds are there, and not some innocent people. But if Stumpy's there, we'll notify the police. Right, Dad?"

"Unless Dowd sees us first," he said grimly.

Nancy said she hoped this would not happen.

"But I suppose they probably will have someone acting as a lookout."

"As I understand it, Nancy," said her father, "the bungalow is in an isolated spot."

"Yes, and there are a lot of trees around it."

"Could anyone inside the house make a getaway by boat?" Don asked.

"Not easily," Nancy answered. "The bungalow is not built over the water. It's some distance from the lake and there's no dock where a boat could be tied." Presently she said, "We're about a mile from the bungalow."

Carson Drew's face tensed. He drove to a point about a tenth of a mile from the lane leading down to the bungalow, then stopped the car in a clearing off the road.

"We'll cover the rest of the distance on foot," he announced.

As Nancy got out the right-hand side of the car after Don she glanced at the luminous dial on the clock. It was three o'clock in the morning!

Walking three abreast, the sleuths saw the bungalow below. It was in darkness.

"I don't see any sign of a car," Don whispered to Nancy, as he guided her by the arm.

Carson Drew was silent, but suddenly he jerked to attention. A twig had snapped. Now they saw a man walking toward the trio through the woods!

As Don, Nancy, and Mr. Drew ducked behind

some shrubbery, they noticed that the man approaching them was carrying a fishing pole and a box of the type ordinarily used for bait.

Passing by the watchers, he walked unhurriedly toward the beach. At this moment the moon chose to show itself brilliantly, and Nancy observed that the man was tall and heavy.

"Hello, Sam," he said, and now the watchers could see a rowboat and passenger gliding out of the shadows.

"I hope the fish are biting well this morning." His voice carried clearly in the stillness.

The fisherman deposited his gear in the boat, and the two companions shoved off. They were barely out of sight when Don whispered hoarsely, "A light in the bungalow."

From the second-story window had come a flash of light. It did not reappear.

"Someone's up there!" Nancy whispered. "Maybe the fisherman alerted him."

"Let's circle the house," said Carson Drew, and suggested that he take the left half of the circle while Nancy and Don took the right. They would meet back at this same spot in a few minutes.

"Be careful now," he warned the young people.

"You too, Dad," Nancy said.

The route Nancy and Don took led past the door into the first floor of the boathouse bungalow. Cautiously they listened at the exit. There was no sound from within. They went on to the beach side.

The two tiptoed among the shadows as far as the center of the rear of the building without incident, then quietly returned to the meeting place. When they arrived, Mr. Drew was not there.

"That's funny," said Nancy, a little alarmed. "Where *is* Dad?"

Just then she and Don heard a low groan. It seemed to come from behind a tree about twenty feet away. Forgetting caution, the couple rushed to the spot. Behind its broad trunk a man lay sprawled on the ground. Mr. Drew!

"Dad!" Nancy exclaimed, kneeling down. She felt the lawyer's pulse. It was steady.

"I think he was knocked out," said Don angrily. "Nancy, you're right about this being a hide-out. We must get the police!"

"And right away!" Nancy agreed, as Carson Drew sat up groggily. In a moment he could talk.

The lawyer said that after leaving Nancy and Don he had started around the bungalow. Someone had come from behind and struck him. "I suppose he dragged me here."

"Stumpy Dowd, I'll bet!" Nancy exclaimed. "And this may mean that he and his wife made a getaway while Don and I were on the other side of the bungalow! Dad, do you feel well enough to try to follow them?"

"Yes, but where did they go?" he asked. "And how? By boat, car, or on foot?"

As if in answer to his question, the three suddenly saw in the clear moonlight the figures of two men and a woman running up the bungalow lane toward the road. Each man carried a big suitcase. Laura's inheritance and Mr. Aborn's little fortune!

"After them!" Don cried.

But Mr. Drew could not make it. He tottered unsteadily and leaned against the pine. "Go on!" he said.

"No!" Nancy replied quickly. "Don, bring Dad's car here, will you?"

As the boy started off, the trio heard the muffled backfire of an automobile coming from the direction of the woods across the main road.

"Hurry, Don!" Nancy urged. "They had a car hidden there."

By the time Don returned, Carson Drew felt better. He suggested that Nancy drive, since she was more familiar with the road. When everyone was in the car, with the lawyer in the rear seat, they took off.

Upon reaching the road, the young sleuth turned right. "I think this is the direction the other car took," she said. "Anyway, it leads to Stamford, where I know there's a state police headquarters."

Carson Drew sat up groggily

The road became rough and was full of sharp turns. Nancy drove fast but carefully, slowing at each curve. There was no sign of another car until Don suddenly cried out:

"I think we're approaching a car!"

Nancy peered forward intently. She saw nothing but the road ahead.

"It's hidden now by that hill in front of us," Don told her.

There was a long moment of suspense, then Nancy exclaimed, "I see it!"

"Do you think it's the Dowds?" Don asked.

"It could be," Mr. Drew replied.

As the car reached a smooth, straight piece of road, Nancy put it to a faster and faster pace.

"We're gaining on them!" Don said exuberantly.

Little by little the Drew sedan crept up on the car ahead. Soon its headlights spotlighted the rear of the other vehicle—a black foreign car! Three figures were silhouetted inside it!

At the same moment Nancy caught sight of a huge black-and-white checkerboard sign at the side of the road. A bad curve ahead! With well-timed precision, Nancy eased up on her speed and gradually used her brake, knowing that abrupt pressure might cause a bad skid.

"That other driver isn't paying any attention to the warning!" Don exclaimed.

The snakelike curve was only a few hundred feet ahead on a steep downgrade. The occupants of the Drew sedan held their breath. Would the others make the turn? There came a violent screech of brakes.

"Oh no!" Nancy cried out in horror.

As she and her companions watched, the foreign car shot off the edge of the road and plunged down a steep cliff!

CHAPTER XIX

Missing Property

STUNNED by the accident to the speeding car, Nancy brought the sedan to a halt at the curve. Everyone inside was reluctant to look down into the ravine below, from which there was not a sound.

But only for an instant. Then Carson Drew urged, "Out, everyone, quickly! We must do what we can for those people!"

Nancy and Don sprang from the car and rushed to the edge of the road. The lawyer was close behind them.

As the three gazed down into the ravine, the first light of dawn revealed that the foreign car had rolled nearly to the bottom of it and overturned against a boulder. A wheel had been torn loose from its axle and the body had been smashed in. There was no sign of any of the three occupants.

A silence held the trio above. It was inconceivable that anyone in the wreck could be alive!

At last Carson Drew found his voice. "I guess we'd better notify the police and emergency squad," he said.

Don agreed, but Nancy thought they should first see if by chance any of the accident victims were alive.

Mr. Drew and Don nodded, and followed Nancy as she scrambled down the incline. Nancy, in the lead, gasped as she saw the body of a strange man, apparently not the driver, which had been flung out of the car into a clump of bushes near the wreck. She also noticed gasoline spilling from a hole in the tank. Vaguely she thought of fire and an explosion.

"Hurry!" she urged.

As the three drew closer they saw a man's leg and a woman's high-heeled shoe protruding from beneath the left-hand side of the car.

With frantic haste Don and Mr. Drew dragged the man out, while Nancy tugged at the woman's body. Stumpy Dowd and his wife! Both were breathing, but unconscious. The victims, cut and badly bruised, were carried to a safe place on the grass.

"Now let's see about the other man, Mr. Drew," urged Don.

As they headed for the bushes where he lay,

Nancy stared at the car. "The suitcases!" she thought. "Laura's inheritance and Mr. Aborn's little fortune! I must get them out before they may be burned up!"

Crawling under the wreck, she began to grope about frantically. Her hand struck a suitcase and she dragged it out.

At that instant Nancy realized how hot the metal was. There might be spontaneous combustion at any second. She must work fast to save the second suitcase!

"It's the only way I can ever repay Laura for saving my life on Twin Lakes!" Nancy thought.

By feeling around she found the bag and triumphantly brought it out, only to be jerked from the scene by Carson Drew and Don.

"Nancy!" Carson Drew cried, white-faced and horror-stricken. "Are you mad? Those suitcases aren't worth your life!"

There was a sudden explosion. Then flames enveloped the car and the dry grass in the immediate vicinity began to burn.

Don Cameron shuddered, but looked at Nancy, admiration showing in his eyes. "You're the most courageous girl I've ever met," he said slowly. "Nancy, you might have been killed!"

As she herself realized what a narrow escape she had had, Nancy breathed a prayer of thanksgiving.

She was shaken and silent as the men threw dirt
on the flames to keep them from spreading. When
they finished, Don told Nancy that he and Mr.
Drew thought the third man would be all right,
although the stranger as well as the Dowds were
injured, perhaps seriously.

"Now I suppose we must get the three of them
to a hospital as fast as we can," he said.

At that moment they all heard the low whine
of an ambulance alarm. This was followed by a
police siren.

Nancy, Mr. Drew, and Don looked at one another hopefully. "Do you suppose—" Nancy began.

She was right. Help had come! A moment later
police and emergency squad cars stopped at the
top of the ravine. Four officers, two stretcher-
bearers, and an intern, clad in white, hurried
down to the group.

"Thank goodness," said Mr. Drew. Introductions were quickly made, then he asked, "How
did you know about the accident?"

An officer, Lieutenant Gill, told him that a
farmer living not far away had seen the speeding
car go off the road and notified headquarters.

"When we heard it was a black foreign car, we
were suspicious immediately," he said. "Can
you identify these people as the Dowds?"

"From pictures, yes," said Mr. Drew, and briefly told the whole story of the Dowd affair up to the present moment.

"And I can testify that they were impersonating the Aborns," Nancy added.

"Anybody know who the other man is?" Lieutenant Gill inquired.

"I believe," Mr. Drew replied, "that he's William Frednich, assistant to the president of the River Heights branch of the Monroe National Bank. He's suspected of removing certain securities from the bank."

During this conversation the intern had been examining the accident victims and the attendants had laid them on stretchers. The doctor reported that the victims had been given first aid and had revived. They would be in good shape after a short stay in the hospital.

"They'll get a nice long rest after that," said Lieutenant Gill, "in the state pen. I shan't try to question them now."

As the prisoners were carried up to the ambulance, with the others following, Lieutenant Gill explained to the Dowds how Nancy had saved them from being burned in the wreckage.

"I don't believe it," said Stumpy ungratefully.

His wife was more gracious. "Thanks, Miss Drew. And I want to tell you I'm tired of this whole business. You're only a kid but you've really taught me a lesson."

Nancy did not answer. She found herself choking up, and tears came into her eyes.

As the ambulance moved away, Nancy, quickly brushing her moist eyes dry with the backs of her hands, turned toward the east. She observed that a beautiful sunrise was beginning to flood the sky with brilliant color.

Don yawned. "What do you say we head for home?" he suggested. "Otherwise, I'll never be able to make my sister's wedding this evening."

"Oh dear!" Nancy exclaimed. "I forgot all about it. Please forgive us for keeping you up all night."

Don grinned. "I wouldn't have missed this excitement for anything!"

"I suggest," said Mr. Drew, "that we go back to Nancy's hotel and the Drews will get some sleep. Don, you take my car and return to River Heights. Later, Nancy and I will take a taxi and pick up her convertible at the Aborns'."

"Thank you, sir. I'll do that."

While the three had been talking, Lieutenant Gill had been wedging open one of the two locked suitcases which Nancy had taken from the wrecked car. Mr. Drew and the others walked over as he lifted the lid.

The bag was jammed with feminine clothing. There were several dresses, a large make-up kit, pieces of lingerie, shoes, and several wigs—a gray one, a black hairpiece, and one which was decidedly auburn.

"That clinches it, Dad!" Nancy exclaimed. "Mrs. Dowd must have gone around in disguise to cash the bonds."

"But where's the money she got?" Don asked.

"It must be in the other bag," Nancy suggested, "together with securities and money belonging to Laura Pendleton, Mr. Aborn, and River Heights bank clients."

Lieutenant Gill opened the second suitcase. It contained men's clothing and toilet articles.

"Nancy, you risked your life for this!" Don exclaimed.

Nancy Drew could not believe her eyes. Had she been mistaken in believing that Stumpy Dowd had put the contents of Mr. Aborn's safe in the bags? Quickly she glanced down at the foreign car. Had Laura's inheritance and other people's money burned in it?

The thought stunned the young sleuth. But in a moment an idea came to her.

"There's just a possibility the papers *are* here," she said.

All eyes turned on the girl detective, as the group awaited a further explanation.

CHAPTER XX

A Surprise Gift

"I'M SURE," said Nancy, "that Mr. Dowd not only put the money and securities in one of these suitcases, but never removed them!"

"Then *where* are they?" Don asked.

Nancy smiled. "These bags may have false bottoms!"

Lieutenant Gill said, "Why, of course. I should have thought of that."

Kneeling down, he soon found that Nancy was right. The bottom of each bag opened up, disclosing packages of thousand-dollar bills and securities.

"Good thinking, Nancy," said Don admiringly. "You're a whiz of a detective, all right."

It took Mr. Drew and the officers several minutes to count the large sum of money and make a rough estimate of the value of the stocks and bonds. When they finished, the officer gave Carson Drew a receipt to turn over to the president of the Monroe National Bank. Meanwhile, he would take the stolen property to police headquarters and send on a detailed report.

A few minutes later Nancy's group said good-by to the officers, and returned to Mr. Drew's car. When they reached the Beach Cliff Hotel, Nancy and Mr. Drew got out. They thanked Don for all he had done.

"Don't mention it." The young man grinned. Turning to Nancy, he added, "I kept my date with you yesterday after all!"

As he got into the driver's seat Don said that when he returned the car to the Drews' home he would tell Hannah Gruen what had happened.

It was now very light. Nancy and her father, exhausted, could hardly wait to get a few hours sleep. They tumbled into their beds and slept until noon, then met in the hotel dining room for a hearty brunch.

"How's your head, Dad?" Nancy asked.

"Sound as ever!" Carson Drew said, grinning. "I don't even have a bump."

"Then we have a date," Nancy told him, waving a note. "This was at the desk. I picked it up. The clerk said Jim Donnell left it a little while ago."

"The date's with him?" Mr. Drew asked.

"No. Laura Pendleton. She says she and the

Aborns are thrilled by the news which the police relayed and would like us to come to their house as soon as possible. What do you say, Dad?"

"We'll go."

As Nancy finished her pancakes and sausages she remarked that she could hardly wait to start for the Aborns' home. "I wonder if the Dowds have confessed everything and what Mr. Frednich had to say."

"In my opinion it's an open and shut case," the lawyer replied.

While Mr. Drew paid the hotel bill, Nancy called a taxi and soon the Drews were heading for Eagle Rock Lane. Reaching it, they got out of the cab and the lawyer paid the driver.

Nancy slid in behind the steering wheel of her convertible, as Mr. Drew got in on the other side. The motor started at once. "Good old Jim," Nancy said with a smile, and drove up the lane to the Aborn home.

As she parked, the front door was opened by a woman of about forty-five. Her pretty face showed humor, kindness, and intelligence.

After the Drews had introduced themselves, the woman said she was Marian Aborn and had reached home "in the wee small hours" because her plane was late. "I've been most eager to meet you two," she added, smiling. "How can I ever thank you for all you've done?"

As the callers went inside, Laura Pendleton hurried down from the second floor. After greeting Mr. Drew she gave Nancy a kiss and exclaimed, "Everything is so wonderful—you've captured the thieves and recovered all the money—and I have the nicest guardians anyone could ever hope for!"

"And Jacob and I have a daughter to love!" said Marian Aborn, smiling fondly at Laura.

Nancy asked how Mr. Aborn felt. His wife said, "Come see for yourselves," and led the way to a small study at the rear of the house.

She knocked, then opened the door, and Nancy heard the steady drum of typewriter keys. Jacob Aborn was seated behind the machine.

The erstwhile cellar prisoner already looked like a new man. His face was flooded with color, and his eyes were alert and happy. Now he stood up, greeted the Drews, and expressed his great appreciation for all they had done in recovering his and Laura's property.

He grinned at Nancy. "First time a girl ever risked her life for me!" he said. "To show my appreciation I'm writing my adventure. You know, writing is my business. If I sell this one to a magazine, I'm going to give the proceeds to Nancy's favorite charity—the River Heights Youth Center!"

"Why, that's terrific!" Nancy exclaimed.

Mrs. Aborn's face sobered. She said that she

had not yet heard the entire story of what had happened. Before anyone had a chance to tell her, the doorbell rang. Lieutenant Gill walked in with Chief McGinnis of River Heights and another man. While Nancy greeted the officers, her father hurried to shake hands with the stranger.

"This is Mr. Seward, president of the Monroe National Bank," he announced a moment later, and introduced the dignified white-haired man.

The president's glance included the policemen as he said, "I want to thank all of you in person for the splendid job you did in capturing the Dowds and the two bank employees involved in the thefts."

"There is a fourth man?" Nancy asked in amazement.

Mr. Seward explained that Alma Dowd's brother, Joe Jackson, had been employed by the Monroe National Bank in their vault department for some time. He and Frednich had cooked up the scheme of taking the securities. They had done this between audits of the bank's holdings. Frednich, in his job as assistant custodian, had known exactly how to place his hands on the valuable stocks and bonds.

"Frednich overheard Mrs. Pendleton's discussion with me about Laura and the large estate she would inherit some day," Mr. Seward said, "and also that Mr. Aborn would be her guardian.

When Frednich learned that Laura Pendleton had a valuable jewelry collection, he instantly thought of a swindle scheme. Frednich had chanced to meet Mr. Aborn one time while vacationing at Melrose Lake. He had been amazed by the strong resemblance between Aborn and Stumpy Dowd, whom Alma's brother had introduced to Frednich. He asked Dowd to impersonate Mr. Aborn and to move up the date when Laura would come to the guardian's home. He even deposited some securities with the bank in Stumpy's name, so there would be no question of Dowd's having anything to do with the thefts."

"Where is Joe Jackson now?" Nancy asked.

Chief McGinnis said he would answer this question. "We caught him cruising by the Drews' home. When we stopped the car, he tried to escape. After the whole story broke, we got a confession from him. He was going to burglarize your home, Nancy, to find the jewels."

"There's one thing I don't understand," said Mrs. Aborn. "Why did the Dowds rent the bungalow when they had helped themselves to this house?"

Nancy grinned. "I'm sure I know," she said. "Dowd was smart enough not to want either Frednich or Jackson to stay here—just in case anyone from the bank traced the thefts to them before Dowd could make a getaway. So he had Alma

Dowd rent the bungalow and convinced Frednich that it was a good hide-out."

After Mr. Aborn and Laura had signed statements for the police, the officers and Mr. Seward left. Nancy suddenly felt a sense of loneliness and realized it was because her work on the case was at an end. Would another mystery come her way to solve? she wondered. And it did. In less than a week, Nancy was facing up to the challenge of *The Mystery at Lilac Inn.*

Nancy and her father now said good-by to the family at Eagle Rock. As Nancy gave Laura a farewell hug, she asked, "When will you come to get your jewelry?"

Laura consulted her guardian, who said the next day would be convenient for them to drive to River Heights. "Will three o'clock be all right?"

"Yes indeed."

The following afternoon Laura Pendleton and the Aborns arrived promptly. After iced tea and some of Hannah's delicious open-faced sandwiches, Laura whispered to Mr. Drew that she would love to get her jewelry from the safe. Excusing himself, Nancy's father left the room and returned in a few minutes with the package, which he handed to Laura.

Nancy, meanwhile, was listening to Jacob Aborn's surprising news that he had finished his story and was sending it to a leading magazine.

"Wonderful!" said Nancy. As she said this, she looked up to see Laura standing before her. In the girl's hand was the beautiful aquamarine ring Nancy had admired earlier in the week.

"I'd like you to wear this," Laura said shyly, "as a reminder that our friendship began on the water." Quickly she slipped the ring on the third finger of Nancy's right hand.

The pretty detective gave an exclamation of delight and admired the gift for a long moment. Then she showed it to the others. At last she turned to Laura and said with genuine sincerity:

"The ring is priceless and I'll always treasure it as a reminder of you—although no one can place a value on a true friendship like ours."

Seeing tears in Laura's eyes, Nancy added quickly with a grin, "Even if we had to be shipwrecked to get an introduction!"